Philip Thicknesse

Memoirs and Anecdotes of Philip Thicknesse

Late Lieutenant Governor of Land Guard Fort, and Unfortunately Father to George Touchet, Baron Audley

Philip Thicknesse

Memoirs and Anecdotes of Philip Thicknesse
Late Lieutenant Governor of Land Guard Fort, and Unfortunately Father to George Touchet, Baron Audley

ISBN/EAN: 9783337267001

Printed in Europe, USA, Canada, Australia, Japan

Cover: Foto ©Andreas Hilbeck / pixelio.de

More available books at **www.hansebooks.com**

MEMOIRS

AND

ANECDOTES

OF

PHILIP THICKNESSE,

LATE

LIEUTENANT GOVERNOR

OF

LAND GUARD FORT,

AND UNFORTUNATELY

FATHER TO GEORGE TOUCHET,
BARON AUDLEY.

DUBLIN:

PRINTED BY GRAISBERRY AND CAMPBELL:

FOR WILLIAM JONES, NO. 86, DAME-STREET.

M,DCC,XC.

TO JAMES MAKITTRICK,

ALIAS ADAIR,

JAMES MAKITTRICK ADAIR THEN,

GREETING,

As it is to you, James Makittrick Adair, to whoſe conduct I am obliged, for the very honourable and reſpectable names, which appear at the head of the following chapters; and who have kindly enabled me (without expence) to vindicate my character, and to defend my honour againſt a baſe defamer, a vindictive libeller, and a ſcurrilous, indecent, and vulgar ſcribbler; you are certainly the propereſt man exiſting, to addreſs them to; for it is you, and me; to whom alone, they can be intereſting. And as you tell us in the preface to your medical medley, that you enjoy a decent competency; and that you publiſhed that cautious performance; not for the ſake of profit, but "to make ſome "compenſation for the manifold errors, you "muſt neceſſarily have committed, in the "courſe of near forty years extenſive practice"

"tice" * ſo I publiſh the following corrections, to expoſe, not the "manifold errors" of your phyſical tranſactions, but the private and dark miſdoings of your cloſet.

Ignorance, might plead ſome excuſe for your medical errors, but impudence and diſregar'd to truth, and juſtice, can only account for your defamatory preſcriptions.

I am ready to allow, that your practice has been extenſive—it is a great way from the northern hills of Scotland, to the burning ſands upon the coaſt of Africa—it is a great way too, from the African coaſt, to the iſland of Antigua, that lovely ſpot, where you gathered the independent ſweets of your retired life, and therefore as you ſo boldly boaſt, of the unpalatable truths, you have told, and how regardleſs you are of the conſequences; ſo I alſo, take up my

* This man obtained his boaſted independence, by black and white practice, among the Negroes in the Iſland of Antigua, where he was known, by no other name, than James Makittrick, but as that was but an awkward name, *to go to bed with*, among *white people*, he returned to England, made a trip to Spa, where he found a very reſpectable practitioner of phyſic, of the name of Adair, and *conſined himſelf*, *into his family* name; in his medical "*morceau*" he has taken care to let us know, that he has ſeen the bed chamber of the Queen of France, but, as if that *arrid Iſland*, upon the ſurface of which, he obtained "*his independence*" had been ſunk by an earthquake, he has omitted to let us know, *that* the language, and manners of the Negroes, was the only living language he could utter a word of, for of the French, he knows no more than the late learned pig.

my pen, to expoſe your unpalatable falſhoods; and will prove, that you have dared to write, to print, and to publiſh; not only a vile defamatory, and falſe libel, but even to ſet at defiance the civil law of this country, by ſending expreſly to me, one of your libels, and writing upon the title page, that it was for the uſe of my council! a libel too, of ſuch a nature, that you have forfeited all pretenſions to the name of a gentleman, or to the ſociety, or countenance of honeſt men, for whatever there may be found from Scotland, I am convinced, there is not in the kingdom of England, or Ireland, a ſingle gentleman, * whether of a civil, or military profeſſion, who will not allow, that to charge an officer, bearing the King's commiſſion in his pocket, with flying from his colours, and that too, in the hour of action, is not aiming a deeper blow, to a ſuſceptible mind, and to an innocent man; than either lead or iron can impreſs; yet you, James Makittrick, ſtruck that deadly blow at my breaſt, you ſtruck it too, in the moſt cowardly and baſeſt manner, for you ſtruck it at a time, that you ſuppoſed I lay upon my death bed. Now I believe I may venture to aſſert, that a charge of cowardice, or even an inſinuation of it, on a military man, is deemed

* Gentlemen Black Legs are excepted.

deemed a matter of as much delicacy, as that of defaming the character of a virtuous woman, I therefore, call upon you James Makittrick, alias Adair, to tell the publick, what punishment you would think due to a man, were he to write, to print, and privately disperse; five hundred pamphlets, as you have done, stating therein, that your daughter, who, for aught I know, is of unsullied fame, and as chaste as she may be fair; had been debauched at Antigua, by a Negroe slave; that she had been delivered of a Mulatto child, and that you had quitted that Island; returned to this, and here taken upon you, a new name, at the age of above three score, in order, the better to conceal, the lewd and wanton conduct of your daughter, * " that a gentleman of respectable " character

Extract from James Mackittrick's Libel.

* " With respect to *your own* narrative, of the flight of you, and " your Friends, from the *runaway* negroes, I have better authority than " yours. A gentleman of respectable character, who had long resided " in Jamaica, related the story very circumstantially, to several persons " in Bath— Th—— had the sole command of the party, and having " consulted his personal safety by an early retreat, the *Serjeant' defeated* " the negroes, and carried several of them prisoners to the guard-house, " almost as soon as the *officer* had told his dreadful tale of blood, slaughter " and defeat." Now who is, and where is, that *respectable gentleman*, who told this tale so circumstantially? where is one of those *several gentlemen* in Bath, to whom he told it? no where! there is but one man, who said it, and thou wretch art that man; for thou hast said it, written it, and assassin as thou art, hath printed and dispersed it.

" character, who had long resided at Antigua, " related the story at Bath, very circumstan- " tially, to several persons," and that this was the cause of your running away from Antigua, quitting the only name you had been known by for upwards of three score years, and taking upon you that of Adair; and yet your false charge against my honour and character, is infinitely more criminal, because your daughter's innocence could have been proved by an hundred living witnesses, but you have dared to go back a compleat half century, to charge me with the most disgraceful conduct, a military officer could be guilty of; and for which, I was liable to suffer death; and you have taken that distant period, falsely to accuse me, in hopes, that I am the only survivor of my own disgrace; and that I should be unable to refute your wicked charge, and expose you to that universal contempt, which is due to so vile a transaction; for not content, with holding me out, merely as a fugitive, to avoid personal danger, by flying from my colours; you have placed me in a still more infamous light, and humiliating condition, by asserting that I was found, boasting of my own personal prowess, at the very instant, that my victorious Sergeant (from whom I had fled) returned, surrounded with prisoners,,

prisoners, and wearing upon his brow, those laurels I had so shamefully blasted. The feeble powers of my agitated mind, render me unable to express the indignant contempt to so base, so wicked, and so infamous a contrivance, but if I shew (AND I AM SURE I CAN) that I had not the sole command,—that I did not run away, —that no prisoners were taken,—no victory obtained, I am sure also, that every man of honor, sense, and humanity, will hold your name, whether it be James Makittrick, or James Adair, in abhorrent contempt, and agree with me; that there is no language, no asperity, I could have made use of, that I might not justly employ, to expose so base a caluminator. It is attention therefore to my very respectable subscribers, and I flatter myself also to many respectable readers, of the following sheets; that I have confined my language to you, within the pale of decency; for if you could suppose, that your "medical morceau" would become a fashionable "powdering book" and that every fine gentleman and lady must make it a toilette piece of furniture, sure I may humbly venture to hope, that these memoirs, may be considered, as a proper pickle to preserve that farrago of self conceit, assuming arrogance, matchless

matchleſs impudence, and daring falſhoods, which ſo ſtrongly mark all your writings.

John, Duke of Marlborough, one of the greateſt Generals, and one of the ableſt ſtateſmen of the times he lived in, and who was well acquainted with the human heart; always gave a young officer who diſcovered any ſymtoms of fear, the firſt time of being in action, a ſecond tryal: and his grace obſerved, that in general, they became good officers: now in the action, from which you have ſo falſely charged me with flying; I was a raw unexperienced boy,——it was the firſt time I ever had been expoſed, to the fire of an enemy, and when I found myſelf (without one moments previous intimation) ſurrounded by a volley of ſhot, poured down from the ſide of a ſteep mountain, coming from an inviſible enemy, and when I had not even a weapon of defence in my hands, and ſaw my men bleeding at my feet, at which inſtant more than two thirds of our party inſtantly run away; I knew too that the fire came not from a generous enemy, who would, if they conquered, give us quarters and treat us with humanity, but that it came from a crew of the moſt ſavage and brutal race of men upon the habitable globe, and whom

whom I alſo knew, often tied their priſoners to ſtakes, and encouraged their children, to treat them with every wanton cruelty they could deviſe, even to that of cutting from them their own fleſh, and compelling them to eat it, I will not ſay therefore that if the ſole command had, at that time, been veſted with me, that I ſhould not have ſought my own perſonal ſafety by flight, as two thirds of my companions had juſt done; but as my commanding officer did not, I ſtood by him, and with him too, for many hours, and if his high ideas of military honor had not overcome his judgment, and good ſenſe, he certainly would have retired alſo, when he perceived, that he was abandoned, by two thirds of his men, and when there was no more probability, of conquering the enemy; than there was of removing the mountain, on which they were concealed. In the following pages, I ſhall prove, that the whole ſtory is the production of our own head, and the promulgation of your wicked heart, and that the vile tale, originated with the publiſher, YOU James Makittrick, alias ADAIR.

The late Mr. Ford, a gentleman well acquainted with the law, and the modes of diſcovering, and detecting infamous villains, was

ſent

ſent for by a foreign miniſter, to trace a villain who had forged his name, and drawn large ſums out of the hands of his banker, Mr. Ford, obſerving that the forged notes, were all ſpelt according to auricular orthography, inſtantly conceived, that the forgery was committed by a foreigner, and ſoon after, ſtrongly ſuſpected, the miniſter's own ſecretary, (then preſent) to be the forger, with that man however he was left by the miniſter, to conſider what were the moſt prudent ſteps to be taken, to make a diſcovery, after a little converſation between them, Mr. Ford propoſed inſerting advertiſements, in all the public papers, offering therein a reward to the diſcoverer, to which the ſecretary very readily agreed; but Mr. Ford, under the pretence of having left his ſpectacles at home, deſired the ſecretary to write, and that he would dictate, and ſo contrived it, that he introduced, into the advertiſement, every word, which in the forged drafts had been ſpelt according to auricular orthography, and as every word tallied to a tittle, Mr. Ford retired, ſatisfied in his own mind, that he had diſcovered THE MAN; the advertiſements were however printed in the public papers, and about a fortnight afterwards, Mr. Ford waited upon the miniſter, but found only the ſecretary at home

home. After mutual civilities, Mr. Ford placed himſelf near, and almoſt vîs a vîs to the ſecretary, who aſked him whether he diſcovered the forger? Mr. Ford looking the ſecretary ſtedfaſtly in the face, replied,—I have; he then perceived ſuch a ſudden change of countenance, that as ſoon as the ſecretary had ſo far recovered his alarm, as to aſk him, who is the man? Mr. Ford, clapping his hand violently upon the knee of the ſecretary, ſaid you ſir, are the man! conſcious guilt ſtruck him to the ſoul, and the window being near and open, he inſtantly jumped out, and impaled himſelf upon the iron rails before the door!——Now James Makittrick Adair, go thou and do ſo likewiſe, FOR THOU ART THE MAN.

AN OCCASIONAL

INTRODUCTION.

SHOULD any book come from the preſs, at a time that ſo great a national calamity has befel us, without offering up our prayers to GOD to remove it? I think not; eſpecially when I ſee with the deepeſt concern, that inſtead of our uniting in ſupplicating the ALMIGHTY to ſtrengthen us, we ſeem threatened with ſtill greater calamities!!

I will therefore ſuppoſe, that there exiſted no abſolute law of this land, that if the father of a family was rendered by the viſitation of GOD, unable to manage his eſtate, or to govern his houſhold; but who had a ſon of full age, and abilities to govern for him, till it ſhould pleaſe God to reſtore his father to his former health, and

and ſtate of mind; a ſet of ſtrangers ſhould take poſſeſſion of his houſe and eſtates; and ſay to the ſon, "Go hence, we have an equal right with you! no law exiſts to deprive us of the power we aſſume, and therefore we will exerciſe it." Suppoſe then the aſtoniſhed ſon obtains a power to convene a council of wiſe and honeſt Judges to eſtabliſh the LAW OF RIGHT; what would be their deciſion? would they not unanimouſly ſay, let the law of GOD, and of NATURE, take place; let the ſon who is to inherit his father's fortune when he dies, manage it during his parents incapacity. It is his inheritance, and he is the moſt likely to govern it with prudence, diſcretion, and moderation.

How much more important then is it, when ſuch a matter is to be determined for a Father, not only of a family, but of a great and mighty Kingdom? Shall the ſon of our unfortunate Monarch, be ſhut out of that temporary power over theſe Kingdoms, and that houſehold to which he is the legal inheriter? GOD FORBID. I am ſure all loyal ſubjects will ſay, GOD FORBID; it is the voice of NATURE; it is the law of GOD, and it is the only reaſon that the law of man has not been exerciſed to confirm it; it would be flying in the face of GOD and NA-

TURE, to controul it. This is not ſubtile Logical, Oratorial language, but it is I hope and believe, the language which will impreſs every honeſt man's boſom who reads it, for it is unadorned truth. I will not, though I am poſſeſſed of ſufficient matter, point out the great mind and elevated underſtanding of the Prince, who muſt be called upon to exerciſe the powers of SOLE REGENT, or I could ſhew how fortunate it is for the nation, that while our KINGLY FATHER is incapacitated to govern; his PRINCELY ſon will hold the reins with dignity to the HIGH STATION he is called to, and with ſatisfaction to his ROYAL FATHER'S LOYAL SUBJECTS.

THE AUTHOR.

Dec. the 25th, 1788.

MEMOIRS

AND

ANECDOTES

OF

PHILIP THICKNESSE.

CHAP. I.

WELL knowing of what compoſition all mankind are compoſed, and that however different our coming into Life, or paſſing through it may vary; that there is no difference between us at the moment of quitting it; I hope to be excuſed, if I deal freely and openly with that part of mankind, whom it has been my lot in life to have been connected with—to converſe with—or to correſpond with; I mean I ſay,

 to

to deal freely, openly, and candidly; and therefore when matter arises, in which I may find it necessary to mention men, whether dignified by birth, or elevated by station; provided I do it with truth and decency, the candid Reader, I trust, will think it justifiable; especially as no man can be more disposed to shew deference and respect to superiors, to whom respect is *really* due. I have nearly consumed a long Life among the busy Crowd, and am now in such a Retirement as to give me leisure to look over with deliberation, my own vices and follies, and the errors and failings of those with whom I have been conversant; many of whom have been deemed great men, but very few of them perhaps have appeared so "*in the eyes of their valet de chambre.*" I do not sit down to write my life, but to relate the outline of a long, a singular, and an exceedingly checquered one; it may be of some use to others, and will, I am persuaded be of some advantage to me; yet it is a measure I have been forced to (for nothing else could) by a late publication, written by an ignorant coxcomb, who never saw me, 'till I was 66 years of age, who knows nothing of me; and yet has put forth a book privately printed, and secretly dispersed; which he calls memoirs of my life:

but which my friends aſſure me, is filled with ſcurrility, falſhood, vulgarity and impudence. I do not know the Libeller's real Name, his profeſſion however, is that of *a Doctor*, his practice has chiefly been among the negroes in the Weſt-Indies, and his degree, I ſuppoſe; as he is a ſcotch highlander, was procured him by a two guinea bribe to his countryman, *Dr. S*—, but before I proceed any further, I wiſh to prepare my readers with an anecdote, and to intreat them to keep it in their *minds eye*, throughout the remaining pages of this book.

A gentleman of high rank and diſtinguiſhed abilities, to whom I have the honor to be known, had an only ſon at ſchool; waiting one day upon his father, I was preſented to the young gentleman, and we had ſome converſation together, of rather a cheerful caſt, after which, the young ſcholar took an opportunity to obſerve to his father, how unlike I appeared in his eyes, to what he had expected from a perſon he had ſo often heard of, adding, that he thought to find me a thin, peeviſh, fretful looking being; inſtead of which, he found me fat, and as much diſpoſed to laugh as any man. His father, from whom I had this information, was pleaſed to inform his ſon, that he believed the latter to be my natural difpofition, but that a great variety of unfortunate events, having fell one after another upon me, had in fome meafure rendered me liable to the imputation of the former. Flattering as that diftinction may appear, I am difpofed to hope there was fome truth in it, at leaft enough to plead for me with the candid reader if he fhould here and there catch me tripping on fome of the *rough roads* I have to travel a *fecond time* over; efpecially, as I affure him I fet out with no fuch difpofition, for though the fprings on which my carriage hung, were not fo exquifite, as many who fet out in life with me, they have held me up a very long journey, without breaking quite down; and if they had, I have been always able to walk upright, without the aid of a crutch, or a woollen fhoe to the next inn, this I am proud to boaft of, becaufe it implies a life of temperance, but I have not only that bleffing to boaft of, but one of more importance, and that is, that I am of an ancient and virtuous family, of which I fhould not fpeak, but that it is poffible all the fcotch doctor's books may not be yet got to the paftry cooks, or to the *cloyfters of darknefs*, for I have now before me a pedigree of the * Ralph Thickneffes

* A Ralph Thickneffe, Lord of Barterley, was flain at Bloar-Heath, fighting under *George Lord Audley*! !

Thicknesses of Barterley-Hall, in Staffordshire, from the 2d year of the reign of Edward the first, down to the present time; and a letter from Mr. Bignall, Somerset, of the Herald's office, wherein he called upon me for it, in order to qualify my son to take his seat in the house of lords, and recommending it to me, to continue it at that office, as nothing he says had been done there relative to it, since the Year 1614.

My father, however was a younger branch of that family, who, after obtaining a good academical education, studied divinity at Oxford, was there ordained, and his uncle soon after (Sir John Egerton, Bart. of Rhyne-hill) presented him to the rectory of Farthingoe in Northamptonshire, a benefice of something more than two hundred pounds a year, which, with another small church within distance was all the preferment or fortune he possessed; the duty of both, he constantly and conscientiously performed, in its fullest extent to the day of his death.* He married Joyce Blencowe, niece to Mr. Justice Blencowe, one of the judges of the court of Common Pleas, and daughter of a neighbouring clergyman, with whom

* He died suddenly upon a visit to Dr. Grey.

whom I believe he had no other fortune than her many virtues. My father died in 1725, in the 55th year of his age, and left my excellent mother with eight children, one only of whom was provided for, viz. a ſiſter married to Dr. Grey, rector of a neighbouring village: and here I hope it will be excuſable, if I relate by what ſtrange incident, that happy connection was formed.

Within a mile of Farthingoe ſtands a beautiful little church, a rectory of 8l. a year, * near to which, in my memory, ſtood the ancient and hoſpitable manſion houſe of Lord Crew, biſhop of Durham, and thither the biſhop came to reſide; being a temporal and ſpiritual peer, and keeping open houſe, he was viſited by all ranks of people far and near, and particularly by the clergy, but it ſo happened that my father, the neareſt of his neighbours, omitted to pay his reſpects at Steane. The biſhop, who was a proud ſtately prelate, was hurt to find a reſpectable clergyman, whoſe reſidence was ſo very near him, to be ſo ſingularly remiſs, and therefore ſent Mr. Grey, his domeſtic

* Dr. Grey obtained Queen Anne's bounty to the little Rectory, and during his life, preached there once a month.

meſtic chaplain, to viſit my father, and to fiſh for the cauſe of what certainly ſeemed a ſlight, but which in fact was not omitted from any want of attention to his lordſhip. It ſo happened, that before Mr. Grey had ſeen my father, he had met my ſiſter, an object which attracted much of his attention, and when he came into my father's ſtudy, inſtead of diſcloſing his buſineſs, he aſked my father whether a young lady he had ſeen in the court yard, was his daughter? my father informed him he had two daughters, and that probably it might; bleſs me! ſaid Mr. Grey, it made my heart leap to ſee ſo fine girl in ſuch a country village. This ſo offended my father, that he felt diſpoſed to have made his *body* and *heart leap together*, out of his ſtudy, had he not quickly perceived my father's diſapprobation, of ſo novel a mode of addreſs. He then explained his errand, and my father finding him to be an ingenious man, began to feel as much partiality to the young parſon, as the parſon had conceived for his youngeſt daughter. Mr. Grey repeated his viſits, and before my ſiſter was well out of her white frock, ſhe became the rector of Hinton's wife, where ſhe may be ſeen at this day, in her 84th year, with many traces remaining, of that beauty which ſo ſuddenly

denly caught the attention of her departed hufband. Nor can I omit repeating a fingular kind of joint compliment Mr. Grey paid her, the day he had obtained (for it was not eafily obtained) my father and mother's confent, to fix that of his happinefs. When walking with my fifter and mother in the garden, he led her upon the grafs plot, and after walking round and round her feveral times, and admiring her perfon, well faid he, Mifs Joyce, I own you are too good for me, but at the fame time I think myfelf too good for any body elfe.*

When my father died, I had two brothers juft removed from the foundation at Eton, to King's College in Cambridge; one upon the foundation at Winchefter, another at the Charter-Houfe, and my eldeft fifter, and next brother at home with my mother, for fome time

I was

* Dr. Grey had alfo the Rectory of Kimcote in Leicefterfhire, was a prebend of St. Paul's, and Archdeacon of Leicefter. His Connection with Lord Crew, probably fhut him out of a Mitre. He died however rich, and left three Daughters, the eldeft is married to Dr. Lloyd, Dean of Norwich, and well known for her genius in working in Worfted. Lord Crew was a ftaunch Friend to the abdicated Family, and as he lay dying upon the Marble Hearth before the Fire, he called out feveral Times to my Brother faying, "*Dick, don't you go over to them, don't you go over to* "*them.*"

I was placed at Aynhoe ſchool, * and then removed with my mother to London, where, by the favour of Dr. Friend, high maſter of Weſtminſter ſchool, I was admitted a *gratis* ſcholar, not a King's ſcholar, and I believe I could at this day ſhew upon the back of my Hands, ſome marks of *the favors frequently confer'd upon them, by that truly beautiful nobleman the preſent Earl of* ———, for as caſh often ran low with me, and *Nan Batchelor's* † tarts and cuſtards were as grateful to my palate, as to any lord's in the ſchool, I did ſometimes ſpend that money which was given me on the *bougie account*, by my mother, rather too haſtily, ſo that I had no other means of *light* for the ſchool, and keeping my mother in *darkneſs*, than expoſing the back of my hand, to a yard and half of doubled wax candle, at ſo *much a cut;* and his lordſhip was of ſo generous a diſpoſition, that I was as ſure of my night or morning's *bougie* from his lordſhip's bountiful hand, as a poor woman is who goes

* Aynhoe, the ſeat of the Cartwrights. In the year 1727, John Cartwright the County Member, who was one of the nobleſt works of God, and who voted according to conſcience (not to the miniſter) never ſpoke but two words in the houſe, viz. *aye* and *no*. Some wags printed his ſpeech, on a large ſheet of paper, and had it cried about the ſtreets of London, one ſide of the paper was Aye, and the other No, and thoſe two words united made Aynhoe.

† See her Epitaph.

goes to the *humane pawn-broker* with her laſt ſhift, to borrow a ſhilling upon, to buy bread for her children; nor indeed was that the only kindneſs I have experienced *from his lordſhip, for he was ſo obliging as to attend, at my requeſt, the houſe of lords upon an appeal to that great and dernier court of juſtice, which I brought thither from the court of chancery.* I muſt however own that ſometimes when his lordſhip was not diſpoſed to make his own exerciſe, that I have had a ſupply of wax candle for the *uſe of my fingers.* Nor was the want of wax candle the only occaſion of my ſmarting at that ſchool, *Vidal*, the uſher, under whom I was firſt placed, did not receive the uſual preſents at *breaking up Times*, from my mother, as he did from the opulent parents, and the wretch was ſo mean, as to let that operate to my diſadvantage: * for I could never keep my place an hour, after a boy of rank or fortune got next to me; nor commit a trifling fault without being *ſhewn up* to Dr. Nicholls; that good old man, I believe, perceived

* Boys who have a little Money in their Pockets, are very apt at School to take it out, eſpecially thoſe who have but little, and ſeldom any. Vidal, when he knew I had, would watch me, as a Cat does a Mouſe, and has frequently detected me in taking it out of my pocket in School Hours, and then never omitted ſending me under a *truſty Guard* to put it into the priſoners box at the gate way, then a priſon at the end of Tothill-ſtreet.

perceived it, for I was not without a box full of ſilver groats, pence, &c. which the generous doctor had given me, perhaps more on *other accounts*, than any merit of my ſchool performances. At this time I lived in St. James's place, and having an exerciſe to make between the morning and afternoon ſchool, my dinner to eat, the diſtance to go, and to return, and my ſlow capacity united; I became unable to do it properly at any time, and often not at all; this ſubjected me to be *fair game* to Mr. Vidal, and at length, fearful of the maſter's *laſh*, and ſmarting often under the noble lord's *bougie*, I played the truant for 10 days together, during which time caſh running low, I *melted down* all my box of little groats, &c. on the eleventh day, *two ambaſſadors* were ſent by Mr. Vidal, to my mother, to know the cauſe of my abſence; here my pretended ſham exerciſes, and all the fibs my idleneſs of courſe produced, came forward, and my mother very prudently deliver'd me up to the hands of juſtice; never did I ſee two officers of ſchool police, more intoxicated with power! I was held by each arm, as ſecurely as if I had been apprehended for murder, and there was ſuch an appearance of delight in their countenances, that I truly believe their joy was equal to my fears, not that they

they were my enemies, on the contrary, they were my boſom friends, but they were boys, *i. e. little men.* When I entered the lobby, and became viſible to all the boys in the firſt fourm, I heard them with one voice as it were, joyfully exclaim, here come's Thickneſſe, here come's Thickneſſe, and their joy ſeemed as general as if the ſecretary of ſtate had juſt procured them a holiday. I was delivered to Maſter Vidal, who inſtantly ſhewed me up to Dr. Nicholls, here was nothing to be ſaid in plea of mitigation: I pleaded guilty, and was inſtantly expoſed to ſhame and puniſhment; after which, however, at the ſtrong interceſſion of Mr. Vidal, all my ſmartings were appeaſed, by the following *ſentence*, for I was told in the language of the court, that my future attendance at that ſchool would be diſpenſed with, a joyful ſentence to me, after I had convinced my mother of the real cauſe of my miſconduct, and obtained her forgiveneſs, for I was one of thoſe unfaſhionable children, who could not perfectly enjoy peace of mind, while I lay under her diſpleaſure; having got hold of a little latin; *being born the ſeventh ſon, without a daughter between*, and indeed having *ſtroked away ſeveral wens*, and ſuch diſorders as are apt to diſappear without medicines, it was thought adviſeable

to

to breed me to a physical profession, and I was placed with a very respectable apothecary in London, whose name was Marmaduke Tisdale, upon what is called *likeing*, and with him I actually resided till I found out that a composition of *aqua mirabilis* and syrup of saffron, was the best cordial his shop afforded; but that mixture, not sitting so well on Marmaduke's stomach (tho' he was a very honest fellow) as it did upon mine, we agreed to part; the truth was, that I had been so poisoned by the glaring colours in which Ogelthorpe had in his printed books, displayed the prospects of his new colony of Georgia, that I was determined to go thither; and at length prevailed upon my mother to consent to it. While this project had filled me with infinite delight, for I then considered myself as one setting out to begin the forming of a new world; my mother told me, that if I chose a verse in the 39th chapter of Genesis, in which there are 33, it would unfold to me the future events of my life, *now it happened to pass in those days*, that the Scriptures were not only believed, but seriously attended to; so I fixed upon the 26th verse, *and when I found that the blessings of my father would extend to the utmost bounds of the everlasting hills, and be upon*

*upon the head of him who was ſeparated from his brethren.** I felt a delight and a faith too, not to be removed; and my mother, *tho' a ſenſible woman, was weak enough to become a partaker with me*, in that heart felt ſatisfaction, ſhe perceived to be ſpread over my countenance; nor could, at that time any offer, however advantageous in appearance, have diverted me, from adding one to the number of the fooliſh Georgia emigrants.

* I was then the firſt of the family that ſeparated from his brethren.

CHAP.

CHAPTER II.

UPON our arrival at Georgia, I was much ſurpriſed to find the town of Savanna, or rather the ſpot where the town *now ſtands*, ſituated upon a high bluff of barren ſand, and directly oppoſite to a low ſwampy iſland; on the muddy ſhore of which (within a ſmall compaſs) I could count at leaſt twenty Allegators baſking thereon! Mr. Cauſton, the chief Magiſtrate, to whom I had letters, received me civilly, and Mr. John Weſtley, to whom I alſo had a letter, ſeemed diſpoſed to admit me among the number of his elect. Mr. Cauſton's Niece, a very pretty young lady, was one of Mr. Weſtley's early prayer attendants at the chapel, after which, ſhe, with ſeveral other young people,

ple, ufually attended Mr. Weftley to domeftic lectures for further edification, at his own apartments, but Mr. Williamfon, a gentleman who came over in the fame veffel with me, paid his addreffes to that young lady, and foon after married her, by which means he was in poffeffion of many pious letters written by Mr. W. to Mrs. Williamfon, but he not approving of that kind of correfpondence, fhe no longer frequented his domeftic lectures, and I believe, like myfelf, became rather flack in attending his early morning prayers. Mr. Hutton, a worthy clergyman, of whom I fhall fpeak more fully hereafter, who had recommended me to Mr. Weftley, I found had been informed foon after my arrival, by Mr. Weftley, that I did not give him *too much* of my company, and to fay truth, I did not covet much of his; and I will give my reafons. Dr. Hutton was a clergyman of worth and character, who could not reconcile himfelf to take the neceffary oaths, whereby he could hold his church preferment, he therefore refigned, and took a houfe in College-Street, Weftminfter, and had feveral boys of that fchool boarded with him; his own family confifted of a wife, a fon, and a daughter; the fon is ftill living, and is, or was, well known

among

among that ſect called Moravians. † My Family were intimate with Dr. Hutton's, and my ſiſter, who was about the ſame age of Miſs Hutton, became ſo far her confidant, that ſhe ſhewed her a great number of letters written by Mr. Charles Weſtley to her, in which the care of her ſoul and body too, ſeemed to claim much of his regard; for I muſt obſerve, that Meſſrs. Weſtley and Whitefield, who were the firſt movers of the methodiſt ſect, were continually at Dr. Hutton's, praying, eating, &c. my ſiſter, who perhaps had more knowledge of the world and mankind, than Miſs Hutton, (for tho' of good underſtanding, ſhe was very deaf) did not approve of that ſpiritual correſpondence, between Mr. Charles Weſtley, and her female friend.

She perceived it made the young woman unhappy, and therefore prevailed upon her, to drop that ſort of correſpondence with him, obſerving to her, at the ſame time, that mankind have various ways of purſuing happineſs

C through

† He was bred a Bookſeller, and opened a Shop near Temple-Bar, from whence he went to Moravia, to fetch himſelf a Wife, of that Nation and religion; but this is not the Age for Bookſellers to make Fortunes by the Sale of Bibles, Prayer Books, &c. and as Mr. Hutton would ſell little elſe, that Buſineſs would not do, and he betook himſelf to one which it ſeems did, that of a Moravian Leader.

through this life to a better, and as I did not find Mr. John Weſtley ſeemed to have any diſpoſition of correſponding with me, and thinking too, that my ſoul was of as much importance to him, as the ſoul of any young lady whatever, I had very little intercourſe with him afterwards. I muſt not however omit to mention a ſingular misfortune which befel him, in conſequence of his zealous endeavors to reform a fair, but *frail lady*, then at Georgia, whoſe immoral conduct had been much cenſured by Mr. Weſtley, and who ſent to deſire him to call upon her; it was natural for him to conclude, his viſit was to pave the way to repentance and future good conduct; he accordingly attended her, but the inſtant he entered her apartment, ſhe laid violent hands upon him, threw him upon the bed, and threatened him with the immediate loſs of life, or what ſome men might deem as dear as life, nor did ſhe diſmiſs him, till ſhe had deprived him of all the Adonis flowing locks, which at *that time*, adorned one ſide of his meek and goodly countenance; yet ſuch was his humility, that he appeared the ſunday following at church, in his partial and ear-crop'd head of hair; the lady perhaps intended to have made Mr. Weſtley a Monk, as the Ducheſs of Montpenſier did

Henry

Henry the third. Let it be remembered however, that a deſire of ſuch ſpiritual correſpondence with the ſex, which appeared in both theſe brothers, might ariſe from the utmoſt purity, and virtuous intentions; however their letters might be conſtrued to convey ſuſpicion of ſiniſter deſigns; thoſe gentlemen were not ignorant, that there never was, nor ever can be, a new ſect formed, (and that was their great object) if women were not engaged to promote it; they knew that *Arius* did more by engaging *Conſtantia*, the Emperor's ſiſter, into his way of thinking, relative to the conſubſtantiality of the world, than he could have done by gaining over a thouſand male followers. The Weſtleys, and Whitefield, firſt ſtarted the methodiſtical plan, but Lady Huntingdon, in reality, is the ſole perſon who has eſtabliſhed its permanency; and there is no doubt but her motives were good, becauſe her life and manners are exemplary, and truly virtuous: ſhe may appear in the eyes of ſome of us, righteous over much, but then remember a text of ſcripture, containing only two words; and from which my father made an excellent diſcourſe, *i. e.* "*judge not.*"

After this, Mr. Weſtley and I ſeldom met, but the day I had embarked with a view of returning to England, I was agreeably ſurpriſed to find him with me, in a ſmall ſloop bound to Charles Town in South Carolina, in which I had engaged my paſſage; he was going to get prayer books printed, and I to find a conveyance to England. Our ſloop commander, proved to be a perfect reprobate mariner, and we, freſh water ſailors, thought he carried too much ſail. I urged him, (for it blew hard) to ſhew leſs canvas, and Mr. Weſtley implored him *to ſwear not at all;* but our prayers prevailed not, more ſail, and more oaths, ſeemed to be the conſequence of our requeſts; by this time we were out of ſight of land, the gale encreaſed, and we run *gunwhale* under water; if there was no real danger, we apprehended much, and Mr. Weſtley, (to my great ſurpriſe) ſaid, well Mr. Thickneſſe, I have a ſmall book in my little trunk here, which I ſhould be unwilling to loſe, and with the utmoſt *ſang froid*, opened his trunk, and put the book into his pocket! now what was I to conceive by this ſingular tranſaction? for though the ſhip, Whitefield ſailed in, to Georgia, *ſtood ſtill* in the atlantic ocean, when all her ſails were *ſleeping*, in a freſh gale of wind, I ſaw

I ſaw no poſſible chance of ſaving our lives, even with *empty pockets*, had the ſloop overſet; nothing but a float of Allegators, with lock ſaddles along ſide, ready to take us on ſhore, could have preſerved us. I did not take the liberty to aſk Mr. Weſtley, his plan of preſervation, or if his book was the *charm*, which contained it; he had but one, ſo I muſt let that remain in enigmatical obſcurity, along with Mr. Whitefield's *motionleſs frigate*. We got however ſafe on ſhore at Charles Town the next morning, where Mr. Weſtley and I parted in good fellowſhip, and therefore, though I have not done with Georgia, I hope the candid reader will excuſe my taking him over to England for a little while to relate my *next meeting* with this very ſingular gentleman, though at the diſtance of near half a century! it is only juſt to croſs the paſſage of the Severn with my old fellow traveller, and then I ſhall have done with him, till we meet, and I truſt and hope we ſhall, where neither ſtorms can diſturb us, waters divide us, and where:—O bleſſed reflection! if we do meet, we muſt all be of the ſame way of thinking. It ſo happened, that from the time we parted at Charles Town, and from our profligate ſalt water Captain, we did not meet again, till within a very few years

ſince,

ſince, and then under the ſame kind of diſaſter, with a freſh water brute; for croſſing the Severn with a female friend, one of the boatmen (I ſhould ſay one of the *Captains*, for they are all Captains) puſhed the *Thyller* ſo ſuddenly *a weather*, that he had nearly thrown my friend overboard. I immediately unſhipped it, and with an appearance of being in earneſt, accompanied by words, not proper to repeat, threaten'd to knock the fellow down with it, this threat brought before me, a goodly looking old man, who with a perſuaſive tongue, and the gentleſt manners, beſought me to ſay no more; the lady, he obſerved, was ſafe, and that in a few minutes, we ſhould be no longer within his reach, that though my provocation was great, oaths, or reſentment, could not mend the matter, and he fully ſucceeded in his attempt, for his manners were captivating, his arguments convincing. At this time I thought I recogniſed my old acquaintance Mr. Weſtley, and it promiſed me pleaſure, in making myſelf known to him, for I had no longer any doubt as to his perſon, having that inſtant heard one of his attendants (for I think he had ſeveral) mention his name: I availed myſelf therefore of ſo fair an occaſion to obſerve that it was not the firſt time he and me had been in

difficulties

difficulties together upon ſalt water: he ſeemed ſurprized! and aſked me when, and where we had been ſo circumſtanced? I then reminded him of our Charles Town Pilot; why ſaid he, what is your Name? and being told, inſtead of kindling thoſe ſentiments, which were warming in my own boſom into a flame, he treated me, and the event, with cool indifference; and ſcarce ſpoke afterwards! now uncle Toby would not have done ſo; would he courteous reader? this was not *Shandean* indeed Mr. John Weſtley; I will not ſay it, looked like want of chriſtian charity, but I will ſay, had not ſuch a want of ſentiment been evident, this tranſaction had never *come on ſhore.* Why I proteſt Mr. Weſtley, that were I to meet even Jemmy Mac Kittrick, alias Adair * fifty years years hence upon the ſevern, I ſhould only jobe him, for printing and publiſhing a parcel of notorious lies, and remind him of *the ambuſh I fell into, "when I had the ſole command" of a detachment of ſoldiers, and a* SENIOR *officer, was one of the party!*

Boccacio

* This lying fellows real name is James Mac Kittrick, as may be ſeen in an obſcure corner, upon a ſtone placed by himſelf over the bones of his own brother in St. Michael's church yard at Wincheſter, "John Mackittrick, 1784."

Boccacio, the Italian wit, obſerved, that nobody, " ſwerved more from the law, than " lawyers; that none obſerved a courſe of diet, " ſo little as phyſicians; and that none fear " the remorſe of conſcience, leſs than divines, " who tho' they lay down ſo many articles of " faith to others, believe but few themſelves." It is true, I believe, that lawyers ſeldom go to law, and that phyſicians ſeldom take phyſic; and I can aſſure my readers, it is true, that the late Lord Chief Juſtice Willes *(I mean not Mr. Juſtice Willes)* adviſed me, when I aſked his opinion about a law matter, to ſit down quietly under any injury or oppreſſion whatever, rather than go to law. I hope therefore, my reader will conſider this piece of honeſt information (for it came from the mouth of as able and upright a judge as ever adminiſtered juſtice) to be worth ten ſhillings and ſix-pence, if he will not, he here has it under my hand, that I have defrauded him of *half a guinea.*

I thought to have done with this *methodiſtical* ſubject, but I cannot lay down my pen, without obſerving, that however ſeriouſly, and in earneſt, many of the leaders of thoſe people no doubt are; yet they are all, men of *warm conſtitutions*, and that if they had been natives

of

of a Mahometan country, where women are excluded, even religious ſocieties, they never would have ſeparated from the eſtabliſhed mode of worſhip. Thoſe who know the hiſtory of the *Mamiliarians* may recollect the ſtory of *Labadie*, who having ſet a female ſcholar to a devout leſſon, and prepared her for inward *recollection*, and mental *prayer*, came ſuddenly to her, *when he thought ſhe was thoroughly recollected*, and put his hand into her boſom: but meeting with a ſevere repulſe, he ſeriouſly beſought her *to confeſs humbly her weakneſs, and to beg pardon of God for having been ſo little attentive to the myſteries of meditation, otherwiſe, ſaid he, you would have been inſenſible to my attempted touch!* And MAREST, (Cardinal Richlieu's favorite wit) owned that he employed his fanatic eloquence among women; purely to deceive, to delude, and to enjoy them; and rather than not ſucceed, he taught them to believe that vice is virtue; and acknowledges that he betrayed God, by miſinterpreting his laws. When Philip the ſecond of Spain aſked the Jeſuits and confeſſors, who were about him, how they could attend ſo many fair penitents, be alone with them, and yet remain chaſte? they informed his Majeſty, that they carried with them a *certain plant*, which always protected

tected them from the danger of uncleanneſs. The King urged them to let him know the name of that precious weed, till they were obliged to own, it was called "*The fear of* "*God.*" That plant might have been growing then in Spain for aught I know, but I am pretty confident, it is not to be found in their botanic gardens at this day; the weedy plant, *arbor vitæ*, has utterly deſtroyed *it*, and when I ſee a female penitent retire with her confeſſor, I always think of *St. Dominic*, who finding a nun in an extacy, he brought her out of it, by anointing her with the *unguentum amoris*; Thoſe who know human nature beſt, know that auricular confeſſion, not only of deeds, but of thoughts alſo, are more than human nature can be ſafely truſted with, when the parties are only two, and of different ſexes.

CHAP.

CHAPTER III.

HAVING eſcaped *ſhipwreck* a *ſecond* time, with my old acquaintance, Mr. Weſtley, and ſeen him ſafely landed on the coaſt of Somerſetſhire; I muſt, as I obſerved above, beg leave to call my reader's attention back again, to the plains of America; in order to introduce him to the knowledge of a very different *caſt* of *men*, from either methodiſts or indigent *wanderers*; who, under the name of *civilized* Chriſtians, went thither, to deprive the Indians of their native rights; and what I fear was much worſe, of their ſimplicity of manners, and frugal mode of living; which is now no longer to be found among them; inſtead of which they have got *diſeaſes*, before unknown to them; ſpirituous liquors, which render them frantic, and they are ſtill ſtrangers to every thing which belongs to Chriſtianity, but *the conduct of Chriſtians to them, and to one another.* It is ſingular, but true, that there are

are no two created beings, more unlike in manners and difpofition, than the red Indians of America, and the negroes of Africa; I could perceive no traces of that bloody and revengeful difpofition among the Indians, of which we have in thefe later days heard fo much. TOMO CHACHI, the Creek Indian King, was not only a very humane man, but I may add, he was a *very well bred man*, for Mr. Ogelthorpe, having fignified to *Tomo*, that he wifhed to build the firft City of his Colony upon the very fpot where *Tomo's Palace* then ftood, he found it no difficult matter to prevail upon his Majefty, to remove his court three miles higher up, on the banks of the fame river. The Bluff, upon which the town of Savanha is built, was called by the Indians, *Yamacra*, and *Tomo Chachi*, was King of *Yamacra*; nor did I difcover any other traces of *a cruel* or *favage* difpofition in King *Tomo*, than thus moving to oblige Mr. Ogelthorpe; and ftepping in between a Criminal, and the Executioner; faying, whip me,—whip me,——when one of our people was under the lafh, for ill-treating an Indian Woman. Their rude drefs, painted faces, fliced ears, *nofe bobs!* and tattooed Skins, rendered their external appearance, to us Britons, fingularly favage; but by making frequent

quent excurſions to the court of *new Yamacra*, and picking up a little of their language, I ſoon became convinced, that my perſon and property was as ſafe at the court of *Yamacra*, as at any court in Chriſtendom; nor could I perceive, that *King Tomo*,—*Cenauke*, his Queen, or *Tonoboi*, their nephew and heir, were not as happy as the princes of the moſt poliſhed courts in Europe. And yet, they had not been long returned, from viſiting the court of Great Britain, where Sir Robert Walpole, or the Duke of Newcaſtle, I forget which, made ſome difficulty, of ſitting down in their preſence! the King's coach, with the Lyon and the Unicorn ſupporters, did not incline them to forget their own ſupporters of Bears and Buffaloes; NATURE, with which they had only been accuſtomed to converſe, ſurpaſſed, in their imagination! all that art could produce. The firſt viſit I made the court of *Yamacra*, their Majeſties were juſt returned in their Canoes, from an *Oyſtering party*, and I had the honor of partaking with them, a *repas*, to which they ſat down with as good an appetite, as ever European princes did, to a barrel of Pyefleet.*

Strange

* The Indians, who dwell within the reach of the ſalt water Creeks, make fires at low water on the Iſlands of oyſters, which are then left high and dry, and roaſt the greateſt part of an Iſland at once. It is

ſaid

Strange as it may appear to us *ratified* Britons; who have been accuſtomed from our infancy, to admire paintings, buildings, jewels, &c. —I am convinced that thoſe Indians at that time were inſenſible to every kind of our works of art, but ſuch as ſtruck their ſenſes with the perſonal comforts the objects would produce, and that King *Tomo's* blanket, which kept him warm, was, in his opinion, more valuable, than the gold watch given him at St. James's. After cultivating a good acquaintance with thoſe children of nature, I ſoon became ſatisfied, whether I met them alone or in company, that I was perfectly ſafe, and therefore I made frequent excurſions into the woods, apprehenſive enough of the danger of rattle ſnakes, but without any from the ſtraggling Indians! and I had many proofs that my conjectures were well founded. In one of my woodland excurſions, and about four miles from Savanha, I found a fertile piece of ground, upon the banks of a rapid Creek, which at high water, was Iſolated; this ſpot, ſo delighted me, that with Mr. Cauſton's permiſſion, I built a wooden, not an iron houſe thereon, and there I paſſed much of my time; my gun ſupplied me

ſaid too, that the *Racoons* and Poſſums viſit thoſe iſlands, and ſlip a dead ſhell into a living oyſter, in order to avail themſelves of the next *tide* to eat what their forecaſt and ſagacity, had made thereby *come-at-able* prey.

me with ſquirrels, wild fowl, &c. and the town only, with rice, to boil by way of bread, the Indians ſometimes *viſited my Iſland* for a day or two, and then I had plenty of veniſon, which they boil'd down, and eat dipped in wild honey, this was a true Robinſon Cruſoe line of life; but it was ſuch, as even in thoſe days, ſuited my romantic turn. In this ſituation I wanted nothing but a *female friend*, and I had almoſt determined to take to wife one of Queen *Cenauke's* maids of honor, I ſeriouſly paid my addreſſes to her, and ſhe in return, honor'd me with the appellation of *Auche* (friend) ſhe had receiv'd a pair of Indian boots, ſome paint, a looking glaſs, a comb, and a pair of ſciſſars as tokens of my love, and one buffloe's ſkin, had certainly held us, had not an extraordinary incident aroſe, which determined me to return immediately to England, and this it was. Walking upon the margin of my creek, and playing upon the flute, ſuch was the effect of an affectionate and warm imagination, that I had a tranſient, but as perfect a ſight of my mother, as if ſhe had actually been before me, in *Propria Perſona.* Strongly poſſeſſed with the talk and idleries which children hear, and many men cannot overcome, its no wonder that a boy, as I then was, concluded it was my mother's

departed

departed ſhade; my ſqua,—my iſland,—and my Robinſon Cruſoe plan, inſtantly loſt all their charms, and though at that time I had an account of a very uſeful ſervant, bound to ſerve me four years, being on his paſſage to join me, I determined to leave the *ſhadow*, and ſeek the *ſubſtance;* and had my mother, whom I found upon my return, in perfect health, died about that time, I might have been a *ſee'r of ſpirits* to this day. I immediately ſet out for Savanha, and on my way thither, having my fowling piece reverſed at my back, I was more *ſubſtantially* alarmed, by a very uncommon rattling at my heels; at that time I had never ſeen a rattle ſnake alive, but I inſtantly ſuſpected, what it proved to be, my fright however, was ſo great, that I drop'd my gun, and run haſtily to ſome diſtance, and when I turned about, I ſaw the ſnake winding her tail foremoſt into a hole in the ground, and though I was exceedingly alarmed, I by degrees ventured to go back for my gun; at a little diſtance from which, I perceived not only the ſnake which firſt alarmed me, but two others, half of each of their bodies out of their holes! and the ſun, which ſhone in between the trees, rendered their backs as beautiful, as their tails were dreadful, but as they did not offer to ſtir, I ventured to lay my

gun

gun upon the ground, and getting their heads upon a line, I ſhot them all three, the largeſt had ſeven rattles, and the other two, had five each: it is ſaid, they are three years old before the firſt rattle appears, and that they have an additional rattle every year, as long as they live! and though I could hear of none in Georgia, which had been killed, having more than ſix or ſeven rattles; I have ſeen in the cabinets of the curious, ſixteen! but perhaps ſome art had been uſed, for it is ſcarce credible, that providence, would give ſo long a life, to ſo dangerous, ſo deſtructive, and ſo prolific a reptile; the leaſt ſtroke however upon *their heads*, with a ſmall ſwitch, inſtantly kills them; and I am aſſured the deer are neither ſtrangers to the danger of the rattle ſnake, nor of the ſafeſt manner of deſtroying them, to effect which, they raiſe themſelves erect, and leap, ſo as to let their hind feet come down upon the ſnake's head, and I once actually ſaw a deer in that action, but I could not find the ſnake, the Indians ſay, if it were not for the great number deſtroyed by the deer, it would be ten times more dangerous than it is, or rather than it *was*, for among the ſettlements I preſume they are rarely ſeen now. The Indians wear ſhoes, called *maugazeens*, they are of one piece of deer ſkin, gathered up and ſewed like a purſe at the toe, with a deer's ſinew; they cover their legs and thighs with pieces of leather, and leave broad flaps which play too and fro' as they walk, at which the rattle ſnakes generally bite, and thereby they avoid the danger. I am to think, however, they ſeldom purſue or bite, but when any living creature approaches too near their young in breeding time. When the Indians are bitten, they tie a leather thong, tight above the wound, and their wives or children ſuck forth the poiſon, but not always with ſucceſs; the limb ſwells immediately, and the patient dies in twenty four hours, perhaps no remedy is of ſuch good effect as olive oil, well and long fomented, with the patients own hands.

CHAP.

CHAPTER IV.

THE Colony of Georgia was, at the time I returned to England, ſtill under the management of certain truſtees, and as I was the firſt of the *Emigrants*, who had returned from thence, I was ſent for to attend thoſe gentlemen, at their office in Old Palace Yard. At that time, Mr. Oglethorpe was juſt nominated Colonel of a regiment to be forthwith raiſed for the defence of his new Colony; and as he had permiſſion to recommend ſome of his friends to ſerve in it, he promiſed me a pair of colours, and I concluded the examination I was to undergo in Old Palace Yard, would eſtabliſh his friendſhip to me, as I went thither determined to anſwer openly, and candidly, to all the queſtions they put to me: ſo, when they ſhewed me *upon paper*, Forts raiſed, where no ground had been broken, and flags flying, where no ſtaffs had been erected, I plainly told them the truth, and though it was ſaid the Queen (Caroline) had worn, on her birth day, a gown made of ſilk, the manufacture of that Colony, I aſſured thoſe gentlemen that I had not ſeen worms ſufficient to reel off a ſingle ſkain of ſilk; the Truſtees, ſeemed perfectly ſatisfied with the account I gave them, but I did not find myſelf higher in the favor of *my Colonel*, nay, on the contrary, I ſoon perceived, if I did not *raiſe my own flag ſtaff*, by ſome more friendly hands, than his, I might probably be only commiſſioned, to ſerve in one of thoſe *paper forts*, I had ſeen elevated in Old Palace Yard. At this time I had two brothers, both fellows of King's College, in Cambridge, both in high favour with the late Sir Edward Walpole, and one, who had ſteadily engaged in the intereſt of the Honourable Thomas Townſhend, then member for that Univerſity. My brothers therefore, united in an application to thoſe gentlemen, and they to Sir Robert Walpole, and obtained that great miniſter's promiſe. Mr. Townſhend, in his reply to my brother, ſaid, " you have a right Sir, to command me upon all occaſions, and I will not be wanting on this." The King, was at that time,

time, at Hampton Court, and my uncle, Mr. Wace, who was firſt clerk in the ſecretary of ſtate's office, ſoon after, informed my mother, that he had juſt filled up a commiſſion for his nephew Philip, and that it would be ſigned by the King the next day, he had given the ſame notice to my brother, who was one of the Aſſiſtants at Eton, and on that day, we both met in my uncle's office at Hampton Court, but inſtead of meeting with my *ſigned commiſſion*, we found my uncle had been directed to put it aſide, and to fill up another for Mr. John Lemon, and that too, by the expreſs commands of Sir Robert Walpole himſelf: this was a heavy blow to them; and to me, it was as bad as a ſentence of death, which my affectionate brother perceived; thus ſtimulated, ſurpriſed, and concerned! he made uſe of a *piece of addreſs*, and got himſelf placed in a paſſage, through which, Sir Robert Walpole was ſoon to paſs, and there, with the loſs of one of the heels of his half jack boots, and a wig with ſcarce a crooked hair in it, he accoſted that great miniſter: by reminding him of his promiſe, to Mr. Townſhend, and to his ſon. My brother's perſon, was unknown to Sir Robert; but his name, from an hundred humourous Eton tranſactions he had heard from his ſons, was

well

well known to him: ſo that the minute he knew his name, he was no longer ſurpriſed at the un—*Etiquetiſh* mode of being *ſo ſtopped*, in the King's Palace; Sir Robert, who in all private tranſactions of life, was one of the moſt friendly and captivating men of the age, took my brother back to his apartments, followed by Mr. Arnold, the deputy Secretary at war, who had under his arm, thoſe very Georgia commiſſions, from which I had been ſo ſuddenly diſmiſſed: he then told my brother, that Sir William Younge, the Secretary at war, who was ill in Cornwall, had ſent Mr. Lemon expreſs to him, for the purpoſe of obtaining a pair of colours in Oglethorpe's regiment, and ſo recommended, that he could not be rejected; 'I ſent ſaid he for Mr. Ogelthorpe, and told him one of the preſent named Enſigns muſt be diſmiſſed, and he obſerved; that *I had put down your Brother myſelf*; and as all the others were ſo ſtrongly recommended, I found it leſs painful to take a liberty *with myſelf*, than with another. This Sir, ſaid he was the caſe, and is the reaſon, your brother was put by; adding, however, in a very pointed manner; but Mr. Thickneſſe, your brother ſhall be provided for; as my brother did not ſeem diſpoſed to retire, Sir Robert turned to Mr. Arnold, and aſked, if

there

there was, in any other corps, a pair of colours, vacant? Mr Arnold informed him there was not, but that a Lieutenancy of an independent company at Jamaica was. Then ſaid Sir Robert, in a manner which *could* not be miſunderſtood, MR. THICKNESSE YOUR BROTHER SHALL HAVE THAT. We ſoon after met Mr. Arnold at my uncle's office, and there, the good old man, thus accoſted me. Come young man ſaid he, next thurſday morning to the war office in White Hall, and then, I ſhall have the pleaſure of wiſhing you joy of a Lieutenancy, inſtead of a pair of colours, with better pay, ſeven years ſervice gained; aye, ſaid he, and a better country and climate to ſerve in, all which was compleatly fulfilled at the appointed time; when I went to return my thanks to Mr. Townſhend, he was pleaſed to ſay, he had rendered me this piece of ſervice, from a deſire he had to *ſerve me*, upon my own account; adding, and I have promiſed your brother to puſh you up to the rank of Captain, to ſhew my regard *to him*. I ſhall in another part of theſe memoirs, ſhew how religiouſly that good man performed his promiſe, even after *I alone* could be ſenſible of the rectitude of his heart, and the amiableneſs of his diſpoſition. Thus become *a captain*,

it

it is with ſhame I reflect, and much more to write, (were it not for the good of other *ſuch captains*) of what importance I conſidered myſelf, but when I had received three months pay, I was quite intoxicated, I quitted my mother's houſe, hired a firſt floor in Dartmouth-ſtreet, Weſtminſter, and had not what I *then* thought a moſt fatal misfortune befel me, took my *honor* a little down, I know not what extravagance or folly I might not have been guilty of. I will therefore relate my misfortune, though it be to my ſhame. Being *a captain*, as obſerved above, I thought it *captain-like* to ſpend my evenings at a certain *female* coffee-houſe, in the neighbourhood of Covent-Garden; and in order to be quite *toniſh*, at twelve o'clock one evening, I ordered a chair to be called, but I was not ſo perfectly initiated into that faſhionable line of life, but that I did not care, even the chairmen ſhould know the houſe I lived in, and therefore, though it rained hard, I deſired to be ſet down at ſome diſtance from my own door, at which time I had twelve guineas and two ſhillings in one pocket, and four-pence of copper in the other, after having given my worthy carriers the two ſhillings, they urged my *honor* to give them ſomething to drink, and though I had not drank too much myſelf, yet

their

their hurry, my own, and the rain, urging diſpatch, inſtead of giving them copper, I preſented *thoſe honeſt fellows* with twelve guineas more! they kindly thanked *my honor*, and were, I dare ſay, a mile off by the time *Betty* had been awoke, and able to conduct me to my bedchamber, but behold! the next morning, taking my breeches by the *wrong end alſo*, I was ſurpriſed to ſee a parcel of half-pence roll about the floor, but what was my aſtoniſhment, when I found they were all that was left me of twelve pounds fourteen ſhillings and four pence! At this inſtant the poſt man brought me a three penny letter from Cambridge, and then, the *captain's honor*, was left with but one penny in his pocket! however I hoped the letter might turn up ſomething favourable, as I knew itcame from a brother, ſincerely loved, but alas, it was to expreſs his concern, leaſt I ſhould be ſailed for Jamaica, before he could be in town, and deſiring, inſtead of a few guineas he might then have furniſhed me with, that I would accept in good part, the following golden rules which he had put down in lieu thereof. The rules it is true, were excellent, but the gold at that time would have proved more acceptable; under this dilemma, I perceived, to make my diſtreſs known to my mother, was not to be thought

on,

on, but after a variety of expedients, I hit upon the only one which could have so well succeeded. The last cash, (I should say the *first cash*, I had received) had been paid me by Mr. Popple, the agent to the eight independent companies in Jamaica, who having receiv'd me with great politeness, induced me to think I might get assistance from him. I accordingly waited upon him, and told him openly, what had happened; and he, instantly perceiving, how exceedingly I was embarrassed in the relation of it, put his hand upon my shoulder, young gentleman, said he, say no more, I know how to make allowances for such youthful indiscretions, and as you are going abroad, I will advance you six months pay, he did so, without *agent deductions*, and the name of Popple has ever since, been respectable in my ears. For till that business was done, I was within *one penny* of being in the same situation of a Frenchman, who frequently wrote to me from one part of London to the other, by the general post, and when I told him of his error, and that he should send his letters by the *penny*, not the *general* post, he replied, *I no dat very vel;* then why do you not send them so? *mai foy, said he, cause me have not de penny to put it in.* Now as these memoirs may be perused, by many *noble captains* like myself, I will

assure

assure them, that the twelve pounds fourteen shillings paid to two chairmen, from Covent Garden to Dartmouth street, Westminster, was the best laid out money of my whole life, for I never visited afterwards, houses which rendered it necessary to be set down *before* I got to my *own door*, and I have scarce ever been within a chair since. It is a machine only fit for women; and nothing but absolute necessity, or want of health, should induce a man, much less a soldier, to be seen in such a vehicle; about four hundred years ago, a Baron of this realm, was to be tried for high crimes and misdemeanors, and among other charges, one was, for suffering himself to be carried about in his *garden*, by two of his own species: this early disaster, put me upon my guard ever since, about *money matters*, or I had probably continued to this day, as indiscreet in that matter, as I have in all others, for I know not any other folly I have guarded against, but that of not being one of those fools, who will be as fine as their neighbours, whether they can afford it, or not. Lord Bateman, who upon many occasions has honoured me with marks of great kindness, once ask'd *me*, privately, (not as the present S——r of the H—— of C——ns ask'd A——l G——r publickly in the rooms at Bath) *how I made it*

out?

out? obſerving at the ſame time, that I had a large family, and was rather diſpoſed to be generous? I told his lordſhip that if I had but fifty pounds a year, I would ſpend but five and forty, and that I was always in a condition to draw upon my banker for twenty; then ſaid my lord, jocoſely, you have the advantage of me, Thickneſse, for that's more than I can do; his lordſhip however, muſt excuſe my reminding him, what *he has choſe to forget*, that he has had ſome years in his poſſeſſion, a draft of mine for *five twenties*, upon my banker, a circumſtance I would not mention, but that I would not have *his lordſhip think, I have forgot it alſo.*

CHAP.

CHAPTER V.

MY *Covent Garden disaster*, taught me to act in future, with more caution, as to money matters; I therefore, not only secured an early passage to Jamaica, in a good river built ship, but paid the captain twelve guineas for my passage, who was to entertain me at his table, and furnish even wine at meals, for that sum, and having soon after procured him another passenger, (a brother lieutenant in the service) we sailed for Jamaica, and by *touching* at Madeira, and staying ten days, at that *half-way house*, we should have enjoyed our good fare, and our civil captain's attention to us, much better, had we not been cursed with the company of *a Mac. Kittrick!* an upstart coxcomb, who called himself a Jamaica merchant, but who in fact, was a Scots pedlar, with a cargo of tagged laces, pins, needles, combs, and scissars; this coxcomb possessed every species of impudence

impudence (except *that of assuming another man's name,)* and whose ignorance was such, that he would have laid his *pack* to a *baubee*, that our commissions were not signed by the King's *own hand*. This "*beggar on horseback*" had been twice before, in Jamaica, and was continually alarming us, with the extreme danger of the climate of that country; it was no uncommon thing, he said, to sup with a friend, one night, and follow him to the grave the next; but when we came in sight of the island, (which from the sea, is rather an alarming than an inviting object) he embraced an hundred occasions, to alarm us; such as, "*God knows which of us may slip his wind first*" *this day seven-night, may occasion great alterations,*—" The negroes will say when you land, *ki massa, me sorry for that poor Bacara*† *him go to the parsons pen,*‡ with a variety of inuendoes, of the same cast; yet it must be confessed the fellow had a little smattering of the *second sight about him*: for for within forty eight hours after we did land, we might have followed him to the grave, for to use his own phrase, he *slipt his wind* first, before his pack had been opened, and we laid claim to twenty pounds worth of his wares, as he had taken a guinea from each of us, to give

† White Man. ‡ The Church Yard.

give us twenty, if our commiſſions were under the King's ſign manual; though he had ſeen it under the great ſeal. Such was his ignorance, but no man could equal his impudence, except an arrogant *aſſuming impoſtor*, who reſides at Bath, and who even *now* dares to ſhew his face among gentlemen, after being expoſed as an infamous liar, a ſcoundrel, and a coward. Fortunately for my purſe, and my perſon too, the company to which I was appointed, was quartered on the north ſide of the Iſland; I therefore, after paying my reſpects to the governor, ſet off the next morning, at three o'clock; (to avoid the violence of the ſun) for my country quarters, and about eight, I found myſelf in *Sixteen mile walk*, a beautiful country, adorned with many gentlemens houſes. Being at that time, very hungry, very hot, and a little fatigued, I aſk'd my *foot guide*, (a negro, who had his hand twiſted in my horſe's tail) who was the beſt gentleman in Sixteen mile walk? for as there are no *country Inns* in Jamaica, every gentleman's houſe is open to all *white travellers*. My guide, conſidering the *richeſt gentleman*, to be the beſt, named Col. Price, and accordingly conducted me to ROSE-HALL. A mulatto ſervant took my horſe, and another conducted me into a

ſpacious

ſpacious hall. A raw boy as I was, thus entering a ſtranger's houſe, did not ſit eaſy upon my mind, but when I heard the *important cough* of my hoſt, from the next room, I would gladly have got out of mine. At length, a tall, grave, ſtately gentleman appeared, with a white hat, deeply charged with *Point D'Eſpagne*, to whom I made an aukward, but ſufficient apology, to extort from him:—*you are welcome Sir*, yet I perceived I was not: and began to ſuſpect that I had been impoſed upon, as to the *travelling faſhion* of the country. The Colonel, however, ordered breakfaſt, and while the chocolate, tea, pine apples, water melons, and a profuſion of good things were ſetting forth, he called for a glaſs of brandy, and invited me to drink another! I then told him, I had been ſo warned againſt drinking any kind of fermented liquors, that I had only drunk two glaſſes of wine, at Governor Trelawney's, ſince my arrival; then pray, Sir, ſaid he, how long have you been arrived? and when he found I was a ſtranger, only of a few days, the miſt was removed, his reſerved countenance vaniſhed at once; and in the moſt obliging manner he expreſſed his concern, that he had received *ſo very a ſtranger* to the country, with the leaſt mark of indifference; add-

ing,

ing, that he had a very large acquaintance, and pointing to a houſe, about a mile diſtant, told me, that it was his ſteward's, a gentleman, to whom he allowed eight hundred pounds a year, for managing his eſtates, and to entertain ſuch travellers as were not of *his* acquaintance. I do not ſay this Sir, to direct you to go thither in future, for I ſhall always expect you to *ſling in a hammock* at *Roſe Hall*; but to explain away that embarraſment, you and I were under, juſt now, for I ſhould have ſaid, that I had told him at firſt, I was going to *Bagnell's Thickets*, to join a company there, to which I was a Lieutenant; he then perſuaded me to drink a dram of brandy, before I ſat down to breakfaſt, and aſſured me, that where one perſon died in that country, by drinking too much, twenty died by too much eating; a truth to which I moſt ſincerely ſubſcribe. After breakfaſt, Mr. Price, ſeeing my *miſerable ſcald horſe* brought forth, for the hire of which I had paid three piſtoles, * he was ſo offended with the owner, and ſo polite to me, that he mounted me upon a fine horſe of his own; then ſhewed me a houſe on the brow of a diſtant mountain, inhabited by his relation, there ſaid he, you will dine, and my

E couſin

* He made the Man return half the Money to me.

coufin will remount you to *Bagnell's*, where I am fettling a new plantation, and I hope we fhall often meet there, and here too; I fhould not have been thus particular, but to fhew the firft fpecimen of the hofpitality I met with, in a country, where the fame would have been repeated, throughout the whole Ifland; and at the houfe too, of the only man in it, who did not ufually receive *ftrangers*. During my refidence at *Bagnell's*, I was frequently fent out with four or five and twenty men, in fearch of the wild Negroes, as the affembly of that Ifland, allowed feventy pounds for *every pair of wild Negroes ears which were brought in*. Juft in the fame manner, as the *tame Negroes*, are allowed a bottle of rum, for every dozen *of rat tails, they bring in*; I thank God however, in *that bufinefs*, I was fortunate; for I never *gathered a fingle pair*. I thank God too, that I very early in life, had perception enough to learn, that however honourable it may be deemed, to invade, difturb or murther men of diftant climes,* it did not tally with my ideas of Juftice. I would fight, and either perifh, or conquer, men, who came from *afar*, to difturb me, from the enjoyment of that land, which my birth, gave me a na-

of

tural footing in; but I feel no diſpoſition, to murther thoſe, who like *Tomo Chachi*, are content with their own. After near a year's duty at *Bagnell's*, I was removed to *Port Maria Bay*, within one mile of a gentleman's plantation, with whom I had been acquainted, when he was a boy in London, * as ſoon as I had ſettled my men, I waited upon my old acquaintance, who received me with the utmoſt marks of kindneſs, and deſired me to be one of his family, while I remained on that ſtation. His houſe was ſmall, having only a large *ſalle à manger*, and two bedchambers beſide out-buildings, for the kitchen, ſervants, &c. I found, at his houſe, his lady, a brother, and his wife, and a Captain Hill; all at bed, and board with him; and yet he urged me to ſtay all night, and when I objected to it, he told me that Captain Hill had a mattraſs, with *a ſheet* laid over it † on the dining room floor, and that it was wide enough for two, for, to tell you the truth, ſaid he, I have lain

* Richard Baſnett, Eſq. a Gentleman well known at Bath and at Southampton, by his amazing Dexterity in ſhooting an Apple with a ſingle Ball; and which I have ſeen him throw up and hit, ten times together.

† Only one ſheet is laid, two, is one too many.

upon it for this week past, but if you will take my half, I can sleep with my wife. Mrs Basnett had given me reason enough to admire her, and therefore I thought it a good reason to accept of the invitation, but before either of us were asleep, I perceived the door to open, and a human figure came in, I told Captain Hill, who observed, that it was probably one of the house Negroes, come to steal *the Plantation* * which always stands upon the side board; but soon after, I found myself pulled by the sleeve, and heard a low voice, say, "*massa me da come*" vastly surprised! I reached out my hand, and put it upon something, as round as an *apple*, but as large as a *pumpkin*, my surprize *encreased* then exceedingly; so I got up,, in a great *passion*, and sent the nocturnal thing out of the room, with a *flea in her ear*, I say *her*: for I verily believe, it was a young negro wench, whom *massa* had ordered to fetch *the Plantation away*, after *Mrs. Baskett* and the family were *gone to bed*, for when I related this circumstance, the next morning, to *Mr. Basnett*; he began to put on some of those *serious looks*, I had, experienced at Rose Hall, before matters were explained, and now I am upon this subject

* Small sour Punch.

ſubject, for I am glad of any ſubject rather than *myſelf*, I may, I hope relate a ſtory of Mr. Anthony Henley; who was thought a great wit, and who poſſeſſed a *Mac. Kittrick* ſhare of impudence. He informed me, that he invited two gentlemen, and their wives, to ſpend a fortnight with him at the Grange. In thoſe days, gentlemen travelled with their own horſes, and Mr. Henley made two days journey, from London to Wincheſter, and knowing that his friends, were no enemy to the bottle, he put a ſmall hamper of claret behind his coach, for the men, and a couple of bottles of cowſlip wine, for the ladies; the narcotic influence of the cowſlips, ſoon ſent the ladies to bed, and Mr. Henley, who was one of the ſtrongeſt, and handſomeſt men in England, ſo plied the huſband's with claret, that by twelve o'clock, the chamber maid was called, to *lead* them to their ladies bedchambers, but previous thereto, Mr. Henley *charged the maid*, to obſerve, that the lady in the green riding habit, belonged to the gentleman in red, and the brown riding habit, to the blue coat gentleman, but either the maid or Mr. Henley, miſtook *the colours and croſſed the huſbands*, but what was worſe, he had made them promiſe to be off by eight the next morning, yet neither appeared till near ten; Mr. Henley, however informed me, that after he *got the Ladies* to the Grange, that they both *owned to him*, no mischief had been done *on the Road*. * The chambermaid, however took the blame *upon herself*, for I believe the chamber maids, upon *that road*, were all in the interest of Mr. Henley, though he did not make use of Mr. Dunning's art, to win them over to him. †

* This facetious gentleman, once asked me to breakfast, at the Grange, and after shewing me *Lady Betty's Cage*, and *other Curiosities*, of his house, I was taken into a light elegant Closet, in which were Corn Sacks, tied up, and labelled, thus. From Southampton.—From Winchester.—From Andover.—From Stockbridge, &c. It was natural to ask the Contents? he informed me, they were Love Letters. I could not said he, *poor Devils!* have the heart to burn them; at another Time he took me to Little Dunford to Breakfast with Mr. Young, Lady Rochford's Father, who had the nick Name of BRASS YOUNG, and it was really entertaining, to see, and hear, those two pieces of *Brazen Metal* sounding together. Mr. Henley, however, was victorious; for he made Mr. Young own, that his Mistress was Young's Cousin; but Young insisted also, that Miss Culliford, was related likewise to Lord Pembroke.

† The young men upon the circuit with Dunning, were always astonished to find, such a mean figure, gained the preference of all the *chaste* chamber maids, his method was this, the minute they alighted, Dunning called for the chamber maid; are you, said he, child, the person who provide the beds? I am Sir: then said he there's a guinea for you, and that *retaining fee*, secured his sheets being always the best aired! and surely such a generous man, was the fittest to oblige. Dunning well knew the *effect* of a fee before hand.

CHAPTER VI.

I Am now arrived at that important period of my life, (yet a compleat half century ago,) that James Mac. Kittrick, alias Adair, hath charged me with having "*the ſole command*" of a party of ſoldiers, when in the woods of Jamaica, and falling into an ambuſh of the wild Negroes; ſecuring my own perſon, by an early retreat, and leaving the battle to be fought, by my victorious Sergeant, who brought many of them in priſoners, at the inſtant that I was boaſting of my own perſonal exploits, I will not call this double named doctor, "a "*beaſt*, a *reptile; an aſſaſſin, and murder-monger*" but the reader will I am ſure excuſe me, in ſaying he is a baſe libeller, a liar, and a wicked defamer, and has no pretenſions to be conſidered as a gentleman, if he has dared to write, print,

print, and publiſh, ſuch falſehoods. But before I expoſe and refute this wicked calluminator; it may be neceſſary to give ſome account of the ſtate of that Iſland, between the years ſeventeen hundred and thirty, and that of thirty nine, when under the government of Mr. Trelawney; who made a permanent peace with thoſe black people. Such who are unacquainted with that Iſland will be ſurpriſed when they are told, that all the regular troops in Europe, could not have conquered the wild Negroes, by force of arms; and if Mr. Trelawney had not wiſely given them, what they contended for, LIBERTY, they would, in all probability have been, at this day, maſters of the whole country. The mountains in that Iſland are exceedingly ſteep and high, much broken, ſplit and divided by earthquakes, and many parts inacceſſible, but by men, who always go bare footed, and who can hold by withes, with their toes, almoſt as firmly, as we can with our fingers. In Governor Trelawney's time, there were two formidable bodies of the wild Negroes in the woods, who had no connection with each other, the weſt gang, under the command of a Captain *Cudjoe*: the eaſt, under Captain *Quoha*. A ſtraggling priſoner of *Quoha's* gang, being taken, he was ſent to inform

his

his brethren, with the conditions Mr. Trelawney held out to them, and which were accepted, by *Cudjoe* long before Captain *Quoha*, had heard any thing of it. At this time, I had been removed from my *Port Maria Bay*, duty, to a place called *Hobbie's*, five miles from the ſea, in the pariſh of St. George's; under the command of Lieutenant George Concannen, a gentleman, who had been long in the Iſland, and brother to Mathew Concannen, then the attorney general of Jamaica. The pariſh of St. George's, one of the fineſt, and moſt fertile in the Iſland, had in a manner been laid deſolate, by the wild Negroes, ſo much ſo, that though it once abounded in ſugar plantations, we were obliged to ſend thirty miles for our rum, and many other neceſſaries, nor durſt we even appear without the walls of our barracks, after it was night, as the wild Negroes ſurrounded us, and frequently, when they heard our centinels call *all's well*; would reply, *ki! ki! Becara* call *all's well*, while we *teeve their corn;* at this place, Mr. Concannen was reinforced with a Lieutenant, and fifty militia men, *black* and *white ſhot*, as they were there termed, and ſeventy baggage Negroes; his orders were to march up a certain river-courſe, till we diſcovered a wild negroe town, ſuppoſed by good information,

information, to be upon its margin, or very near it; after two or three days march from Hobby's, towards the fun fetting, we came to a fpot, on which the impreffion of human feet, of *all ages*, were very thick upon the fands, as well as dogs, &c. We were certain therefore, that the object of our fearch was near, but as there is very little twilight in that country, it was determined, that we fhould lie quietly all night upon our arms, and make our attack at the dawn of day, the next morning; and before the fun appeared, we perceived the fmoak of their little Hamlet, for the Negroes, always have a fire burning in their huts to drive away the *mufquitoes:* we therefore flattered ourfelves, that we might take even them, *napping*: if thofe people, ever ftand their ground, it is upon fuch, as is almoft inacceffible by white men, and the firft notice of their attack, is a heavy fire, from invifible hands! however the little Hamlet I am fpeaking of, was not a principal town, but a temporary *fifhing* and *hunting villa*, if I may be allowed the expreffion; it was fituated on the margin of the river, acceffible every way, and confequently not teenable: and therefore the inhabitants, who had difcovered our approach, were gone off in the night, or perhaps but a few minutes before we entered

their

their town, for there were ſeventy-four huts, and a fire burning in each, but no living creature in it. *Here* the duty, upon which we were ſent, was *compleatly* performed; but Mr. Concannen, thought it then became his duty, to communicate to us, the orders he had received, in the governor's name, from Captain JAMES ADAIR, (*not one of the Adairs of the Highlands of Scotland*, but really CAPTAIN ADAIR) * brother to the late well known, and much reſpected, William Adair, of Pall Mall, Eſq. when I ſaid *conſulted us*, I meant myſelf, the lieutenant of militia, and our young Scotch ſurgeon: I do not know what Mr. Concannen's *own opinion was*, but he adopted ours, which I am ſure was a very weak one, and that was to burn the town, and purſue the enemy; both which, we inſtantly put into execution, and followed the very track, which the Negroes had, in ſome meaſure made paſſable, by cutting the buſhes before us. At every half mile, we found *Cocoes*, *Yams*, *Plantains*, &c. left artfully by the Negroes, to induce us to believe, they were in fear of our overtaking them, and at length we found a fire, before which they had *left* ſeveral *grills* of wild hog, *probably well ſeaſoned*

* Killed before *Bocca Chica*.

ſeaſoned for us, we continued the purſuit, till near night, and then, hearing their dogs bark, we concluded they had heard us alſo, and we gave over all hopes of ſeeing or hearing any thing more of them: we had marched with great expedition, the whole day, and were much fatigued; but ſoon after, we got upon, the margin of *Spaniſh River*, * where we intended to enjoy ourſelves, and reſt that night, and the next morning, to follow the Stream, to the ſea ſide, in order to find our way back to Hobbies: for the ſtream only, could have directed us which was our courſe back again. As I was the ſecond in command, my ſtation was, in the rear of the whole body of men, baggage Negroes and all; and as ſoldiers on that duty, can only march *Hedge-faſhion* one after another, I may venture to ſay, I had been all the former days, a mile at leaſt from Mr. Concannen, who marched in the front, except a ſerjeant, and twelve *black* and *white ſhot*, which preceded him: but as all idea of ſervice was over, I deſired Mr. Concannen, to permit the militia Lieutenant, to bring up the rear, that I might have the pleaſure of his company, and converſation, on our way down to the ſea ſide? this being agreed to, after drinking

* The Rivers in Jamaica, are the beſt Paſſes for Foot paſſengers, except in heavy Rains, and then they carry all before them.

drinking our wild ſage tea, we gave our fuzees to the drummer, and moved forward. The Negroes, ſome of whom, had been in our rear, all the preceding day, and others before us, had placed themſelves, from top to bottom, on a very ſteep mountain, thickly covered with trees and buſhes; on the other ſide of the river, under which, they knew we muſt paſs, as the water was too deep on our ſide, and as that mountain was not an hundred and fifty yards from the ſpot, on which we had ſlept, they had an opportunity of knowing our numbers, and ſeeing which of us, were the *Grandé-men*, for as to external dreſs, we were all very much alike, in courſe jackets and trowſers. The Negroes therefore, permitted the advanced ſerjeant, and his party, to paſs unnoticed, but the minute *us Grande-men* got under their ambuſh, a volley ſhot came down, which muſt have killed or wounded moſt of us, had they taken any aim, but they are ſuch cowards, that they lie down upon their bellies, ſtart up to fire *per hazard*, and then ſink down, to *re-load*; ſeveral of the ſoldiers, for the militia were at ſome diſtance, though not out of gun ſhot, were mortally wounded, and the drummer, at our elbows, was ſhot through the wriſt: at this inſtant, the baggage Negroes, (ſeventy) who had

had but juſt got their loads upon their heads, threw them down, and run away; and the militia, to a man, their officer excepted, (whom however we did not ſee) followed them. The wild Negroes at the ſame time, firing and calling out, *Becara* run away—*Becara* run away, it is probable too, that we ſhould have followed, but fortunately, there were ſome large maſſes of the mountain which had caved down, and which lay in the middle of the ſtream, juſt under the foot of the ambuſh, and we took ſhelter behind them, but though we could hear the Negroes and even converſe with them, not one was to be ſeen!! our original ſtock of ſoldiers, did not exceed thirty, and to the beſt of my remembrance, we were not above ſixteen or ſeventeen behind the rocks, nor was it in our power, to reſtrain, that handful of men we had, from firing at the *ſmoak only*, of our enemies, till they had not a ſingle cartridge left!—The Surgeons inſtruments, and all the ſpare ammunition, with the proviſions, &c. was caſt down in the river above, and to ſay the truth, we durſt not run away, for the Negroes, only fired, when they could ſee a head, or an arm of any of our people, above the rocks, and there we ſtaid, more out of fear, than from any hopes of victory, up to our waiſts in water

for

for four hours and a half, with a burning ſun upon our heads, and in momentary apprehenſions, of being all *taken alive*, for I believe *that fear*, overcome the fear of immediate death, I own it was ſo with me, and at length, however, one of our men, was ſhot through the knee! it was impoſſible that he could have been ſo wounded, from the ambuſh ſide, and therefore we naturally, and fearfully too, concluded, the Negroes had croſſed the river, either above or below us, and that they would inſtantly puſh in upon us, and take us alive, we therefore agreed to quit our place of ſhelter, and take our chance of their reſerved fire; and put the beſt face we could, upon our enemy, on the other ſide, with *preſented, bnt unloaded arms*, for Mr. Concannen, myſelf, and the ſurgeon only, had a few ſpare cartridges, we accordingly haſtily paſſed over the river, which was not forty yards, from the thicket, and was as thickly *be-ſpattered* on our retreat, as by their firſt ſalutation, the men who were mortally wounded, and who perhaps never intended to move from the ſtones in the river on which they were repoſing for death, were ſo alarmed, to think that their laſt minutes, were to be ſpent in the poſſeſſion, of *ſuch enemies*, defying their wounds, their agonies, and their miſeries, jumped

jumped up and followed us, and one in particular, who had been ſhot through the body, at the firſt fire, received another bullet in at his back, and out at his belly, and yet not only went over with us, but actually clambered up a ſteep mountain, and *there* beſought *us* to diſpatch him. Before we had been two minutes in the oppoſite wood, the militia lieutenant joined us, he had concealed himſelf behind a tree, for what elſe could he do? and as we dreaded a purſuit; we aſcended as faſt as crippled, fatigued, and for myſelf, I will add, frightened men could aſcend, the ſteepeſt mountains, during which we heard the horrid ſhouts, drums, and rejoicings of our victorious enemies in the river below; not only rejoicing over our ſalt beef, bread, hams, &c. &c. but bearing as we afterwards found, the heads of our dead men in triumph. The run away militia, got among the ſettlements the ſame evening, and had not their *hinder* wounds, contradicted their *forward* declarations; they would have made their neighbours believe they had fought valiantly, I believe that a report had prevailed, that Mr. Concannen, and the whole party, had run away, * that report aggravated Mr. Concannen's

* I never heard of any party, whether of militia, or regulars, that could ſtand againſt the ambuſhes of thoſe people.

cannen's friends, and then it was as wickedly propagated that because Mr. Concannen, the attorney general, and Mr. Trelawney the governor, were upon bad terms, that the governor had sent his brother, the lieutenant, upon this hazardous expedition, with a handful of men, to sacrifice him to the private resentment, he bore to the attorney general. I am happy even at this distant period, however, to say, that Mr. Trelawney, was too wise, too good, and of too noble a disposition; to be capable of any base, mean, or spiteful action. The town being found according to the information given us, is sufficient to prove, that it was for the good of the service *only* that such orders were given, and that *us, younger counsel of war,* whom Mr. Concannen consulted, led him into that disasterous situation, in spanish river, Mr. Grenville, had a statue erected to him, when he quitted his government of Barbadoes, where there were no wild Negroes to subdue; and if the inhabitants of Jamaica, had been as wise, as they were generous, they too should have erected one, to Mr. Trelawney, before his door, at *St. Jago*, as the preserver of the Island, and the author of their present quiet possession of it. I must now return, to my brother officer, and fellow sufferers, in spanish river; Mr. Concannen, by standing so many hours in the water, with a perpendicular sun upon his head, and a mind deeply suffering no doubt upon many accounts, was suddenly seized with a violent fever. Before we ascended the first steep mountain, but we thought it prudent, if practicable, to ascend to the very highest, and with great difficulty, and crippled as we were, did so; the poor drummer, who had been wounded at the first onset, got a ball through each thigh, when we retreated, and called loudly for water, or he could proceed he said no further; Mr. Concannen, was in the same distressed condition, but not a drop of water was to be had, my friend, and brother officer, then lay down, and desired me to make the best of my way, with such men as were able to follow me, and not to sacrifice the whole to two or three, miserable wretches unable to proceed. One of the soldiers, had a little hammock, made out of a barrack sheet, at his back, and flinging that between two trees, we with much difficulty got Mr. Co[illegible]cannen into it, for he was a tall bulky [illegible]an; he then procured water, *but of his o[illegible] making*, in his hat, and from time to [illegible]e, *moistened his mouth with it*, I say *moistene[illegible]* [illegible]or he durst not indulge his appetite in s[illegible]owing it, for want

of

of the ſame powers of ſupply! the night approached, and as a profound ſilence was neceſſary, every man bore his wretched condition, without a groan, though we were all in a condition, *I hope* as bad as thoſe ſufferers in the hold at Calcutta, which has been ſo pathetically related, by a ſtill ſurviving, and reſpectable ſufferer, Governor Holwell. For myſelf, I lay down upon my back, by the ſide of my brother officer, with my tongue out, and praying to god to let that dew fall, which is conſidered fatal to thoſe who expoſe themſelves to it. The next morning, providentially, we found an enormous cotton tree, the ſpurs of which, grew ſo fantaſtically, that they had formed a reſervoir of rain water, it was as black as coffee; but it was more acceptable, than a treaſure of gold, on the evening of that day we got to the ſea ſide, and among ſome inhabitants where hoſpitality and humanity was not wanting, notwithſtanding the preſent *hue* and *cry* about ſlavery, cruelty, &c.

Jamaica is an iſland as remarkable for longevity as any part of the known world, and I hope and believe, there are many people living there, and here too, who will remember this tranſaction, not only as it occaſioned much

 converſation

conversation among the principal people of the island, relative to the slanderous reports about the governor and the attorney general, but as being our last act of hostility, as will appear in the next chapter, between the wild Negroes, and the civil inhabitants, a most important Æra, in the annals of that wonderful, beautiful, and I will add, plentiful and luxurious island.

CHAPTER VII.

NOTHING but a mind rouzed to recollection, and awaken'd by the grossest falsehoods, could have recalled so perfectly to my memory, transactions, which from the great distance of time, seemed to me but as a dream, though it may be observed, that people in age, frequently forget the events of the year, and even the day in which they live, yet have a perfect recollection of what passed in their youth. About three months after this unfortunate *run-away business* in Spanish river, Governor Trelawney, like the Duke of Marlborough, honoured me with a *second tryal*, for I was again ordered out with a party of three hundred regular troops, under the command of Captain Adair, we were in possession of a prisoner, one of Captain, Quoha's people, and he too was one of their *hornsmen*, and under-

took

took to lead us to their principal town, for at this time Quoha did not certainly know, that Cudjoe (the captain of the west end of the Island gang) had submitted upon Governor Trelawney's terms. It was utterly impossible that those two parties could have any kind of communication or correspondence with each other; our prisoner, the *hornsman*, was well assured however, that the western gang had laid down their arms, and were in possession of *that* for which they contended; LIBERTY, he assured us too, that we should fail, if we attempted to possess ourselves of their town by force: it was so situated, he said, that no BODY of men, or scarce an individual could approach it, that they would not have five or six hours notice, by their detached watchmen, or out centinels; nothing but ocular demonstration, can convey a perfect idea of the steep and dangerous precipices we passed, and which men, wearing shoes, could not be so secure as Negroes, who being bare footed; had *toe fingers*, as well as hands, to secure them from falling. After two or three days fatiguing march, the *hornsman*, conducted us to the foot of a very steep and high mountain, where we found in the vale beneath, a plantation of yams, plantanes, &c. he informed us that on the

the other side, equally steep to descend, stood their town, and the only accessible way to it, was up a very narrow path, that holes were cut, from place to place, about four foot deep, all the way up, and down, with crutch sticks set before them, for the entrenched Negroes, to rest their guns upon, and that the first man who appeared would be fired at, and another Negroe ready loaded, to take his place for the next comer, in short, that it would be impossible to lead our men in force, even to the top of the mountain, where the Negroes, who knew of our approach, were waiting for us; Captain Adair perceiving that force of arms would not do, to my great satisfaction, ordered the *hornsman* to sound his horn; the Negroes then were at no loss to know that their missing companion was with us, and they returned the salute, by sounding theirs, but all this while, not a man of them was to be seen! we then hailed them with a trumpet, and told them we were come to agree, not to fight; that the governor had given *Cudjoes* people freedom, and that the same terms were open to them; this account tallying exactly to that which the poor *Laird* of Laharret had communicated to them, had much weight, but when they were informed, that we were *sol-*

diers,

diers, not militia, they were alarmed, obſerving, that ſoldiers had *no tatta, no mamma, and that one ſoldier dead, 'tother tread upon* him, however, after a long *trumpet parle*, they agreed to ſend one of their Captains, in exchange, for one of ours, in order to ſettle *preliminaries*, and this being agreed, to our utter aſtoniſhment, we ſaw in an inſtant, an acre of under wood cut down, and that acre covered with Negroes! every man having cut down a buſh at one blow in the twinkling of an eye! ſoon after, terms being agreed to, we marched, or rather ſcrambled up the narrow path, and found at proper diſtances, the holes and crutches exactly as deſcribed by the *hornſman*; when we had deſcended a *path* equally ſteep and narrow on the other ſide, and approached the town, it became wide enough to march our men in, two a breaſt, under the beat of drums, this novel appearanee, to their women and children, ſeemed ſo terrible, that they could not ſtand it, but taking their children by their arms, run away with them into the woods; however, when our drums were ſilent, and the men inactive, they returned, one, or two, at a time, till all was quiet, as I was the hoſtage, and firſt in their town, I took up my abode at Captain *Quoba's* habitation, and it

was

was ſome amuſement *then* to obſerve, with what deteſtation his *peccananes* (children) were bred, to feel againſt white men; for though they ſaw their father in civil converſation with me, they could not refrain from ſtriking their pointed fingers, as they would knives if they had been permitted, againſt my breaſt, ſaying in deriſion, *a. becara—becara—i. e.* white man! white man! and here I had the mortification of ſeeing the poor *laird of Lahar-rets** under jaw, fixed as an ornament, to one of their hornſmen's horn, and we found that the upper teeth of our men, ſlain in Spaniſh river, were drilled thro' and worn as ankle, and wriſt bracelets, by their *Obea women*, and ſome of the *ladies of the firſt faſhion in town*; however, upon our informing *Quoba*, that ſuch objects were very painful to us, they did not appear the next day, I was very inquiſitive to know in what manner the poor *laird* was put to death, but all I could obtain, upon that ſubject, was, that he had pleaded his own cauſe, and the Negroes too, ſo well (for he was a man of ſenſe, and learning) that *Quoba* told me, he had put bracelets upon his wriſts, and determined to have ſent him down to Governor

Trelawney,

* The lairds teeth were ſo very particular, that ſome of our men could have ſworn to the identity of the jaw bone.

Trelawney, with offers of submission upon the same terms, the *laird* had assured him, *Cudjoe* had accepted; but said *Quaha*, when I consulted our *Obea woman*, she opposed the measure, and said, *him bring becaria for take the town, so cut him head off*. But God knows what the poor laird suffered, previous to that kind operation. The old *Hagg*, who passed sentence of death upon this unfortunate man, had a girdle round her waste, with (I speak within compass) nine or ten different knives hanging in sheaths to it, many of which I have no doubt, had been plunged in human flesh and blood; the susceptible reader therefore can better conceive, than I can describe, what my feels were, who had so lately escaped from some of her horrid operations in the use of them. But in the midst of this calm, and when we had reason to think all was peace and security, an event took place, which had not only nearly lost us the honor of making peace, and the islands the benefit of it, but involved us in a civil war, for a militia colonel, was out at the same time, with a large party of his men, and hearing by some straggling negroes, that Mr. Adair had brought the negroes to terms, he joined us at Trelawney town, and being of superior rank to Adair, insisted upon it, that the terms of peace should

be

be sent down in his, not Captain Adair's name; and this dispute, between us regulars, and the militia officers, arose to such a height, that Adair had put us all under arms, and if the militia colonel had not submitted, I verily believe we should have come to blows. The negroes could not be indifferent spectators to a scene of such confusion, and so big with mischief, and it was with some difficulty we could prevail upon *Quoba* to consider himself, and his people safe, between two contending parties of white men; and if *Quoba* had not been a *plantation slave*, who knew something of the customs, and manners, of the white people, all had been lost, it was clear however, that the peace was the act of Captain Adair, though the militia colonel might assume, upon our junction, the command of the whole, but even that, Captain Adair would not submit to. As *Quoba* spoke tolerable good English, and seemed a reasonable man, I questioned him very closely about the transaction in spanish river; and the fate of those wounded men whom we left there, but he answered my questions so cautiously, that it was plain the *truth* was not to be told, but when I asked him what mischief our random fire at *their stockade* had done; he sharply replied, "*massa you no see this hole in my my cheek? one of your ſhot bounce again my gun, him flly up, and makeum,*" and he was the only man who loſt a drop of blood on their ſide, on a day that we ſuffered ſo ſeverely, both in body, and mind. One of the liſtening negroes, to my converſation with *Quoba,* then told me he had obſerved me in particular, after we quitted the ambuſh, for when we left the river, and got into the thicket, I found a little keg of ſhrub, which one of our baggage negroes had caſt from his head, in the firſt flight, and a ſoldier near me, having a little tin pot at his girdle, we all took a *potation* from it, and a moſt ſeaſonable relief it afforded, after ſtanding a long time up to our hips in water, with a vertical ſun upon our heads. I then queſtioned the negroe where he was at that time? it ſeems he and another negroe, had been hunting wild hog, and was not with the negroes in ambuſh, but the reports of our firing, had brought them to the ſpot, and they had concealed themſelves behind a large cotton tree, and ventured to fire only once, upon us, before we had left the river, and then it was, that the man was ſhot in the knee, and that ſhot it was, which determined us to quit the river; finding that we were fired upon from both ſides, and apprehenſive that the negroes would have ruſhed in upon us, and taken us alive,

alive, for that *only* was our fear, we would have compounded for immediate death; but we dreaded the ſentence of death, and the executions of it, from the hands of that horrid wretch, their *Obea woman*. I have been thus particular, as to this part of the buſineſs, because the ingenious author of the hiſtory of Jamaica, in ſpeaking of the peace made with the wild negroes by Governor Trelawney, has not mentioned it as *two diſtinct acts*, and with two ſeparate bodies of men, under different leaders, and quite unconnected, but as if it had been *one* act of grace; to *one* body of people; whereas, it was as diſtinct a matter, as making peace with the French, without including the Spaniards, or the Spaniards without the French. This great and important ſervice rendered to that iſland, ſhould have been marked by the aſſembly with a ſtatue at St, Jago, before the governor's door, to the man, who preſerved their lives, and properties; and as they are a generous, a brave, and an hoſpitable people, I hope, when they ſo properly place a ſtatue to Lord Rodney's memory for ſo gallantly defending them from an attack by ſea, that they will not forget, what they owe to him who ſecured them interior benefits of equal importance to their purſes and perſons. Though it is fifty years

years ſince theſe tranſactions took place, there can be no doubt but that there are many perſons now living in England, and in Jamaica, who perfectly remember the two events I have been forced to relate in vindication of my military character, and if the falſe defamer, Mackittrick, does not produce the gentleman of "*reſpectable character*, nor thoſe to whom that *reſpectable gentleman told it to at Bath*, to confirm, that I had the *ſole command*" that I run away, that my ſerjeant obtained the victory, while I was boaſting of my own proweſs". the candid reader will I am convinced agree with me, that the charge was baſe, wicked, cowardly, and ſuch as no man, not utterly void of every ſenſe, of honor, conſcience, or rectitude! would have dared to have publiſhed.*

CHAP.

* Let Mr. Mackittrick produce *that* gentleman of character, or the gentlemen to whom he related ſo *circumſtantially* this matter, and if they are really men of character, I hereby promiſe to acknowledge my ſhame in the publick papers; but I ſhall expect Mr. Mackittrick for ever to hide his head among the barren hills, which gave ſuch a wretch life, if he cannot, and I tell him he cannot; the man does not live who can ſay it, not even he who wrote it, durſt not.

CHAPTER VIII.

IN conſequence of theſe two *ſmarting* expeditions againſt the wild negroes, and hearing that there was a talk of raiſing ten regiments in England, I applied to Mr. Trelawney for ſix months leave of abſence, and having obtained that indulgence, Captain Wyndham, of the Greenwich man of War, was ſo obliging, to give me a paſſage home with him, in which ſhip I bore my ſhare in two of the greateſt calamities, to which mariners are ſubject:—FIRE, AND WATER; for in the windward paſſage, during very fine weather, and ſmooth water; the cooper dropped a lighted candle into a half puncheon of rum, which was *ſtoed* in the *after hatch-way*; and which ſtood upon many others. The fire burſt forth with great fury, even to flame up to main-top! all command instantly ceased, and such a scene of confusion took place, as is utterly undescribable. Captain Wyndham, and his first lieutenant Mr. Crookshanks, (now living) assisted by the other officers, and such men as were not deprived of reason (for I saw many who were) exerted all their skill and prudence, in extinguishing the flames, by covering the spirits with water, for had they stopped the bunghole, as some proposed, it is probable the air within, would have been so rarified, as to burst the vessel, and set all the dry materials on fire also. Fourteen sail of Merchantmen, which were under our convoy, seeing the condition we were in, and knowing that our guns were all shotted, stood off. The men had left the wheel, and the ship, with her sails set, took her *own* course! during this time, or a great part of it, I was the only person upon the quarter deck, for there were more about the fire than could be of service, and I experienced a *second tryal*, almost equal to that in spanish river. In bad weather sailors will obey orders, but in a ship on fire, it is every man, *a dram out of his own bottle*, and I believe many bottles were poured down during that time; for either a temporary madness, or extreme drunkenness, seemed to have taken place, among the greatest

part

part of the crew. Some were crying, many were raving, some laughing, while others were endeavouring to get the boats over the side; yet I am firmly persuaded, had the ship been burnt, those men who preserved a little reflection, and resolution, would have been saved. The water was perfectly smooth, and though the Merchantmen stood off, all their boats would have been out, the minute the ship had blown up, not only to save the people, but many loose things which such a sudden explosion, must necessarily set on float; it was a trying time with us all, and as I had nothing to do, but to consider my own safety, I secured an oar, and laid it upon the netting of the quarter deck, determining, if the fire gained upon the ship, to perish by water, rather than fire, or to save myself by swimming, and floating with my oar. However the good sense and prudence of those about the fire got the better of it, and peace and order again took place. As we had not only Commodore Brown, the late Sir William Burnaby, and several ladies passengers, the society on board was very agreeable, and much heightened by the obliging conduct of Captain Wyndham; one of the best bred gentlemen in the british navy, but when we got into the latitude of Bermudas, we were taken by a gale of wind, or rather by a furious ſtorm, ſuch as landmen cannot conceive, and ſuch as few ſeamen ever experience, if I miſtake not, we run eleven knots (miles) under our bare poles, we then attempted to lye to, but the ſhip would not bear it, and we were obliged to run before it, a under fore ſail, while we were in this ſituation, the mountainous ſea which followed us, becalmed the fore ſail, and the ſea made a breach over us, and with ſuch force too, that the poop, the cabins beneath it, and all the upper works were ſo ſtove in, that the great cabin was laid quite open, and fluſh with the main deck, Sir William Burnaby's hammock and mine, flung ſide by ſide, at this time, in the gun-room, and the ſea, which came pouring down the hatch ways in ſuch quantities, induces us to believe, that the ſhip was under water, and that we had no longer to live, than till ſhe was filled between decks, but as I ſat in my hammock, with my face to the tiller-head, the canvas having been beat in, I perceived light, for it was juſt at break of day that this *pooping ſea* had broke over us. I then got out of my hammock, and with difficulty, in my ſhirt only, gained the deck, but good God! what a ſight did it exhibit, there lay poor old Commodore Brown;

Brown; ladies, both black and white, naked among the fragment of furniture, bedding, sheets, blankets, all *helter-skelter* without any covering, but their wet shirts and shifts, and poor captain Wyndham, a cripple with the gout, holding himself from being blown overboard, by the main-sheet; I crawled, (for I could not walk) to Commodore Brown, and asked if I could render him any service: he said a few dry blankets, would be of use to the poor ladies, and as Sir William's hammock and mine, were perfectly dry, I got down again into the gun room, and having secured two or three blankets, and a pot of ginger (which cost me seven pounds sterling) I attempted to make my way up again, but a sea broke over us which not only threw me down the hatch-way, but broke my pot of ginger, which *the jacks*, sopped as it was, in salt water, and dirt, devoured in an instant. It is very singular, that though all the *after* cabins were washed away, and even the bedsteads on which some of the passengers lay were splintered, no one was maimed, wounded, or washed overboard! The passengers, ladies and all, were got down into the purser's cabin, and bread room, and the gale continued in its greatest force, I think for more than eight and forty hours; I have been much at sea, and in what has been called by ſeamen very hard gales of wind, but they were mere breezes to this Bermudian gale. Upon my arrival in England, I found ten new regiments were to be raiſed, ſix of marines, and four of foot, my brother, who was then at Cambridge, ſent me a letter to Mr. Townſhend, and directed me to deliver it myſelf, either in town or country, and upon enquiry, I found Mr. Townſhend was upon a viſit, with that great and good man, Mr. Poyntz, at Mitcham, and thither I went with poſt horſes, for no ſuch thing as a poſt chaiſe exiſted in thoſe days, it was very ſevere weather, and I arrived there ſo froſt bitten, that I could not have returned even to Reading. Mr. Poyntz therefore humanely invited me to ſtay a day or two, as he kindly termed it, to warm myſelf, and then ſaid he, part of my family, who are going to London, can give you a corner in my coach, and I went back, with an open letter in my pocket from Mr. Townſhend to Sir William Younge. This letter (was not written in a court favor ſtyle) but to deſire I might be promoted in the new raiſed corps to the rank of captain, which was accordingly done, being appointed Captain lieutenant to Brigadier Jefferies's marine regiment of foot, for at that time the marines were independent of the admiralty

board.

board. Our head quarters was fixed at Southampton, and after two or three months successful recruiting, I was ordered to quarters. A few days after my arrival there, fourteen or fifteen officers, all strangers to each other, were collected to eat our first *regimental dinner together*, and here I hope I shall be excused, if I relate a very unfortunate circumstance which arose even before I had drank a glass of wine with my brother officers. I am well aware that events of such a nature ought not to come from the pen of either party, but as *Jemmy Makittrick* has charged me with want of spirit among the *blacks*, I hope to be pardoned, if I relate part at least, of my conduct among my *white brethren* at Southampton, for previous to our sitting down at dinner, observing one of the company to have his hand supported by a black silk sling, I asked by what accident he had suffered? he replied that he had been involved in a fray at Portsmouth the evening before, and that two of his fingers had been cut off. It was natural to ask him what company he had been in? he named several, and among them Lieutenant Briggs, a gentleman whom I knew and esteemed, and who was just appointed to that vacancy, which my promotion had made in the company at Jamaica. I was astonished, and concerned, observing that Mr.

Briggs

Briggs was my friend, and particular acquaintance; he may be your acquaintance, replied the wounded gentleman, but I aſſure you he is not your friend, for he abuſed you in the groſſeſt terms, *intimating at the ſame time that it was lucky the wind was not eaſterly, or he would have been ſailed for Jamaica.* I underſtood by this *hint*, what was expected, for it ſeems the abuſe Mr. Briggs had beſtowed upon me, had been imparted to all the company. And here I muſt obſerve that this young man had run out a very pretty fortune, and was ſo diſtreſſed, as to go over to Jamaica, a *cadet* in the company to which I belonged; that I had pitied his condition, that he eat often with me, was ſometimes aſſiſted with a little pocket money from mine; and that we never had the leaſt difference together, that I had rejoiced to hear he had ſucceeded me in the commiſſion I quitted, and that if I had been aſked his character, I ſhould have mentioned him as a genteel well bred young man, for whom I had a real eſteem and regard.

The reader may eaſily conceive my ſituation at dinner, with fourteen or fifteen gentlemen, who would never have eat again with me perhaps, had Mr. Briggs been ſailed, I therefore

made

made a ſhort meal, drank the gentlemens healths, and deſired them to ſuſpend their judgment for a few hours, as I underſtood Mr. Briggs was ſtill at Portſmouth, and that I would endeavour to ſee him before I ſlept, or eat again. I was at this time a very young man, and neither the *colony of Georgia*, nor the mountains and *wild negroes* in Jamaica, had given me much opportunity of knowing how to conduct myſelf, upon an occaſion ſo very novel and unexpected; but as the late General Sir Richard Lyttleton, was one of the company, and though not older than myſelf, I knew he had been page to the Queen, and much better acquainted with life than me, I ſent for him out, and deſired him not only to honor me with his advice, how to proceed at that time, but to give his aſſiſtance throughout the whole affair, provided I acted with that ſpirit which I ought, and which he approved. Mr. Lyttleton ſaid many polite things upon the occaſion, thought himſelf particularly honoured, and being ſingled out from ſo many brother officers, equally zealous to ſerve me, and then obſerved, that Mr. Briggs muſt be a paltroon, to have ſo *nearly timed* his indecent attack, upon an abſent gentleman, therefore ſaid he, do not challenge him but cane him ſoundly, and tell him he will find

find you ready for him whenever he is at leiſure to call upon you at Southampton; adding, that I ſhould thereby interrupt his preſent voyage, and render him *the challenger.*' With theſe inſtructions I inſtantly took my leave of Mr. Lyttleton, and ſet off for Portſmouth, it was in the month of April, and the day that Admiral Cavendiſh gave a ball, upon being elected member for that city. I did not find the young gentleman at his lodging, but while I was waiting for him at the coffee houſe, I ſaw him ſtanding at the King's Arms Tavern door, very elegantly dreſſed, for the ball, and to do his perſon juſtice, he was a very elegant man, he had a ſword on, and a cane in his hand, and as I had only a ſword, and a ſmall riding ſtick, I drew a more ſubſtantial one out of a bundle, which ſtood to be ſold at the next door, and without ſtaying to pay the owner for it, I determined to pay Mr. Briggs *with it*, I believe he ſaw me draw it out, for before I got over to him, he was as white as the paper I am now writing upon, my word, and my blow went in uniſon, at his head, and brought forth blood enough to ſpoil half a dozen brocade waiſtcoats, he did not draw his ſword, but ſtruck at me with his cane, I then followed my blows, till I had ſhivered my ſtick to pieces

over

over him, and then I took him, ſtick and all, and laid him at full length in the gutter of the high ſtreet, before the King's arms door, gave him a blow or two with his own cane, and told him he would find me at his ſervice at Southampton whenever he had any further commands for me. Portſmouth being a garriſon town, we were both, in an inſtant put under arreſt by the Governor, and the next *morning* according to *Eliquette Militaire* brought before him to *ſhake hands and be friends*, and then we were ſet at liberty, but as Mr. Briggs was not in a *condition* to *take notice* of his *dreſſing for the ball*, at that time ſo I told him again, where I was to be ſpoken with, and returned to Southampton. The next morning I was informed Mr. Briggs was dangerouſly ill, indeed it was with difficulty he could be brought before the governor, to perform the *Etiquette Militaire*, to take off his arreſt; I then returned to Southampton, again letting Mr. Briggs know, where I was to be found, ſhould he *hereafter* have any commands for me, but before I had been two days at quarters, (where I was very well received by Captain Lyttleton, and my brother officers) notice came up, that Briggs was dying. Captain Smyth, a natural ſon to Sir Thomas Lyttleton, and conſequently a *natural brother* to Captain

Captain Lyttleton, was then commander of a ſhip of war, at Spithead, and bound for Newfoundland, Captain Lyttleton therefore went down to Portſmouth, to procure me a *birth* with his brother upon that ſtation, till it might be deemed ſafe for me to return, in caſe of Briggs's death, however about a fortnight after I received the following letter from my adverſary. "Sir, I came laſt friday in expectation "of ſeeing you, but being diſappointed in my "deſign, I ſend you this, which is to acquaint "you, that the ill treatment I have had from "you obliges me inſiſt upon ſeeing you to mor-"row, the 11th of May, 1741, between the "hours of ten in the morning, and two in the "afternoon, and that you will ſend me word "by the bearer what hour, and what place, "otherwiſe you may depend upon my poſting "you in every place I come in."

HUTTON BRIGGS.

May 10, 1741.

"*P. S.* If you come alone or bring a friend, "let me know."

The reader will perceive that the poſtſcript to Briggs's letter conveys more than *meets the eye*, conſidering the rough manner he had been treated

treated at Portſmouth. After conſulting Captain Lyttleton, I replied that I would meet him upon Titchfield common the next day at one o'clock, that Captain Lyttleton would honour me with his attendance as my ſecond, and that I ſhould bring a caſe of piſtols, and a ſword, and expected him to do the ſame, ſoon after our arrival upon the common on horſe back, and conſequently booted and ſpurred, Mr. Briggs, dreſſed like a dancing maſter, appeared in a chaiſe and one, accompanied by a Lieutenant Morgan, who propoſed to Mr. Lyttleton, that if I would aſk Mr. Briggs's pardon, the matter might be *ſo* ſettled, this not being agreed to, Mr. Briggs, who was a good ſwords-man, and had often given me inſtructions with *florets* in Jamaica, was aſked where his piſtols were? he had none he ſaid, his arms were on board of ſhip, that a ſword was a gentleman's weapon, and began to bind up his right arm with a ſilk handkerchief; being in boots and ſpurs, and my adverſary in pumps, I objected much to deciding the matter with ſwords, and Mr. Lyttleton offered Briggs his choice of three caſes, his own, mine, or his ſervants, but Briggs abſolutely objected to uſe either, and flouriſhed his ſword; Mr. Lyttleton, then obſerved to me, that he was a coxcomb, and that he believed he was a coward

coward alſo, however ſaid he take him with his own weapon; I accordingly did ſo.—For the reſt many of Sir Richard Lyttleton's friends are ſtill living, to whom I know he related the tranſaction; * and therefore I ſhall only ſay, *that Briggs did not kill me*; here I muſt obſerve, that three months afterwards, Mr. Briggs did me the favor of a viſit at Southampton, to know my commands for Jamaica, and then I aſked, him, what could have induced him to ſpeak ſo diſreſpectfully of one who had always eſteemed him? now it is to be obſerved that his chriſtian name was Hutton, and that he had a rich aunt of that name in Weſtminſter, who was a very intimate acquaintance of my mother and ſiſters; ſo intimate, that the fooliſh neighbours, imagined the old lady had left her whole fortune to my mother and ſiſter, and as Mr. Briggs found ſhe had been told, ſome extraordinary tales of his extravagance, he had conceived me to be the tatler of thoſe tranſactions, in order to deter his aunt from leaving it to him, but he had been ſince convinced, that I did not even know they were related, and beſide his aunt was then dead, and had proper-ly

* Lord Barrington, was at that time a particular Friend of Sir Richard's, and I believe Mr. Monckton, now an eminent Surgeon at Southampton, was behind the Hedge. Lord Barrington is no Friend of mine, but he is a Man of truth and honor.

ly diſpoſed of her fortune to her own relations, not to mine; this ſtory ſhould not have appeared *here*, if I had not been ſo baſely charged with running away from the wild negroes, and beſide, however wrong duelling may be deemed, for ſlight offences, there are ſome, which according to the preſent mode among mankind, and particularly among military men, which cannot be decided otherwiſe; had Briggs been ſailed for Jamaica, I might ſoon have been in the ſame Situation with ſome officer of my own corps.

ANECDOTE

OF

LORD CHANCELLOR THURLOW.

HAVING tired myſelf, and my reader with too much on one *inſignificant Being*, which I hope will be pardoned, as it is a juſtification of my military character. I ſhall change the ſubject to a man of the firſt importance in the kingdom, and relate the ſingular manner in which Lord Thurlow did me the honor of making me perſonally known to him. It was at Bath, in the year 1780, when he came thither for the benefit of his health. It may prove uſeful to many others, both in a phyſical and political light,

for

for at that time I had no knowledge of his lordſhip, further than that he had been with my reſpectable friend Mr. Madocks, one of my council at the bar of the court of chancery, and the houſe of Lords, in an unſucceſsful cauſe, whereby I loſt ten thouſand pounds, contrary to the opinion, not only of both thoſe able men, but of the late Lord Chief Juſtice Willes, and Sir Dudley Ryder. His lordſhip came ſo ill to Bath that the general opinion was he could not recover, his diſorder was bilious in an high degree; he however walked up to my hermitage, in company with a lady, and ſeemed much pleaſed with a romantic ſpot I was then building a *hermit's neſt upon.* Excluſive of his rank, I was charmed with his free and eaſy manner of converſation, he obſerved that I had choſen a bit of ground to which nature had been very liberal, and ſuch as might be improved to advantage; I then told his lordſhip if I poſſeſſed any talent, it was the earlieſt and humbleſt of all; that of *cottage making*, and informed him, that I once bought a thatched cottage for five and forty guineas, which had ſince been ſold for two thouſand. Why ay, ſays my lord, that is Feliatow cottage, is it not? adding, I know it, and by my faith I think it worth but five and forty pounds now: I thought this but a courſe compliment,

compliment, so I *roughed* him again in my turn, which he not only took in good part, but replied, you will come and dine with me notwithstanding that; nothing could betray better sense, or better temper than such a reply from such a man as his lordship, to such a *man as me.* Upon further conversation, I observed, that by his lordship's complection, and other symptoms, he certainly had stones in the gall bladder; how should you know that? because I am the first and best gall doctor in England:—who made you so? five and twenty years dreadful sufferings under that most painful of all disorders, and if your lordship will permit, if you have that disorder, I will not ask, but tell you what the symptoms are you suffer under. He desired I would breakfast with him the next morning, and was satisfied he had every reason to believe my conjecture was well founded. I then informed him I had passed seven and twenty gall stones in one day, and assured him that art, not physic, was alone to be used to remove them; he desired me to explain it, and after assuring his lordship, I pretended not to possess any physical or anatomical knowledge, but what extreme personal sufferings had woefully instructed me with; I observed that the coagulated bile concretions generally formed with

with irregular mulberry like external surfaces, and consequently when nature (which is always aiming to discharge morbid matter) forced them into the gall duct, their rough coats irritated the duct so as to create not only exquisite pain, but frequently imminent danger; that the first thing therefore to be done was to render the externals of the gall stones perfectly smooth, and that could only be effected, by a hard trotting horse. I then enquired whether he walked, or trotted his? he walked him, for trotting he observed hurt him; for that very reason he should ride one of his coach horses, observing that were I to put some par-boiled peas into a bladder, and hook to my button hole, I could ride a horse from London to York, without crushing them, but that I could not *trot* from London to Turnham-Green, without reducing them into one mass.*

* The gall stone is a disorder unknown to the ancients, and very little known to the modern physicians, till about the year 1750, when Doctor Coe, of Chelmsford, wrote a very ingenious treatise upon that subject. My mother died of that disorder, and I had suffered grievously under it for many years, before I knew the cause, yet it is, and probably always was, a very common disorder,

I am the more particular in this relation, because I am confident I am right, and that horse exercise, keeping the body gently open, and a free use of laudanum, twenty, thirty, or forty drops, every hour, when the stones are passing, and a tepid Bath, is all that can be done, to relieve the intolerable pain, and save the patient, I am convinced too, that stones, or coagulated bile, which a trotting horse either passed, or separated, was the cause of his Lordship's rapid recovery, for he trotted himself from that day, in a few weeks, to be so well recovered, as to desire all my family, to do, as I had

order, and consequently mismanaged; drams, and all hot things are mischievous, among the many curious anatomical preparations of the late ingenious Dr. Frank Nicholls is the gall bladder of a woman much extended, and quite full of innumerable gall-stones, three *mulberry coated* ones are in the duct, which caused her death, yet they are not one third of the size I passed with smooth surfaces, I am assured that few men die who have not concretions in the gall bladder, in the *Hotel Dieu* at Paris, all who die there are opened, and in all, gall stones are found, Mackittrick has laughed at Coes book, Dr. Heberden has highly commended it, and if I mistake not, has acknowledged himself instructed by it. The Rev. Mr. Smith who died lately at Bath, according to the account of Dr. Parry, a very ingenious and observing physician, had two thousand nine hundred gall stones in the gall bladder, yet he never suspected it to be the cause of his disorder, as the stomach is the seat of life, may we not naturally conclude, that a due and regular flow of bile is the first and principle concoction in the preservation of health? it seems by its situation, to be better secured than even the heart, from any external injury, and is in a great measure out the reach even of medicine, and can be operated upon only by that which effects the whole frame, opium.

I had frequently done before; to eat a parting dinner with him before he left Bath. I cannot be ſo vain, as to ſuppoſe a man of his abilities, could find any entertainment in my company, and therefore I may fairly impute the many *tete à tete* dinners I was honoured with at his table, aroſe from an idea that I had contributed to the preſervation of his health, and life.

Before his lordſhip left Bath, he took occaſion to mention the ſenſe he had of my attention to him, and mentioning the *unfortunate* cauſe he had been a party in, on my behalf, at the bar of the houſe of Lords, aſked me in what he could ſerve me? Soon after his Lordſhip's return to London, I took the liberty to mention to him a young Clergyman, the ſon of my particular friend, a young man of uncommon good parts, of much learning, and of irreproachable character, and hinted to his Lordſhip, the affecting ſtory of Swift's two ſcholars, one of whom, *(a ſcrub,)* who became high in life, while the virtuous man, of learning and abilities, died an obſcure vicar, and was ſaid after ſtarving out a long life, " *to* " *have* been thought *a notable man in his youth.*" Now ſaid I my Lord, if you knew this young man, as well as I know him, he would not want ſuch an advocate as I am, if therefore your Lordſhip will give him a living, *I will furniſh him with a wife.* Lord Thurlow anſwered my letter by the ſame poſt, he approved much he ſaid of my plan, " *but doubted whe-* " *ther he was then able to ſet him up*" ſuch a reply, from ſuch a man, as the Lord Chancellor, to ſuch a man as myſelf; I conceived, and alas! *ſo did more than me*, to be a promiſe, his Lordſhip however did not think it ſo; becauſe his enemies allow, that among his many good qualities, one is, that he never breaks his word. His Lordſhip's letter however kept the young man and *two more* in ſuſpenſe for ſome years; my daughter indeed was *more fortunate*, for ſhe has been provided for by that unerring LORD, of the WHOLE UNIVERSE, who ſees what is beſt for his creatures, and whoſe DECREES are unalterable. That my readers may not ſuppoſe I have been *boaſting* of higher marks of his Lordſhip's partiality, and favor, than becomes me; I here preſume to give a copy of one of the many polite marks of his Lordſhip's attention to me, while he was on his valetudinarian viſit at Bath.

" BATH, *Aug.* 26th, 1780.

" The Chancellor preſents his beſt reſpects to " Mr. Thickneſſe, and returns him many

" thanks

" thanks for a very agreeable morning's amuse-
" ment, and for the many important advices,
" and useful truths, he met with. It seems to
" be the most useful way of teaching; but it
" certainly is the most pleasant to hear the *sage*
" *ridentum dicere verum*"*.

After impatiently waiting a year or two, I determined to go abroad, and desired his Lordship would permit me to have the honor of waiting upon him on my way through London to Brussells, to which request I received a flattering answer, and as his Lordship had often considered a wonderful piece of art in my possession, as the first of its kind, and the only one in England, I took it with me to town, and desired his permission to put *another man's head* into his house in a country, where I had at that time, no place to put my own in! just as I came to his door I found his Lordship preparing to go in form, to the court of chancery,

* The above card was wrote by his lordship, after reading the Valetudinarians Bath Guide, wherein the mode of getting *rid* of the gall stones, is particularly pointed out, and which by his Lordships permission I dedicated to him, I may say with truth too, that I have had a large correspondence with many gentlemen and ladies, to whom I am not personally known, on gall stone complaints, and have the satisfaction of knowing the methods I have used, have been successfully tried by many, nay by all.

ry, I therefore concealed my *two heads*, till he was gone, and then made my deposit in his library, where I found, and confounded, the Bishop his brother, by the sight of it, I then took my departure from Brussells, and saw nor heard any more of his Lordship, while he was Chancellor, but on my way from Spa to England, I met Lord Thurlow at the Hotel de Bourbon at Lisle. He received, me with marks of freedom and favor, and told me my deposit was safe and at my service in great Ormond Street, whenever I chose to send for it. The truth is, I never intended to have sent for it, had he not given me this hint to remove it, but I understood by that hint, his silence, and indeed his being out of power, that I had reckoned without my host. His Lordship however, honoured me with his name as a subscriber to my *Pais Bas* Journey, and sent me his five guinea subscription, soon after, loose his grooms leather breeches pocket, in a manner I thought rather indelicate, from a great fortunate Lord, to a little unfortunate private gentleman, and I shewed my resentment to it, by a very severe letter, which I dare say he threw into the fire, without reading it, as he has done hundreds of letters from men of rank and consequence. About a year after, I received

received the following post letter with a bank note of twenty five pounds enclosed.

"This comes from one who esteems you, " and has been obliged to you, though he has " reason to believe you think otherwise, the " enclosed note he hopes will discharge the pe- " cuniary obligation, and he wishes he could " with the same ease discharge that of grati- " tude. This is a secret, and it is desired it " may remain so, when he sees you he will " reveal himself."

The letter I had wrote to his Lordship, when he sent me his five guinea subscription, and another not less severe upon the *untimely* death of my daughter, shut out all idea *then* that the bank note came from Lord Thurlow, and as any man's guesses in *such a case*, must be confined to a few, I wrote to those few, whom I suspected, but it still remained in enigmatical obscurity. Lord Keppel was one whom I suspected, not from his generosity, (for I knew he had none) but from his justice, however he was obliged, by the last letter he ever wrote, to say "*it was not me.*" At length I suspected it came from a GREATER MAN, and wrote to his private secretary, stating the particulars,

and

and as it is said silence gives consent, I must conclude, from the polite diction of the card, and its accompaniment, it came from Lord Chancellor Thurlow, and I therefore thus publickly render him my thanks; he treated me, I thought with neglect, I resented it with Severity, but as he is, I verily believe, in his judicial Capacity, such as I have represented him to be in the dedication to the valetudinarians Bath Guide, long may he live to send the vanquished suitors away, satisfied by the arguments they have heard, that they had been mistaken in their claim; such a life, entrusted with a place of such infinite importance to equity, and justice, is invaluable, and if I contributed to the lengthening of it, I have been amply rewarded. I confess I was led to expect, from the partiality I had experienced, something more; for when a very powerful man, says to his inferior, you have been unfortunate, self-love construes it into a favorable turn, when I solicited a mark of that good man Lord Rockingham's favor, alas! at the last levy he appeared, he held my hand between his, and added, to my arguments, what his Lordship thought still stronger, than what I advanced, by saying "*aye Mr. Thicknesse, and the father of a Peer.*" No looks, no

face;

face; no words; could imply a more determined resolution to fulfil his intention, and a certain nobleman soon after told me, that his Lordship's death was a fatal blow to me, as well as a great national loss, for surely if there ever lived a truly good man, the Marquis of Rockingham was such.

ANECDOTE

OF

A WILTSHIRE ESQ. NOW LIVING.

ABOUT the year 1749 Mr. QUIN came into the lobby of the rooms at Bath, it was after dinner. Quin was what he would call in another man, *ſack-mellow*; at this time I was in converſation with the Eſquire to whom Quin walked as ſteadily up, as he could, and putting his heels upon the Eſquire's toes, made them *craſh again!* and then without ſaying a word, walked off. Whether pain, ſurpriſe; or timidity, overcome the Eſquire's *upper-works* I cannot ſay, but as ſoon as he could ſpeak, he aſked me whether I had obſerved Quin's conduct, and whether I thought it was an *accident*, or done

done with deſign to affront him? I recollected, that upon ſome occaſions, the truth was not to be *ſpoken*, and thinking this one; I replied, that Quin had been drinking and probably did not know, what he was about; but the next morning, meeting him on the parade, I aſked him why he ſo treated a good natured man, with the whole weight of his *body corporate?* d—n him, replied the comedian, putting on one of his moſt *contunding* looks; the fellow, ſaid he, invited me to his houſe in Wiltſhire, laid me in damp ſheets; and ſeduced my ſervant: fed me too, with red veal, and white bacon; ram mutton, and bull beef; adding, and as to his liquor, by my ſoul it was every drop ſour, except his vinegar, and yet the ſcrub, had the impudence to ſerve it upon dirty plate, I believe Quin's twinge on the toes of that gentleman, is to this day viſible in his face, if a face it can be called, yet I ſhould not at this diſtance of time, have ſhewn in what manner Mr. W—fed his friends, in the year 1749* had he not in the year 1778, made his ſix feet high young wife, write a very extraordinary letter to a certain "*copper faced Captain.*" This gentleman's firſt wife, was more *honorable*

* The *year* 1745, and 1749, were the moſt important years in the Eſquire's life.

honorable than her husband, for she was a Lord's daughter, and made her husband and servants, call her *your ladyship*, it so happened, that Johnny her husband, being out with the Wiltshire hunt, observed a military gentleman, with a black crape about his arm; this being a novel sight to Johnny, he enquired the cause? why replied a *wag*, do not ye know! he married a Lord's, not an Earl's daughter, and it is by that means *only*, his wife's rank can be made known; the next day Johnny appeared at the hunt, with his wife's black *insignia* twisted about his arm: by his second marriage, Johnny has no *external* badge of distinction, except a fine boy, begotten in the seventy seventh year of his age, with a carrotty pate and a turnip complection.

N. B. When Johnny's first wife's daughter died, that lady caused to be inscribed upon the monumental stone. Here lie the remains of Williamelia, Leonora Charlotta, W— the only daughter of the honourable Mrs. W— by her husband *John.* I will not add that which a *wicked wight* tacked to it with his chalk, for she was a good woman, as the world goes, only laid too much stress upon her *quality*, pray Mr. Thicknesse said she, in the rooms at Bath,

Bath, who is that lady? I do not know madam; I ſuppoſe ſhe is an Earl's daughter ſaid ſhe, becauſe ſhe cut the cards before me! at another time, Johnny and my lady being upon a viſit at a friend's houſe, Johnny was indiſpoſed, and taking a little buttered ſmall beer, went to bed at nine; and about eleven, found himſelf in a nice breathing *perſpiration*, that was the word, for my lady would not hear the word *ſweat* mentioned, as ſoon as her ladyſhip had got all off, to her under petticoat, ſhe called upon Johnny to get out of bed;—out of bed my lady, why I am all over in a *perſpiration*—*perſpiration* or no perſpiration, ſaid my lady, you muſt get up, for it ſhall never be ſaid that the Hon. Mrs. W—n, went to bed to a Shepherd's grandſon; though I believe it was his father, not his grandfather, who was a Shepherd at

"I——r on the Down
"Three miles from any Town."

I wiſh I could with the ſame propriety, relate an anecdote, whereby the laugh would take the other turn, and in which the comedian was much more dirtily treated. Let it be remembered however, that Mr. Quin poſſeſſed among his many failings, ſome great

and

and excellent good qualities. His ill nature, and wit, are only recorded; becauſe he carefully conceal'd the inumerable acts of benevolence and generoſity he daily committed. A brother of mine, it ſeems had been offended by Quin behind the ſcenes, not by treading upon his toes, no man durſt have done that, but it was an offence my brother thought he merited reprehenſion for; and ſoon after, a very dirty *recipe* was ſhewn my brother in M.S. called " *maw wallop a ſoop*" to which he deſired permiſſion to add half a dozen lines, four of which I have forgotten, but the two pinching ones, which I retain were,

" With a nice pippin paring, and all finely ſhred,
" Which lay where that lay, that Quin eat o' bed."

I will not tell where the pippin had lain, but every body at that time knew, and Quin ever after, preferred a John Dorey, to a golden pippin. Being one of four, who ſpent an evening or rather a night with this facetious entertaining man, at the White Hart in Bath, and Lord Kilmorrey being one of the party, I may venture to ſay, that it was a pleaſant evening to the other two, who were brothers. Towards day light, Lord Kilmorrey, who ſuſpected a motion would be made to part, obſerved,

ſerved, that it was probable we four might *never meet again*, and ſo ſaid he, *let us call for a bill and go.* My Lord knew that Quin would object to this motion, as it ſtood, and make the amendment, of a *bottle* and a bill. The bill paſſed, nem. con. The next time I met Mr. Quin, he expreſſed the great ſatisfaction and pleaſure our *partie quarre* had given him, adding, I will put down that jolly fellow *Jack Needham* in my will, and did ſo: * Quin never broke his word, not even with Daniel Lackie the ſcotchman, who taking the opportunity of aſking him, when he was drunk, to whom he would leave his gold watch when he died? he replied, to you Daniel, and did ſo, in the following words, as may be ſeen in his will. "I leave, according to a fooliſh promiſe made, "my gold watch and ſeals to Daniel Lackie." This was throwing a bone which would have made a dog cry.

ANECDOTE

* Lord Kilmorrey will excuſe this Freedom, it was a name equally reſpectable in thoſe days, to Lord Kilmorrey in theſe.

ANECDOTE

OF AN

EXTRAORDINARY KIND OF PAROQUET, ITS UNTIMELY DEATH, AND THE CONSEQUENCE THEREOF TO TWO YOUNG LADIES OF FASHION AND FORTUNE.

MOST people, at leaſt moſt people who have honoured me with their names to this trifling publication, have heard of my favorite fellow traveller, *Jocko*; but few have heard of Mrs. Thickneſſe's; this bird, which had the uſe of his wings as perfect as any bird whatever, travelled from Marſeilles to Calais, quite at liberty, in an open chaiſe, and moſt part of the day ſat upon Mrs. Thickneſſe's ſhoulder or boſom; or hung by his bill at her tippet; and he he would ſit by her for hours at the Inns, *gilding his eyes* with ſuch delight, that it would almoſt induce one to believe the tranſmigration of ſouls, and that the bird was animated by the ſpirit of a departed parent, or a deceaſed lover, for to me he was a determined enemy! Upon my return to Calais, where I took a houſe, ſome ſtranger entering the room, while the bird was ſitting in the open window, he flew out and was abſent a day or two, for the boys had hunted him from tree to tree all round the city, till at length he returned to the very firſt tree he had alighted upon when he flew from the window, and ſoon after found his way in again, and perched upon the boſom of his miſtreſs; it is needleſs, I preſume, to ſay, that this bird was of ſo ineſtimable a value to her, that no ſum of money could have induced her to part with it. At this time there paſſed through Calais, a friend of mine, a gentleman of faſhion and fortune, with four daughters, who had been ſome time in a convent at Paris, and as an unfortunate diſagreement had taken place between him and his lady, a woman of beauty and virtue, he found it very aukward to be encumbered with four daughters, and two or three ſons at his houſe in town, and as I was then in

London for a few days, he desired I would write to Mrs. Thicknesse, and ask her if it would prove agreeable to let the two youngest of his daughters spend the summer with her at Calais: this being agreed to, I was to conduct the ladies over; the eldest was of the age of fourteen, the youngest between eleven and twelve, both lovely handsome children, but the youngest of uncommon vivacity and beauty. I was a little hurt to find in the arms of the latter, the day we set out, a favorite dog, and hinted to her, that I feared that dog would be attended with great inconvenience to her, and me too; however we all set off in good humour, and to avoid their sleeping at a Inn, I got them lodged with a family at Canterbury for whom I had much esteem, where the dog gnawed the carved clawed feet of the mahogany chairs, and did much injury, the next night however, we were so lucky to be landed at Calais, and at supper, the dog was placed in the charming little girls lap, but I observed that I too had a favorite dog, who had travelled through Spain with me, but that I did not permit him to *sit at table*, and desired she would put hers down, this request was complied with but reluctantly, and I found I had given much offence to one whom I wished to oblige, and with whose animated disposition

ſition I was highly delighted. The next morning, the dog was put into the cloſet where the bird rooſted, and he there eat for his breakfaſt, what fifty louidores would not have purchaſed. I need not ſay how much I was irritated at this, and how it was aggravated by ſeeing Mrs. Thickneſſe in tears, but I leave the reader to imagine, what we both felt, when in the midſt of this diſtreſs, the little ſpirited girl, with a ſingle feather ſticking in her hair, began to hum lady Coventry's minuet; I then called for the dog, and threatened to cut his throat, but was told if I did, ſhe would cut hers, and I offered her my pen knife as being better adapted to the purpoſe than her own, I however ſent my ſervant with the dog to the packet, and returned him to England, and then within the ſame half hour, I told the young lady that before the expiration of one hour more, ſhe ſhould be in a convent, till the pleaſure of her father was known; and turning to her elder ſiſter, deſired to know whether ſhe would accompany her ſiſter in the convent, or honour Mrs. Thickneſſe with her company till we had heard from England? ſhe replied with great propriety, and good ſenſe; that ſhe loved her, and would not part from her, a reply as much to her honour, as it was to my ſatiſfaction, and ſo giving each a *bras*, I conducted them to the convent door; where, ſoon after, obtaining a *Parlè* with the Lady *Prieur*, I told her the young ladies were the daughters of a gentleman of faſhion, that a little miſunderſtanding had happened between them and Mrs. Thickneſſe, and therefore I deſired her to accommodate them with every comfort, the inſide of her convent could afford, to allow them a fille de chambre, and in ſhort every indulgence that could be granted them, excluſive of liberty, till their father's pleaſure was known, and there I left them, not doubting but that their father's letter would liberate them in a week or ten days at fartheſt, but circumſtanced *as he was*, and knowing that they were in perfect ſecurity, he ſuffered them to remain there, I think near three years, a conduct I could not diſapprove, yet a puniſhment, as it originated with me, I could not but lament. A young French lady my *vis â vis* neighbour, told me that if I pulled out a few bricks from the wall of a ware-houſe which belonged to my houſe, I ſhould have a view of my little *temporary nuns*, I did ſo, and often ſaw, and always lamented, that inſtead of conducting them daily as was agreed upon, in their *ſhayſe and one*, I could only ſee *them encaged* and deprived of liberty; this tranſaction rendered

me

me for ſome time very odious in the eyes of all the family, except their father; but time and truth, overcomes all falſe reaſoning, and I have the ſatisfaction to live in friendſhip at this day with their mother and all the family. I cannot cloſe this little unfortunate narrative without lamenting that the young lady, when ſhe was juſt arrived at an age, to have beſtowed her own irreſiſtible charms, to ſome worthy object, died; much lamented by all who knew her, and by none more than he who had *convented her*, for a haſty inconſiderate act, which her youth, vivacity, and heedleſſneſs might be juſtly pleaded in extenuation of, if not thoroughly excuſe.

ANECDOTE

ANECDOTE

OF A

MINIATURE PICTURE, NOW IN THE POSSESSION OF HER MAJESTY THE QUEEN.

MR. Ford, Mrs. Thickneſſe's father, having bought the Dutcheſs of Kendal's houſe and furniture at Iſleworth, among other pieces which he ſent to his own, was a very curious commode dreſſing table of exquiſite workmanſhip, this table being placed in his daughter's bedchamber, and having a great variety of private drawers in it, there was found in them, two or three curious miniature pictures, on one of which was the portraits of the Prince of Wales, the preſent King's father, and his three ſiſters, ſitting

ſitting in the ſtage box at the opera. The picture is the ſize only of a common bracelet, and no doubt was a preſent of the King's to the Ducheſs. * When it became my property, by marrying the poſſeſſor of it, ſtruck with the talents of the artiſt (for it is exquiſitely painted) and with reſpect for it, both as a ſervant and ſubject to the family it belonged, I ſet it round with brilliants, and my wife wore it upon her wriſt as a bracelet, but unfortunately, having the picture in my pocket one morning, when I was upon a viſit to Mrs. Forreſter, the widow of the late Governor of Belliſle, and finding with her, Mr. Dutens, a French clergyman who was ſhewing her ſome of his brothers pariſian trinkets† I fooliſhly produced my picture, at length Mr. Dutens admired it exceedingly, and obſerved what an acceptable preſent it might prove to the Queen, I confeſſed I had more than once conceived it might be ſo, but at the ſame time obſerved it was matter of great delicacy, and hinted at the ſtory of King James, giving a great turnip, as a very proper

* Miſtreſs to George the Firſt,

† Mr. Dutens is a native of Paris, of a good catholic family, his brother is now a ſilverſmith at Turin; Mr. Dutens was left by Mr. Mackenzie, *Charges des Affaires*, with a ſalary of ſeven hundred pounds a year at that city.

rebuke

rebuke, to a subject who had presented him with a fine horse, yet I could not help thinking that as I was the first subject who welcomed her Majesty to these dominions, and in possession of an *original family picture, not to be purchased;* it might, if properly offered, be kindly accepted, Mr. Dutens then told me he had *a friend* who saw the Queen every day, and that if I would trust the picture a few days to his care, it should be shewn to her Majesty; to which proposal I foolishly complied, he then asked me what was to be said if her Majesty seemed disposed to accept of it? I desired that his friend (whom I supposed to be a person of fashion) would say, that I was perfectly sensible of the great impropriety of a man in my low station, to offer a present to so exalted a personage, but that being the first subject who has received her Majesty on her arrival to these dominions,† and accident having put me in possession of such a family picture, I humbly hoped her Majesty would excuse the liberty I took in offering to restore it to a family to whom it more properly belonged; a day or

two

† The Author was the Lieutenant Governor of Land Guard Fort, and announced her happy Arrival, by the Report of one and twenty two and forty pounders, under the fire of which the yatch passed into the harbour of Harwich.

two afterwards, Mr. Dutens informed me that the Queen, on ſeeing the picture, was much ſtruck in perceiving ſo ſtrong a family likeneſs, and aſked if ſhe might ſhew it to the King? her Majeſty was then informed it was wholly at her diſpoſal, provided it was deemed worthy of her acceptance. The Queen then aſked whoſe property it was? and being told, ſhe was pleaſed to ſay, I know Mr. Thickneſſe, he ſent me off ſome refreſhments at ſea, when I arrived upon the coaſt; truth however obliges me to ſay I did not, but I had Lord Anſon's thanks for having fired nightly, minute guns, in dark tempeſtuous weather, when her Majeſty was expected upon the coaſt, that the frequent exploſions might ſhew the bearings of the fort, and him how the land lay; and his lordſhip was pleaſed to ſay it was a good piece of *land ſeamanſhip*. Not hearing for ſome days, I concluded the Queen had accepted of the picture, but Mr. Dutens then informed me by a note, that the King and Queen were very deſirous of keeping the miniature picture, and yet could not receive it as a preſent; but if I would name a price they would be equally obliged to me. In reply, I told Mr. Dutens, he had ſet me too arduous a taſk, I knew not where to draw the line; too high, or too low a price, a price, might be deemed equally improper, and therefore I again urged their Majesties acceptance of it, as a mark of the most respectful offering of a subject and servant; but instead of succeeding in my humble request (which I very much suspect was not properly delivered) I received a threatening card the next day, from the Rev. divine, informing me, if I did not name a price, "*by nine o'clock* "*the next morning*," the picture would be returned! To this, I replied, I could only lament, that what I had offered with the humblest respect, should have met with so unfortunate a termination, and therefore concluded, before nine the following day, Mr. Dutens would have returned me my picture, but no picture, nor message was sent me. I then was allowed the honor of levying Mr. Dutens, (and very often waiting a hour before I had an audience) at the house of Mr. Mackenzie, but even then, I could not learn in whose hands the picture remained, nor by whose hands it had been conveyed to the Queen, but as I certainly knew the Queen was too just, and too good, not to wish the picture might be returned to the right owner, I was determined not to sit down under the displeasure of the Queen on one side, and the loss

of

of my picture on the other; therefore, tired of levying this *ingenious foreigner*, and alarmed about the fate of my picture, I waited upon Mrs. Forrester, and told her the situation I was in, from the confidence I had placed in her friend, and required her to let me know, who Mr. Dutens friend was, who *saw the Queen every day*, but who was likely to continue forever, a stranger to my eyes, and she soon after informed me, it was Dr. Majendie, her Majesty's language master, I then had the honor of levying another foreign divine, but with no better success; he had carried the picture to the Queen he said, but he knew not in whose hands it now was, he supposed however it might be in the *hands of those German women*, meaning I suppose Madame Schwellanbergen, or some of those foreign ladies about the Queen's person, and in short, gave himself many of those *lively airs*, which an elated Frenchman may easily be conceived to exhibit, who had the honor of "*seeing the Queen every day*." I could not but again observe, that as he knew the Queen had declined accepting the picture, her Majesty most certainly understood, it was to be returned to the owner, and asked him to whom it could be given, but to him who had first produced it? and therefore I required him

him to return it to me, but I could not make this celebrated language maſter underſtand my language, "*he knew nothing of the matter* "*not he*" and I left this ſecond upſtart, with a determination, rather than loſe my picture, to go to court, and break through all etiquette, by throwing myſelf at her Majeſty's feet for an explanation, and accordingly went thither, to ſee what could be done; but ſeeing in the drawing room the late Dutcheſs of Portland, to whom I had preſented a miniature of Lewis the fourteenth by Petitoe, and whoſe daughter was then holding the Queen's train, I told her grace my errand to court, in hopes that ſhe might feel for my ſituation, and offer me her aſſiſtance to regain my loſt picture. The Dutcheſs however politely aſſured me that when Princeſſes received preſents, they were generally put by in a drawer and no more heard, or thought about them; juſt in the ſame manner I ſuppoſe, as her grace had put up the enamelled Petitoe I had preſented to her: I felt agitated and diſappointed, till turning my head aſide, I ſaw that honeſt, open, and noble countenance ſhone upon me, of the late Dutcheſs of Northumberland, and having formerly been well known to that truly good lady, I claimed the honor of her acquaintance, and

told

told her my name, her ladyſhip (it was before ſhe obtained that high rank ſhe afterwards did honor to,) ſaid ſhe remembered me very well, and was glad to ſee me, then madam I believe you will be glad to ſerve me, if you will permit me to relate my preſent embarraſſment, I then repeated what I had juſt before related to the Dutcheſs of Portland, and though I had never preſented her ladyſhip with a miniature picture, ſhe inſtantly expreſſed her ſurprize, that ſhe had neither ſeen, nor heard of ſuch a picture having been ſhewn the Queen; * adding, however you ſhall not loſe your picture Mr. Thickneſſe, for I will aſk the Queen in whoſe poſſeſſion it is, and if you will call at Northumberland houſe in a day or two, you ſhall have certain information about it, and there it was I learnt that the picture had been returned *ſix weeks before* by her Majeſty *(not to theſe German women)* but to that Rev. Divine *who knew nothing of it!!* with this good intelligence, I waited a ſecond time on the Rev. Doctor, whom I found a little *creſt fallen*, and who informed me, I had done him a great injury, by going to the drawing room at court, and complaining of his conduct relative to the miniature

picture,

* Her Ladyſhip was then one of the lady's of the Bedchamber.

picture; for at this time, he did not *know all the information* I had obtained at Northumberland house: but instead of hearing *his* grievances, I desired he would redress mine, and deliver me up the picture, he replied, *that the Queen would he believed have given it him,* that very morning, had not the King came in just at that minute, but said he would bring it me to morrow. In the afternoon of the *same day* however, I met the Doctor in the street, his hand was in his side pocket, and I believe the picture was in his hand, I accosted him, for he seemed lost in a Reverie, but as soon as he recovered his recollection, he brought forth the picture, saying, "*There sir is your picture; I* "*wish you success with it, but I fear you have lost* "*all chance of presenting it to her Majesty*" looking with eager eyes, upon my recovered jewel, and observing that all the colours were as vivid, as when I foolishly parted with it, I told the Doctor I thought I had been successful; by recovering my picture again, and took my leave of him with a salutation; I will not repeat here, because the man is gone *elsewhere*, now the reader will be astonished, at least I was, to know that soon after this transaction, Mr. Dutens wrote to Mrs. Forrester to express *his* surprise, that I had treated his friend Merjendie so rudely!

ly! if I did treat him rudely, I treated him justly, if I did not, I call upon Dutens to defend his departed friend, it is his duty, and if he has truth on his side, he has capacity so to do, and ought: but let him not forget, that his defence may fall under the eye of a LADY, who is ALL TRUTH, and goodness, and who will not, CANNOT BE MISTAKEN, the picture being returned to the arm, from whence it went, was again worn by Mrs. Thicknesse, but on the King's Birth day at Paris, when all the English were celebrating it, at the table of the late Earl of Rochford, his Majesty's ambassador to that court, it was taken from her arm, handed round in a gold plate and much admired by all the company present, I then related the out line of the above story, and Lord and Lady Rochford both seemed to think it a pity it was not again offered with propriety to the Queen, I therefore waited upon his Lordship the next morning, observed that as he was going to spend a fortnight in England, I begged leave to present the picture to him, hoping that her Majesty might be prevailed upon to accept that from his hands, which could not be taken from mine, Lord Rochford objected to accept it as too valuable a present, but said, had it been a family picture of his own, he would

not

not have refuſed it, I had taken it out of the ſetting, before I went, and to cut the matter ſhort, I aſſured him, that if he would not accept of it, I would call for a peſtle and mortar and ſmaſh it in his porters lodge, * and I would certainly have done ſo. This peremptory declaration, ſettled the buſineſs, Lord Rochford cauſed it to be elegantly ſet in plain gold at Paris; took it with him, and without deſiring an audience of her Majeſty; requeſted one of thoſe *German women as Merjendie called them*, to deliver the picture in his name to the Queen: his lordſhip ſent for me ſoon after, to dine with him, and informed me, that when he appeared at court, the Queen paſſed all the foreign miniſters, came up to him, and thanked him for a picture ſhe had once ſeen, but had deſpaired of ever ſeeing again; he then told her majeſty from whom, and how he had received it, and I have the ſatisfaction of knowing that the picture is now in her Majeſty's poſſeſſion, *without being paid for*, but at the ſame time I may be allowed to ſay, that ſome time after, inſtead of my poſſeſſing ten thouſand pounds, which all the greateſt lawyers in this Kingdom, but ONE, had

* The Rev. Mr. Fountaine then chaplain to the embaſſy and Mr. Higden his Lordſhip's domeſtic ſecretary, probably remember this circumſtance.

had been clearly of opinion belonged to me, and that inſtead of receiving ſuch ſum, I had ſix hundred to pay *for law*, I then humbly ſtated to her Majeſty, that what I had once reſpectfully declined to receive, would now be acceptable; but in *money matters*, throughout life, I have been unfortunate, *i. e.* if it can be deemed unfortunate, to have been confined to one good diſh of meat, inſtead of two;—if it can be deemed unfortunate;—to have eſcaped the gout, which *two* diſhes might have conducted me to, or if it can be deemed unfortunate, to have been confined to a life of temperance, to the ſeventieth year of my age, without feeling any of the infirmities which generally belong to ſuch who attain a length of days, to which not one man in fifty thouſand arrive; nor one in a hundred thouſand, without finding ſuch an age, render life, rather a burthen, than a bleſſing; I will not therefore allow that my LIFE has been unfortunate, becauſe I have more than I can eat, and conſequently ſome to ſpare for thoſe who want it, accompanied with health, ſpirits, and powers as fully to enjoy it, as at any period of my life, and that too, at nearly the full age of man, "THREE SCORE YEARS AND TEN."

ANECDOTE

OF

GEORGE THE FIRST, AND HIS COLONEL,* FATHER OF THE LATE UNFORTUNATE ADMIRAL KEMPENFELT.

MR. Kempenfelt came over to England with King George the first, who having been his friend in private life, deemed him worthy of his protection when he became a King. The King, who had tasted of the sweets of social and private life, continued to enjoy his evenings, according to his wonted manner, and Mr. Kempenfelt was often of the party, when the King smuggled in a Savoyard girl, to sing him a *German song*, accompanied with her *vial*, Kempenfelt,

* The King always called him *his Colonel*.

Kempenfelt, was an expenſive man, and the King, having made him a lieutenant Colonel, (for he often ſaid he had not *intereſt enough* to procure him a regiment) more than once paid his debts, at length however he was ſent over, lieutenant governor of Jerſey, where he died, leaving behind him a widow and four children, two ſons and two daughters, with nothing elſe to ſupport them but the mother's penſion; when I was appointed a lieutenant of an independent company at Jamaica, I found my old ſchool fellow, the late Admiral, a melancholy midſhipman in Port Royal harbour, lamenting that he was without friends, without intereſt, and without money; yet I think he was under Captain Knowles command, in the diamond, his brother Guſtavus Adolphus, got a commiſſion in the army, but I believe he obtained no higher rank than that of a Captain; much merit is due to him, for the filial affection he ſhewed to his mother and ſiſters, without which they could not have ſupported themſelves ſuitable to their condition in life. The Admiral was a man of great nautical knowledge, very reſerved, and ſhy even of thoſe he eſteemed, when upon half pay, he generally ſpent his winters at Marſeilles, to avoid the ſeverity of this climate, and I have often wondered, who it was, who had knowledge enough of him to know, that he not only poſſeſſed great nautical abilities, but with it, an enlarged and enlightened underſtanding, for he was very careful to conceal it, nothing but a long acquaintance, and a confidential correſpondence, could bring it forth. His Will I ſuppoſe ſunk with him, and his brother, my ſchool fellow alſo, I preſume poſſeſſes the fortune he left. Admiral Kempenfelt was in all things original, I never left his company without hearing things I had never heard before. I ſent a young man on board his ſhip to him, who was very ingenious, but friendleſs, but as he was a good mathematician, a good draughtſman, and underſtood the theory of navigation; inſtead of aſking his admiſſion on board the victory as a favor, I deſired the Admiral to *thank me* for having ſent him ſuch an ingenious young man to provide for; he accordingly thanked me, and ſhewed the young man particular marks of his favor; and afterwards put him on board with that honorable and gallant captain, George Berkly, that he might have a chance of prize money. I never knew any other naval officer to whom I would have ventured ſo to expreſs myſelf, except the late Admiral Medley, who, upon all occaſions, ſeemed as much delighted to ſerve young men of merit,

as

as they could poſſibly receive by being provided for. When I ſailed with him to his Mediterranean command, a ſingle inſtance of his politeneſs to me, and his readineſs to reward merit, I cannot help relating. A ſeaman on board of the fleet, had married a Southampton woman; and he learnt that I alſo had married one of the ſame city; this kind of *country kindred*; he conceived to be ſufficient, to claim ſome notice from me, and deſired I would recommend him to the Admiral as one who merited a better *birth*; the ridiculouſneſs of the claim, induced me to relate it at dinner; but the Admiral immediately obſerved, that it was probable the man felt in his own boſom, unrewarded merit, adding, I will therefore learn his real character, and after dinner made a ſignal to ſpeak with his Captain, and finding that his ſuggeſtion was ſtrictly true, made him gunner of a ſeventy-gun ſhip. Being wifeſick, I left this gallant Admiral three months only before he died, or probably he had left me a large ſhare of his fortune, for though he readily conſented (after I had ſerved one year under his command) to let me depart, he took it unkind of me, for he had repeatedly told me, thoſe to whom he intended to leave his fortune, had never ſent him even a barrel of Yorkſhire

ale,

ale, though he had ſupplied their cellars with wine, and we both parted with wet eyes, the Admiral loved a preſent; moſt men who are liberal themſelves do; and I was glad he lived long enough to receive a little token from me, as a mark of the many ſingular and pointed ones, of his partiality and kindneſs, during the pleaſant year I ſerved under him on board the Ruſſel. This gallant Admiral, who could drop a tear at parting from a friend, had a tear alſo for his country, for I ſaw him weep, for want of an opportunity to regain the loſt credit of the navy, which he thought had been greatly ſullied, by the conduct of Leſtock; when under the command of Admiral Mathews; it is with pleaſure I thus regiſter, after a diſtance of forty three years, the excellent good qualities, which Mr. Medley poſſeſſed, becauſe a haſty diſpoſition, had created him many enemies; he threw his wig in Admiral Buckle's face, but the provocation was great, and I have heard him over, and over, make ſuch apologies as any other man, (under ſuch high obligations as Mr. Buckle * was to him) would have deemed ſufficient; but Buckle would not forgive either him, or me; becauſe when he told me the

* He was the Admiral's Captain, who took him from the Command of the Spence Sloop.

the next day, he would resign his ship, I replied not I hope to fight the Admiral, for I will take care you shall not; and as he was an excellent officer, urged upon him not to give up eight hundred pounds a year, in pursuit of a phantom, nobody said I, can doubt the personal courage of either, and beside, he could not send the admiral a challenge, nor the Admiral accept it (at that time) if he did; yet I verily believe, had Mr. Medley lived to return to England, Admiral Buckle would have called *him out*.

ANECDOTE

OF

DOCTOR DODD.

WHEN I confider the real character, and conduct of this unfortunate man, as well as the conduct and character of a great variety of other men and myfelf, I am apt to fufpect, we have complimented ourfelves, with what does not perfectly belong to mankind; are we I fay to myfelf *rational creatures?* I fufpect we are not: Dr. Dodd was one of the beft tempered men I ever knew; his talents; his time; and even his purfe, when he had any money in it, were at the fervice of every claimant, for affift-

ance

ance or pity; he was a man of strong passions, expensive to an high degree, void of all prudence, possessed of extreme sensibility, and went through (long before he suffered death) a torture of mind, between hope and fear, which was worse than a thousand deaths, if therefore he had been pardoned, he would not have escaped without an adequate punishment for his manifold sins; and some little allowances might have been made in consideration thereof; he once visited me, when I was the inhabitant of a gaol; and though it was neither for debt, nor treason, yet it was *a gaol*, and I thought myself bound to visit him, under such dreadful circumstances; and having done so once, I could not refrain from repeating it, while I thought my visits, could either alleviate his sorrow, or assist him in his wants, the first visit I made him, I found Mrs. Dodd with him, but delirious in a fever, he told me he had not closed his eyes all night, because they had been unriveting the fetters of a number of criminals, who were executed that morning; adding, that every blow which was given, struck him, as with an ELECTRIC SHOCK; after Mrs. Dodd left newgate, I contrived to call at those hours, she was *not usually with him*, but the last time I saw him, was in a situation, neither to be described

ſcribed nor conceived, it was after he knew his *certain fate*, and when Mrs. Dodd was taking her everlaſting farewell of him; they were alone; and at the upper end of a long room, I walked up to them, and found their hands locked in each others, and their minds as much departed, as if they had been both dead; after being almoſt as *loſt* as they were for about a minute, and plainly perceiving, that they neither ſaw me, nor one another; I quitted the room. This was the only minute of my life, I coveted ſovereign power; I would have been a beggar all my future days, to have poſſeſſed kingly authority for one minute, I returned home, and wrote him a letter, wherein I gave advice, not ſuch as a *rational man* would have given, and the following is his anſwer to it.

"Dear Sir,

"I am *juſt at preſent* not very well and inca-
"pable of judging, I ſhall communicate your
"kind paper to my friends, my brother will
"be at Mrs. Porter's this evening; many
"thanks for your attention,—I rather think
"it would *do hurt* and be deemed a mob."

Your's in great miſery,

W. D.

Dodd

Dodd was the firſt mover in the reconciliation between me and Lord Orwell, and preſſed me to apply to him, to ſign his petition to the King, as Vice preſident of that charity which Dodd had inſtituted, but his Lordſhip denied the boon ſeemingly with reluctance, for at the ſame time he declared, he wiſhed he might obtain the King's pardon, though he could not recommend him as an object, who in *his opinion* had any claim to it; perhaps as a MAN he might not have been an object of mercy, but as a *Clergyman who had been a public*, and an admired preacher, it might have been prudent to have made him the Botany bay curate. Dodd was an excellent companion, when he fell into ſuch company (as he called it) whom he *could truſt*, and I have heard him, after making all the old women cry at church in the morning. make his *truſty friends* laugh, as much in the evening, by ſinging a ſong, of Adam and Eve going a journey, *and ſtopping in the land of nod, to have their horſes ſhod*, a matter more excuſable, in my opinion, than that of him, and his wife, dining *tete a tete*, at one tavern, in the moſt voluptuous manner, and ſupping in the ſame ſtyle, on the ſame day at another! but which I am aſſured they frequently did. That a man who ſuffered ſo long

long the fear of a dreadful death: and then death itſelf, ſhould have given his friends particular inſtructions to endeavour to re-animate his body, is to me the moſt extraordinary part of his conduct, ſurely to covet reſtoration to *ſuch a life*, as his muſt have been, was as *irrational*, as the hopes were abſurd. Mrs. Wright, the wax modeller (a crazy pated genius) modelled his head, as ſhe informed me, and carried it to him under her pettycoats, in order to favor his eſcape, by the uſe of it; a thing certainly (as he was circumſtanced) not impracticable. His room was large and long, the fire was at the further end of it, and the entrance door oppoſite to it, at his fire ſide ſtood a large table covered with books, on a carpet; now as he was without irons, had eight or ten of his friends came in one after the other, ſo as to have all gone out together, he might poſſibly have gone with them, if he had dreſſed up a figure in his night gown, with Mrs. *Wright's head thereon*, for his keeper only appeared at the door when he rung the bell, and then, ſeeing his figure ſitting at the table with his hat flapped, and his head reclined, he would not have regarded the number who went *out*, being *ſure* he left his priſoner ſafe *within*, ſhe ſaid, Dodd had not courage to attempt it,

nor

nor am I clear ſhe had reſolution ſufficient to have aſſiſted him, and beſide, it would have been in Dodd, a worſe *forgery* upon Mr. Akerman's humanity and indulgence, than that committed on the noble Lord's purſe; whoſe tutor he had been, with whom he had often eat, and drank, and been merry, and who, when Dodd went to viſit him at Geneva, rode ſeveral miles to meet him in ſuch weather, that he was froſt bitten on the way, and when he arrived there, gave him a round of dinners, to all his friends, preſented him to them as his chaplain, &c. in ſhort Dodd ſeemed to lament his want of that pity from Lord Cheſterfield, which he ſaid he had ſome right to expect, for having faithfully, as his tutor, done his duty towards him, and loved him perſonally. Dodd has aſſured us, he died in charity with all mankind, but he certainly did not *live* in charity with his Lordſhip, had Dodd lived to this time, he would have called himſelf probably the britiſh *Nuncamar*, had Dodd's friends, been half as powerful as his enemies, he might have eſcaped: I have been told by one who lived in great intimacy with the ingenious Ryland, who ſuffered alſo for forgery, that if he were to name the moſt friendly, benevolent, and good hearted man a long life had made him acquainted

quainted with, he ſhould in truth and conſcience name Ryland the engraver!—ſuch is the unaccountable mixture, of good, and bad, in the compoſition of that wonderful being, MAN —a lock was forced, and an out building in my garden was entered lately in the night, a tea box and other trifles were taken away, I know the robber, and where the tea box is, but knowing that it was perſonal ſpite to me, and that the man's profeſſion is not that of houſe breaking, has ſaved him from the gallows, becauſe I felt in my own boſom, a perſonal reſentment to him, his execution therefore (however conſiſtent with the law of the land) would *in me, and by me,* be deemed malice prepenſe, a certain Lord, ſaid he was going "*a parſon hunting*" ſoon after Dodd was taken into cuſtody! I hope therefore he was in at *the death*, but *Uncle Toby* would not have ſaid ſo—would he *Yorick?*

ON

ON THE

AQUA MEPHITICA ALKALINA,

OR THE

SOLUTION OF FIXED ALKALINE SALT, SATURATED WITH FIXIBLE AIR, IN CALCULOUS DISORDERS, AND OTHER COMPLAINTS IN THE URINARY PASSAGES.

THAT these *ſelfiſh* and inſignificant ſheets may be ſtamped with a few pages of the utmoſt importance to the good of mankind, I ſhall publiſh (for no publication ſhould I think come from the preſs without mentioning it, till it is univerſally known) ſome account of this medicine, and more eſpecially as Doctor Munro has, in his pharmaceutical chemiſtry, been *pleaſed* to ſpeak of it ſo ſlightly; to have given its preparation ſo imperfectly; and to ſay he knows of but *one* inſtance of its efficacy; will

will the learned Doctor permit me to ask him why he did not know of more instances? his own bookseller, Cadell, could have furnished him with many, under the names too, of men as eminent for TRUTH and CANDOUR, *as the Doctor himself.* Is this the way in which a chymical physician, treats a discovery of the first importance to mankind? it is the way indeed that Mackittrick treated Mr. Tickell's Æther, and may be *the way* of some of our northern practioners; but it is highly reprehensible, and therefore I earnestly recommend to him, the perusal of Mr. Colborne's experiments, and the cases published by Doctor Falconer. Does the learned Doctor know, that Mr. Colborne is a gentleman of Bath, of large and independent fortune, of great chymical knowledge, who has for many years been indefatigable in trying, by various chymical experiments, the means to relieve himself, and others from their sufferings in calculus complaints, and who has, I can venture to say, not only wonderfully succeeded, but generously given the public, the means also of preparing, at a trifling expence, a medicine of the first importance, and the last to have been expected in the materia medica; for if it be not a solvent for calculi already formed in the human bladder, it will unquestionably

unquestionably prevent such concretions from forming or enlarging, after they are formed. I know nothing of physic, but I have heard, and seen, such extraordinary accounts of the efficacy of this medicine, both in M.S. and print, under the respectable names of those who have made their grateful acknowledgements to Mr. Colborne, that I speak from UNQUESTIONABLE AUTHORITIES. I have the honor too, to call this gentleman my friend nor could he have bestowed it upon one who esteems him more, not only for his philanthropic disposition, but for the amiableness of his general conduct, and the many virtues I have for years past, known to be inherent in his numerous family; to all of whom, God has given length of days, and affluence of fortune, sufficient to DO AS THEY WOULD BE DONE UNTO. Those who would see particular instances of the efficacy of this medicine, will find it at Cadell's, by Dr. Falconer of Bath; I shall therefore only give one incontestible proof of the effect this medicine has in correcting any acrimonious disposition, in the urine, because it does not appear among the cases published, but proves past all doubt, what a wonderful change it occasions in that excrement. A boy, I think of seven or eight years of age, had been cut for the ſtone, and for ſeven years afterwards, could not retain his water, all the phyſical people concluded, that the ſphincter had been cut in the operation, and that the boys condition was paſt the reach of either medicine or art. Mr. Colborne thought otherwiſe; he gave him this medicated water, and the boy can now retain his, as well as any perſon whatever; this proves beyond a doubt, that the want of retention, did not ariſe from any injury done to his perſon in the operation, but from an acrimonious irritating diſpoſition of the urine itſelf, which the medicine corrected; now if the proximate cauſe of calculi, (as ſome great phyſicians have aſſerted) originates from a tartarious ſalt, conveyed out of the blood, into the ſmall ducts of the kidneys (for it is the nature of theſe ſalts, to contain a conſiderable quantity of that ſubtle matter which Sir Iſaac Newton has ſhewn to be the cauſe of coheſion of bodies) this grievous diſorder is accounted for. If therefore the kidneys furniſh a *nucleus*, when that nucleus gets into the bladder, it cannot fail of being daily augmented by additional *lamelæ* like the coats of an onion. I ſhall therefore only tranſcribe accurately, the method of preparing the medicine from Mr. Colborne's own receipt, and as the glaſs apparatus may be had compleatly made for the purpoſe, at Parker's warehouſe Fleet-Street, nothing more need be ſaid, as every man in theſe caſes, may become his own DOCTOR, even without the advice *of Doctor James Mackittrick late medical cautioner of Bath*, and formerly one of the *Quorum* of Antigua, from whence he lately returned.*

——————— all arrid dry,
Like the parched ſtubble in a *dog-day* ſky.

The exact method of preparing the medicated water, from Mr. Colborne's directions.—"Put two ounces and a half troy weight of dry ſalt of tartar into an open earthen veſſel, and pour upon it five quarts, wine meaſure, of the ſofteſt water; ſuch as is clean and limpid, and ſtir them well together, with a piece of wood; after ſtanding twenty four hours, carefully decant, from any indiſſoluble reſidium that may remain, as much as will fill the *middle* part of the glaſs machine for impregnating water with fixed air. The alkaline liquor is then to be expoſed to a ſtream of air, according to the directions commonly given for impregnating water with that fluid. When the alkaline

 ſolution

* The true engliſh, and meaning of this *cautious* Doctor is, to frighten all womenkind, if not all mankind, from taking any kind of medicine without the advice of a phyſician, and conſequently *if they are wiſe*, to take his.

ſolution has remained in this ſituation till the fixible air ceaſes to riſe, a freſh quantity of the fermenting materials ſhould be put into the lower part of the glaſs machine, and the ſolution expoſed to a *ſecond* ſtream of air, and this proceſs repeated twice more. After the liquor has continued forty eight hours in that ſituation, it will be fit for uſe, and ſhould be carefully bottled off in pints, cloſely corked, and put with their bottoms *upwards* in a cool place, it will then keep good ſeveral weeks. About eight ounces of this medicated water have been taken thrice in twenty four hours, for a conſiderable time together, and hath agreed well with the ſtomach, appetite, &c. but a pint in twenty four hours, will be ſufficient to begin with."

☞ The Marble Powder, Oil of Vitriol, and proper Inſtructions to uſe the Machine for Impregnating Water with fixible Air, may be had at Parker's Glaſs Warehouſe, and I think the Medicine ready prepared alſo.

ANECDOTE

OF AN

UNFORTUNATE SERJEANT, SHOT AT LAND GUARD FORT, FOR DESERTION.

HAVING resigned the command of the Garrison to Major Debrisay, of Hudson's regiment, with an intention to spend a winter month or two in town, I met at the late Duke of Cumberland's levee the General, who informed me it was his Royal Highness's commands, that I returned, in order to resume my command, while the Major sat as president of a court martial upon a sergeant for desertion. A general court martial upon a sergeant for such a crime, implied death upon

upon the firſt face of it, and as I had been informed that the priſoner bore a good character, and that his deſertion was owing to his poſſeſſing an unuſual ſhare of ſentiment, I attended his tryal. The charge being read to the priſoner, he was aſked whether he pleaded guilty or innocent? to which the brave man replied, guilty to be ſure; it would be impertinent in me to trifle with your honours by denying it. Then what have you to ſay, aſked the preſident, before the ſentence of death is paſſed upon you? to the beſt of my remembrance the following noble, but alas! fruitleſs defence was made.—Gentlemen, ſaid this Sentimental Soldier, I was in a manner born a ſoldier, my father was a ſoldier before me, and I have been all my days, as it were of the ſame profeſſion, and ſince I have been a ſerjeant, I appeal to my captain, and the officers of the company to which I belong, how I have acquitted myſelf, but as I did not aſſociate ſo much with the private men, as other ſerjeants do, in order the better to ſupport my own authority, or to carry the orders of your honours into execution, I was rather diſliked by the rank and file-men, and as my wife had been accuſed (whether guilty or innocent I cannot ſay) of ſtealing a handkerchief,

the

the men when I was doing my own duty, or obeying the orders of your honours, were continually calling out from every corner of the garrison, *Hep*—whose wife stole the handkerchief?—whose wife stole the handkerchief? And this insult, being daily and constantly repeated, it so overcome me with wretchedness, and misery of mind, that in a fit of despair, I took the fatal resolution of going off, which I could have done, with the company's money, to whom I was pay master serjeant, since which, I have been a miserable wanderer, and almost starved, for I knew not how, or where to get my bread but in that line of life to which I had been accustomed, this is the truth gentlemen, and I submit my case to your honours consideration, in hopes that my life will be spared, and my future services useful, the man was condemned to be shot to death!! when the fatal day of his execution arrived, I chose he should not die under my *immediate* command, and therefore quitted the garrison, desiring an old trusty sensible invalid soldier, for whom I had much good will, to attend the execution and let me know *every particular*, that passed at it. He promised so to do, but not without assuring me, he would not have seen such a *deadly blow*, if I had not desired it.

Upon

Upon my asking him how the old serjeant behaved? he replied, sir, he went out as bold as a lion; but recollecting, that by saying so, I might conceive him to, have gone out with an hardened unbecoming boldness, he recalled those words, and said, he died sir like a MAN: observing, that the prisoner was the *only* man present who did not tremble! what said I, did Major Debrisay tremble? yes they all trembled, Major, officers, and men. The Major then asked the prisoner whether he acknowledged the justice of his sentence? the prisoner said he did; have you then any thing to say previous to its being put into execution? yes:—he had a small favour to ask of his honour, and it was, that his fellow prisoner, whom he had just left in the black hold, for a trifling offence, might be forgiven and released? he was promised a compliance to his request, and then, after refusing to have a cap put over his eyes, but to face his hard fate, he was shot to death, according to his sentence. The body was buried in the warren, a spot to which my old invalid, who was my trusty warrener also, and I often visited. After it had lain there seven years, we two, took an early hour, to dig up his bones, as I was determined to preserve the skull of a man, which possessed better brains,

than

than a majority of his court martial members. Upon turning the lid of the coffin over, I was exceedingly ſurpriſed, to find the ſkeleton, blanched as white as ſnow, by the ſalt ſands and lying in the moſt perfect order, of a perfect ſkeleton but with the back upwards! I then obſerved to the old ſoldier, that the man had been buried before he was quite dead, and had turned himſelf in the coffin. This for a while ſtaggered my chum's recollection alſo, but at length he accounted for it, by obſerving, that the Major had ordered him to lie buried, face downwards, as a further mark of infamy! but I will venture to ſay that he buried a man with his face downwards, whoſe ſhoulders wore a head, and whoſe body ſupported a mind, equal to that of any Major, or General in Europe. This was the time, and the only time, I coveted rank ſufficient, to claim an audience of the King† in which caſe, I would have urged not only the preſervation of a brave ſoldier's life, but his promotion to a higher rank in the army than that of ſerjeant, for I might have wrote over his remains; "here lies a cromwell guilt-"leſs of his country's blood" I placed the ſkull of this ſentimental ſoldier at Felix-tow cottage hard

† It was in the late King's reign.

hard by, but with a different inscription under it. A circumstance which rendered me obnoxious to many military men, whose understandings were placed *below* their *shoulders*. And here let me observe, though I would not be thought superstitious, that before the revolution of one year, Major Debrisay, died a more violent death, for his body was so torn to pieces, that the fragments could not be collected together for the burial of it, even in a rabbet warren! The life of an old soldier, should not be put in the power of young officers, who perhaps may think they stamp an importance upon themselves, by exercising it within the limits of martial law; it is an easy matter to sentence a man to death, or to inflict a thousand lashes upon his bare back, but it is terrible to endure; during the fourteen years I commanded Land Guard Fort. I made the old invalids do their duty like soldiers, and I have a certificate under all their hands that I did so, and that no man during that period ever had his shirt stript from his body, or a lash upon his back.

When Lord Barrington wrote me such a letter, that I thought I could no longer serve with honor in a military capacity, I waited upon his Lordship

Lordſhip to know the cauſe, and aſked him whether I had been guilty of treaſon or cowardice? he replied no; he believed me to be an honeſt man, but added, he had recommended it to the King to write me ſuch a letter, for ſaid he, Mr. Thickneſſe, there is ſomething very peculiar in your temper, I acknowledged the charge, and produced the certificate, obſerving that there certainly was ſomething *peculiar in my temper*, and beg'd his Lordſhip to peruſe the certificate, ſigned by the maſter gunner, quarter gunners, and every man then under my command, and I defied his Lordſhip to produce ſuch another certificate from the governor of any Garriſon either, at home or abroad. I would not have mentioned this circumſtance, but to apprize my ſucceſſors, that old ſoldiers ſent to ſpend the dregs of a hard fated life in Garriſon, ſhould not be brought under the *drummer's laſh*; no port liberty; confinement in the guard room; turning their coats, double duty, and other gentle puniſhments, will have a better effect; when I was tried upon eight heavy charges by a court martial at the horſe guards, * one of them was for ſpoiling and deſtroying the King's ſtores, it was proved; the charge was for ordering down an invalid ſoldier, whom I found upon coming into

* The Duke of Northumberland was one of my Judges.

into the fort, mounted, in the ſixty fourth year of his age, upon the wooden horſe, with his hands tied behind him, and four heavy firelocks tied to his heels! for ſeeing this horrid ſpectacle, and hearing the ſufferer call upon me for pity, I not only ordered him to be taken down, but the ſoldiers to break up the wooden horſe and burn it, that no temporary commanding officer, while I was out of the fort, ſhould again repeat ſuch wanton acts of cruelty; it is a dangerous puniſhment for young men, but to age, it occaſions diſorders which ſoon carry them beyond the reach of tyrants, and I hope to ſee the day that picketing the horſe ſoldier, and *riding the foot*, be utterly aboliſhed from the britiſh army, no ſoldier in France receive corporal puniſhments for petty offences, and yet good diſcipline is preſerved. It has been inſinuated by my enemies, that the King diſmiſſed me from the government of Land Guard Fort, and a froſty faced attorney, of Ipſwich, ſaid he had ſeen the letter of my diſmiſſion, but the truth is, I had the King's leave to reſign it in favour of the preſent lieutenant governor, Mr. Singleton, who paid me two thouſand pounds down, and *promiſed* to inſure his life for four hundred pounds more, which he paid me with intereſt at fifty pounds a year for eight years afterwards;

afterwards; this indulgence and unprecedented transaction however, was brought about by that virtuous, friendly, and excellent man, the late Marquis of Rockingham, whose conduct all good men admired, and whose memory I revere.

ANECDOTE

OF

NATHANIEL St. ANDRE,

HE WHO THE SAME NIGHT MR. MOLLINEUX DIED, WENT OFF WITH LADY BETTY, HIS WIDOW, AND MARRIED HER.

IT was the faſhion at Southampton, in the year 1743 and no where elſe in the Kingdom, to viſit Lady Betty and her huſband St. Andre, who was conſidered *there*, by many of the *then* inhabitants, as a miracle of wiſdom and knowledge of every kind. St. Andre was a German, and bred a fencing maſter, but finiſhed his *education*, by travelling with an itinerant doctor. Thus qualified, he arrived in England, called

called himſelf a great Anatomiſt, and ſpeaking the native language of George the firſt, was not only introduced to his Majeſty, but was appointed the King's Anatomiſt, and actually attended his Majeſty to inſtruct him in that occult art! by this extraordinary ſituation he became noticed by many people of faſhion, and among others, by Mr. Mollineux, ſecretary to the Prince of Wales, and by means of his baſs viol, fiddle, &c. (for he poſſeſſed all thoſe *travelling accompliſhments* in a tolerable degree) he wriggled himſelf into his favor, and at length, from his *anatomical knowledge*, into Lady Betty's; and then into their houſe *en famille*. That he was ignorant to a degree ſcarce to be conceived, may be ſeen in his ſilly pamphlet, written to prove that the impoſtor, Mary Toft, of Godalming rabbets, were præternatural human fætus's, in the form of quadrupeds, which pamphlet he afterwards, bought up, and ſo effectually ſuppreſſed, that I was twenty years in ſearch of it, before I could obtain a ſight of one. I do not know who killed poor Mr. Mollineux, but I have been aſſured that *he* who publiſhed, lately, the ſecond edition of that curious performance, killed St. Andre, be that as it may, it is pretty certain, that his fooliſh book, and Sir Richard Maningham's illiterate one, upon the

the ſame dirty ſubject, ſhews the wretched ſtate of phyſical practice and Anatomical ſkill, in this Kingdom, bout ſixty years ago. Soon after, indeed, a REAL GENIUS in this way appeared; Doctor Frank Nicholls, who by his ingenious public lectures, and curious Anatomical preparations, put an extinguiſher upon the heads of a train of ſuch impoſtors on one ſide, and pretenders on the other. After Maningham had been as much impoſed upon, as St. Andre, and another high German Doctor whom the King had ſent down to Godalming, to examine Mrs. Toft's rabbet warren; he too, wrote a curious pamphlet, to ſhew how that impoſtreſs was detected, but without ſaying a word, to ſhew how, ſo many *great men* could have been impoſed upon, by a very ſimple wicked woman, and by the moſt obvious fraud that ever was attempted; however I give him credit for the truth of *one* aſſertion in his ingenious "Diary "of what was obſerved during a cloſe attend-"ance upon Mary Toft the pretended rabbet "breeder, from Monday the 28th of Nov. to "December the 7th, 1726, by Richard Man-"ingham, Kinght, fellow of the royal ſociety and "of the college of Phyſicians, for ſays this fel-"low of the royal ſociety, on Tueſday the 6th, "Sir Thomas, (meaning Sir Thomas Clarges the

" the justice) threatened her severely, and began to appear the *most properest* physician in her case, and his remedies took place, and seemed to promise a perfect cure, for we heard no more of her labour pains" was Sir Thomas a fellow of the royal society I wonder? he certainly ought to have been, as the *most properest one*, of any of the doctors.†

It is not a *quite* singular case that Mary Toft should have made so shameful an attempt to impose upon mankind, and so debase her sex and nature; for a young girl lately in France (in order to destroy her quandam sweet heart) declared herself pregnant by him of toads, and was delivered, *like Mary Toft*, of several, and some with life enough, to make it a matter of doubt with her *Parish Priest*, whether they should, or should not, *be christened!*

M Notwith-

† In Justice to these two *great men*, it ought to be observed, that it was their ignorance, not wickedness, for they were both imposed upon, by that simple wicked wretch, who had made them, and Mr. Howard the Godalmin man-midwife believe, that rabbets had danced in her *Uterus* for many weeks together to the *tune of fourteen or fifteen!* The whole Kingdom was *in talk* upon this extraordinary delivery, and St. Andre, with Mr. Limborch, another *High German* Doctor, were sent down expressly by the King, to examine into these *uterical matters*.

Notwithſtanding the high eſtimation St. Andre ſtood in, as a man of knowledge among his Southampton admirers, I ſtrongly ſuſpected he was at bottom, an empty ſilly fellow, who would pretend to account for every thing, by uſing a few technical terms, applied with much aſſuming, confident, and arrogant manners. I therefore tried the following experiment *upon him.* Having ſplit an apricot ſtone, and taken the kernel out, I fixed in its place, a ſmall convex *lens*, and gumed it together, in a manner that it was not eaſy to perceive, it had been opened, and making two ſmall holes on the ſides of the ſtone oppoſite each other, it had of courſe a very conſiderable magnifying power; toſſing this ſtone for a conſiderable time up, and catching it in my hand, while I was walking before the coffee houſe door at Southampton with St. Andre, I at length put it to my eye, and holding up my finger before it, obſerved to him, how extraordinary it was, that there ſhould appear ſuch magnifying powers, from thoſe two holes, merely from the cavity within, and deſired him to obſerve, and explain it? he accordingly applied it to his eye, and elevating his finger before it alſo, could no longer doubt of the *truth* of my obſervation, and upon my aſking him the cauſe,

he

he was pleaſed to inform me, " *that the kernel within, had periſhed, and that the concavity of the ſtone, cauſed the rays of light to expand in the vacuum*, and *thereby preſent the rays of light in globular forms between the eye and the object, &c. &c.*" this nonſenſe bringing to my mind the ſaying of a fine lady, who being aſked if ſhe drank milk in her tea, replied, yes; *becauſe the globular particles of the milk render the accute angles of the tea more obtuſe*, I burſt into a loud laugh, and attempted to go into the coffee houſe to relate *my manner of magnifying matters*, but St. Andre, then ſuſpecting that I had learnt the art of *concealing embryoes* of Mary Toft, endeavoured to prevent me, and deſired me not *to tell;* It was a *kernel* however I could not but crack, as I knew it would become *nuts* to many of the company, though it finiſhed for ever, my correſpondence with that very eccentric and ſingular genius; yet I confeſs that it deprived me of great pleaſure, for Lady Betty, his wife (whatever *errors her paſſions* might have led her into) was certainly one of the moſt entertaining ſenſible women then living, and ſaid to be (by Queen Caroline, before ſhe was forbid the court) the beſt bred woman in the Britiſh dominions.

ANECDOTE

OF

THE DUKE OF SOMERSET, THE FATHER OF THE MARCHIONESS OF GRANBY.

THERE happened such a contest at King's college, Cambridge, in the year 1742, between the equally divided Fellows, in their choice of a Provost, that neither party could prevail; my brother, who was of the whig party, but a moderate man, and esteemed by both, was desired immediately to take his doctor's degree, and that they would unite, and elect him. As the King was just setting out for Hanover, my Brother was obliged to go immediately

diately to London to get his mandamus, and to apply to the Duke of Somerſet, who was chancellor of the univerſity, the inſtant he arrived in London, which happened to be on a Sunday, he was utterly unknown to the Duke, but wrote him a ſhort letter the copy of which now lies before me, the Duke, to his great ſurpriſe, ſent to deſire his company at dinner, my brother accordingly went, was kindly received, and his requeſt complied with; previous to the dinner being ſerved up, the company, conſiſting of ten perſons beſide the Duke, were ſitting in the great Hall, a ſervant entered, holding a ſilver ſtaff in his right hand, ſomething like a Biſhop's croſier, and bare headed, announced the ſplendid repas three times thus; *Forte,—Piano,—Pianiſſimo.* My Lord Duke of Somerſet.—My Lord Duke of Somerſet.—My Lord Duke of Somerſet. Your Graces dinner is upon the table. I believe my brother was the only undignified clergyman who was ever admitted to ſuch an honor, and as he died ſuddenly, a few days after, he died without knowing why this ſingular mark of attention was ſhewn him, and therefore I will venture to account for it, from one expreſſion in his letter to the Duke; it is, "nothing could in-

"duce

“ duce me to give your Grace this trouble up-
“ on a Sunday, but the King’s going ſo ſoon
“ abroad” The Duke perhaps did not lay much ſtreſs upon *the day*, but he was gratified; and perhaps flattered, to find a clergyman who ſuppoſed he did. Mentioning this matter ſome years afterwards, to the Dowager Lady Bateman, I obſerved that the pride of the father, ſeemed very conſpicuous in the deportment of his daughter, Lady Granby, for ſhe appear’d to me to walk in a more ſtately manner, than I had ever ſeen any Lady move. Lady Bateman, who was intimately acquainted with the Marchioneſs, and who admired her for her many virtues, and above all, for being far above any pride but ſuch as was becoming her rank, laughed at me for having conceived an idea ſo contrary to truth; as to her manner of walking ſhe obſerved, that might be eaſily accounted for, for ſaid ſhe, Lady Granby never was ſuffered to walk alone, till after ſhe was married, nor even to go up or down ſtairs, without being ſupported by a groom of the chambers, or ſome gentlemen, adding, you ſhall go with me ſome morning and breakfaſt with Lady Granby, and ſoon conferred that honor upon me. I here acknowledge my miſ-

take,

take, for I found Lady Granby as devoid of pride as she was covered with irresistible charms, and I was as proud of my extraordinary introduction to the Marchioness, as my brother could have been to the noble Duke her father.

supposed he did. Mentioning this [illegible] years afterwards, to the Dowager Lady Bateman, I observed that the pride of the father, seemed very conspicuous in the deportment of his daughter, Lady Granby, for she appeared to me to walk in a more stately manner, than I had ever seen any Lady move. Lady Bateman, who was intimately acquainted with the Marchioness, and who admired her for her many virtues, and above all, for being far above any pride but such as was becoming her rank, laughed at me for having conceived an idea so contrary to truth as to her manner of walking she observed, that might be easily accounted for, for that Lady Granby never was suffered to walk alone, till after she was married, nor even to go up or down stairs without being supported by a groom of the chambers, or some gentleman, adding, you shall go with me some morning and breakfast with Lady Granby, and to [illegible] conferred the honor upon me [illegible] acknowledge my mi[illegible]

ANECDOTE

OF AN

ITINERANT PLAYER, &c.

ABOUT eight or ten years ſince, a young man was brought to me, who was thought to poſſeſs ſome Theatrical talents, and the ſpecimens he gave of it were ſuch as induced me to recommend him to the manager of a Theatre who employed him, either upon my opinion, or his own, at a ſmall weekly ſalary; at this time, the man, who I think had been bred a coach maker, owed ſome money, and honeſtly propoſed to his creditors, to give them up a moiety of his little income, till they were paid, but

but that propoſal was rejected, and he was obliged to fly to France, and there remain without his ſubſiſtence, till he could be what, is, I think, called *white waſhed;* I thought his caſe hard, and his creditors unreaſonable, and therefore gave him a letter to a french officer, and a weekly allowance to maintain him there out of my own pocket till the *whiting had been put on.* The officer, to whom I had written in his favor, being very deſirous of obliging me, went to him one morning in a great hurry, and informed him, according to the french manner of expreſſion, *that he had procured him a penſion,* meaning thereby, a family to board with; procured me a penſion, replied the young comedian! you aſtoniſh me! pray Sir how much is it? forty pounds a year for you and your wife.—Good God Sir, how ſhall I reward you? you have laid me under an everlaſting obligation, what a lucky man I am, firſt to find a friend to ſend me into a foreign country, and there to find a ſtranger to ſerve me ſo eſſentially. The frenchman who had been too much accuſtomed to hear ſuch expreſſions made uſe of, for trifling favors, did not perceive that the Engliſhman, was thanking him for procuring him and his wife a penſion dur-

ing

ing life, of forty pounds a year; but after a little further conversation, the matter was explained on both sides. If this man was not so lucky, on the *other* side of the water, as he had for a while believed, he has had it amply made up to him on *this* since his return, for he now holds a place under government, said to be worth a thousand pounds a year, and yet his name does not appear among the list of my subscribers! he sent *it* indeed, but not *properly*, and beside, it is not the first time that he has reminded me of a very just observation; viz. that ingratitude is a crime of so deep a dye, no one was ever found hardy enough to acknowledge himself guilty of it; * tho' I am apt to believe, he was intimidated from doing it by his comedian master, who I have often seen in his blue sleeves, dipping candles in a grease tub; but that was all fair, and should not

* When the late Duke of St. Alban's married, he sent *one* wedding favor to Lord George Beauclerck. Lord George returned it, and desired the servant to inform his grace, that *two* or *none*, should have been sent to him, Lord George having just before married *his lady*, so this fortunate comedian sent me *one* mark of *his gratitude*, but as I had subscribed to him and his *wife too*, during the *white washing business at Calais*, I declined the favor, agreeing with Lord George that two favors, or none should have been sent, one to me, and *one* to my wife, for we had both *subscribed to them*.

not have been mentioned *here*, had he conducted a negotiation between a *father and a son* with truth, candour or justice, but low birth, however cultivated will always have a smack of it, neither good company, nor good luck; can do them quite away. The wife of the first artist in this Kingdom, nay, of any Kingdom, and who frequently earns fifty guineas before he sits down to dinner, carries this beggarly disposition to a pitch scarce to be conceived. Her husband who is by no means young, constantly stands upon his feet during five or six hours every day, and then before dinner walks into the park for a little fresh air, or into the city upon business, by which time, he becomes so *foot sore*, that he takes a hackney coach to return home, but he durst as soon eat his *palate* as be set down within sight of his own door, for fear of *another set down*, from a little bit of *red flesh* which grows in this Scotch woman's mouth!! what renders it worse too, is, that the husband is as generous, as he is ingenions, and feels those dirty doings at his finger ends, for no man living possesses a *cunninger finger*, nor a more beggarly and mean spirited jealous pated wife, who would rather deprive him of the company of those friends who sincerely

love

love him, for his many good qualities, and who admire him for his inimitable talents, than that an *extra* bottle of wine, or a bit of roast mutton should be eat at his table, and yet this woman has an annuity settled upon her for life, four times more than she has spirit to spend, or genius to enjoy, nor is this the meanest instance I could with truth advance, but instead of which, I will relate one of an English *Farmeress*, who died worth thirty thousand pounds, and who was my nearest neighbour *of fashion* at Land Guard Fort. On my first journey to that garrison when I came to Walton, a village only three miles from it, having been previously told there was no neighbourhood near it, I was delighted to see a magnificent house, and an Atchievement over the door! a few days, after having walked up to the village, an old hag, resembling one of the witches in Macbeth, came forth from this goodly looking mansion and thus accosted me.—"*Your servant your honor, I "hope we shall serve you with butter, eggs, and things "in our way, we always served Governor Hayes "your honor, &c.*" upon enquiring of the parson, I was assured that this woman was worth a great deal of money, and that in the last ill- [illegible] ness [illegible] ness of her husband; the old man, when he found himself *going*, said "*wife if thee wouldst,* "*I will send over to Ipswich for Dr. Venn, for indeed* "*I am deadly bad.*"—send for Dr. Venn replied the wizard, why you *auld feule* you, what signifies your *thrawing* away your money upon Doctors stuff, when you *knaw* you cant *bauld* it above a day or two, but as the Doctor was not sent for, the old man told *Thomas*, who was going with the teem to Ipswich market, to bring him a bit of veal, and *Thomas* would have brought it; but that she privately forbid him, unless it could be had at five pence a pound! the old man died a few days after, without the assistance of Dr. Venn, or Dr. *Veal;* yet this man, who submitted to be thus treated by such a mean *animal*, for she merited not the name of a woman, I am well assured, had the spirit to give my predecessor, a handsome horse whipping. When it came to the old woman's *turn*, to *have nothing more to do with butter and eggs*, she sent for the *Layer*, to make her will, and the following conversation passed between them. Your servant Mr. *Kilderbey*,—your servant Madam,—to be sure Mr. *Kilderbey* I am deadly bad;—to be sure Madam you are;—to be sure I have a great deal of money to leave behind

me

me Mr. Kilderbey;—to be ſure Madam you have;—and I am very unwilling to part with it;—to be ſure Madam you are; then lifting up her eyes for the firſt time to heaven, (previous, to her doing what ſhe had never in her life done before) ſhe obſerved, that a ſalt gooſe hung in the paſſage, and deſired Mr. Kilderbey to put it into his pocket; and he did ſo, for Mr. Kilderbey finding that ſhe was diſpoſed to leave all her money, where he wiſhed it to be left, he would have put *her* in his pocket rather than have thwarted the old lady at ſuch a critical time, for he too perceived, that neither Dr. Venn, nor *Dr. Veal's* aſſiſtance, could make her *hauld* it above a day or two, and ſo poor Mr. Kilderbey, after having made her will, was content to ride thirteen miles home with a ſalt gooſe in his pocket, the very emblem of the hag, whoſe will he had made, ſo much to his own ſatisfaction, being in favor of his friend, a reputable Farmer in the neighbourhood, who had a very large family, we have heard of high life above ſtairs, and high life below ſtairs, but where ſhall we place the lives of two ſuch Jeſabells as are above delineated? if the reader ſhould be diſpoſed, either to laugh, or to cry,

at

at fuch inftances of human depravity, for here is matter for both, he is required not to doubt, the truth of either, for I have the BEST AUTHORITY to fay they are TRUTH ITSELF.

A FEW REMARKS

ON

SLAVERY.

THAT Englishmen, who boast of more freedom than perhaps they possess, should countenance slavery, is a shame, but that they have taken the matter up all at once, with too much ardour, and perhaps too, it originated with some sinister views there can be no doubt. That the Negroes are a species of the human race, I cannot deny, but that they are an inferior and a very different order of men, I sincerely believe; I have seen and conversed much with them, in what we call their state of slavery, and

and yet by living long among them, in the Island of Jamaica, it never was my lot to see those acts of cruelty and oppression, with which the native white men, of those climates, are now accused; warmth of temper, the climate certainly conveys to them, but it is accompanied with generosity and humanity in a great degree, and the life of their slaves, appear in my eyes, much preferable to the *white slaves* among us, for what else are the day labourers of England, Ireland, and Scotland? they indeed serve a variety of masters, instead of one; but does that mend their condition? there is an old Negro servant now living at Bath, to whom I put the following questions, do you know the condition of your countrymen in slavery in our West India Islands? I do perfectly;—do you know the condition of the day labourers in this country? I do perfectly;—then put your hand to your bosom, and tell me truely, which of the two kinds of life would you prefer, were you to live your time over again? that of slavery said he ten to one; if a race of blacks were to be placed under the frigid zone, they would continue as black as under the torrid? * do the Indians

 of

* The bile of the Negroe is black, that of the white man yellow, but there are many other proofs of their being a very distinct race of the human kind.

of north America, or any nation under the ſun, beſide the Negroes, traffic in human fleſh? the condition of the Negroes of our Iſlands in ſlavery, is preferable to their freedom in their own, if a life of perpetual fear of the hands of the greateſt and crueleſt tyrants upon the earth, can be ca lled freedm. Do the advocates for ſlavery believe, that if a gentleman emancipated his whole plantation of ſlaves to day, and deſired their labour *for hire* to morrow to cut down his canes, &c. that they would ſerve him? if they do, they are miſtaken, not one of them would; and if they were all to come to this country, which God, and the Parliament forbid, no man would ever ſee them either hedging, ditching, or ploughing;* they would be either domeſtic ſervants, or ſtreet beggars, and the Engliſh nation would in another century, degenerate into a race of Portugueſe. If they are to be free, let it be to return to their own country, not to this. The prudent policy of the French nation ſhould not be overlooked, they will not ſuffer a Negro to land in their Kingdom, therefore we ſhall ſoon be *peopled* with them from *all* quarters. The giving freedom to the Negroes,

* Did any man ever ſee a Negroe in England at work? I never did except now and then to ſerve the maſon or bricklayer, with mortar.

Negroes, and giving up our West India Islands, are synonymous terms, if we give them freedom, and compel them to work, they are no longer free, and while the earth there will produce yams, plantains, cocoes, &c. Negroes will only plant *them*; white men cannot bear the violence of the sun in those climates, even without labour, but God has given the Negroe hair to protect him from the *Coup de Soleil.* The manner of their being brought down the rivers of Africa some hundred miles, their package one upon another, and the cruel treatment on the way by their own complectioned tyrants, is too dreadful to relate, but it is contrary to the interest, and I hope to the disposition of our guinea traders in general, to treat them cruelly on ship board, here and there, white tyrants arise, whose delight it may be, to extirpate whole nations. This nation has set Mr. Pitt, by their numerous petitions in favour of the blacks, a most arduous task for granting it, he must ruin the West India Islands, and declining it, he may rouze the Negroes into a general rebellion as they all now consider the whole british empire are united, in wishing to set them free. I have seen the slavery of the West Indies, and the slavery of the Galleys, but the *veriest slaves* I have ever seen, are the day labourers of England and Ireland, and the *all work* maid servants of London; while such a hue and cry is made about the freedom of black slaves, hundreds of free born Englishmen are actually in slavery under the barbarian moors in Africa who are not thought of! the late Mr Henry Grenville when he was Governor of Barbadoes, contrary to the custom of the country, told me, he dined with his coat on, and expected all whom he invited to his table to wear theirs; for what said Mr. Grenville, is a King in his waistcoat? may we not go a little further, and suppose him without any covering whatever, and then who would be able to distinguish which is the King, and which was the slave. Lord Chesterfield's observation is very just, when he said, "dress is a foolish thing, yet it is a "foolish thing not to be well dressed," the wisest men cannot conquer that absurdity, and the multitude are governed by it, to a man. A pickpocket under the character of Prince Justinian, with his son, and princess, lived eleven months splendidly, at Spa, in Germany, without a single farthing in his pocket, or scarce a shirt to put on; merely

by

ment, by dint of the ſun and ſtars being embroidered on an old coat bought of a *Friperie*, at Paris. When I ſee on Lord Rodney a ſtar, and ribband, I conſider it as an ornament due to the great and eminent ſervices he has rendered his country, but when an Iriſh Earl makes uſe of that badge to introduce himſelf and his wife into my garden, or when I am not at home, to aſk impertinent queſtions of my ſervants; I look upon him with contempt, and embrace this public occaſion, to deſire he will not take that liberty with me again, nay to tell him, HE SHALL NOT; his coat, his ſtar, and his ribband; are as inſignificant in my eyes as he is.

☞ There are in our Weſt India Iſlands, particularly in Jamaica, a great number of free Negroes and Mulattoes, who poſſeſs ſlaves of their own, and it is among them only cruelties are exerciſed! I was *more* than an eye witneſs to the following affecting ſcene in Jamaica. A gentleman at whoſe houſe I was upon a viſit, had ſtruck his head boyler, a very old man, rather too heavy a blow, and the *only* blow the man had during his long life received. The man was hurt in body and mind too, and ſeemed to be in danger, his ſorrowful maſter and miſtreſs daily viſited him, and ſhewed him every mark of attention in their power, the old man was ſenſible of their kindneſs, and often ſaid he hoped to recover ſo as to boil off the preſent crop and get out again, but in a few days relapſed and died. The day of his funeral his maſter, his miſtreſs, and myſelf; were lookers on at this melancholy ſcene, for it was a more melancholy ſcene to us, than it ſeemed to be to his numerous relations and companions, when the bearers had carried him to the margin of the grave, they run ſuddenly away with the corpſ, ſaying *him no ſave go to the grave.* A conſultation was then held, as to the cauſe! oh, he he had not taken leave of his friends, the body was then carried to the door of every hut in the Negroe town, and ſome one ſpoke for the deceaſed thus, farewell *tatta*, farewell *mamma*, &c. he was then a ſecond time carried to the grave, but a ſecond time alſo, *him no ſave go*, and a ſecond conſultation took place, when it was *found*, that he had not taken leave of his Maſſa and Miſiſs, ſo up a high hill the corps, and the crew were mounted, and the *Sheridan* among them, thus harrangued us three *Beccaras*. Good bye *Maſſa*, good bye *Miſiſs*, good bye *gemem*, me always ſerve you true *Maſſa*, my heart burn true Maſſa, and *you never beat me no more than once*, me ſorry to die before me boil the crop; ſo *Maſſa* and *Miſiſs* went crying away, and ordered the bearers a large jug of rum, and then poor *Quamina* went as quietly to the grave, as could be expected!

AN

AN

OBSERVATION

OR TWO, ON THE

MODERN DOCTRINE OF LIBELS.

A BURNT child (ſays the old adage) dreads the fire; I have *been libel-burnt*, I therefore aſk the candid part of my countrymen, whether it can be juſtly ſaid, we live in a free country, while every man among us a few only excepted, is liable to be tried by a jury, who may be perſuaded to find his Peer guilty of *publiſhing only*, and then leave his *unknown* puniſhment to the court of King's Bench. Is not a man ſo convicted, left to the mercy of Judges, who may

may nail his ears to a pillory; nay, who may cut his ears off? who may imprison him for life, or sentence him to find such high securities, as may detain him for life in a prison, and that too, for a crime, which if the punishment had been left to the bosoms of his jury, would neither have deprived him of liberty, or fined him five pounds. I will state my own case, because it is applicable to many other FREE BORN Englishmen. Lord Orwell, afterwards created *Earl of Shipbroke!* * was appointed president of a court martial upon the tryal of a military, or rather an *unmilitary* officer of his own corps, but under my command in a frontier garrison; in war time, and at the time the Queen was hourly expected to land at, or pass under the very muzzles of the cannon of that garrison. This officer quitted his duty without my leave, contrary to repeated and positive public garrison orders, I sent a serjeant to the place he had retreated (thirteen miles off,) to order him to return to his duty; yet in defiance to all military discipline, to duty, and decency to the person of his sovereign, he would not return; but aggravated his crime by absenting himself two days more; unwilling to embarass government.

* He served an apprenticeship to a Mercer.

by trying such a *militia culprit* at a court martial, I put him first in arrest, and gave him twenty four hours time, to consider of his improper conduct, in hopes, that he would make such an apology as he ought, or at least, such a one (for I would gladly have accepted of any) that might save appearances in me, and spare trouble to the *folks above*, but finding he did not apply to me! I applied to him, and asked him whether he had any reasons to offer, why I should not lay his very extraordinary conduct before the secretary at war, in order to receive the King's commands*? but this obstinate country Esquire (Captain Lynch of Ipswich) had none!! nay, he considered himself so *ill used*, that he *insisted* upon being tried at a court martial! Lord Orwell, and twelve more of his *respectable corps*, sat in judgment upon *us both*, for they rather tried *me*, than him; and after (what might have been done in one hour) three days *mature deliberation*, the *honorable court* found the prisoner *not* only, *not guilty*, *but acquitted him with honour!!* The King however could not, as appears by the Judge

* I had desired the Serjeant to tell Mr. Lynch that I expected him to let me know whether his going without leave was owing to his contempt to discipline, or *to me?* the latter part of which rather alarmed the noble Captain, and induced him to prefer the matter being settled by his Brother Officers, than *between himself and me*.

Judge advocates letter, confirm this very extraordinary and *honourable acquittal*, " becauſe the " charge ſtands CLEAR, * and UNCONTRADICTED " by the priſoner" ſome time after this ſentence, The *noble lord* was preſented with a wooden cannon; by a wag, who thought it I ſuppoſe, a proper field piece for ſo *reſpectable a corps*, for it made, when *let off*, as much *noiſe* as an iron one, and when his lordſhip was a candidate to repreſent the town of Ipſwich in parliament, a paper was littered about the ſtreets to which the following querie was tacked.†

His Lordſhip, determined to preſerve the *ſpirit* and *honour* of his corps, fixed upon me, as the *ſender* of that wooden piece of ordnance, and the author alſo of the aukward kind of querie annexed to the *election ſquib*. I was tried at St. Edmund's Bury, as the author of thoſe libels by an

* Extract from the judge advocates Gould's letter.

† " If a man be proved guilty of wilful and premeditated perjury can " any ſet of people be ſo mean to elect ſuch a villain to repreſent them " upon any occaſion, without ſubjecting themſelves to be conſidered en- " couragers and promoters of a crime the moſt impudent and the moſt " infamous," &c. Here was neither name nor the initials of a name, it was, as Mr. De Grey juſtly obſerved in court, as applicable to any man in that country, or in that court, as to the proſecutor, or was it ſaid he (turning to the noble Lord who ſat by the judge) that your conſcience retorted it upon you? Mr. De Grey had ſixty one guineas for his attendance.

an almoſt ſuperanuated judge, and a ſpecial jury of twelve gentlemen, and who thought themſelves bound in honor to find me guilty in court, though they thought me innocent enough out of one, to do me the honor to invite me the next day to breakfaſt with them, and to expreſs their concern. Six or eight months after Mr. Lynch had eſcaped *his puniſhment;* I was brought to Weſtminſter Hall to receive mine; it was to be impriſoned three months; to be fined one hundred pounds; to find ſecurity ſeven years for my good behaviour, two friends to be bound in five hundred pounds each, and myſelf in one thouſand, for the maintainance of it.* Now had the puniſhment for theſe heinous crimes, been left with my jury, would they not have naturally concluded, if impriſoning my perſon had been mentioned by any one of the number, that ſuch a mode of proceeding might ſubject me to the pains and penalties of TWO puniſhments for ONE offence? which I have been told is contrary to the ſpirit and law of the land; did the court, who paſſed this ſentence upon me *then* know, that the King would, as indeed he MOST GRACIOUSLY DID, overlook my incapaci-

ty

* A printer and my ſervant was alſo proſecuted, the expences of all coſt me at leaſt a thouſand pounds.

ty to do my military duty for the ſpace of three months I was ſhut up in a priſon? if they did not, then they laid me open to a DOUBLE puniſhment for ONE offence; but I know, that the day I was committed, one of my judges ſaid to his clerk, this military man muſt have been mad, for he will loſe his commiſſion, and I certainly ſhould (for that was the main aim of my enemy) had his Majeſty been as regardleſs of JUSTICE as the Judge mentioned above, was deſtitute of candour. Why was I not fined double, nay quadruple the ſum, and not have been deprived of my liberty? but that was not the object of my proſecutor, he had declared that he would never quit me till I was undone, and I knew CERTAINLY that Mr. W. Ellis, then Secretary at war, received an anonymous letter, while I was in durance, to the following effect, and nearly in theſe words, "Sir, Philip Thickneſſe the Governor of Land Guard Fort is muſtered *abſent with the King's leave*, but it is expected that you ſir, muſter him abſent where he really is, *i. e.* in the King's Bench priſon, for publiſhing a falſe ſcandalous and infamous libel on the Right Hon. Lord Orwell." Yours, &c.

Veritas.

This

This letter was treated with that contempt which was due to ſuch an ungenerous attack, but in juſtice to the noble *Lord's valour* I muſt own, that *after* I obtained my liberty, but bound with my friends to keep the peace for ſeven years, he did ſend Governor Tonynin to invite me to a breach of it in Hyde Park and yet, when by the advice of Mr. Cornwell the ſpeaker of the houſe of commons, I pointed out a ſafe way of accepting this extraordinary invitation, the noble Lord *prudently obſerved the laws of the land*, and declined going over to Calais with me, on account of *his gout*. At the time that this ſentence was paſſed upon me, or rather at the time I was to have the doors of a priſon thrown open to me, ſuppoſe I could not have found two friends (for they muſt be really friends) who would have been bound in five hundred pounds penalty for ſeven years, I muſt then have been a priſoner for life, or until I could. I had ONE brother, whoſe affection I could not doubt, but I had not TWO, I had a thouſand acquaintance, among whom I hope were many who wiſhed me well; but I could not ſay I had any right to expect one of them, to ſubject himſelf to the payment of five hundred pounds as a proof of it. Is not therefore a man found guilty of a

libel

libel by a jury *of only publiſhing it;* liable to impriſonment for life? and if he be, is he; can he be ſaid to be a native of a free country, who can be tried and puniſhed only, by twelve honeſt men his Peers, and countrymen? I have not the honor to be known to Mr. Bowes, but I have the pleaſure, (if it can in the leaſt be pleaſing to him,) to know, that I feel deeply for the length of time he is ſentenced to be ſhut up, with ſo many *ſons* and *daughters* of woe, for that of itſelf, is a grievous puniſhment to a ſuſceptible mind. †

† In the ſequel, I ſhall relate the ſtory of the WOODEN GUN, as I flatter myſelf it may convey ſome uſeful hints, I am ſure it will ſome extraordinary events, and ſhew as Lord Bacon juſtly obſerves, what a fire may be lighted only from a ſpark.

ANECDOTE

ANECDOTE

OF

HENDERSON.

AT the time that Palmer allowed him only a guinea, or a guinea and half a week, there were people at Bath, who were not ſtrangers to Henderſon's great powers as an actor, and ſtrength of underſtanding as a man. Lord Bateman, who firſt ſaw him at my houſe in private, was ſo much offended with his manners, (for he poſſeſſed neither modeſty, nor ſentiment) that it was with difficulty I prevailed upon his Lordſhip to ſee him in any other character than his *own*, yet he was ſo much

much delighted with his ſtage endowments, that he deſired me when we met in town, to bring Henderſon to dine with him; as we were on our way up Oxford road, it occurred to me that Lady Bateman would be more diſguſted with Henderſon's uſual table deportment, than my Lord had been, I therefore took an occaſion to tell him, that Lady Bateman poſſeſſed a good underſtanding, and was very delicate as to the propriety of the behaviour of thoſe who came to her table, and as it was probable Lord Bateman might, after dinner, deſire him to give her ladyſhip a ſpecimen of his ſtage abilities, entreated him, as he could act *even* the part of a very ſhy modeſt man, to *play it*, both before, and at dinner, obſerving, that then, whatever he was kind enough to do after dinner, would come forth with double force. Henderſon played the part of the *knife and fork*, *always* in *the beſt manner*, and during the time of dinner, *I ſaw him in a new and ſingular character*, if he did not diſplay much good breeding, he was in all other reſpects, *the thing*. My conjecture too, proved right; for Lord Bateman obſerving that as Lady Bateman had not been at Bath in his time, he would gratify her curioſity by a little ſpecimen either comic, or ſerious, of an aſſumed character, from that

inſtant

inſtant, Mr. Garrick, not Henderſon was at the table! neither Gainſborough, nor Rey- nold's; could have given ſuch a portrait of that firſt of all actors; they could only give his face, eye, and perſon; but Henderſon, al- moſt *without face, eye, or* perſon † gave us the LIVING MAN tho' *outred* to the extreme, in every part. That Henderſon ſhould be unable to with-hold ſuch very extraordinary powers of mimickry, and thereby endeavour to ridi- cule the only rival he had, is not much to be wondered at, but that he poſſeſſed effrontery enough to *take off Garrick*, TO Mr. GARRICK, which he did in the ſame manner, will ever remain a wonder, but to thoſe who knew him as well as I did, and will ſufficiently juſtify me, for giving him the *Oxford Rodd Hint*. Mr. Gar- rick was ſhocked when he ſaw himſelf in Hen- derſon's Mirrour, and only ſaid, (as well he might) "*What! is that me?*" When I aſked Henderſon how he could be prevailed upon to do it, he ſaid Mr. Garrick deſired him! Did Henderſon then poſſeſs either modeſty or ſen- timent? † but what muſt we think, when I aſ-

O ſert,

† His perſon was void of elegance and his own face bad.

† He poſſeſſed however the firſt of all virtues, that of filial affection to his aged Mother in a high degree.

ſert, that I have ſeen ſeveral letters from Mr. Garrick to Henderſon, while he was an early performer on the Bath ſtage, wherein Mr. Garrick had given him ſuch kind and important hints, as to his conduct on, and off the ſtage, that they appeared to me not only friendly, but as parental admonitions; Mr. Henderſon however ſlighted them, as puerile and uſeleſs. Mr. Ireland, the ſenſible, honeſt man, who wrote Henderſon's life, was his firſt and beſt friend, yet Henderſon *took him off*, ſtill *better* than he did Mr. Garrick! for when Mr. Ireland failed in buſineſs, and failed too, in all probability, from the expences Henderſon and his aſſociates had led him into (for Mr. Ireland's houſe was his *only* home) he was his *only* creditor alſo, who refuſed to ſign his certificate! and yet with what candour and ingeniouſneſs has Mr. Ireland written Henderſon's life, ſince Henderſon was *taken off himſelf*. *

ANECDOTE

* When Henderſon was ſeriouſly complaining of his loſs by Mr. Ireland's failure, a wag in company, who knew that he had got all Mr. Ireland's myrtles and bough-pots from the window's in maiden lane, obſerved, why what would you have more; have you not got all his timber?

ANECDOTE

OF

A LORD, A MONK, AND A FOOL.

THE Earl of Coventry, to whom, I was neither known nor obliged, further than that he had honoured me with his name, and a guinea, as a subscriber to my journey into Spain, meeting me at Bath soon after my return from thence, was pleased to inform me, and to surprise me also, by telling me it was in my power to render him a service which no man else in England could! he then gave me a list in latin, of the name of every tree, shrub, and flower, which the extraordinary mountain of Montserrat produces, and desired I would write to my friend Pere Pascal, to cause the seeds and bulbous roots it produces, to be collected at the proper seasons of the year, and sent to him, and that whatever expence attended it, he would most thankfully pay, and feel himself highly obliged; I immediately wrote in the most pressing terms to the good Monk, and told him they were for a nobleman of my country, of high rank, and great fortune. This request opened a correspondence between me and the good old man, one year, *before* the Spanish war commenced * and continued one year after for Pere Pascal, lived in peace with all mankind; in his reply to me, he expressed such a willingness to oblige his Lordship, and such regard to me and my family that it *unmanned* me; if bringing a tear or two in my eyes when I read it, be *unmanning*, such poor beings as the best of us are. My only concern said the Monk is, "least we should not fulfil "thy commands with that zeal and ardour we "wish, as our apothecary is the only man in "whom we can confide." After two years expensive

* The Spaniards I suppose mean to shew their respect to their correspondents, by enclosing their letters in several covers, or perhaps (as in Spain they pay by weight) to prevent wear and tear, in foreign letters their paper being very thin, for my letters often had double covers.

expenſive correſpondence to the Monk, and myſelf alſo, he informed me that he had that day ſent to Mr. Macdonald their Agent at Barcelona, two boxes, one, containing ſeventy four parcels of ſeeds, all properly marked and numbered; and the other, filled with bulbous roots. "*When this valuable cargo arrived*" Lord Coventry honored me with a letter of which the following is a copy.

Dear Sir,

"I am this minute favoured with your "moſt obliging letter, I return you a thouſand "thanks for the trouble you have been at on "my account, I hope you will ſee next year "the produce of your own bounty, though it "muſt appear in an infant ſtate, I am really "thankful for what I could not have obtained "by any other means, and whatever expenſe "may have attended this valuable cargo *in its* "*paſſage to England*, I ſhall moſt gratefully pay "to your order, it is the only ſhip that I wiſh "may eſcape Admiral Rodney's vigilance, for "under every adminiſtration I muſt always "wiſh well to that of Britain, I return you "the Monk's letter * and join in his bleſſings, being

* All the Monk's letters were tranſlated and ſent to his Lordſhip with the originals.

"being dear Sir, your most faithful humble
"Servant,"

COVENTRY.

PICCADILLY,
March the 4th, 1782.

As his Lordship only seemed by this letter, desirous to pay the expences of the *sea passage, of this valuable cargo*, I replied, by pointing out, the only means I knew of, to transmit some gratuity to the Monk's and the Apothecary, who had, as I did then, and do now believe, traversed a mountain sixteen miles in circumference in the hot autumn of Spain to collect them, and to the Monk who had parceled them, numbered them; provided boxes for them, and sent them all properly packed up, to their agent forty miles, from Montserrat, to Barcelona. I therefore informed his Lordship that as it was war time, if he transmitted his donation to Mr. Walpole the british minister at Lisbon, that gentleman might be able to convey it by some safe means to Montserrat. His Lordship did not honor me with any reply to that letter, but soon after, called upon Mr. Brown, my bookseller, the corner of Essex Street and gave him *a guinea!* for their reward, and desired I would remit it to them, I did not remit it; but I did not

not keep it, but gave it to a Spaniſh priſoner who was almoſt naked, and pennyleſs, and there the matter had reſted in ſilent aſtoniſhment in my own boſom, had I not a year afterwards, met with a Spaniſh gentleman at Bruſſels, who *delicately hinted* to me (for he was juſt returned from Montſerrat) that the Monks were much ſurpriſed, that a britiſh nobleman, (HOMO RICCO,) ſhould have offered ſo ſmall *a return* for their trouble and expenſe! I too, was not only ſurpriſed, but deeply hurt, for as his Lordſhip had ſeen *all* the Monk's letters, he could not but have obſerved one remarkable expreſſion in them, towards the cloſe of our correſpondence, viz. "I ſhall be always glad to oblige you, but I muſt inform you, that the poſtage of your letters have coſt me eighteen *pecettoes* (ſhillings,) which is a great ſum out of a poor monk's pocket."† Upon this alarming and painful hint, I wrote to Lord Coventry and told him I would vindicate myſelf, not being able to endure the moſt diſtant ſuſpicion, of having

† My letters were all a ſingle ſheet of the thinneſt paper I could procure and ſealed with a thin wafer; the reader will therefore judge of my expenee of poſtage when I aſſert that the replies were always in two and ſometimes three covers!

having behaved either ungratefully or unjuſtly to ſtrangers, who had received me with kindneſs and treated me with much hoſpitality; his Lordſhip in return, by a letter dated Croome, Sept. 22, 1782, ſays, "Sir, the reaſon of my leaving a guinea with Mr. Brown for the uſe of the Spaniſh Apothecary, was becauſe you told me a few ſhillings would be a ſufficient gratuity, and I really meant to be liberal, I have not the ſmalleſt objection to depoſit another guinea or two with the ſame perſon when I go to town next winter and I ſhall certainly do ſo, though I never bought docks and weeds at ſo high a price; the gentleman certainly did not collect them upon Montſerrat, but probably before his own door without going a yard to procure them. The Hill is known to contain ſome curious plants, of which I troubled you with a catalogue, but inſtead of thoſe productions the contents of the box were preciſely what I have deſcribed as ſeveral of the beſt botaniſts can teſtify, who have ſeen this whole cargo. When I left the money with Mr. Brown I fully explained the purpoſe for which it was intended, and told him that you had no other concern in it than being the vehicle of it to a poor Apothecary at Montſerrat,

it

it is therefore, ſurpriſing that there ſhould have been any miſapprehenſion about it."

I am Sir, your obedient Servant,

COVENTRY.

But with all due reſpect to the noble Earl, may I not ſay, that I had not only been *the vehicle* to procure " *the box*" but to procure TWO BOXES from Montſerrat, that I had been at ſome expence, and had ſent, beſides poſtage of letters, a preſent to the Monks, in conſideration of their kind attention to my requeſt, and was not repaid, nor even aſked what expences I had been put to, I was therefore obliged to trouble his Lordſhip with another letter from Bruſſells, to expreſs my concern, that I ſhould at the uſe of my intereſt, the expence of my purſe, and the moſt ardent deſire to ſerve his Lordſhip, incur his diſpleaſure! his Lordſhip in reply does me the honor to ſay " Sir, Nothing could ſurpriſe me more than your letter of the 4th. inſt. interpreting a former letter of mine to convey that I was *highly offended with you*, could I be offended with a gentleman who being almoſt an entire ſtranger to me, obligingly undertook to write into a foreign country? could I be offended with him for having punctually executed that commiſſion?

ſion? as to the expence of collecting the ſeeds I always underſtood that I was to pay it, and I think ſo ſtill, with that idea I applied to you to know what demands there were upon me, and received in anſwer only a few ſhillings to a poor Apothecary who had the trouble of gathering the ſeeds, I thought I could not ſend him leſs than a guinea, which ſum I left with Mr. Brown, your bookſeller, fully explaining for whoſe uſe it was intended, and fully ſtating, that I believed you would be kind enough to remit it to Barcelona, having myſelf no correſpondence with that place. The charge attending poſtage of letters I confeſs did not occur to me, but if you will let me know what may be due on that account and what you *now* think a proper gratuity to the Apothecary, I will readily ſet right the miſtake and pay the money to any perſon in London who may be appointed to receive it."

I am, Sir,
Your obedient humble Servant,
COVENTRY.

CROOME,
October the 12th, 1782.

After an additional trouble, and expence in a freſh correſpondence with the monk at Bruſſells,

ſells, I returned to England, and living within three or four doors of Lord Coventry, and conſequently often ſeeing his Lordſhip, I again took the liberty of ſtating to him that I was ſome pounds out of pocket, for having *punctually executed* his Lordſhip's commands, and even offered to ſwear within the mark to the ſum expended; a day or two after, meeting his Lordſhip in Piccadilly, he was pleaſed to tell me, if I would call at his door, his porter had a note for me; as I had never in my life been within his Lordſhip's doors, I declined that honor, but ſent my ſervant for the note, and thus it was written, in his Lordſhip's own hand, "If Mr. Thickneſſe will call at Mr. Cun-"ningham's, Hoſier, the corner of St. James's "Street, *the day after* he receives this note he "will find his demands enquired into and ad-"juſted" but I declining *that honour* alſo; and Sir John Miller called at my houſe a few days after, and ſaid he had brought ten guineas, which he was deſired to deliver to me, from Lord Coventry, as a *douceur* for the Monk and Apothecary; here again I was under the neceſſity of declining this *ſubſtantial offer*, but I informed Sir John Miller, that if he would pay it to Don Virio, ſecretary to his excellency the Marquis Del Campo, the Spaniſh Ambaſ-

ſador

ſador, I was very ſure that he would remit it to the Monks, it was accordingly paid to him, but it arrived alas! too late for Pere Paſcal to know how the matter ſtood. The Prior of the convent however informed me, that he had received the ten Britiſh guineas, and that he would not part with them, till he had my inſtructions how they were to be diſpoſed of, I therefore deſired that after deducting the eighteen *pecettoes* for the poſtage of letters, the price of the boxes; their carriage; and embarkation at Barcelona, for the uſe of the convent; that the remaining ſum, ſhould, if he pleaſed, be given to the Apothecary, who collected the miraculous *docks and weeds* on a mountain where flowers *only grow*, and I have ſince received a letter from *Don Joſe Ferret Boticaria de Montſerrat en Cataluna*, acknowledging the receipt of the balance, and offering me his future ſervices in the moſt polite and friendly terms; and now I have only to lament, that Pere Paſcal, who ſhewed me and my family ſo much attention in the moſt romantic and retired ſpot upon the habitable globe, died without being thoroughly ſatisfied, that I had not been diſhoneſt or ungrateful, for the ſingular attention he ſhewed me and my family, during our ſtay at his moſt enviable

habitation

habitation, and that my ſincere and expenſive endeavours to oblige Lord Coventry, ended in my being ſent to a *Stocking Grocer*, on a *fixed* day, to have my demands "*enquired into*, "and adjuſted." That Lord Coventry may be thoroughly ſatisfied that no part of his bounty remained with me, the following extract from Don Virio's letter, dated London, the 30th of July, 1785, will ſhew.

Dear Sir,

"I received ſix weeks ago an anſwer "from my friend at Madrid about the affair of "Montſerrat, he had delivered the ten britiſh "guineas to an agent of that convent with "a particular charge, that this ſum ſhould be "paid to the Apothecary, as unluckily our "good Padre Roderego Paſcal is no more. Not "ſatisfied with this anſwer, I wrote to my "friend, that he ſhould inſiſt on having an "anſwer with a proper acknowledgment from "the perſon that was to receive the money, "and conſequently, by a meſſenger juſt ar-"rived, I received the encloſed letter †

"which

† The letters was from the Prior of the convent as mentioned above, who had received the money, and paid the balance to the Apothecary.

" which I dare ſay will give ſome better infor-
" mation, &c."

Subſcribed,

J. Virio.

THE

THE STORY

OF THE

WOODEN GUN,

AS IT WAS HASTILY SKETCHED OUT FOR THE INFORMATION OF A LADY, NOW RESIDING AT BATH, AND LONG BEFORE THE RELATOR HAD ANY IDEA OF PUBLISHING IT.†

IT is very natural Madam, that you ſhould wiſh to hear the particulars of a ſtory, now you are grown up to years of maturity, which you ſay excited much of your curioſity, even when you was a child, for I verily believe, that during ſome years, the wooden gun was a topic

† The Lady of Admiral G——r.

a topic as often touched upon in Britain, as the Iron maſk was in France, and perhaps, is at this day as little underſtood; I ſhall therefore Madam, as well as my memory can, without any minutes to aſſiſt it, comply with your requeſt, in relating the moſt material points of a quarrel, which commenced by what the French call *un mal-entendu*, and which, though trifling in the beginning, was attended with very ſerious conſequences to the two principals, and even involved many other perſons into very diſagreeable and untoward ſituations; ridiculous as ſuch a narrative may appear, at the diſtance of full twenty years ſince its commencement it may have its uſe, by ſhewing in what manner, little miſunderſtandings may become productive of fatal conſequences, and how neceſſary it is not to be too quick in forming opinions, by conceiving rudeneſs or incivility is meant, when attention, and the utmoſt propriety only was intended. The circumſtances ariſing from the diſpute between Lord Orwell and myſelf, has clearly convinced me, that it is much ſafer to have a miſunderſtanding with a ſenſible knave, than with a vain proud, of weak honeſt man; and here it may be neceſſary to obſerve, that the conſequences, and cenſure, ought to fall on the firſt

aggreſſor,

aggressor, and I flatter myself Madam, however partial I may insensibly become by relating facts, in which I was so seriously an interested party, that you will believe I cannot deviate so much from candour and truth; but that you may be able to see your way; to form a just judgment; and determine on which side the weakness, the wickedness of the prosecution (I was going to say persecution) preponderated. I believe Madam that you and every person of sense will allow, that military knowledge, cannot be conveyed by the King's sign manual, and that nothing but inspiration can impart the knowledge or duty of a soldier, the minute the sovereign is pleased to confer a military command. In this situation however, Colonel Vernon, the late Lord Orwell, and since, Earl of Shipbrook stood, when his Majesty appointed him to the command of the Eastern Battalion of the Suffolk militia; but before I proceed further, it may be necessary for me to observe, that Colonel Vernon was the nephew of the *renowned Admiral Vernon*, and singled out from his other nephews, to be his sole heir, and that as I had served in the fleet at Jamaica, under that Admiral's command, and not approving of his conduct to the soldiers under mine, I had rather a dislike to the name, and therefore, when Mr. Vernon came to take possession of the Admiral's house and estates, in the neighbourhood of Land Guard Fort, of which garrison I was then Lieutenant Governor, *I did not visit* him, but meeting him one day near a little cottage I then possessed, in a very narrow lane, I pulled off my hat as we passed; soon after which, he stop'd at a little farm of his own, and describing my person, asked the farmer what officer it was he had just met? and being informed, he rode back to my cottage, and without alighting, entered into a very civil conversation with me, and when he went away, said he should be glad to see me at NACTON; and though I was far from feeling any personal dislike to Mr. Vernon, after this conversation, it so happened, that I did not visit him, but soon after, Mr. Vernon was appointed Colonel of the Suffolk militia, consisting of eight companies, four of which were sent to do garrison duty under my command. It then instantly occurred to me, how negligent I had been, in not visiting *Mr. Vernon*, and how necessary it was instantly to visit *Colonel Vernon*, as he could not, without much aukwardness to himself, and to me too, see that part of his corps under my command, without taking some civil notice of one, who

who had seemed to slight his acquaintance; and as he was at that time in London, I wrote to his Adjutant, with whom I was well acquainted, to let me know by a special messenger, the first day the Colonel arrived at Nacton that I might pay my compliments to him; and this the Adjutant accordingly did, and on that very day I waited on him, and was received with the utmost civility. Colonel Vernon then expressed how much he was pleased with the situation of his corps, one part being at Ipswich, the other at the Fort, and his own house between both. Before we parted, I desired him to name a day to visit that part of his corps I had the honor to command, and hoped that he would eat a Barrack dinner with me when he did, this being settled and the day fixed, he came accompanied by his Adjutant, and returned, as the Adjutant afterwards informed me, pleased in every respect, and said several civil things of me. He soon after, invited me to dine with him, entertained me and some of his own officers, with great hospitality, and I returned, not less pleased from Nacton, than I understood he returned from the Fort. From this clear state of facts, it seems evident, that the utmost good will prevailed on both sides; confident I am, it did on

 mine,

mine, and therefore a few days after, on my way to Ipswich, I made Colonel Vernon a third visit; at which time, he observed, that a knowledge of garrison duty would be of service to his whole corps, and therefore said he, when the four companies now under your command have been two months on that duty, I will relieve them, by sending the other four in exchange; I was not much surprised, that a gentleman whose *first* commission gave him the command of a Regiment, should propose such a thing, but I was very sure the secretary at war would have been infinitely surprised, had I permitted such an exchange to have taken place without his knowledge, nay I know, that my character as a soldier, and my bread was at stake, if after I had received the King's command to admit the troops *then* in duty, I had permitted any others, even of the same corps, to relieve them, but by the same authority, *i. e.* an official letter in the King's name from the War office. This I mentioned with all imaginable civility, as an irregular mode of proceeding, but the Colonel told me with some seeming warmth, that he had mentioned his intentions to Lord Ligonier and to Mr. Charles Townshend (then Secretary at war) and *that they had both consented*

to

to the exchange proposed; Nevertheless Sir, do not I beseech you said I, urge me to consent also, to an unjustifiable measure, but either write yourself to the War office, or permit me, as I should be sorry to see the troops from Ipswich arrive at the garrison gates, and then be obliged not to receive them. Upon which Colonel Vernon struck his hand violently upon his breast, and with a face as red as crimson, again *asserted that he had permission* to change them, and change them he would; wondering that I *doubted* his word! he then asked me *hastily* if I would drink chocolate, but in such a manner, that it plainly implied, *a parting cup*; I took the hint, and retired, but much hurt, that he should have so misconceived my real sentiments; for I had no more doubt but that he had mentioned the matter to Lord Ligonier and to Mr. Townshend, and that they had both consented to it, than if I had been present when they did; but the Colonel could see it in no other light, than that of *doubling his word!* and therefore from that minute determined to begin playing the low game of cross purposes with me. His first *move* was, to kill a Buck, send it to his officers, under my command, to be divided among them, and to overlook me, the division of which was made

made in my kitchen, in order to *roast me* instead of the venison. The next move was, to order his Major, to prepare the men for *his Review*, on a certain day, on the *outside* of the garrison; and consequently beyond the reach of my command; and therefore I took the liberty absolutely to forbid that mode of reviewing the troops of the garrison, under my command, not his, till he sent to me, to ask it as a favor, and promise that the men should return to their duty, the minute the Review was over, for I found in all points of military Etiquette, he was as ignorant, as he was of common good manners; he accordingly, but reluctantly complied with my requisition, and the men were marched out for his review, during which time I took my horse and rode to my cottage hard by, without taking any notice of the Colonel who was *then under my command.* From that minute, I fancy the Colonel began to suspect, that matters might brew into a *tête a tête* review between him and me, for as soon as I was gone he entered the garrison, left his name at my door, and sent his Adjutant after me to desire I would eat a cold pasty, with him and his officers at his neighbouring farm, but as he had *so sorely disappointed my venison appetite* for a bit of a hot haunch just before,

fore, I desired to decline that honor, but I should have observed, that after I had the last interview with him at Nacton, I wrote to Mr. Townshend, a short letter, to tell him Colonel Vernon's inclinations relative to the change of men, and asked him whether I had the KING's *permission* to let that exchange take place? and it seems the Colonel too, had wrote a long letter of complaint against me, on the same subject. In reply to my letter, Mr. Townshend honoured me with a private answer, under his *own* hand, beginning thus. "I return you thanks for the attention you upon all occasions shew to me, and to my office, Colonel Vernon mentioned this matter to me before, and I am sorry to find he is grown all of a sudden, so jealous of the war office; but as you have not that jealousy, its a matter of indifference to me in whose name orders are brought to you." If I was a little too much elated in receiving such a particular mark of approbation, and attention from such a man as Charles Townshend, it cannot be wondered at, I shewed his letter to every body, and pointed out the implied censure it contained of Colonel Vernon's conduct, which greatly encreased his resentment, and soon after an event happened, which he weakly flattered himself, would enable him to gain a compleat

pleat victory over me; here it must be observed this was in war time, when I commanded a frontier garrison of importance, and at a time too that the Queen was hourly expected to land at, or pass under the walls of the Fort, into Harwich Harbour. Notwithstanding which, I had observed several of Colonel Vernon's officers, absented themselves from their duty without my leave, and even to be absent all night, I therefore repeated my former orders, in stronger terms, and positively forbid any officer of that garrison quitting his duty without first obtaining his own superior officers leave, and then mine; nevertheless Captain Lynch, one of Colonel Vernon's Corps, a man possessing a better heart, than good manners, or attention to military discipline, took his horse, and before my face rode away in defiance of all *civil* or *military attentions*, I sent to the Major who commanded, to know whether the *noble Captain* was to return that night, and if not, ordered a serjeant to follow him, and to require his immediate return to his duty, or, to let me know whether his absence was owing to contempt to *my authority*, or to discipline, and his own duty? this message was delivered the same evening to him at Ipswich, but the Captain did not return to his duty, till two days afterwards,

and

and then, I was under a neceſſity of either putting him under an arreſt, or giving up for ever all chance of ſupporting that neceſſary authority my duty and ſafety laid me under; * Captain Lynch was therefore put under an arreſt, as ſoon as he entered the Fort, and when he had continued ſo twenty four hours, I ſent to know whether he had any reaſons to offer why I ſhould not (for I was very unwilling to give ſo much trouble above) lay his conduct before the ſecretary at War! but the Captain, being of the ſame wrong headed line with his Colonel, had none he ſaid, ſo far from it, that he inſiſted on being tried at a Court Martial!! encouraged no doubt, in ſo *laudable a cauſe*, by his noble Colonel, though it muſt be obſerved, that there was no good underſtanding in a political line, between the Captain and Colonel, who was then member for Ipſwich, where the Captain was much eſteemed, and had no ſmall ſhare of electioneering intereſt to beſtow, the Colonel therefore, with ſome chance of ſucceſs, flattered himſelf that by being named Preſident of the Court Martial, he might, by ſhewing ſuch *kind attention* to the *unfortunate priſoner*, and ſuch

contempt

* I contrived to meet the noble Captain upon the Road, the Day he returned, but he paſſed me without even the Salutation of the Hat.

contempt to the *disciplinarian Gov*r. as to kill two birds with one stone, and gain a victory in the field of battle, as well as in the rotine of election; a scheme better conceived, however than executed, for he failed in both. However the day of tryal arrived, and the Colonel with a train of his officers, arrived also at the Fort; they came directly to my house, and the Colonel asked me why I took the liberty of putting out the name of two officers whom *he* had appointed members of the Court Martial, and putting down the names of two others? he was informed, by the same authority that he is now ordered out of that house, into the chapel, where the members were to assemble, where I would bring the prisoner, and support the charges for which he was confined, * observing at the same time, that I, not HE commanded within those walls, and that within them, I knew my own authority and importance as much, or I did my insignificance without the walls. The officers were accordingly assembled, the Adjutant, mentioned above, was named judge advocate, and the members were by him SWORN to administer justice

* He was so ignorant as not to know that if all the Colonels or Generals in the Army had come into that Fort upon duty, they would be under my command.

justice according to the rules and articles of War, he however, was as ignorant of his duty as a judge advocate, as his Colonel the prisoner were of military discipline, for he proceeded to try the prisoner before the warrant, signed by the Arch Bishop of Canterbury, and all the regency was read, for that being read, could alone constitute them a legal court, but that warrant remained (where it now is,) in my pocket. The court however *thought* themselves competent to try, and did try the prisoner, and the President often attempted to try me too, using very indecent and improper expressions, such as "*you disciplinarian* you, *Mr. Governor*, &c. &c. I will not trouble you Madam with the minutes of this very extraordinary tryal, further than to say, that the prisoner, who at bottom is a very honest man, acknowledged that he did go without my leave, that he did, the same night, receive my orders to return to his duty, but that he did not return till a day or two afterwards. You will naturally wonder then that such a military culprit, should have insisted upon being tried at a Court Martial, but I must instantly recall your wonder to another, and a greater matter!! The cour (I believe unanimously) found him NOT GUILTY, AND ACQUITTED HIM WITH HONOR!!! The sentence

ſentence of Courts Martial, are never made public till the King has approved, or diſapproved the ſentence, yet, having no doubt *how* the matter had been decided, I followed their *proceedings* to London; and entreated the favor of Mr. Townſhend, not only *to read the ſentence,* but to caſt his eye over the minutes; he replied I have, and I really am at a loſs, ſaid he, to know what advice to give THE CROWN (that was his expreſſion) and then obſerved, it is not right, to diſcloſe the ſentence of a Court Martial.—But to acquit a man who acknowledges himſelf guilty, is * Soon after his Majeſty's pleaſure was known, the judge Advocate informed me, that the King *could not confirm* the ſentence by which Captain Lynch had been acquitted, " *becauſe the charge ſtands clear, and uncontradicted* " *by the priſoner!*" a very gentle but prudent manner ſurely, of ſetting the *gentle judges down:* however Captain Lynch, in conſideration of his *long* and *cloſe* confinement, (for he *had only the range of the whole garriſon to breathe in,* was releaſed, and Mr. Townſhend with great propriety, moved Colonel Vernon's corps from Land Guard Fort, and replaced it, with part of Sir Armine Woodhouſe Norfolk militia, who with his officers, came into that duty, (in ſpite of all

all the prejudices, endeavoured to be raised against the commanding officer) with the utmost good temper, good discipline; and polite behaviour; a conduct which distinguished them wherever they went, and which will always be remembered by me with the utmost satisfaction, gratitude, and respect. Soon afterwards however, to the astonishment of every body! Sir Armine's corps was removed, though they professed to like their quarters exceedingly, and Colonel Vernon's, then just created Baron Orwell, returned to their old quarters!! If Mr. Townshend's *previous conduct*, would tally with his future, one would think he had returned Lord Orwell's corps, on purpose to make a smoak blaze, which he knew had long been on the eve of bursting forth, for I had by a variety of provoking inuendoes intimated, that the *disciplinarian Governor* would not sit down quietly without *that sort of* satisfaction, which one gentleman expects from another, or an acknowledgement, and an apology for such impertinent behaviour; but the person of his Lordship was almost as difficult to be seen as the grand Turks. It was necessary however, that the new created Lord, should become re-elected as member for the borough of Ipswich, and

as

as all is fair game at an election, the following printed hand bills were dispersed by my servants, my friends, and his enemies.

ADVERTISEMENT.

Shortly will be published, and generously given gratis, for the benefit of that extensive family (now in the utmost distress) the family of the Wrongheads, of Wronghead Hall, in the county of Suffolk, a letter

To the Wrong Honorable,
Mr. President Upstart,

Giving a full and particular account of the origin of a late *militious* quarrel—The first wrongheaded cause of his Wrongship's taking umbrage—His Wrongship's private views miscarry—The discipline doctor's prescription read in public—It is *taken*, and brought up again,—The shame and woe that has already arose from young Esq. Wronghead's obstinacy —A surmise how much more may—He alone answerable—His military exploits—Mr. President Wronghead's sanguine expectations miscarry—The young Esquires *secret* cause of disobedience,

bedience, known only to himſelf and *one more*, ſome account of an old ſong, ſung at a late Camp,—The offence it gave, and why—The downfall of a Major, and the upſtart of a Captain; Some notice of a letter from Camp giving an account of a wrong honorable entertainment, The ingratitude of the writer,—A new method (much improved) of ſeparating wine by a piece of chalk* How to know Port from Claret at a certain table without taſting either.—A fray among the grave ſtones—Four challenges and no blood ſhed! with a curious plate and references of a new invented piece of ordnance weighing only four pounds, made without either *iron or braſs*, the whole illuſtrated with ſerious and humourous remarks, by a diſbanded militia man without a head, but in poſſeſſion of a very good tail piece.

N. B. To be lett or ſold a new erected manſion houſe, known by the name of *Wronghead Hall*, fit for a man of honor, being very near a Blackſmith's ſhop and a Church.—great plenty of game, but *unfortunately* it is not the man, [illegible] nour [illegible]

* His Lordſhip had Claret for the upper part of his table and Port for the lower, and Captain Lynch chalked how low the Claret was to deſcend.

nour houſe. Enquire at Admiral Vernon's *head* in P—p—t Lane.—The only reaſon the preſent poſſeſſor parts with it, is, the air being too keen for the gout, and the ſituation rather too near a powder magazine.

Quere. If a man be proved guilty of wilful and premeditated perjury, can any ſet of people be ſo mean to elect ſuch a v——n to repreſent them upon any occaſion, without ſubjecting themſelves to be conſidered encouragers and promoters of a crime the moſt impudent, and the infamous? ſurely if ſuch a repreſentative ſhould be made choice of, they will ſhew his face on the day of election through a *round hole*, inſtead of clapping his ba—k—ſ—e on a *cuſhion*.

This balderdaſh grub, being local, could only be underſtood by the *then* inhabitants of Ipſwich, but one part is neceſſary now to be explained, to the well underſtanding of what is to follow, *i. e. the fray among the grave ſtones*; for it ſeems, that Lord Orwell had ſaid to the Bailiff of Ipſwich, that he would not carry the addreſs of that borough to the King, in company with ſuch a ſ——l as Mr. S——n, Mr. S——n being told this, *buckled himſelf on* to

an

an old ſword, and ſent to Lord Orwell to meet him in the Tower church yard, Ipſwich, and there demanded ſatisfaction, but this was declined, and his Lordſhip retired to Scarborough. I muſt now return to the Fort, where Major Negus commanded the four companies of Lord Orwell's corps, and who, either from ſimplicity, or obſtinacy, ſet the garriſon orders at naught, which I did not at that time much attend to, as Lady Betty, my late wife, was in a very alarming and dangerous ſtate of body and mind, nor ſhould I have attended *then* to his mere diſobedience to orders, had he not drawn his men up in *array*, under her bed chamber window, and made them fire their pieces, ſo as not only to alarm my wife, but ſo terriſied her, that ſhe did not recover her right ſenſes till three days afterwards. Indeed the paſſion ſuch an inſult, offered to her, and to me, under ſuch afflicting circumſtances, drove me almoſt mad, and I plainly told the Major, I would confine him in the black hold, if he did not inſtantly diſmiſs his men, and keep ſilence, which he then did. Lady Betty ſurvived this inſult about three weeks only, and the night I had followed her to the grave, after my ſervants and the Chaplain were gone to bed, I wrote the Major a letter, requiring

 him

him instantly to meet me at the back of it, and give me satisfaction for so basely violating the dictates of humanity, and disobeying garrison duty; as I could see into his apartments from mine, I perceived he was up, and I concluded for a considerable time, that he was preparing to meet me as I had desired, but upon my sending a *second* Letter, he returned me the following answer, the original of which now lies before me.

Sir,

" You will excuse my giving you satisfaction in the manner you require, and at the same time give me leave to assure you that I never intended any insult either to the departed Lady or yourself, and further give me leave to condole with you for the late Lady Betty whom I esteemed for her many virtues.

I am Sir,
Your most obedient
Humble Servant,
WM. NEGUS.

LAND-GUARD-FORT,
Just past Two o'Clock in the Morning,
April the 8th, 1762.

Thus

Thus warmed by resentment, and depressed with affliction, I rashly sent a letter to the St. James's Chronicle wherein I observed, that where an officer first disobeys the orders of his superior, aggravates it by disregarding the dictates of humanity, and when called upon to answer for such insolent and wanton conduct, writes the following letter, little spirit or services could be expected from such a man, when called forth into public service. The Major's letter, thus published, and so severely prefaced, induced Lord Orwell, who hated him, to call forth a consulation of his Corps, the result was, that the eldest Captain, should wait upon him, and tell him he must either fight me, or resign. The Major declared he would not fight in a wrong cause, and that as he was, or seemed to be, the aggressor, he would rather resign; by this time however I had been almost convinced that what the Major had said in his letter was true, and that it was rather an inconsiderate act than an inhumane one; he had ladies with him, and he had a mind to shew himself to advantage, and how well his men could perform their Evolutions, so that the only part of my conduct in this long contested business, which at this day gives me any sensible concern, is, my being the cause of the

Major's resignation, a gentleman to whom I believe the pay as Major was of some importance to his family; but they had insinuated that the first time I met him in public I intended to insult him; to obviate which, I wrote to him, urged him not to resign, and assured him that whenever we did meet, he should receive no incivilities from me, but all I could say availed nothing, he would he said resign, and did so.

After this long preamble Madam, you will naturally ask, but where is the wooden gun, and what has all this to do with the pith of the dispute? why Madam the gun was all this time a *Scare-crow* on board of some collier's ship in the ocean, but being washed over board, or drop't over by some accident, it was driven at my feet, on the sea beach near the Fort, while I was taking my evening walk; and at that instant, it occurred to me, that it might prove a piece of suitable ordnance to accompany the noble Lord's regiment, as they were just going to camp. I therefore took it home with me, tied a label round what is called the *Cornish-ring* of an iron cannon, and the following address.—With Major Negus's compliments to the right Honorable Lord Orwell to be left

in

in *the Tower church yard* 'till called for; that being the place where Mr. Stanton had invited Lord Orwell to a *pointed* interview, which he had declined; but though the addreſs on the gun was in Major Negus's name, the direction was of my hand writing, and it went to Ipſwich with me; ſtood ſome hours viſible in my chaiſe before it took its ſtation on the tomb-ſtone, in the Tower church yard, and had been viſited by hundreds in both places, till at length, a ſtay maker who lived there, took it into his houſe, and ſhewed it to the curious, at a penny per perſon. As ſoon as the news of this piece of artillery arrived at Nacton, Lord Orwell, who very well knew the *train* in which it came, pleaded ignorance, and wrote to the major to aſk him whether he had ſent it? he replied, *by aſſuring his Lordſhip he did not!!* I then took occaſion to obſerve, in the coffee-houſe at Ipſwich, and in the preſence of ſeveral of his own officers, that if he would make the ſame enquiry of me, which had been made to Major Negus, I would inform him *who* ſent it, and *why* it was ſent; but to my great aſtoniſhment, I found the next enquiry was at the bar of the King's Bench, where he ſwore that I had ſent it to reflect on his courage as an officer, and to render him ridiculous in the eyes of his Majesty's subjects, that he believed the hand writing to be mine, and that I had dispersed a paper at Ipswich, during the time of his election, intimating that he had been guilty of wilful and premeditated perjury on the tryal of Captain Lynch.

This business came to tryal before a special jury, some months after at St. Edmund's Bury, where (though I acknowledge I was guilty of the whole charge) I protest I was convicted by the most impudent p——y; but not procured, I verily believe, by Lord Orwell. The late Sir William Bunbury, father of Sir Charles, had very kindly invited me to spend a week at Barton, near St. Edmund's Bury, previous to that tryal with a view, I believe, of shewing the court, and the country gentlemen what *his opinion* was of

‡ Tenacious as those Gentlemen were for the *honor of their corps* upon seeing their Major held out in the St. James's Chronicle, there had appeared in the same paper, a much severer Letter, a Letter which *reflected highly* upon the conduct of their *mock Court Martial*, and when I had occasion to go to London, and leave the Command of the garrison *to that honorable corps*, I pasted up *that news paper* upon one of the pillars in the chapel, and told the commandant I expected it to remain there, and there I found it upon my return !! but if there had been a single grain of true spirit among them, they should have tossed up which of them should have had the honor of tearing it down, there was not then, nor is not now another corps of militia in the kingdom, who would have suffered such a paper to have stood a single minute, where it remained for months.

of the prosecution, for some people called it a persecution, and the jury who found me guilty, did me the honor to invite me to breakfast with them the next morning, and I am very certain had the *punishment* as well as the *guilt*, been left to their determination, my sentence would not have been imprisonment three months in the King's Bench, a hundred pound fine to the King, and securities in two friends, of five hundred pounds each, and myself in a thousand, to keep the peace for seven years! As my man servant and my printer were likewise prosecuted on the same libelous matter, the expences of which all fell upon me, I may justly say, first and last, it was not less than a thousand pounds expence to me, and a much greater sum I dare say to his Lordship. The tryal came on before Mr. Justice Denison, at a time that he seemed almost superanuated, Mr. De Grey however was one of my council, to whom I gave sixty guineas for attending it, and Mr. Willes was his Lordship's. Lord Orwell, contrary to the advice of his friends, appeared in court, and sat upon the judges bench, while I, the poor culprit, was below the bar, with nothing but a little model of the wooden gun in my hand, and Mr. De Grey's brilliant talents to protect me, and to be sure he gave the noble Lord, a good

good ſixty pounds worth of chaſtiſement. What ſaid he! the nephew of the renowned Admiral Vernon; who took PORTO BELLO with ſix ſhips *only*, to bring a gentleman into this court to vindicate his courage; it cannot be my Lord, I am aſleep, it is a dream, ſaid he, but if I am awake, I muſt ſay, that if I had preſided at any court whatever, and could have put my hand to my heart, and have ſaid I had conſcientiouſly done my duty like an honeſt man, I would never have conſtrued a dirty bit of paper, thrown about at the time of an election, a paper as applicable to any man in this court, or this country, as to Lord Orwell, to have been an inſinuation that I had been guilty of wilful and premeditated perjury, or was it ſaid he (turning his eyes to Lord Orwell,) that your conſcience my Lord retorted it upon you? and as to your courage my Lord, that ſtands juſt where it did. But my Lord, turning to the judge, I now recollect it is a family failing, for I remember I was council for a poor man brought into this court by Admiral Vernon himſelf, for ſaying (tho' he had juſt before taken Porto Bello with ſix ſhips *only*,) that he was a traitor to his country! after about two hours harrangue in this way, Mr. De Grey thought, and ſo did I, that he had given me

a lumping

a lumping pennyworth for my penny; and Mr. Juſtice Deniſon, then degenerated into an old w——n, began to ſum up the heads of the charges, but not without two clerks as prompters one at each elbow; and thus he began.—Here, here—what is the Lord's name?—Orwell?—here, here, it ſeems that Lord Orwell has been throwing about in lanes, alleys, and ſtreets, certain libelous papers and — —no my Lord, not Lord Orwell, he is the proſecutor,—and who is the other? Governor Thickneſſe, aye, aye, *General* Thickneſſe, I thought he was a Lord, but it is no matter, he is clearly guilty, and ſo the jury muſt find him. About ſix months afterwards, I appeared in Weſtminſter Hall to receive the judgement as mentioned above, and had the honor of being put into the cuſtody of a Tipſtaff, who however took my word for going *alone* to the priſon of the King's Bench; ſome time in the evening of the ſame day, but before I had been twenty four hours in durance, I was thunderſtruck with reading in ſeveral of the morning papers the following paragraph. "Yeſterday Philip Thickneſſe, Eſq. who was committed to the King's Bench Priſon for publiſhing a falſe, ſcandalous, and infamous libel, on the Right Honorable Lord Orwell, made his eſcape from the

the ſaid priſon, was re-taken, and brought back again." Whereupon I ſent to eight different printers who had inſerted that falſehood, to know by what authority they had publiſhed it; and ſeven of them ſent me Lord Orwell's letter, containing the above falſehood, and inſiſting that they inſerted it in their papers, and that he would be anſwerable for it. Whereupon the Tipſtaff, to whoſe care I had been delivered, went before the Lord Mayor, and ſwore that the whole was falſe, and his affidavit ſoon after made its appearance in the ſame papers. After having ſpent part of the months of February, March, April, and May, with great mirth and feſtivity, at my *Town-Houſe* in St. George's Fields, the then Marſhal, who had treated me with great kindneſs, threw open the priſon doors, and I had the *honor* of being huzza'd out by the priſoners, at the head of whom, was a juſtice of the Peace, and at the tail, the Cock-lane ſcratching girl, her father, her mother, and the celebrated young ſcotchman Dunn, who was confined for attempting to aſſaſſinate Wilkes. I then returned to reſume my command at Land Guard Fort, and Lord Orwell retired to Nacton, in perfect ſecurity as to his perſon, but he did not find *his mind* in a much better ſtate than before Tryal. He had juſt

built

built a fine houſe at Nacton, and I had juſt bought a cottage built in the form of a country church directly oppoſite it, it was called High Hall, and as every man has, thank God, in this land, a right to decorate his own houſe in what manner he pleaſes, it pleaſed me to mount a very formidable two and forty wooden pounder, between the windows in the Tower of High Hall, with the following doggrel lines in legible characters beneath it.

ALTHO' I ne'er with thunder broke,
Nor hid a coward in a ſmoak;
Although no man e'er ſaw my fellow,
At Carthagene or Porto Bello;
No gun that e'er was made of metal,
Nor tinker with a brazen kettle,
Nor gun that ever dealt in blood,
Or ever croſſed the briny flood,
Did ever make ſuch loud report,
At death of men, or joy at court,
As this ſame gun which here you ſee,
Although of mock Artillery;
Which by the tide was hap'ly ſaven,
By floating into *Orwell Haven*,*

Sav'd

* The Harbour of Land Guard Fort is ſo called.

Sav'd by the favor of the tide,
Lo! high I hang to ſhew my pride,
The pride of Nacton, happy ſtation,
A village fam'd throughout the nation;
For though I'm only heart of oak,
I ſpeak it not by way of joke,
I coſt in money hard and ſound,
The ſum of fifteen hundred pound,
And every year for ſeven to paſs,
Shall every lad, who with his laſs,
Of Nacton pariſh join their hands,
And no *Upſtart* forbid the banns,
Shall find within this homely cot,
A hearty welcome to the pot,
A pudding ſmoaking on the board,
And all that houſe and hoſt afford,
Nay, not to baulk them of their fun,
A lodging found them at THE GUN,
Provided that the maiden ſay,
I'll have it Roger, on the 7th of May.*

The novelty of the houſe, the ſingularity of the wooden gun, and the oddity of the paltry lines on the front of it; brought an infinite number of people to ſee it, beſide all thoſe who viſited his Lordſhip; for there was not a window in the front of his houſe, which had not

* The day I came out of priſon.

not High Hall in view. Here was no libel; no King's Bench Bar to fly to, nor any breach of the peace; what then was to be done to heal this dreadful eye sore? Why a Petition to the King, to remove me to some other garrison; but even that might not remove High Hall. At length however, Mr. Welbore Ellis was pleased to send me a verbal message, desiring *when it was convenient, to see me in Town*, and when I arrived there, to follow him into the country as far as Twickenham; and there, in the house of the *departed* Mr. Pope, I found the *living Mr. Welbore Ellis*, who not thinking I had not spent quite money enough among lawyers, in a prison, &c. honoured me with this little jaunt to see his Villa, and to receive *the King's command's*; and so with that *gentleness of manners*, and *inconceivable address which has rendered him the admiration of all the world for half a Century*, he told me that the king had not taken any notice of my incapacity to do my military duty, that his Majesty knew I had a large family, and as he believed I was a man of some abilities, he was disposed to overlook my past conduct to Lord Orwell, provided I would give my word of honor never more to disturb the peace of his Lordship; observing, that we were both servants, as well as subjects, and that his Majesty

Majesty expected to be obeyed. I expressed how happy I should be upon all and every occasion, to pay obedience to the King's commands, and observed also, that if I had not been so particularly honoured, by being called two hundred miles from my home and my family, a letter would have enjoined me as steadily to my observance, as the personal interview I was then honoured with; and beside, that I flattered myself I had laid Lord Orwell's conduct so compleatly before the public, that it would have appeared downright cowardice in me to meddle with him any further; and after again expressing my *obligations to Mr. Ellis*, which *I shall never forget*, I took my leave, and returned once more to my duty at Land Guard Fort. I well knew that Lord Orwell could not have the face to tell Mr. Ellis in what manner High Hall was embellished, but being tired down with the weight *of metal*, though not of gold, in this business, I determined to take down the wooden gun, blot the doggrel lines and to think no more of Nacton Hall, its Lord, nor of High Hall. I accordingly housed my Cannon, and burnt my *varses.* This move, I have reason to believe removed from the noble Lord's mind, a great deal of deep oppressive matter, for he told every body, that I had

I had done more than I was enjoined to do, and that he flattered himself he should be able to enjoy the remainder of his days in peace, for I have good reason to believe, though he loved money, he would have given half his fortune that the peace had not been broken between us. However, this permanent peace in appearance, was but of short duration; a parcel of fools took it into their heads, that they could draw up charges against my military conduct, which would fall heavier upon me than my late *civil* prosecution, but then it would be attended with an expence they could not afford; they had prepared the charges, and very weighty ones they appeared on paper, and very heavily they must have fallen upon my head, had any of them (for they were eight in number,) been well founded. Those charges were shewn to Lord Orwell, and they met with his approbation and *encouragement* to proceed upon them, and so I once more experienced the *attention* of Mr. Welbore Ellis, who obligingly sent me *extracts* of those charges, to hear what I *had to say* to them *before he took* the King's commands, by laying them before his Majesty? in reply, encouraged by a conscious innocence, I humbly besought his Majesty to grant me a tryal before a Court Martial, and that it might not be be privately at Land Guard Fort, but at the horse guards where my innocence or my guilt might be more publickly brought forward; the charges all affected my bread, and character, and some of them my life, one of which was for "*spoiling and destroying the King's stores*, the english of which however was *stealing them*; and here I cannot help making a digression, to shew what an escape I had, for innocence does not always protect a man against a combination of knaves, and it was a combination of knaves, who had formed the eight charges against me, though they knew that there was but *one* on which they hoped to convict me. It must be observed as said above, that though I was fully *guilty* of the libel on which I was tried at St. Edmund's Bury, yet the witness who convicted me, did it by the most impudent perjury, for he swore possitively that I told him, when he asked me who I meant by the perjured villain, mentioned in the printed paper, and dispersed at the election, relative to the *Wronghead family*, that I replied, I mean Lord Orwell, and he is a perjured villain. No person therefore in the court but myself could be sure, that G——n was a perjured villain, and therefore upon his testimony alone, the jury were obliged to find me guilty. It will be necessary now

to

to give some account of this Mr. Goniston, he had made *himself useful* to Lord Ligonier, who was then at the head of the board of Ordnance, and when his *Lordship's age* rendered Mr. G——n's *talents* no more necessary, he was rewarded by his Lordship with the appointment of Master Gunner and store keeper under my command at Land Guard Fort; he was a fellow of some abilities, which he employed in secreting, selling, and stealing the King's stores, in such a manner, that within the first year of his trust, I was able to procure seven affidavits of his shameful and wicked conduct, which I sent up to the board of Ordnance, and desired a Court Martial might be ordered to try him, as it was my duty to do, for I was called upon to sign the expenditure of stores as used in the King's service in the garrison under my command, which I could not have done, without being as guilty as G——n who had not been wanting, in endeavours to make me share with him part of his plunder. At this time I believe Lord L—r was dead, for Lord Granby was then at the head of the Ordnance, but there was also an inferior officer who for many years had the lead at that board, and that gentleman for reasons *best known to himself*, was very unwilling to let G——n appear at a Court

Martial, perhaps he thought an enquiry into the conduct of a little rogue, might open a field to enquiries of a higher nature, certain it is, he prevailed upon Lord Granby to write me a letter wherein his lordship said "*he could rather* "*wish Goniston was not tried*, as the tryal would "be attended with much trouble even to *Go-* "*vernor Thicknesse himself*, and therefore he "would remove him to some other garrison "and *beg'd leave* to recommend Mr. John "Walker, who had served in the blues under "him, and who was he said an honest man, to "my countenance, and favor" all this was very innocently done by Lord Granby; he did not see, nor was it probable he should, how danger-ous it might prove to me to let such a lion loose, who knew what steps I had taken to punish him for his roguery, but as I knew "*the rather wish*," of the COMMANDER IN CHIEF of his MAJESTY'S TROOPS, was a polite way of conveying an absolute command, I was obliged to acquiesce. It was in revenge therefore that Mr. Goniston appeared so useful to Lord Or-well's cause at St. Edmund's Bury, and he then *served* the Ordnance at Chatham, and was no longer under my command. Now Madam, the first time I went to the horse guards, where I was soon to appear as a culprit for *spoiling*

and

and destroying the King's stores, the first person who caught my eyes was Mr. G——n, and then, and not till then, I own I was seriously alarmed, for knowing what he had done, I well knew what *he could do* in the swearing way, and pray Mr. Goniston said I, what has brought you hither? *I don't know your honor;* here I am, and rubbing his hands with a smile of insolence and contempt, added, they have brought me here to be an evidence *against your honor I think;* here too, it became very necessary for me *to think*, for I plainly perceived, unless I could defeat Mr. G——n's evidence, I was utterly undone in character, bread, and perhaps to be exposed to an ignominious death. At this minute that I am relating the tender pivot on which my fate was wavering, I tremble, to think of my escape. Fortunately I had preserved Lord Granby's letter, wherein his lordship acknowledged the receipt of the affidavits sworn against G——n's frauds, and *his wish that* he might not be tried at a Court Martial; I therefore instantly wrote his Lordship a letter, informing him that I was on the eve of a tryal at the horse guards, on eight heavy charges, one of which, was for *spoiling and destroying the King's* stores, and that to my great astonishment, Mr. G——n, whom his Lordship had preserved, would probably effect my ruin,

 for

for he was the *only* evidence produced to convict me of the ſame crime! but I plainly told his Lordſhip, that I muſt give him the trouble to attend the Court, and there give HIS REASONS, why, he *rather wiſhed* to ſave a notorious villain from puniſhment and inſtead of diſmiſſing him from the King's ſervice, remove him to a place where he might carry on the ſame practices, leſs liable to be detected. No reflection is meant here on the memory of that brave and liberal minded Nobleman, he had been *requeſted* to *ſign* that official letter, and did it probably in the rotine of buſineſs, without conſidering much about the matter; but he now ſaw the conſequences in the cleareſt light, and Mr. Thoroton was directed to let me know, that *his Lordſhip was confined to his bed with a ſore throat and cold*, but could have no objection to my producing his lordſhip's letter at the Court Martial, if it could tend to be of ſervice to my acquital. I replied, that the proceedings muſt then be ſtop't, till his Lordſhip's health was reſtored, for I could not let Mr. G——n's evidence appear at the horſe guards againſt me, till his Lordſhip had informed the court, why I was to be tried for a ſuſpicion only of ſpoiling and deſtroying the King's ſtores, and G——n ſpared, againſt whom there

was

was proof poſſitive in his Lordſhip's poſſeſſion by ſeven or nine affidavits. Here Madam, you will perceive that Lord Granby ſtood in almoſt as aukward a ſituation as I did, for he muſt have perceived how unjuſt it was that G——n ſhould be permitted an evidence againſt me, before he had been cleared of the ſtrong evidences againſt himſelf; the next day however, I happened to ſee at the horſe guards, Mr. B——, a gentleman belonging to the board of Ordnance, with ſome papers *under his arm*, and in cloſe converſation with Mr. G——n. I did not hear a word that paſſed, but I was ſo convinced of the converſation that did paſs between them, that I *then* conſented to take my tryal, and to let Mr. G——n appear as an evidence, without calling upon Lord Granby to attend, for I concluded Mr. B——, came to aſk Goniſton his buſineſs there? and being told; he would naturally obſerve, that Mr. Thickneſſe would never ſubmit to have his evidence given in Court, while there were ſeven affidavits now under his arm, wherein it is poſſitively ſworn, that he had ſtole and ſold the King's ſtores, and he might add, what have you to do with Mr. Thickneſſe, or he with you? or why are you fiſhing in troubled waters, which may overwhelm yourſelf? This,

or

or ſomething like this, I was ſo perfectly convinced paſſed in that converſation, that all my apprehenſions of danger from G——n's evidence ceaſed, and I ſoon had the ſatisfaction of finding they were well founded, for Mr. G——n, to the aſtoniſhment of the phalanx formed againſt me, knew nothing, not he, of my having ſpoilt or deſtroyed the King's ſtores, I had frequently he ſaid, made uſe of ſpades, pick-axes, &c. of the King's at my cottage, but that I had always given a receipt for them, and regularly returned them into the ſtores when I had done with them; this being ſo directly contrary to what he had declared he would ſay and ſwear to; that he was not ſuffered even to eat, as he had before done, with his chums in iniquity, for it muſt be obſerved, that though eight charges had been brought forth, it was *this one only* they laid any ſtreſs upon, for G——n had boaſted that he did *my buſineſs* at St. Edmund's Bury *for me*, and would compleat it at the horſe guards; but failing with this their ſheet anchor, they all got a ground on a ſandy bottom, and ſunk; for I was neither *ſhot, broke nor* ſuſpended. At this tryal too, Lord Orwell attended, and gave his evidence, tho' he had often declared he would never drop me till he had ruined me.

And

And now Madam, you will think perhaps that the meaſures of my perſecutions were at an end; no ſuch thing; I had a much more arduous piece of buſineſs to go through, for I had no ſooner defended my innocence, than I had another perſon to try before the ſame Court Martial. Mr. Welbore Ellis had ſent down a Captain with the King's warrant to command Land Guard Fort during my tryal; this man, was weak enough to believe, that if I was broke, he might probably ſucceed me; I had accommodated him with two parlours in my houſe, with a bed in one, and ſuch other conveniences as were neceſſary to a temporary reſidence, for a ſingle man, and had not only locked, but nailed, and ſealed, the door which led into eight other apartments, becauſe the pipes of an organ I had pulled to pieces, were laid in proper order, and almoſt covered the floors of two of the rooms. *Nails*, *ſeals*, and *locks*, created a ſuſpicion that ſome of the King's ſtores might be concealed on the other ſide of them, and this man as I ſaid above, was weak enough to break the ſeals, locks and nails, in order, *he ſaid*, to give the ladies a ball in my dining room, ſo that my Organ, my liquor, and my papers were now all at his mercy! and he or his man made very free indeed with what

what they found convenient, or agreeable; but no King's ſtores could be ſeen, but they found a vaſt cedar cheſt, ſeven feet long and four feet broad, which was quite full, and very heavy; and there no doubt they concluded the King's ſtores were concealed. Some attempts were then made to force the locks and bolts of the cheſt, but not ſucceeding, they unſcrewed the cheſt, which was dove-tailed together, and got the front ſo to open at the bottom, as to examine part of the contents, but could not ſhut it up again, without taking out ſeveral parcels of pamphlets which were tied up to the number of ſeven hundred and fifty, in parcels of five and twenty each, and by thus drawing them from the bottom, a ſnuff box rolled down, from the top, which contained a gold medalion of the preſent King, which coſt me fifteen guineas, a five moidore piece, and ſeveral ſmall pieces of old gold, to the value of about forty pounds, no part of which I ever ſaw afterwards, and was thankful to find my plate ſafe, which was lapped up in a blanket with the ſnuff box, but that alone had fallen down. I therefore drew up four charges againſt the Captain commandant, one of which was for behaving in a ſcandalous infamous manner, ſuch as was unbecoming the character of an

officer

officer and a gentleman, by breaking open my doors, whereby I had sustained considerable loss, and *specified the particulars*. This officer being chosen by Ellis to command in my absence, and he who thought eight heavy charges against me, not too many to defend, found four against the Captain, too many for him, for he informed me that the *King had ordered* the Captain to be tried on two of them, but *had reserved the other two for his further consideration*. At the Captain's tryal I clearly proved, by the girl who made his bed, that one of the seven hundred and fifty pamphlets which came out of the chest (for not one had been published) she had seen, read a part of, and even quoted almost *verbatim*, a card addressed to Lord Orwell, and sent by Mrs. Thicknesse, wherein she asked him "if he "intended being at the assembly at St. Ed-"mund's Bury that night, for if he did, she "would meet him there *as sure as a Gun*." The court however only found the Captain *indiscreet* in breaking open my rooms! But why he was not broke for doing it, or I for charging an *innocent man* with behaving in a scandalous infamous manner, must be determined by General Parslow and a majority of the members who tried him, and who heard the charges, for according to my weak judgement, both ought not

not to have born the King's commiſſion, *one muſt have behaved infamouſly;* but neither of us was puniſhed!! and here let me obſerve, and with gratitude and reſpect acknowledge it, that had it not been for Lord Walkworth, now Duke of Northumberland, and Lieutenant Colonel Darby, both utter ſtrangers to me, I had certainly been undone at this Tryal, for there was not want of P——y ſufficient to have demoliſhed half a dozen innocent men, but thoſe two worthy perſons, either from poſſeſſing ſuperior parts, or feeling more attention towards the guilt or innocence of a priſoner before them, took uncommon pains to get to the bottom of every circumſtance; one of which, was managed with ſuch addreſs, that I cannot forbear repeating it. In the ſummer time, I generally reſided at a little cottage three miles from the Fort, and when my ſervant there, informed me, while I was in London preparing for my own tryal, that my rooms had been broke open, I inſtantly went down, and took him with me to the Fort, and then ſaw that my cheſt had been forced alſo, but cloſed up again, for it had many marks of violence viſible enough. Now in order to ſhew that the Captain commandant had not broke open the cheſt, evidence was brought to prove that I came one

morning

morning at four o'clock *alone* into the Fort, and ſhut myſelf up in my own houſe for two hours, and conſequently *robbed myſelf*. I then poſſitively aſſured the court that I was not there either morning, noon, or night; and that if it could be proved I was, I would allow they could not be too ſevere upon me in their cenſures, obſerving that the draw bridge was conſtantly drawn up every night, that it required eight men to lower it, and conſequently ſome of them muſt remember lowering it at ſo early an hour; and my paſſing at the ſame time cloſe to two centinels. But this viſit of mine was to be proved, by the only *viſible* proſecutor of me when I was tried, viz. his wife's and his maid. This was one Enſign Agnus Macdonald, an Enſign who could neither read or write, but who, got a pair of colours in America, by the favor of Lord Townſhend. To prove this early viſit of mine to my *own houſe*, his ſcotch ſervant, a girl of very uncouth appearance, was firſt examined. Did you, ſaid the Court, ſee the Governor on a certain day come into the garriſon? *yes;* what time of the day was it ſaid Colonel Derby? a little after four only? How did you know the hour? I looked at the clock;——and what did you then? I went into my miſtreſs's room, and ſaid

lord

lord Madam, the Governor is come into the Fort; aye, what o'clock is it? *a little after four.* —Colonel Darby then took his watch out of his pocket, and bid the girl tell him what hour it was by that? but ſhe ſeemed totally unacquainted with the machine. He then ordered her to be taken down *between two truſty men*, to ſee the Horſe guard clock, a clock exactly ſimilar to that at which ſhe had *read the hour ſo exactly by* at Land Guard Fort; but that too, was above the capacity of a poor illiterate, ignorant, wicked girl, who had perhaps never ſeen a clock, till ſhe arrived by the ſea at Land Guard Fort. Colonel Darby then aſked her what coloured coat I had on? after a little pauſe (for that matter had not been previouſly ſettled between the miſtreſs and the maid) ſhe replied *a red one.* The next witneſs was her miſtreſs another *Highland Lady*, almoſt as uncouth, and full as *well* inſtructed as her maid. Being aſked whether ſhe had ſeen the Governor on the ſame day her maid had ſworn to? *yes* ſhe had ſeen him, but not till eight o'clock, for ſaid ſhe, I have a young child which I ſuckle myſelf, and my maid brought it into the room and ſaid, Lord madam, the Governor is come into the Fort! why what o'clock is it? *almoſt eight*; what could bring the Governor *ſo early* into the Fort?

and

and after many shrewd questions put to this *good* lady by Lord Walkworth, and Colonel Darby, they asked her also what coloured coat I had on? this being a point *not settled* between Madam and her maid, she replied a *green one*: in short the prevarication of Macdonald, his wife, and his scotch maid were such, that the audience *groaned them*, and the President told him, that he was ashamed to ask a man who had the King's commission in his pocket, whether he knew the nature of an oath, "but said "he, you prevaricate so, that your conduct is "scandalous, I had almost said infamous" yet this observation is omitted in the minutes I required, and received at the Judge advocates office! for notwithstanding what the President, General Parslow said to Mackdonald, he seemed far from being disposed to favor me, either at my own tryal, or on my prosecution of the Captain commandant; and I verily believe he wished to find matter sufficiently strong to crush me if possible. I was an utter stranger to the General and so was the Captain commandant, and he could not have treated me with such severity while I stood a prisoner before him, and when my life, bread, and honor was pending, if he had not been induced to believe by somebody that I merited no favor from

from the Court. One inſtance will ſuffice, to ſhew his unguarded partiality to the Captain commandant, and I could produce a dozen. The Captain in order to ingratiate himſelf in the neighbourhood, had given a ball on a ſaturday night to the neighbouring ladies, the Chapel, a *conſecrated one*, was appointed for the dance; the Communion table for the punch and the negus; and about four o'clock on *ſunday morning*, the ball broke up, but not before Sir John Barker and many of the Gentlemen, were compleatly drunk. Doctor Smyth, the late *worthy rector* of St. Giles's and his wife, were witneſſes on behalf of the Captain commandant on this tryal, and after the Reverend Doctor, then only a country Vicar, had given his teſtimony, I had him to croſs examine, and did ſo, as follows.

Was you at the ball which the Captain commandant gave at Land Guard Fort? no; you was at the Fort however during the ball was you not? yes—and your lady I think danced there? yes, where was the dance given? in the chapel; did the Captain aſk you whether there was any harm by dancing in the chapel? he did; what was your reply? I told him there

there was none; here the numerous by standers gave the Rev. Divine some heavy groans. As many of the members of this court never were at Land Guard Fort, pray inform them what kind of place the Chapel is?—It is a great room,—has it not at one end a desk, a pulpit, and Pews? yes, and what is at the other end? why a great window—and what is under that window? a table—for what use? to administer the sacrament from,—and is it not elevated above the floor and railed off? it is,—and pray where was the negus, punch, and wine put? I believe upon that table; here another universal groan took place!! but General Parslow with a *look of the greatest complacency*, observed, that wherever the ladies were assembled for dancing, there must be refreshments provided. An observation however that did not pass without a more unanimous groan than any which had been bestowed upon the Reverend Divine, and I am very sure it must at *this hour*, if he reflects on his conduct AT THAT; cause sensations of a very different complection in his bosom. And I was well assured that the same day that the Rev. Divine had given his evidence, and had been *cross examined* even till he burst into tears, that Lord W—h said when he return'd to Northumberland house that Parson

Parson Smyth is the d—dest rascal I ever met with. † He however married a great man's cousin, and was made Rector of *St. Giles's.* I shall conclude this narrative with a few observations, for though, much foreign matter from the wooden gun has already been introduced, yet it all originated from that source. The libel prosecution, cost me a thousand pounds, and the Horse guards Tryal some hundreds, and at length, determined me either to sell the government of Land Guard Fort, or resign it, and disentangle myself from fools and knaves; which by the favor of that good man the late Marquis of Rockingham, during his short administration I fortunately effected, and got two thousand four hundred pounds for what I would have sold for the four hundred pounds only, rather than have continued in such a service, to be persecuted and unprotected in the evening of my days, after an active life in different parts of the globe, where I had served the King, to the best of my poor abilities. And now Madam, I think I hear you say, but how happened it that for some years

† The doctor died lately at Bath, with an income of above sixteen hundred pounds a year, and yet before he was *earthed*, his house at Norwich was entered, his goods seized by his creditors, and many of them are become great sufferers.

before Lord Orwell's death, he and you were upon good, nay even upon visiting terms!! To make the story compleat, I will tell you; you may remember that I was bound to keep the peace for seven years, with all his Majesty's liege subjects, but just at the conclusion of those seven years, a decision was made against my claim in the court of chancery; and in the house of lords afterwards confirmed,† by which I was deprived of ten thousand pounds, I thought my property from the clear opinions of Sir Dudley Rider, Lord Chief Justice Willes, Mr. Madocks, and in short most of the ablest lawyers in the kingdom (Lord Mansfield excepted) for they tho't it as clearly my property, as that the sun shines at noon day; so that instead of my receiving ten thousand pounds, I had six hundred pounds to pay to lawyers, a heavy blow, and which determined me to leave my native country with a resolution never to return to it. At this time I was informed that Lord Orwell was preparing to go to the south of France, the very Rout I also was taking, I therefore wrote him a letter, and observed that as he was going southward for the

† Earl Powlet moved to have the opinion of all the judges, but that being over-ruled!! he took his hat, and with indignation in his looks quitted the house, and other Lords followed his example.

benefit of his health, and I the ſame road for the convenience of my purſe, I hoped we ſhould meet there, and then ſettle that *little matter* which had been ſo long *pending between us.* To that letter you may conclude I received no reply, but when I came to London, I met in the park, the unfortunate Doctor Dodd, who told me he had dined the day before with *my friend Lord Orwell*; and I told him of the letter I had written to his Lordſhip; I have ſeen it ſaid he, and though I cannot juſtify his conduct towards you, I cannot help conſidering that letter cruel towards him; I do not think ſaid he, Lord Orwell will live ſix months, and you have hindered his ſouthern expedition, he will not go, leſt you ſhould follow him, obſerving at the ſame time, that he, who often attended ſuch high creſted men in their ſickneſs, or on their death beds, could better perceive their real condition than I could, and conſequently was more diſpoſed to pity and feel for them, for I muſt obſerve that Dodd was as good and pleaſant a tempered raſcal as ever lived, or as ever was hanged, and I left the Doctor fully determined, though I did not tell him ſo, to write another kind of a letter to Lord Orwell, and went to a coffee houſe directly and did ſo. The ſubſtance of which

was,

was, that though I had once aſked him to forgive me, when he had the ROD OF JUSTICE HIGH LIFTED OVER MY HEAD, he thought proper to refuſe that requeſt; yet I felt myſelf thoroughly diſpoſed to forget and forgive all that was paſt, wiſhed him a good journey, and a perfect re-eſtabliſhment of his health, adding, that perhaps neither he or I had long to live, and that I was willing to die in perfect forgiveneſs of all thoſe who had injured me, and in hopes that thoſe whom I had injured would do ſo likewiſe. Not dating my letter from any particular place, Lord Orwell was three days before he could find my addreſs, and then he wrote me a very handſome and proper letter, in which he thanked me, for mine, and aſſured me both as a Chriſtian, and a gentleman, all his reſentment ceaſed, and good will and wiſhes ſucceeded it. I met with him at Lyons on my way out, and found him at Aix in Provence on my return from Spain, and while he reſided at Bath, we ſometimes viſited each other, and now and then he ſent me ſome game; but as he was a very rich man and had materially injured my family, and was without any children of his own, the candid reader will perhaps think with me, that one, or all my children ſhould have found a place in his Will; he was the firſt aggreſſor, and acknowledged himſelf to be ſo. That fatal quarrel to him and to me too, began juſt as his fortune and honours fell upon him, and from that time till his death, he had but little peace of mind, or bodily health; probably the bottle was his conſtant reſource, for he died a martyr to the Gout, and perhaps too, without a friend to cloſe his eyes. He was a man of a violent vindictive temper, paſſionately fond of money, but far from being void of conſcience or moral rectitude. When Dodd was under ſentence of death, he deſired me to prevail on his Lordſhip to ſign his petition to the King for pardon; I did apply, and Lord Orwell refuſed my requeſt, but with great propriety and ſentiment, I wiſh ſaid he to oblige you, I wiſh too, that Dodd may be pardoned, but I cannot give it under my hand, that I think him an object worthy of it, becauſe I know tranſactions of his, infinitely worſe than that on which he ſtands convicted, but do not ſaid he tell him ſo; and as he certainly wiſhed to oblige me, and to ſerve the man, who though by mere chance, was the cauſe of our reconciliation, it is but fair to conclude, he refuſed my requeſt merely on the ſcore of conſcience. I ſhall now finiſh this long Narrative with a copy of a letter

ter I wrote to Lord Orwell, at the earneſt request of that good man, the late Lord Litchfield, previous to my receiving the judgment of the Court of King's Bench, a letter that all *his* friends, and all mine agreed, he ought to have rejoiced at receiving, and to have been happy to have accepted; but paſſion and reſentment prevails often over prudence and even good ſenſe, and though Lord Orwell did not poſſeſs either in a high degree, he lived to ſincerely repent his refuſing to comply with ſo reaſonable a requeſt, a requeſt ſo binding on my part, and ſo triumphant on his; yet that letter made part of his Counſels Brief to aggravate my guilt, when I received the judgement of the Court of King's Bench.

But peace to his manes.

It is probable he obtained the Earldom and took the title of Shipbrooke, merely to drop the well known title of Lord Orwell, becauſe that name was conſtantly connected with the *Wooden gun.*

Copy of a Letter to Lord Orwell, previous to my receiving the Judgment of the Court of King's-Bench.

My Lord,

"I ſhould have taken this method of addreſſing your Lordſhip much ſooner, had I not depended (I now find too much) on the promiſe of ſome powerful friends,* to uſe their utmoſt endeavours to put an end to a difference which I hope aroſe from faults on both ſides, but which I am ſenſible has far exceeded the bounds of decency on mine.—Thoſe who are quick in anger are often led into indiſcretions they become ſorry for, and I am not aſhamed to ſay this is my caſe; and therefore I flatter myſelf your Lordſhip will conſider the very great expence, and the painful ſuſpence, of a proſecution that has already coſt me more than double of my whole years income, to be a ſufficient puniſhment to me, and a ſufficient reaſon to your Lordſhip not to carry this matter any further. Your Lordſhip has a manifeſt advantage over me; by waving which you muſt either forever lay me under an obligation to behave towards you, as to one I muſt think

* Lord Bute had undertook for a while to ſtop Proceedings, and did ſo, for reaſons hereafter to be mentioned.

think myself obliged to in so doing, or I must for-ever lye under the imputation of acting contrary to sense, decency, and gratitude, I profess too, my desire is, (exclusive of the consequences of this prosecution) to be laid under that obligation; and as it has been my case to offend against the laws of my country in general, and against your Lordship in particular; it may be yours to forget and forgive the latter, that I may appear in Court, with a better grace, to receive the judgment due to the former.

I have the honour to be your
Lordship's most obedient,
And hope to be your most
Obliged humble Servant.

P. THICKNESSE.

Lord Halifax, Lord Litchfield, and indeed all the friends to both parties agreed, that the above letter was sufficient to bury in oblivion even the greatest injuries; Lord Orwell alone thought otherwise, but lived to repent it, and at length became thankful to accept that forgiveness from the writer, which he had so injudiciously rejected when a prosecutor. It must be observed however that I erected a

printing-

printing-office in my own houſe, and that my preſs teemed with *ſquibs*, *crackers* and inuendoes innumerable, and that many of the very provoking means I made uſe of to inflame and irritate Lord Orwell, do not appear in this narrative, a narrative I meant to have related as a matter of mirth, and in another mode, but the many ſerious circumſtances attending it, reſtrained that vein of pleaſantry with which I was diſpoſed to have given it, for alas! what do all the moſt important things end in? why with a

Hic jacet Lord Orwell,
Hic jacet Philip Thickneſſe.

Neverthleſs Madam, I will not conclude this long winded ſtory ſeriouſly, but finiſh it with a ſong from my own pen and preſs, which you may ſing if you pleaſe, To the tune of "*A Cobler there was &c.*"

THE

THE WOODEN GUN,

A NEW SONG TO AN OLD TUNE.

I'LL ſing you a ſong of a RIGHT NOBLE PEER,
Whoſe manhood of late, has been queſtion'd we hear,
But leſt this aſſertion ſome people may doubt,
I'll tell you good folks how it all came about.
DERRY DOWN, &c.

When DISCORD was raging in L—— Orwell's Corps,
And nothing but BLOOD SIR, wou'd HONOUR reſtore,
Dame fortune o' cruel! was pleas'd to declare,
His L——p ſhou'd alſo come in for a ſhare.

A CHALLENGE in form, he receiv'd the next day,
The heart of a COWARD, his face will betray,
Had you ſeen but his looks, which diſcover'd his fears,
You'd have ſworn it was Garrick, when BANCO appears.

For

For learned hiſtorians have joyntly agreed,
His L——p is ſprung from the true V——n breed,
And like a good CHRISTIAN, thinks fighting a ſin,
For what the world talks of he cares not a pin.

Now ſatyr who neither regards RICH, or poor,
Began to let fly at the PEER, all his ſtore,
Not many days after, to heighten the FUN,
His L——p receiv'd *(as a preſent)* a GUN.

This gun made of BRASS, STEEL, or IRON, was not,
Nor ever had ſwallow'd ball, powder, or ſhot,
But harmleſs and ſimple, a mere country ELF
All wood, neatly varniſh'd and GILT like himſelf.

Enrag'd and confounded, the donor ſuſpecting,
And thinking this gun on his *honour* reflecting,
To Council he haſtens, lays open the caſe,
And aſks if an ACTION here, may not take place?

The grave man of *Law* ſoon pronounc'd '*Eſt probatum*,
I'll prove right or wrong it is SCANDAL MAGNATUM,
For Lawyers you know, never let ſlip good prizes,
So the Gun's to be *tried* at next *BURY Aſſizes*.

His L——p's the firſt, I may venture to ſay,
Who on oath has had Courage, his fears to betray.
And while to his ſhame, there is light in the SUN,
He'll be the TOWN ſport—aye, as ſure as a GUN.

DERRY DOWN, &c.

As

As the interpoſition of Lord Bute, to put a ſtop to Lord Orwell's proceedings, has been hinted at above, it ſeems neceſſary to mention the cauſe, eſpecially as it is ſaid his Lordſhip has lately received a gratuity from the Lord *know who; for the Lord knows what.* Soon after Lady Mary Wortley Montague's letters were publiſh'd, Mrs. Forreſter, the widow of the late Colonel Forreſter, a woman of ſuperior underſtanding, and poſſeſſing a much better heart, having determined to ſpend the remainder of her days at Rome, put into my poſſeſſion, letters and pieces of poetry of Lady Mary's correſpondence with her for more than twenty years, and gave me a diſcretional power to publiſh ſuch of them which I thought proper. Thoſe letters were not, like the Conſtantinople correſpondence, intended for the eye of the public, and therefore I conſidered them, and ſo did my bookſeller too, a very valuable acquiſition, and I proceeded to print off the firſt thouſand ſheets; but upon giving them a ſecond and more attentive reading, it appeared to me that many parts thereof might prove painful to Lord Bute or ſome part of his family. Lady Mary had in many places been uncommonly ſevere upon her huſband, for all

her

her letters were loaded with a ſcrap or two of poetry, *at him*, * I therefore wrote to Lord Bute, and told him that ſuch papers were in my poſſeſſion, and that the firſt thouſand ſheets had been printed off, but that upon more mature conſideration, I thought it prudent not to proceed in a matter of ſo much delicacy, without previouſly acquainting his Lordſhip; yet at the ſame time, I cautiouſly avoided letting him know, whether her Ladyſhip's correſpondence was with a *male* or a *female* friend. Upon the receipt of my letter, his Lordſhip employed the late Sir Harry Erſkine to uſe all his *perſuaſive arts* to prevail upon me to fold the letters up, to wait upon Lord Bute, and then ſhewing me the abject attitude, of *uplifted ſhoulders, and a downcaſt head*, how he would, were he in my place, preſent the original letters to Lord Bute, for he aſſured me Lord Bute never omitted to ſerve eſſentially thoſe who obliged or gratified him, of which truth ſaid he, I am a living example. Upon my obſerving that my Friend had not given me power to beſtow upon any one the original letters, Sir Harry's ſhoulders again gave a hint of *what he would do*, though

* "Juſt left my bed a lifeleſs trunk, and ſcarce a dreaming head."

though he would not he ſaid pretend to dictate *to a man of my ſenſe;* for what has honor, truth or juſtice to do, when a Prime Miniſter is to be gratified? Notwithſtanding Sir Harry's *candour* and *friendly* advice, I would not let him catch that which he was fiſhing for, namely, whether Lady Mary's correſpondent, was a *male* or a female, for that was a matter I believe of great importance to be known. Having received no letter from Lord Bute, I did not depend much upon *Lord Harry*, and I aſked him how Lord Bute came to turn me over to him? why ſaid he his Lordſhip writes to nobody, but he ſuppoſed we ſoldiers all knew one another, and ſo it proved, for my Regiment had *the honor* you know of being *under your command at Land Guard Fort.* In ſhort it was Sir Harry's way, *as he aſſured me*, to be quite candid and open, ſo he preſſed me to drink a glaſs of Champaigne, tho' it was neither after dinner nor after ſupper, for he was kind enough to diſpoſe me to be as *open* as himſelf. I then obſerved that though it was true that we ſoldiers knew one another, yet that the *great ones* did not know what the little ones often ſuffered, that I had been proſecuted, and perſecuted too, for want of a proper ſupport, in doing my military duty with propriety as a ſoldier,

ſoldier, and with decency as a ſubject; and then I told Sir Harry my ſituation with Lord Orwell, *and a Lord of trade alſo*, and wiſhed Lord Bute's interpoſition relative to putting an end to that expenſive buſineſs. Lord Orwell and Lord *M—d too, were ſpoke to*, and my receiving the judgment of the court of King's Bench was, *ſome how or other*, poſtponed to ſee what could be done, for another term or two, but which only added to my expences; during which time Sir Harry often viſited me, and I him, and in one, (for I have many,) of my unguarded minutes, I happened to read to him part of a letter I had juſt received from Mrs. Forreſter, for he was always fiſhing for the name, or ſex of my correſpondent. Upon reading part of her letter he obſerved, that my friend muſt have made ſome figure in the republic of letters *himſelf*, for he did not ſuſpect, either by the ſtyle or ſubject, that it was a female friend, but aſking me where my friend was, at a time that my head was where it ſhould not have been in ſuch company, I replied at VOREE upon a viſit to *Monſieur Helvetius*, I inſtantly perceived I had *ſhot my fools bolt*, and that the negociation was at an end. Sir Harry then wrote to know what Engliſh gentleman, of erudition, was upon a viſit at VOREE,

his

his anſwer was no one, for the Lady was overlooked; conſequently I had ſaid the *thing that is not*. Sir Harry then renewed his viſits to me, and obſerved, that even Lady Mary's hand writing was a curioſity, and his *curioſity* led him to aſk to ſee a ſpecimen of it, I had ſuſpected that would be the caſe, and had put ſeveral notes into my pocket book for the purpoſe, being ſuch as no one could tell whether they were to a male or female correſpondent. Sir Harry was then ſure I had ſome of the Lady's letters and that convinced him I might have more; ſo another expreſs was ſent, to make further enquiries at Voree, and then, it was found, that Mrs. Forreſter a *Scots woman, and a Scotſman's widow too*, had been there upon a viſit, and was juſt gone from thence to Rome, but as ſhe had left an unmarried daughter behind her in London, Sir Harry judged his viſits to that young Lady, might prove not only more efficacious, but certainly more agreeable, as ſhe was a very accompliſhed ſenſible young woman. Sir Harry therefore *wiſely* dropt me, I had the honor of being placed in my *winter quarters* in *St. George's Fields*, where ſoon after Miſs Forreſter viſited me, and informed me at that viſit, that if any advantages were to ariſe from Lady Mary's letters, (the property of

her

her mother) ſhe, not me, was certainly beſt entitled to it; and at length told me, that if I would return the letters to her, ſhe could obtain a penſion. Eſteeming her and knowing that while her mother lived her fortune was but ſmall, I thought it juſtice ſo to do, and ſhe accordingly obtained the penſion, which ſhe now enjoys, and I the expence of printing off a thouſand copies of what was never publiſhed. I then wrote a ſecond letter to Lord Bute, told his Lordſhip the candid manner in which I had acted in that buſineſs, and obſerved that as by my *gentle ſentence*, I was to pay a fine of one hundred pounds to the King. I entreated his lordſhip (he was then, I think THE MINISTER) to procure a remiſſion of that fine, as I thought I had ſuffered enough on both the noble Lords account; but in *mony matters*, I muſt repeat it, I have hitherto been unfortunate, though I am in daily expectation of a packet of bank notes being foiſted upon me, by the Lord knows who, eſpecially as it is now I find to be the *ton* to act in that clandeſtine manner. I often perceived with what contempt *Lord Harry* held me when he found I made any ſcruple to ſhurk up my ſhoulders, and beſtow on Lord Bute, that which I could not with propriety beſtow; for what ſignifies

propriety

propriety when it is to oblige or ſerve a miniſter of ſtate, or a *King's Friend?* Let a man who will not do that ſtarve in a corner, he deſerves no better condition in this life, and ought to be d—d for a fool in the next, and thus ends the ſtory of the *Wooden Gun*, and the Golden Lords. I know how to value good men, who by rank, and great fortune, are placed high on earth, but I know too, thank God, how to look down with indignant contempt on thoſe who act otherwiſe, upon Score of, I DARE.

ANECDOTES

OF

GEORGE TOUCHET, BARON AUDLEY, AND PHILIP HIS BROTHER.

IT was my determination, when I began to write theſe memoirs, to have left unnoticed, and to their own *courts of conſcience*, two wretched and undutiful ſons, the eldeſt, ſhamefully negligent of his duty to a father who moſt affectionately loved him, the younger, infamouſly abandoned and wicked; but the poſt boy having juſt left a letter with me, addreſſed to Philip Thickneſſe, and the word *junior* being obliterated by the red poſt mark, denouncing it FREE, Audley, I opened it by miſtake; and found

found in it the following poſtſcript.—*So, we are to have the memoirs of a certain gentleman er'e long, in which I make no doubt, you and I are to have our ſhare of abuſe; but we have this ſatisfaction, that neither you nor I care.*" As it is then, a matter of indifference to the two *young gentlemen*, I will honeſtly own, it is a matter of great importance to me, and to my affectionate brother and ſiſter, that I publickly acquit myſelf of the imputation of having merited neglect from the former, or having attempted to defraud the latter; a crime which the wicked infamous and abandoned wretch, has flatly charged me with! If I were to name the greateſt crime a ſon could commit againſt a father, I ſhould not ſay it would be to aſſaſſinate, and murder him, becauſe in that caſe, the parent would be ſoon out of his pain, but that it would be the ſon who accuſes an innocent parent with a crime of a deeper dye, than even forgery, murther, or aſſaſſination; yet ſuch a crime has Mr. Philip *Touchet*, the brother to the *Right Honorable Baron* Audley, been guilty of. Charges of ſo black a nature coming from a ſon againſt a father, cancels all relationſhip for ever, and even Lord Audley's neglect of a father who ſincerely loved him, is almoſt obliterated by the villainy of his brother's conduct.

With respect to the former, therefore I shall only acquit myself, by shewing that he thought of no want of paternal affection on my side, as the following letter of his to me, will evince, written when he was an Ensign with three and sixpence a day at Gibraltar, and I a wandering exile at Barcelona; because from the receipt of that letter, till he had been a peer, with an ample fortune two or three years, I neither saw or heard one word from him, though I frequently solicited that *honour* by many affectionate letters!

Dear Pappa.

I cannot express the happiness and satisfaction your letter gave me, after so long a silence; the last I received from you was dated the 19th of February, I answer'd that and wrote again in about eight weeks after, and not hearing from you, wrote to Lord Bateman, desiring him to let me know where you were, in his answer he said you were gone abroad, but to what part of the world he knew not, so that I have been ever since expecting to hear from you from some part of France. My surprise was great indeed when I saw your letter dated from Barcelona, I all along imagined you were gone to the south of France, as I have

have heard you and my dear mother ſpeak of it as a country you prefer'd to any other, it is with grief and horror I reflect on the late circumſtance that muſt for ever make you diſlike *that* you have left, I wiſh much to ſee your two letters to that infernal raſcal * * * * who I and all my family ſhall ever have reaſon to curſe. I ſaw a letter in the *C—s* ſigned *J—s*, which if he had any feeling, muſt have made him ſhudder at his villainy, but I'm afraid he is as great a ſtranger to *feeling*, as he is to *juſtice*, and then nothing can affect him. How happy would it make me, if I could by ſea, or land, come to ſee you at Barcelona, but it is utterly impoſſible, as the Hanoverians, who are to relieve us, are expected here daily, they are to relieve three regiments, *ours is one*, ſo that in all probability we ſhall be in England ſome time in December. If Sir Thomas Gaiſcoine comes here before we embark, I will ſhew him every attention in my power, and will write to you on his arrival, but if the tranſports come before, will write immediately on their arrival in the bay, I'm afraid we ſhall have a terrible voyage, as we ſhall be in the channel in the very depth of winter, however, as I am never ſea ſick, I don't much mind it. How very unlucky it has turn'd out, that on your arrival

in

in Spain, I ſhould be juſt quitting it, had you come to Barcelona three months ago, I could have come up with the greateſt eaſe. I am happy to hear my mother is well after travelling ſo long a journey, pray aſſure her of my tendereſt love and affection, I ſhall ever be bound to love her for her many kindneſſes to *me*, excluſive of her unparallelled love for my dear father. I long much to ſee poor Charlotte and Ann, my love to them both, pray where is Phil. and Ralph. do let me know in your next letter, that I may know where to find them in England, you remember I uſed to be troubled in England with a difficulty of breathing, it is now grown ſo bad that I cannot lie down in my bed, ſometimes for three nights, but am obliged to take the little ſleep I can get in a great chair; indeed I have been ſo bad with it and the want of ſleep together, that I have wiſhed myſelf dead above a hundred times ſince I came to this place. Lord Bateman in his letter to me ſeemed very much hurt that you never went to ſee him before you came away, he ſpeaks of you with great regard and I am ſure loves you much. I write to him by this poſt, and ſhall let him know you are well. He ſays he ſent after you in London ſeveral times, I receive

two

two letters a year from Lord Caſtlehaven with *draughts* for thirty pounds in each, which enables me to do very well, your letter has been thirteen days coming *here*, but I imagine it was longer on account of the roads being ſo bad after the rains, do pray let me hear from you by the return of the poſt, as I may then poſſibly receive it before we embark for England, I have only one officer under me in the Regiment in two years, a very *ſlow beginning*, but I hope to have three or four ſteps when we get to England, the firſt leave of abſence I get in England I will be with you, whether in *Spain* or *France*. I have nothing more to ſay but to aſſure you of my tendereſt affection, and that I ſhall ever remain

Your dutyful Son,
GEORGE THICKNESSE.

GIBRALTAR,
Thurſday, 15th *November*, 1775.

Now may I not aſk, whether it is poſſible for a ſon, to write a more affectionate letter to an unfortunate father, (who was driven out of his native land from *misfortunes* not his *faults*) than the above, or whether it is probable, I could have done any thing towards a *lordly ſon*, to merit ſuch ſilent contempt, *after* he became a peer? but

but it ſeemed as if he was ſo addled with his own uncommon elevation, that he choſe to TRIUMPH IN IT, over his father's no leſs ſingular depreſſions; or why elſe did he not, as he would viſit, me, eſpecially as I was for a full year, at no greater diſtance from him than Calais? I have ſeen a fooliſh book as large as a church bible on the influence of climate * upon mankind, but I could wiſh to ſee one from a good pen, on the influence of unexpected honours and riches; yet after all this miſconduct, when he had involved himſelf in ſuch difficulties that he could not, as he declared to me, ſhew his face in London before his creditors, I received again to my breaſt, the *prodigal ſon*, and gave him a thouſand pounds, which I now repent, as I may live to want the intereſt of it, ſhould he die before me, but enough; or I could add much more; but I leave him to thoſe horrid reflections which age cannot fail to imbitter his latter days with, when I am forever beyond the reach of feeling his miſdoings. I am ſorry to add too, that he is the only one, among many learned, ingenious, and virtuous men, bred at St. Paul's ſchool under my brother, and *his uncle*, who do

* By Dr. Falconer of Bath.

do not honor, love, and respect him. "*How* "*does that good man my master and friend your bro-* "*ther do, said Mr. Francis* to me, *just before he* "*went to India?* adding, does he want any "thing? for I could enjoy nothing I have if "he does;" yet this brother so loved and respected by all his scholars, and who for eight years, had been as kind as an uncle, and master as he could be to a nephew and a scholar; has found it necessary to tell this *young nobleman*, that if he did not quit the name of Thicknesse, and take another name to tack to that of Audley, he would change his, and I will venture to say, that those who KNOW MY BROTHER, will agree, that such *a recommendation from him*, conveyed more contempt in those few words, than I could say were I to fill a ream of paper upon the subject. I must however render him justice in this point, he took the hint, dropped the name of Thicknesse, and took that of Touchet, and I am happy to know that it is a name no longer connected with mine; but George Touchet, *Baron Audley*, two words, which have stood in the roll of infamy, from the reign of Charles the second UNTO THIS DAY. As every young Lord you can make a genteel bow, give a frank, and put on a forced smile upon an occasion, must have the preference to an old and obscure parent

parent in all polite circles, there is no doubt but that with ſuch people the *old fellow* muſt be the aggreſſor, I am therefore urged to inſert a letter I received from a clergyman of Odiham, in Hampſhire, whom I never ſaw, but whoſe character is as reſpectable as any clergyman, of any rank, in Britain, to ſhew that the old, nor the young, have eſcaped the keeneſt miſery from this *accompliſhed young nobleman.*

Hot-Wells, *Briſtol*, *Aug.* 12, 1780.

SIR,

I have juſt received your letter, which by its date, has lain ſome time at Odiham, or I ſhould have anſwered it ſooner; I have been at this place for three weeks, in hopes, vain hopes, of eſtabliſhing my poor girl's health, which Lord Audley's treacherous conduct has too violently affected, it muſt touch even *his* heart, was he to perceive the diſtreſs and unhappyneſs he has brought on one of the beſt girl's, and on one of the happieſt family's in the world—But the ſubject is too tender for me to enlarge upon—I can only lament with you the cauſe of both our diſtreſſes; 'tis ſhocking to loſe a favorite child, even though ſo much innocence and goodneſs muſt be rewarded.—

You

You Sir I fear are too ſenſible what it is to be the father of ſuch a ſon as Lord Audley.

I am Sir, &c.

GEORGE WATKINS.*

Upon receipt of the above letter, I went over to Briſtol to congratulate the young lady upon her eſcape from ſuch an huſband, but alas! the maſter of the ceremonies congratulated me, that I was too late to ſee youth, beauty and innocence ſinking into the grave, ſhe had that morning left Briſtol to return to her affectionate father's home, and from thence to HEAVEN. Mr. Watkins, I hope and believe, will excuſe my inſerting this letter, he will not take a bow frown,

* Till I received this letter from the father of a beautiful and virtuous young lady, to whom L. A. had told me he was engaged to marry, and who ſhewed me a fine pair of buckles he had bought to preſent to her, I had ſome hopes of reclaiming a young man, naturally of a good temper, who from ſuch a ſudden elevation might be allowed a little *worldly intoxication*, but when ſuch reſpectable characters as Mr. Watkins and his whole family had been ſo deeply wounded, I gave all over as *a loſt caſe*. I will not aggravate this ſtory by ſaying for what particular reaſon Lord A. *conceal'd himſelf* at Mr. Watkin's houſe, where that unfortunate connection was formed, and ſo ſhamefully violated, it is enough that he knows it, nor ſhould I have related the above but to ſhew, that I am not a *ſingle complainant*.

frown, nor aſk a frank of *Lord Audley.* And now for the young gentleman his brother Philip Touchet, for he too ſhall *wear* the true Audlean name, not mine, Philip Touchet then, having been left all the perſonal fortune of the late Earl of Caſtlehaven, Baron Audley, in caſe he arrived to the age of twenty one years, but to go to Lord Audley, his brother, if he *died under age*, was ſo offended with his Brother's conduct to me, and to himſelf; that at the age of nineteen or twenty, he went before Mr. Wright, the Mayor of Bath, and made an affidavit that he never would viſit or even ſpeak to Lord Audley during his life, and charged him in the ſaid affidavit with ſetting him upon a run away horſe, *before he was of age*, a horſe whom even his groom could not ride, though he knew him to be a very indifferent horſeman; when this *young gentleman* came of age, he received about five thouſand pounds, a moiety of his uncle the Earl's legacy, and then made me a preſent of one hundred pounds, and I believe preſented and idled away many hundreds more within the firſt year; and in a few more years, when all was nearly ſpent, he *plumed* himſelf with a wife, a *prettyiſh* Bath milliner girl, of the name of *Peacock*, and ſome people ſay ſhe has the worſt of the bargain, but

I muſt

I muſt do him the juſtice to own, that till *all his love* was beſtowed upon her, he had given me many proofs of his affection and duty, and among others, a note of hand in the following words; to make uſe of when *he married*, by way of enabling me to marry off one of his ſiſters.

"I promiſe to pay to my Father Philip "Thickneſſe, Eſq. or order, on demand, for "value received, Five Hundred Guineas, as "witneſs my hand this third day of January, "one thouſand ſeven hundred and eighty "two.*

PHILIP THICKNESSE, Junior."

At the time he gave me the above note, he had *determined to marry* a young lady of large fortune† then reſident at Bath, and had given her foot boy a crown to deliver that lady a letter *ſecretly*, wherein he let her know *his determination;* the letter was accordingly delivered, but the *ſtrange infatuated girl was ſo weak* as to reject

* At that time I had not conceived even the idea of ſelling the Hermitage or going abroad, it was a ſudden reſolution upon *Eſq. Hooper's* telling me he would let the land all round my houſe to a parcel of Beggars on purpoſe to perplex me.

† Miſs Scr——r.

reject the propoſal with civil contempt, and he was ſoon after honoured with the hand of Miſs Polly Peacock, whoſe father and brothers are eminent menders and makers of ſhoes, in the city of Bath, whoſe mother is an *upper ſervant* to a reputable Pawnbroker, and whoſe ſiſters are very induſtrious in the millinery way, for farmers wives and the lower claſs of country wenches. *Three months* after this note of hand for *value received*, had been given me, I determined to go abroad, and by way of ſecuring ſomething to my ſon for the preſent, as the other half of the Earl his uncle's legacy depended upon contingences, I ſold Mr. *Philip Touchet*, the Hermitage, my preſent reſidence, and aſked him only five hundred pounds for it, though it had coſt me much more; to that price he generouſly objected, and inſiſted upon giving me ſix hundred, and paid me that ſum on the *very day* the writings were executed, by a draft on Meſſrs. Hoare. Upon my return from Bruſſells, finding that he had done every thing that could be done, to render a very pretty ſpot as *outré* as money and incapacity could render it, I re-purchaſed it of him, and ſecured to him an annuity for ever of thirty five pounds a year, equal to near double the money he had paid me; but ſoon after, hear-

ing

ing that he was about to *enter into trade* with his *induſtrious wife's relations*, and knowing on *whom* that *ſilly buſineſs* would *fall*, if the *Co-partners failed in Trade*, I deſired Mr. Lucas, of York-houſe, to tell the young man, *i. e.* young Mr. Touchet, that he muſt pay me the five hundred guineas on his note, but that he ſhould have the INTEREST during my LIFE, and the PRINCIPAL at my Death; and this I did to ſecure that ſum from being *ſunk in Trade*. When Mr. Lucas made the demand, though he had ſeen the note, he mentioned it by miſtake as for five hundred *pounds*, not guineas, Mr. Touchet affected much ſurpriſe, and replied, if my father has ſuch a note of mine, it muſt be a forgery! Such a reply could not but ſurpriſe Mr. Lucas alſo; he then obſerved, that he had read the note, and though he was not ſufficiently acquainted with his hand to ſay it was of his writing, he knew mine well enough to enable him to ſay it was not of mine, during this *want of memory* in young Mr. Touchet, and aſtoniſhment of Mr. Lucas; he aſked the young man whether any note of hand had paſſed between us relative to the purchaſe of the Hermitage? and *then*, and not till *then*, the young gentleman *recollected* that he had given me that note for the payment of it, but had forgot

forgot to take it up,* and immediately retired and wrote the following letter to Mr. Goodall, a very honeſt man, my Attorney, of Bath.

SIR,

I muſt beg again to trouble you to go up to the Hermitage, in conſequence of a note I received from Mr. Lucas; the cauſe why my father has made all this confuſion and diſturbance with me, is I find in conſequence of his having in his poſſeſſion a note of hand on me for five hundred *pounds* dated ſome time in January 1782, which it ſeems is on demand for value received, this note I *now* recollect was for the purchaſe of the Hermitage ſoon after I came of age, he *aſked five* hundred, and I gave him *ſix* hundred pounds, *one more* than he acknowledges he demanded, but never having the leaſt idea that *my father* would have been led to have made his advantage upon a ſon a *ſecond time*, for what had been more than paid, I from not harbouring ſuch an ungenerous ſuſpicion of a father, never thought of taking the note up when I paid him the five hundred pounds and gave him a hundred pounds more too it as a free gift; but ſince

* Near five years want of memory, and the note for neither the ſum aſked, nor the ſum offered!

ſince I find that it is the caſe that though he has this note againſt me, all that I ſhall now ſay is that if he thinks by this *double dealing* to make me comply with his unauthoriſed commands, namely, that unleſs I will quit Bath he will put it in force againſt me, I repeat it again that I will not, and that he may reſt aſſured, that if he demands a *ſecond* payment of the ſame note, I am determined to ſtand the trial, for I have got ſufficient acknowledgment under his own hands to confute him, nay I will even *defy* him to demand it as a *juſt debt*; and now ſir once for all I beg you will inform my *father* that I will conſent to relinquiſh the trumpery, eleven ſhillings *a year* which he has made ſo much work about, on the following conditions being complied with on his part, I would not have made them but, that I have had now a ſufficient proof that there is no truſting even him; what can I ſay or think of a father who has ſecreted for near five years a note *of hand* againſt a ſon, after that note had been truly diſcharged, only for to make uſe of it a ſecond time againſt me I leave you to judge. I will relinquiſh the eleven ſhillings on the condition that my father will give me a ſecurity under his hand, that he will not on any pretence whatſoever in future diſpute the due payment of my rent, but that it ſhall be regularly performed every quarter without any further deduction ſave the eleven ſhillings, and that he will deliver me up the note of hand; the latter he very well knows he cannot in juſtice detain, for he will pleaſe to recollect that he was very careful to make me return *his* note of hand for one hundred pounds that I lent him for a diſtreſſed gentleman, on theſe conditions I will perform that which he deſires, I will namely give up all my claim to the eleven ſhillings, but as to my leaving Bath I plainly will not, I ſhould be glad to know whether he thinks that becauſe he is my father that he has a right to reign in an arbitrary manner over me, or that I am obliged to obey him, if he does I can plainly tell him I ſhall not obſerve his unauthoriſed commands. In ſhort I repeat it once more, that if he does not chuſe to come into the above terms he is very welcome to proceed with me as he thinks fit and I will ſtand it in the face of the public, and then I hope it will be clearly known who has been the aggreſſor, as this is all that I can propoſe that is juſt and equitable, or I will leave

my

my father to uſe his own pleaſure, and I ſhall follow mine.

I am Sir,

Your moſt obedient Servant,

PHIL. THICKNESSE, Junior.

THURSDAY MORNING,
July 27, 1786.

Before I proceed further, I muſt here obſerve, that he not only *forgot* the note, but he forgot alſo, the ſum it was for, a ſum which was neither aſked, nor paid for the purchaſe, for he ſays to Mr. Goodall, my father aſked five hundred pounds, and I gave him ſix, how then could the note be for the payment of the Hermitage? but having committed this wicked and infamous deed, he was bound to abide by it. The firſt ſtep he then took, after he knew I had made an affidavit, and that there were *then* two other perſons living, to refute his aſſertions upon oath alſo; he quitted the Eſtabliſhed church, and enliſted himſelf to a ſect of people, called I think, INDEPENDENTS, among whom he found a ſubtle man, who had been educated at the Bar, but finding *that practice* would not do, betook himſelf to *Independency*, and this *conſcientious changling* was promoted to the honor of being a committee man among the *Independents* of his new mode of faith, and found a diſcarded lawyer, converted to hold forth the laws of God, ready enough to aſſiſt him, and who more than once attempted to bully me, to deliver up the note, though I repeatedly offered to cancel it, if he would ſwear to the truth of his letter to Mr. Goodall; nay, to give it to Mr. Goodall for that purpoſe, if he would attend him and his new PASTOR, to the altar of his Independent meeting houſe, and at that altar, and in their preſence only, ſolemnly declare before them in the name of God, that the note was given for the purpoſe he had declared in his wicked and infamous letter. His *law friend*, was then forced to find out the following feeble apology for his declining it, viz. that doing ſo, after knowing that his father had ſworn the contrary, would be indelicate! Could any thing ſuch a wretch could ſay or ſwear at the Altar of INDEPENDENCE be indelicate, after ſo groſs a letter to Mr. Goodall? even if the note had been given for the purpoſe he ſaid it was, conſidering I could no ways be intereſted therein, it was highly criminal; for why did he not *firſt* apply to me

and

and point out my *wicked conduct privately* before he *exposed me for* committing *so infamous a deed?* but to give one specimen out of many I could produce of this young man's *delicacy*, I shall present my reader with the copy of an anonymous letter this *delicate wretch*, wrote to me in his own plain hand writing, a letter which even baffled his *Priestly Father and Lawyer*. *

NOV. the 6th. 178(.

SIR,

"Low life abuse and falsehood is too contemptible to be offended at, and I should have supposed it had equally have been beneath the dignity of a man of understanding and a gentleman, but I find it is not, I shall therefore only observe, that you would do much better to send your younger son to sea, than to abuse *his* as well as *your* benefactor, though God forbid that he should undergo the hardships and ill treatment that I his brother have experienced from the age of eight years to twenty six, through the means of an unnatural Father."

And

* The minute his *Noble* Brother heard of this misunderstanding, resolutions, and oaths were laid aside, and a friendly correspondence has subsisted ever since! between the *two Brothers*.

And yet this ſon, who had been ſo cruelly treated by an *unnatural Father*, from his infancy, up to manhood; no ſooner became of age, than he preſented his *unnatural Father* with an hundred pounds, always addreſſed his letters "Dear and Honoured Sir," gave him a hundred pounds *more* for the Hermitage than was aſked! and at the full age of man, and totally independent of that *unnatural* Father with whom he by choice lived, gave him a note of hand for five hundred guineas, and for value received too, three months before the date of the writings! *not as a free gift*, but *for the payment of*, *and in full*, *for value received*, for an Eſtate not conveyed, nor even mentioned in the note! If any perſon wiſhes to ſee what an ingenious *Independent Lawyer*, and his young committee man, have ſaid on this ſubject, when I called upon them in the Bath Chronicles and Journals to defend themſelves, they may find a long correſpondence between *an* unnatural *Father*, and a *dutiful* ſon, in thoſe papers.* A Letter to Cruttwell, the Printer of the

* No ſooner was this tranſaction known to the *Noble Lord* Audley, but he immediately commenced a correſpondence and afterwards viſited his dear brother at Bath, though there had been a total ſeparation for above five years, the young gentleman who was ſo delicate about contradicting his father upon oath, had no objection to break his own, when it

the Bath Chronicle, from Mr. *Philip Touchet*, Lord Audley's Brother, now lies before me, in

it was to lead to a reconciliation with his dear brother who, said he had mounted him upon a run-a-way horse at one time, and who had nearly buried him alive in a stone quarry at another before *he was of age.* I forgot too to observe that Ensign Thicknesse when at Gibraltar, addressed me as his *Dear Papa*, but when he became a Lord and had jockeyed me out of a thousand pounds, I was kept at a proper distance by "*Honoured Sir*" and his dear mother was become "Mrs. Thicknesse," and that too when he wrote a shameful excuse for not paying me the interest of the thousand pounds I gave him. Several wise and friendly men of rank and probity, have advised me not to publish the conduct of these *two Brothers:* because they are my sons, they *were so;* but their shameful conduct has canceled all those ties which are so binding, between Parents and Children, and shall I not defend myself when charged by a son with a crime even worse than forgery? because not done at the risque of my life, and is not Lord Audley as criminal in giving countenance to a Brother, whom *before* he had no connection with, the minute he heard of his conduct to me? Before I published the queries to this young *Nobleman*, I sent them to him for his serious consideration, and gave him a fortnights time, but he immediately returned them to me at the *expence of a shilling for their postage!* and even his servants wrote me insolent anonymous letters, nor would he pay me the interest of the thousand pounds, till I had been at his door in Pall Mall, and sent him in a pistol to shoot rather than starve his Father, and yet Palmer of the Post Office, was the go between, previous to the sham reconciliation on his *Lordship's* part, declared to me that Lord Audley promised to evince his sincere contrition, by settling two hundred pounds a year upon me, and yet even after I had given him the thousand pounds, it was with the most marked Reluctance, that he signed the necessary Security which Mr. Madocks thought he should sign. Now should this *Noble Lord* die before me, an event, considering his wretched state of body, and mind, by no means improbable, I lose fifty pounds a year; and I at present possess another fifty, which hangs upon a tenderer thread, if therefore these two events happen, I may live to want; should not Lord Audley therefore have insured his life against mine, for I could not have wanted this interest, had I not so weakly

in which *that ingenious* young man, ſays, *If I will leave a note with the Printer under my own hand writing, and therein pledge my honor that I will believe what he ſwears, and that I will neither ſpeak of it, nor print any thing about it afterwards,* he will then ſwear that the note of hand was given for the payment of the Hermitage. Provided I acknowledge at the ſame time, and in the ſame paper, that he was *only eighteen* when he made an oath never to ſpeak more to his Brother, and that the oath was made with my conſent. This needs no comment, but I acknowledge that I did approve of his never ſpeaking to or viſiting his Brother, for the *reaſons*, (whether true or falſe, I know not) he had

weakly given away the principal, but Lord Audley may truly ſay, have I not ſettled an hundred pounds a year on Mrs. Thickneſſe after my Father's death? He has ſo; it was what I compelled him to do, when I found he was ſilent about the two hundred pounds a year promiſed to be ſettled upon me, but it is a grant of ſo little value, that it is at his ſervice for two years purchaſe. Previous to the thouſand pounds being given to him, this *affectionate Lord* ſat in *my Lap*, curl'd *my hair*, and told me he had been ſo unhappy that he thought he ſhould have *piſtoled himſelf*, but now ſaid he, I ſhall recover my health and ſpirits. If therefore I have not acted the part of an *unnatural Father*, remember READER, that the relation of this ſad tale may ſave ſome other unguarded Parents from the treachery of their children, and remember too, what Swift often ſaid, viz. I never knew a man who could not bear the afflictions and misfortunes of his neighbours, *perfectly like a chriſtian*, and then put your hand to your heart and ſay, would it not be THE SAME WITH ME?

had given me, but I deny that it was when he was only eighteen, as I think he was, if not quite, near twenty years of age.

I ſhall cloſe this ſad, and unexampled ſtory, with a copy of a letter from Lord Audley, to the "*Dear Papa*" of Enſign Thickneſſe, who thereby meant to teach me to keep my diſtance, by ſuch an affected manner of diſplaying his own. And now in the name of that INCOMPREHENSIBLE BEING, who gave me life, I ſolemnly declare, that ſad, ſevere, or wrong as this narrative may appear, to ſuch "*who can*" "*bear the misfortunes of others, perfectly like*" "*chriſtians*" that I am not actuated by malice, or reſentment; but to hold up a Picture of the *Preſent times*, before the riſing generations of men, in hopes that it may never be copied; and if thereby I preſerve one Parent from the bitter pangs which I have endured for years, even to that of BURSTING and BLEEDING from the moſt IMPORTANT CHANNELS OF LIFE, I ſhall glory in having told this diſmal tale.

Honour'd Sir,

It has given me great concern, not being able to ſend you a draft for the half years intereſt ſooner, but my Grovely Tenant who is

a year

a year and a half in arrear to me, has ſo often diſappointed me, that I have been much diſtreſſed. I now incloſe a draft on Horlock, for twenty five pounds, which I hope you will receive to-morrow, as I ſend it by the coach. Mr. Riely has not proſecuted, and the Term ended yeſterday, he is ſtill in town, but I have never ſeen him in public. I will try and find Count O'Rorke, and will ſhew him any civilities that lies in my power, as it is your deſire. The letters I forwarded, and have incloſed ſome franks for Mrs. Duff, I have been far from well for ſome time paſt, I have ſome thoughts of going abroad, as ſoon as I have ſettled my affairs, but will tell you more of that when I have the pleaſure of ſeeing you, which I hope will be ſoon. My love to Mrs. Thickneſſe and my Siſters.

Believe me to be with the greateſt regard,

Your affectionate Son,

AUDLEY.*

ANECDOTE

* This was the laſt letter I ever receiv'd from *Lord Audley*, and the firſt Intereſt he paid me, the next was at the *Piſtol Recommendation!* in Pall-Mall.

ANECDOTE

OF

T. CHATTERTON.

WHEN he was only five years of age, somebody made him a present of a little penny toy in plaister of Paris, representing a Lion or a Horse, I forget which, but seeing a great variety of figures in the Vender's basket, he urged the presentor to change it, if there could be found among them such a thing as an Angel with a trumpet; as the Angel could not be found, he cried, and being asked why he was so desirous of that particular figure; he wished for

for an Angel he ſaid to *trumpet about his* FAME!! when he went to London, to ſeek his future fortune, he told his mother and ſiſter, he had only to lament that he did not underſtand latin and greek. If ſaid he I were acquainted with the Claſſics, I could do enough to be remembered a thouſand years, adding, I have already done enough to be remembered three hundred.

It is to me as wonderful, even as wonderful, as Chatterton himſelf was wonderful; that the leaſt doubt could ariſe between learned and ingenious men, that Rowley and Chatterton were not *one and the ſame perſon?* Are not all his writings pretended tranſlations from the Saxons or other mens works? Poor fellow! he thought that the writings of a young blue coat boy could not attract notice, but he hoped that *his writings* under an antient and a borrowed name might, and therefore he borrowed Rowley's; but unfortunately finding that neither would ſufficiently provide for a man of his extenſive and aſtoniſhing genius; he borrowed that life from HIM who gave it, and who I doubt not will forgive the unwarrantable deed of a ſoul, who could not bear its preſent manſion, in want of the neceſſaries to ſuſtain life, and ſenſible that he merited more. By his de-

ſire

ſire of fame, one would be apt to think he imitated Alexander the Great, who coming to the tomb of Achilles, ſighed, and cried out, "O fortunate young man! who had an Homer to *trumpet out* thy fame."

ANECDOTE.

ANECDOTE

OF A

FEMALE GREEN GROCER AT SOUTHAMPTON.

HAVING landed at Southampton about the year 1752, from the Iſland of Jerſey, and lodging in that city, oppoſite the market houſe, I was daily accoſted by a remarkable well looking woman, who had a ſtand there for the ſale of Aſparagus, Greens, Fruit, &c. with, "*nothing in our way to day ſir?* in ſhort this woman's captivating manners were ſuch, that I had no idea of dealing with any one in any other way but herſelf. Upon my aſking her one

one morning the price of her Aſparagus, ſhe made ſo high a demand, that thinking myſelf at the Jerſey, inſtead of the Southampton market, I replied in French, *c'eſt trop.* Indeed ſir, replied my elegant *fruitereſs,* "*I have not drank a drop to day.*" I inſtantly recollected my miſtake, explained it, and aſked her what ſhe ſuppoſed I had ſaid to her? She replied, (ſtill preſerving her temper and the utmoſt addreſs and good manners,) I thought ſir, you ſaid I were drunk, I begged her pardon, and expreſſed my ſurprize! that ſhe could have ſuppoſed I could have ſaid ſo rude a thing to ſo a handſome, and ſo well behaved a woman, and we parted both perfectly ſatisfied. A Southampton friend who dined with me that day, commending her Aſparagus very much, I thought a little commendation due alſo to the accompliſhed vender of them; related what had paſſed between us, and deſired he would obſerve her appearance from the window as ſhe was ſtill at her ſtand in the market. Do you know who ſhe is ſaid my friend? that woman Sir, ſaid he, is the Siſter of the preſent Ducheſs of Chandois!! I determined early the next morning to give her *handſale,* and the following dialogue paſſed between us. Pray Madam ſaid I, are you Siſter to the Ducheſs of of Chandois? yes Sir, I am; and does your Sifter take no kind notice of you? yes Sir, fhe takes a proper notice of us all; we are many Sifters: what fort of notice does fhe take? why fhe fent for us all up to London, cloathed us fuitable to our ftations in life, fent a fervant to fhew us fuch things in London as were moft likely to amufe fuch ftrangers, put fome money in our pockets (obferving that the Duke is not rich,) and then paid our journey back again: adding, what elfe could fhe do? for we were not fit to be fet down at *the Duke's table!* What an inftance was here of good fenfe and refined judgment; it were a pity thought I that *there had* not been another good tempered Duke, to have bought this woman alfo of her hufband; * for fhe too was certainly worthy of *gracing* any man's table.

* *Her Grace* when a girl of fourteen years of age, ferved as *Pot Girl*, to an old woman who kept an ale houfe near the entrance gate of the city of Winchefter, and when the old *Harridan* was told of the fudden, and exalted fituation of her quandam maid. Aye—aye—faid fhe, I always told her, "Nan *you'll come to good:—you'll come to good Nan.*"

A FEW

A FEW

R E M A R K S

ON THE PRESENT SITUATION OF

GEORGE BRIDGES, BARON RODNEY.

IT is impoſſible for a man of reflection to look over the many eminent ſervices this gallant and able Sea officer has rendered to his King and country, not only in the late, but in former Wars, without recurring to the numerous inſtances of public ingratitude of Greece and Rome, or our ſurpriſe would be greater, to obſerve with what neglect the preſent men in power *only*, treat, a Nobleman of ſuch diſtinguiſhed merit! I ſay in power *only*, for the nation at large look upon Lord Rodney as an officer who has laid at the foot of the THRONE, more and larger Branches of LAURELS than any Admiral of the paſt or preſent Century, but it is a melancholy reflection, though not a new one, that the crime of INGRATITUDE TO PUBLIC BENEFACTORS, is as old almoſt as the world. Bodies of men will do that which each individual, muſt condemn, and what the poet ſays, *Ploravere ſuis non reſpondere ſavorem ſperatum meritis*, is applicable to the valiant and wiſe of moſt ages and countries. "When TIMOTHEUS had by a deciſive and victorious battle at ſea, compelled the Lacedemonians to acknowledge the Athenians ſuperior in that element, what was his reward? His countrymen *puniſhed him by fine*, at the inſtigation of a baſe, a mean, and an artful faction; and may we not ſay, as the friends of SCIPIO did? That two of the greateſt Cities in the world have again been found, highly ungrateful at the ſame time, to their chief commanders! Count de Graſſe, after having loſt upwards of four hundred men killed outright in the VILLE DE PARIS, and himſelf more than once left almoſt alone upon his quarter deck, was received by his King with *ſullen ſadneſs!!* and Lord Rodney; either by the

the careleſſneſs, or treachery of office, has been as ill fated in this!! The King indeed, ſenſible of his eminent ſervices, has in the moſt gracious manner and without expence, made him noble, and marked his perſon with a badge of diſtinction; a badge, which ſhould never appear, but upon the breaſts of military Heroes; but ſurely while every pariſh in the Iſland of Jamaica are inſtructing their repreſentatives, to confer ſome diſtinguiſhed and ſubſtantial proofs of their eſteem upon this great ſea officer, for ſecuring to them their lives and poſſeſſions; Lord Rodney's *private property*, ſhould not be neglected at home. To ſee a gentleman who has ſo juſtly deſerved the applauſe and eſteem of mankind; of poliſhed and refined manners; of great political and nautical knowledge, grown old in the ſervices of his country, not made as eaſy and happy as age and infirmities can render him, is indeed a melancholy reflection. It is now I think ſix years ſince the flag of France ſtruck to that of Britain in the Ville De Paris, and yet though *keel* after KEEL, of ſhips of War have been laid, the loſs of that noble ſhip has not, nor *would not*, have been revived here, had not a land, not a ſea officer, been placed at the head of the Admiralty. A wiſe reſolution of Mr. Pitt's. That ſeat ſhould never be filled with a seaman; of the justness of this seeming paradoxical assertion, we have lately had sufficient proofs, too recent, and too painful to be repeated. I am under no other obligation to Lord Rodney but as an individual of that Kingdom, which owes to him so MANY high OBLIGATIONS; but I have been urged to say thus much, from my indignant contempt to an anonymous *writer* (who calls himself *an officer,)* of a pamphlet manifestly calculated, and I dare say wrote *for hire* by a *garretteer book maker;* the drift of which is, to steal from the brow of Lord Rodney, some of those branches of Laurels he so bravely gathered, in order meanly to tack them to a man to whom they do not belong; whenever great actions are performed, it is always under the eye of envious men, who are never in want of the word IF.

This *pamphlet officer* is fond of that word, and I too will use it for once, and say, IF Lord Rodney had seen the whole fleet of France, and had twenty two sail of copper bottom ships under his command, though he might not have thought it prudent to have given them battle, he would not have given an order to twenty two British Captains, commanding line of bat-

tle

tle ſhips, to put out their lights, leave their anchors and Cables behind them and run away! inſtead of which, he would probably have ſtood out to ſea all night in a cloſe line of battle, and cloſe upon the wind, in hopes of finding himſelf by the morning to windward of the enemy, but had he found the enemy even in that ſituation, he would not have ſhrunk from a prudent bruſh with them, though they poſſeſſed a few more ſhips of the line.

" BIRDS OF THE SAME FEATHER, FLOCK TOGETHER."

I did not intend to have ſtained a ſingle page more of this work, with the odious name of Mackittrick, as it has been too often held up to ſhame already; and becauſe more powder and ſhot has been beſtowed upon it, than ſuch a Carrion crow was worth; had not Mr. Tickell's ſecond edition of the caſes and cures effected by his ÆTHERIAL ANODINE SPIRIT, rendered it neceſſary, becauſe that gentleman has proved beyond the power of contradiction, that his medicine has ſucceeded in a great variety of caſes; after the beſt advice, and all other powerful medicines have failed, I ſhall therefore

therefore annex to this chapter, a single and most extraordinary cure effected thereby, because I have seen it under the patients own hand, and it does not I think appear in Mr. Tickell's second edition, but I must first observe, that it has been my province to expose the impudence of Mackittrick, it has been Mr. Tickell's, to exhibit his ignorance; for in both instances (his friends if he has any) cannot—durst not, attempt to defend him. Doctor Falconer was the only *medical pigeon*, among more than twenty ingenious residentiary Physicians at Bath, with whom Mackittrick could form any acquaintance, but Falconer, finding him a man capable of writing, printing and publishing whatever falshoods his malevolent disposition urged him to, he used him as a proper tool to work with, *i. e.* to say, and write, such things which he had not spirit to do himself. I had, some years before, called Dr. Falconer to an account, for writing, printing and publishing, POSITIVE ASSERTIONS, in what he calls *his analysis* of the Bath waters * that LEAD was *soluble therein*,

* This *learned chymist* says, that the chief efficacy of the Bath waters arise from the great quantity of fixed air contained in them. Dr. Priestly (acknowledged to be the ablest chymist in Britain,) says the Bath waters do not contain more fixed air than his common pump water at Calne in Wiltshire.

in, and thereby founding a serious alarm to the public. I asserted that it was a false alarm, by a letter in the St. James's Chronicle, leaving my name with the printer, in case the Doctor should call for it. The Doctor possessed himself of that information, and in the true *Mackittrick style* and *manner*, thns replied in the same paper.

SIR,

I observed in your Paper of the 20th of last Month, a Letter addressed to me by Name, on the Subject of the Bath Waters which I understand is the Production of Mr. Philip Thicknesse. I do not think either the *style* or *matter* of this curious Epistle worth any answer from me, but as part of it relates to an affair of public concern, on that account only, I offer an explanation.

In the Year 1770, the stone which covers the lead cistern in the middle of the King's Bath, and which cistern lies about two feet and a half under ground, was taken up in order to clear the cistern of sand, which had accumulated so much, as to clog the pipes that convey the water to the Pump-Room at the King's Bath.

Bath. By accident a piece of the upper part of the ciſtern, about a pound and a half weight, was broken off, and was brought into the coffee-houſe in the Grove, and there examined by ſeveral perſons, and myſelf among others, who all agreed, that the ſurface of it that had been next the *water*, appeared in a ſtate of having been acted on by the *water*, from the furrows or irregularities that appeared upon it. Dr. Harrington, who I believe brought it into the coffee-houſe, can vouch for this fact; this was the foundation of what I advanced as a caution, and not as an aſſertion or inſinuation of actual danger, but merely to *obviate ſuſpicions of that kind*. This was all meant by a recommendation of the change of the pipes from lead to wood or iron, and ſo every candid reader has underſtood it, and I doubt not will do ſo.

As for Mr. Thickneſſe's aſſertion, that the inſide of the ciſtern is now in a pure and perfect condition, I aſſert he ſpeaks what is not matter of fact, to his knowledge, as he has never ſeen more of it than a ſmall piece, about two or three ounces in weight, * which was accidentally

* Yet the *penetrating* Dr. has ſeen every part of it! See page 299 of his eſſay; where he ſays, *the corrodings are viſible in every part on the inſide of the ciſtern!*

accidentally broken off, as the ciſtern itſelf has not been taken up or examined, but remained covered with a foot and a half thick of earth at leaſt.

As for his belief concerning the ciſtern *having been more expoſed to examination now than ever before ſince it was put down*, every perſon who is acquainted with the baths, can inform him, that it has been *opened* every two or at moſt three years, and *laid open* juſt as much as lately, except only about eight inches of gravel, which were lately removed, but which did not bring to light any part of the ciſtern, which was ſtill under ground at leaſt a foot and a half below the deepeſt part lately dug up. *

Had he made the proper enquiries before he formed this article of his faith, he would not have betrayed his ignorance of this well known *fact*. Having thus, as briefly as I could, ſtated the matters of *fact*. I ſhall trouble myſelf no more on this ſubject.

I am, Sir, &c.

W. FALCONER.

Dec. 8, 1781.

Extract

* I do aſſert that I have ſeen the ciſtern, and that the water is capable of operating on both ſides, for the truth of this aſſertion I appeal to Mr. Baldwin the Bath Architect, to Dr. Lee, General Johnſton and many other gentlemen who ſaw it alſo.

Extract from Falconer's Book.

" The action of this metal (lead) *has* BEEN
" SUFFICIENTLY PROVED, and that it is possible
" that the unfavorable symptoms sometimes
" produced on drinking them, which we know
" not *how to account for otherwise*, may be pro-
" duced by some such impregnation as this me-
" tal, though its effects are sometimes latent,
" is seldom inactive, it may be perhaps owing
" to this cause that some disorders of the Spas-
" modic kind as *Opisblotonus* seems sometimes
" rather enhanced by drinking the waters,
" when bathing alone is of great service."
Reader; observe what is said in the above extract from his *own book*, and compare it with what he has said in his *own letter*, and consider whether I, or he, have said *the thing that is not.* If I have, I will ask his pardon, if he has; he should long since have asked mine, instead of setting a mad dog to bark, because he durst not bite; nor is this the only falshood he has printed and published; for I do assert that Doctor Harrington DID NOT bring the piece of lead into the coffee house—that Doctor Harrington, will not vouch for the fact.—It was not the foundation of what Falconer advanced —nor

—nor was it an aſſertion to obviate ſuſpicions. To Doctor Harrington, I appeal, a gentleman of the utmoſt probity, reſpectable as a man; able as a Phyſician, and an accurate obſerver of every thing worthy of notice, I appeal; whether that very piece of lead, was not brought into the coffee houſe by Mr. Atwood, a plumber, to prove the very reverſe of what Mr. Falconer has aſſerted in the St. James's Chronicle? Mr. Atwood brought it to thoſe gentlemen to ſhow, that the ancient plumbers caſt their ſheet lead upon very courſe rough ſand, and conſequently, the underſide would be very irregular, the upper perfectly ſmooth, and the piece brought into the coffee houſe being exactly in that ſtate, after having lain ſome hundred years in contact with the Bath waters, appeared in the ſame inſoluble ſtate * for the indents of the courſe ſand were perfect on one ſide, the other perfectly ſmooth, and proved beyond a doubt, that the water had not altered its original form, to all who poſſeſſed either eyes to ſee, or faculties to conceive; that

LEAD

* This fooliſh and alarming idea had got into France, and the *Falconer of Paris*, Monſieur *Sheele* has ſaid *que l'eau diſtillé*, diſſalovit le plomb, Que ce metal reſt ſimplement en ſuſpenſion dans l'eau, &c. but it has been proved in France as well as in England; que ces aſſertions and les terreurs qu' elles ont produites ſont egalement fauſſes.

LEAD *is* NOT SOLUBLE IN THE BATH WATERS: yet Falconer has had the temerity to ſay it "*has been proved*" and to deny that he has ſo ſaid!! and that too in as perfect a *Cook maid ſtyle*, as theſe ſheets, or any other traſh which ever came from the preſs. If the above extract from his analyſis does not prove it to the ſatisfaction of the reader, he is referred to the book itſelf, or to a book I publiſhed, addreſſed to this man *of mettle*, in the year 1775, in which I have voted him a *medal of lead*, as a reward for his extraordinary talents, at *ſaying*, and *unſaying*; and *ſince which* he has united with Mackittrick, to decry a medicine, which all the other Phyſicians at Bath, have the candour to acknowledge to be a valuable acquiſition to the *Materia Medica*. One proof of which I ſhall inſert here, having as I ſaid above, ſeen the account under the patient's own hand; beſide, I have experienced the efficacy of the Ætherial Spirit in my own perſon, as well as the ſkill, attention, and abilities of Mr. Tickell, during a diſorder in which I was in imminent danger, and during which (ſuch was my confidence in Mr. Tickell's abilities) I did not call in any other aſſiſtance; ſurely therefore, if I entruſt a medical gentleman with that which is of moſt importance to all men (LIFE.) I have a right

to

to ſpeak of his abilities as a man, and of his medicine (of which I know the good effects) with confidence; yet that was the cauſe *only*, of bringing two mighty *Doctorial Gentlemen's* vengeance ftom the *preſs*, who did not conſider, that they were to endure the *pain*; and therefore I do again aſſert, that Mr. Tickell's Ætherial Anodyne Spirit, poſſeſſes antiſpaſmodic virtues in an eminent degree, and that it lately ſucceeded in a moſt obſtinate rheumatiſm, attended with ſuch frequent and intolerable ſpaſms, as rendered life abſolutely a burthen; but happily the patient poſſeſſed a moſt equable temper, and many chriſtian virtues.

The ſpaſm, or if you will, that ſubtile humour which violently irritated the nervous ſyſtem (and ſudden in its tranſition as the gouty) generally made its firſt attack in the lower extremities, rapidly paſſed up the hinder part of the leg and thigh, and terminated about the loins, where it exerted its cruel ravages on the ſpine. The duration of extreme pain was but ſhort, for if it had laſted many ſeconds, no human patience could have been equal to the conflict. The waters of Buxton had proved unſucceſsful, nay rather increaſed the complaint, and thoſe of Bath were made trial of with

with no better effect. Such medicines alſo, as might naturally have been concluded, would have afforded relief, proved altogether ineffi-cacious. Salivation was at laſt propoſed, and the ſuffering patient, readily ſubmitted to make the experiment, during the height of the ptya-tiſm, the ſpaſms totally ceaſed; but as it dimi-niſhed, they returned with equal violence. Under theſe circumſtances, the Ætherial Spirit was recommended, and from the time of taking the firſt doſe, to the end of a week, there was not a ſingle attack. The ſpaſms afterwards return-ed, but were neither ſo violent nor ſo frequent, and as neither drinking Bath water nor bath-ing, appeared to be of the leaſt ſervice, the gen-tleman by ſhort ſtages returned home, and took no other medicine but the Ætherial Spirit, which he continued once or twice in twen-ty four hours, till he remained perfectly free from this diſtreſſing complaint for ſeveral days. On any ſlight return, the patient had again recourſe to the ſame Spirit, repeating the doſe, five or ſix times. The attacks became more ſlight, and leſs frequent, and when he wrote the laſt account of himſelf, he had been perfect-ly free from any ſymptom of ſpaſm for two months, had regained his uſual ſtrength and health,

health, except now and then, a trifling remembrance of the rheumatic affection.*

Having found such frequent occasions to produce instances of ignorance, impudence, and falshoods, not only in this chapter, but in the preceding ones, the reader may conclude I might naturally reflect on the conduct of that King of impudence and falshood, whom I have more than once heard hold forth in my younger days near Lincoln's Inn Fields; I mean the celebrated Orator *Doctor Henley*, of whom the following story seems *apropos;* Henley challenged any two disputants to meet him on a certain day, to propose their own subjects of discussion, and declared that he would meet them, and determine the merits of the cause, with the strictest regard to impartial justice. Two ingenious and spirited Oxonions, fixed with the Orator, and on the appointed day, went well supported with a party of their friends; and being called upon by the Orator to propose their *Themes*, one of them told him he had undertook to prove the impudence of the Orator himself, adding, and my friend here,

* Since this sheet has been at the press, I have seen a letter from Dr. Bree of Leister, wherein he says he has performed two very extraordinary cures, with Tickell's Æther and holds the medicine in high esteem.

here, has undertook to prove your ignorance. Henley had a private way from the *Rostrum* into his own house, through which he prudently retired, postponing the award to a future day. May I not now say, that I have proved the impudence and falshoods of two great *physical philosophers*, and that Mr. Tickell has proved their ignorance, and that if an instance of their *modesty* could be offered, it is, that one has retired from his *Rostrum* at Bath, and hid himself in a little village near Portsmouth, called Titchfield, where he may "snarl and bite and "play the dog," and that the other, has frequently put forth in the Bath and other papers, a fulsome panegyric, which was sent him with the Fothergillian medal, to which I could wish to add a companion to it, of insoluble lead, wherein I would have the two medical philosophers heads vis a vis, and underneath them, I DARE.

ANECDOTE

OF THE

ARCHBISHOP OF CANTERBURY.

I HAVE been told by a very great man, and a very proud man too; that proud men are always particularly humble to their inferiors. If that obſervation be a juſt one, the Arch-Biſhop of Canterbury is not a proud man, and therefore I am convinced his Grace will excuſe my relating the following tranſaction, which I will endeavour to do with all imaginable reſpect to his preſent high ſtation.

I became

I became firſt acquainted with Mr. Moore at the houſe of my Brother in law, Dr. Richard Grey at Hinton in Northamptonſhire, where I found him *Garcon de famille*, much eſteemed by my Brother and Siſter, and much admired, I dare ſay by their four daughters, for he was a very handſome young man, and if I miſtake not he admired one of them *particularly*; as it was during the Aſtrop ſeaſon, it there fell to his lot and mine, to decide the fate of a pool at commerce, each of us equally anxious, for the Lady on whom the luck was pending, and I had then an early ſpecimen, of the great ſuſceptibility ſo trifling a matter excited in Mr. Moore's boſom, relative to a deciſion, on which neither of us were otherwiſe intereſted, than on behalf of our fair friends.

It was about that time I believe, that the late Duke of Marlborough (whoſe truly princely and noble diſpoſition will never be forgotten,) aſked my brother Grey, whether he knew an ingenious learned young Clergyman, or a fellow of a College, of character ſufficient, to be taken into his family, as Tutor to his ſon Lord Charles Spencer? Doctor Grey did—for he knew Mr. Moore—and recommended him in a pointed and particular manner, as an unexceptionable

ceptionable perſon, and fully qualified to execute ſuch a truſt with fidelity and abilities. I will not, I need not ſay, how fortunately, or I might ſay it (conſidering the high ſtation his grace now ſuſtains, with the ſame credit he did his low one) that ages may not produce the like again. It was natural for me, knowing this, to imagine ſome little attention was due from Mr. Moore, through every ſtation of his future fortune, to the relations of Dr. and Mrs. Grey. After Dr. Moore became a Prebend of Durham, I had the honor of ſpending ſome time with him at Shobdon Court, the ſeat of Lord Bateman, in Herefordſhire, we daily rode out together, and he afterwards honoured me with letters couched in the moſt friendly terms, and deſired me to procure him a ſingular weather cock of my own conſtruction, which I ſent him, and which coſt me ſomething more than a guinea. When he was appointed Biſhop of Bangor, I took the liberty to tell him a cauſe of great importance to me, and my family, was ſoon to come on before the houſe of Lords; ſent him I think, the caſe of the appellant and reſpondent, and entreated him to (what I preſume was his duty) attend it. To this requeſt I received a very ſhort reply indeed! it was a "*Sir, and an humble Servant*" letter to tell me he he *could not!* I concluded therefore, ſome other Dr. Moore had been appointed to the See of Bangor, and that I had addreſſed a ſtranger, for I did not till *then* know, that it was improper to addreſs a Biſhop, or congratulate him upon his good fortune in the ſtyle of a friend who rejoiced to hear it. The event in the houſe of Lords is WELL KNOWN, and *will be never forgotten.* I ſoon after went *a wandering* into Spain, and upon my return to Calais, I again addreſſed the Biſhop of Bangor in a *proper manner,* for my requeſt was complied with in the following manner.

"Sir,

Yeſterday brought me the favor of your letter upon the ſubject of your intended publication, through France and part of Spain, I ſhall be one of your ſubſcribers"*

And am your moſt obedient

Humble Servant,

J. BANGOR.

Soon

Soon after my return to England, and after my firſt volume had been *delivered* to the Biſhop, being at my Bookſeller's ſhop, (Brown's the corner of Eſſex Street) the Biſhop accidentally came in, and noticed me with—" your ſervant *Captain Thickneſſe*," and then turning to the bookſeller, ordered his paper, &c. to be ſent to BANGOR and retired. I was aſtoniſhed! I conſidered myſelf an unfortunate man and no way obliged to the Biſhop. I had received *his guinea* indeed, but ſo had he the weather cock. After he was gone, the bookſeller and his boys expreſſed their ſurpriſe alſo, for they it ſeems had heard the Biſhop ſpeak of me as one I had the honour to be well known to, and by his repeated enquiries for the book he had ſubſcribed to; and Brown could not help ſaying I thought you had been well known *to my Lord Biſhop* and intimate friends. And I replied I thought he had been mine; but as I now had reaſon to think otherwiſe, if he would furniſh me with a ſheet of paper, I would take the liberty to aſk his Lordſhip, what ſin I had committed, or what ſin I lived in the commiſſion of, that he ſhould treat me with ſuch diſregard, as to occaſion the bookſeller and his boys to obſerve it? I will not repeat more of the contents of my letter, though a copy of it lies before me, me, becauſe I muſt own it was written in anger, and in very intemperate terms, but my boſom heaved as his Lordſhip's did, at the pool of commerce, for inſtead of receiving ten thouſand pounds, a ſum I had for twenty years before been aſſured by the ableſt lawyers in the Kingdom would become my property, I had at that time ſix hundred pounds to pay for my vain efforts to recover it, and I thought I ſhould have met the Biſhop with a better face, if I had, like him, been a fortunate man.

Nothing could be more temperate than the Biſhops reply, for he declared that he was not conſcious of any ſlight or neglect of civilities due to me, but as he was, even after he had paid his ſubſcription, rather in my debt, than I in his, I told him he owed me a guinea, for I could not aſcertain the exact ſum I had paid for the weather cock, and deſired it might be paid; this was accordingly done, a guinea encloſed between two cards, and another very temperate civil letter accompanied it; though I muſt own, neither of my letters merited ſo much politeneſs.* And now I may obſerve, how

* I carried it to Dr. Dodd in Newgate.

how cautious even the greateſt men, either by birth, or high ſtation ſhould be, in their conduct to their inferiors, for would not the reader conclude that *here* the buſineſs ended, Will he not ſay, there is now for ever an end to all correſpondence between the Biſhop and *Captain* Thickneſſe? Certainly he will think ſo, but no ſuch thing! it was only the beginning! For a few days after, I dined with Mr. Bateman (Lord Bateman's brother) and there related, what had paſſed between me and the Biſhop of Bangor. I related it perhaps with a degree of warmth, natural to my temper, and when I had ſo done, Mr. and Mrs. Bateman ſaid they were not ſurpriſed, for that his Lordſhip had ſhewn the ſame ſlights and want of attention alſo to them. If they were not ſurpriſed, I was; for however inſignificant I might appear in the Biſhop's eyes, it was wonderful to me, to find that a reſpectable and honorable gentleman, *nearly related to the Duke of Marlborough*,† could have been overlooked by any man, much leſs by Dr. Moore. I then told Mr. Bateman that my anger and reſentment was at an end, and that I would that very day write to the Biſhop, and humbly aſk his

† Mr. Bateman's mother was Siſter to the late Duke of Marlborough.

his pardon for the warmth expreſſed in my former letters; and did ſo, for I had juſt learnt, I ſaid, that he had ſlighted alſo near relations of the Duke of Marlborough, and therefore I had not the moſt diſtant pretenſions to be hurt by his overlooking or ſlighting me.

My letter upon this point, ſeemed to give his Lordſhip pain indeed, he left his name at my door, the next day, and urged me ſtrongly, to let him know (if I were not bound to ſecrecy,) by whom of the Duke of Marlborough's family he was ſo accuſed? adding, that if he were guilty, he ſhould think himſelf the moſt offending man alive. In reply, I informed his Lordſhip, that though I was not bound particularly to ſecrecy, I conſidered myſelf not at liberty to diſcloſe private converſation which paſſed at a friend's table, but aſſured him that they were people of veracity, and therefore I could not doubt the fact, and that the reader may not doubt this relation of it, I will obſerve that though my reſpectable friend Mr. Bateman is dead, his lady is ſtill living. This buſineſs however ſeemed to give the Biſhop deep concern, and he determined not to drop his enquiry, till he found within whoſe doors the complaint was lodged; and knowing that I

had

had the honor of being often with Lord Bateman, he feared the complaint originated there, but upon enquiry found it did not; yet there perhaps, he got a hint that it lay in Hartford Street, for thither he went alſo. Mrs. Bateman would not be ſeen, but Mr. Bateman acknowledged the charge, nor did the viſit and apologies, which no doubt were made, occaſion any renewal of their acquaintance. I have the Biſhop's letters before me, one of which his Grace I am ſure will excuſe me in preſenting to my readers, as it is relative to the preceding part of this tranſaction, eſpecially as I ſent the propoſals of printing my memoirs to *his Grace, and to the Duke of Marlborough, who upon a former occaſion honoured me with his name*, and who upon no occaſion can notice any man, who has more reſpect to his aimiable character. †

SIR,

" It is not much like a proud man to write to you again after the letters I have received from you. But it is like a man who knows how to excuſe even injurious treatment from one

† His Grace is ſtill a few ſhillings in my debt, and therefore from the tenor of the following letter, filled with *good wiſhes*, it rather diſappointed me, as I preſume it will every candid reader.

one he wishes well to; when he sees that treatment was the effect of resentment grounded on misapprehension. You ask me, if I did not know that you had lately a very great misfortune and great injustice done you? I did not, nor od I know at this moment what you allude to. I was also ignorant, till I received your letter, of the other events you mention, that a title and fortune had fallen to your children. The truth is, my thoughts and time have been engaged for some time past solely with a very near relation, and a friend, both in a very bad state of health, and I have heard little, and attended less to what was going on in the world. And now Sir let me ask you a question in my turn, where is the crime in my not having been acquainted with those circumstances? or how are you justified in loading me with opprobrious accusations, for not having taken notice of them when I met you? You will do better to keep your anger for those who deserve it, I do not deserve it; I am really and unaffectedly sorry for your misfortunes, and the injustice that has been done you, of whatever kind they may be, and I am still capable of receiving a sincere pleasure, from hearing of any good fortune that befalls you, or your children, and the greater the extent of it it is, the greater will be my pleaſure. This is the truth; and I expect to be believed, and that for the beſt of reaſons, becauſe you never in your life could charge me with untruth. You tell me again and again of my obligations to your family, I am ready to acknowledge a thouſand obligations to Dr. and Mrs. Grey in a long friendſhip of many years, particularly to him whoſe advice I have profited by, and may as long as I live, if it be not my own fault, but not one of thoſe he has left behind him will tell you, I have forgotten thoſe obligations. But enough of this, I will put an end to this letter with repeating the advice, don't be affronted at the word, it is not meant to affront, I have given once before in it; diſtinguiſh between thoſe who are diſpoſed to behave inſolent to you, and thoſe who are not—between your friends and your enemies, I can never have a place among the latter, and perhaps it may be immaterial to you whether I have any among the former or not.

I am Sir,

Your Humble Servant,

J. BANGOR.

It is many years ſince I read the above letter, and therefore it urges me now to obſerve upon it, that it certainly is written with a temper and diſpoſition ſuitable to a wiſe man, and a chriſtian Biſhop, it is true alſo, that my ſiſter now eighty four years of age, and her three daughters, ſpeak as highly of his grace as any of his friends; and think as highly too, nay I know my ſiſter has left him a picture worked by her daughter, Mrs. Lloyd the Dean of Norwich's wife, of real value, merely becauſe the Bullfinch which is pecking at a bunch of grapes in a cabbage leaf, was copied from a Bull-finch, Mr. Moore ſhot; but may I not ſay in my turn, that Dr. Grey has three daughters, who have ſons at the univerſity unprovided for, and a daughter married to an ingenious young man, who has no other ſubſiſtence than the ſmall Curacy of Uphill in Somerſetſhire, and then may I not aſk, has his grace conferred any mark of favor further than *civil words*, upon any part of Doctor Grey's family? two of whom would at this day have been in holy orders, if they had the leaſt hopes of any preferment, yet before this chapter went to the preſs, I wrote to my Niece, the widow of the Rev. Doctor Bowles, and youngeſt daugh-

ter

ter of Doctor Grey, and asked her the state of her family, and whether the Arch Bishop had taken any notice of her, or any of her family. In reply she was *quite silent*, as to the latter Querie, but says, "as you was pleased to enquire into the state of my family, I shall trouble you with a small account of it. I have four daughters and three sons, the eldest of which is designed for the Church, and is of Trinity College, Oxford, he is not yet in orders, but might have been some time ago, as he is neither wanting in knowledge, character or abilities; his present view is to be fellow of the College, to which I imagine he will succeed the first vacancy, my second son is as you know, in the physical line, and my youngest is bred to the law; if you can form any idea of the expence of a university education, I presume you will easily see why there was only one sent thither, my eldest daughter married without our knowledge or consent, a Clergyman of very small fortune indeed, he is Curate of Uphill in Somersetshire, where they now live." This is the situation of Dr. Grey's daughter and grandchild, the Uphill Clergyman has thirty pounds a year, and the eldest son might have been in orders, but being *without a patron*

tron or a friend, waits to obtain a fellowſhip of Trinity College! and yet his Grace of Canterbury tells me, "that not one of thoſe" (meaning Dr. Grey's family) "whom he has left behind, will tell me he has forgotten thoſe obligations" it may be ſo, but I can tell his Grace, that not one of thoſe, have yet benefited by the goodneſs of his memory, and I hope at leaſt the poor Curate of Uphill, who certainly cannot deal with the *Village Butcher* above once a fortnight; will be remembered *effectually*. I never ſaw him nor his wife; but I flatter myſelf his Grace will not let a grand daughter of Dr. Grey's ſtarve, when a Vicarage of four ſcore pounds a year would make him and his wife happy, for fortunately, they have no children.*

I might

* The late Dr. Garnett, an Iriſh Biſhop, and the Author had been intimate friends in their youth, long before the Doctor had any idea of wearing a mitre, many years however ſeparated them, till chance threw them together at a muſick meeting in London.

The Author thought it was his old friend, but not being certain, after looking ſtedfaſtly at him, and not being able to make up his lips for the utterance of the two words, MY LORD; he thus addreſſed the worthy Prelate. *Is it you, or is it not;* for I proteſt I am not ſure? Yes ſaid he, it is me, (and taking one of my hands into both his) nor will we part ſaid he till we have ate and drank together. This was manly, if not prieſtly, and when this good man died, he directed his

Executors

I might aſk his Grace in my turn too, (were not the queſtion ſo high above my reach) whether if he had not been full as ſuſceptible of ſlights, neglect, or ill breeding, even in a rapid line of proſperity, as I might be found in adverſity, why, when a certain old Ducheſs *beparſoned* him at Blenheim, he inſtantly took his horſes and a French leave, and went to Durham, and from thence made his excuſe to the Duke of Marlborough and deſired permiſſion to *return* when the Ducheſs *left* Blenheim? If he did ſo, ſurely I might have been excuſed if I diſliked being *be-Captained* in a bookſeller's ſhop! I could aſk his Grace another queſtion, and relate another extraordinary anecdote, but which I with-hold, out of HIGH RESPECT TO OTHER PERSONS to whom it might give great pain, though no ways diſhonourable to any perſon *now* living. †

Executors to ſend me the Portrait of a Brother of mine; which had hung thirty years in his houſe, and yet that brother had no hand in leading him to an inſtallation, but he had been his friend, when in an humble ſtation, and when a Curacy of fifty pounds a year would have made him happy.

† Since this book has been in the preſs, Mrs. Bowles has been honoured with more than one letter from the Arch Biſhop; expreſſing an unbounded regard for her and her family, and has promiſed to provide for the Curate of Uphill and her ingenious ſon, *(now in orders)*

at

at Oxford, for I muſt own I did anonymouſly remin'd his Grace of the ſituation of my widow niece and her large family, and thereby procured ſome notice to be taken of them not only by letters, but by his Coach ſent from Lambeth, to fetch ſome part of the family to dine at the Palace. It is near a year ſince, but I have not yet heard of any other place, than a place in the Coach of Lambeth,

A N E C D O T E

OF THE

PRETENDER, PRINCE CHARLES.

LADY Mary Touchet a beautiful Engliſh woman, and ſiſter to my late wife, made her firſt public appearance at a ball at Paris, given by the Pretender juſt before his expedition into Scotland, in the year 1745. The Prince not only attracted by her perſonal charms, but being the ſiſter to a Engliſh Catholic Peer; took her out, as his partner, and before they parted, he communicated to her, whither he was going, and the importance of his expedition. I cannot tell, but I can eaſily conceive, to what a pitch a pitch of enthuſiaſm, a beautiful young Engliſh woman of the ſame religious principles, and ſo particularly honoured at that time, might be led to ſay upon ſo trying an occaſion; but whatever it were, he inſtantly took his pen knife from his pocket, ript the ſtar from his breaſt, and gave it her as a token of his particular regard, and I doubt not that *ſhe* concluded, ſuch an external mark of his partiality, had he ſucceeded, was given as a prelude to the offer of a more precious jewel which had lain under the ſtar *within* HIS BOSOM. As that beautiful woman, died at the age of twenty, the ſtar fell into the lap of her ſiſter, and as ſhe ſoon after fell into mine, I became poſſeſſed of that *ineſtimable badge of diſtinction*, together with a fine Portrait of the Prince by Huſſey. Being a whig and a military man, I did not think it right to keep either of them in my poſſeſſion, and a ſimple old Jacobite lady, offered me a conſiderable ſum of money for them, but having three nieces, whoſe father had lived in intimacy with the *late Sir John Dolben*, I preſented both to them, and I believe that *valuable relict* of the departed Prince Charles, is now in the poſſeſſion of Mrs. Lloyd, my eldeſt niece, and wife to the preſent Dean of Norwich. Lady Mary Touchet, was the first woman who appeared in England, in a French dress, about the year 1748, which was *then*, so particular, that she never went out at Bath, the place of her constant residence, without being followed by a crowd; for at *that* time, the general dress of France, was deemed so *outré* in this, that in most eyes, it diminished the charms, of both her face, and person; which she otherwise had the utmost claim to. She danced on the Friday night ball, and died the Sunday following, a lady who assisted in laying her out, told me she could scarce believe she was dead, for that she never saw so much beauty in life, and that she exceeded in Symmetry, even TITIANS VENUS. That this unfortunate man was in London about the year 1754, I can POSITIVELY ASSERT, he came hither, contrary to the opinion of all his friends abroad, but he was determined he said, to see the capital of that Kingdom, over which he thought himself born to reign. After being a few days at a Lady's house in *Essex Street in the Strand*, he was met by one, who knew his person in Hyde Park, and who made an attempt to kneel to him, this circumstance so alarmed the Lady, at whose house he resided, that a boat was procured the same night, and he returned instantly to France. Monsieur

Massac,

Maſſac, late Secretary to the Duke De Noailles, told me he was ſent to treat with the Prince relative to a ſubſequent attempt to invade England. Mr. Maſſac dined with him, and had much converſation upon that ſubject; but obſerved that he was rather a weak man; bigotted to his religion, and unable to refrain from the bottle, the *only benefit* he ſaid he had acquired, by his expedition among his countrymen into Scotland.

An Iriſh officer with only one arm, formerly well known at the *Caffee de Conti* in Paris, * aſſured me that he had been with the *Prince* in England, between the years, forty five and fifty ſix, and that they had laid a plan of ſeizing the perſon of the King (George the ſecond) as he returned from the play, by a body of Iriſh chairmen, who were to knock the ſervants from behind his coach, extinguiſh the lights, and create confuſion; while a party carried the King to the water ſide and hurried him away to France. It is certain, that the late King often returned from the theatres in ſo private a manner, that ſuch an attempt was not impracticable, for what could not a hundred

or

* Mr. Segrave.

or two, desperate villains effect, at a eleven o'clock at night, in any of the public Streets of London? Ten minutes start would do it, and they could not have failed of a much greater length of time. He also told me that they had more than fifteen hundred Irish chairmen, or that class of people, that were to assemble opposite the Duke of Newcastle's house in Lincoln's Inn Fields, the instant they heard any *particular news* relative to the pretender. I cannot vouch for the truth of this story, but it may be right to relate it, to prevent such an attempt, should any other pretender start up, for I have the BEST AUTHORITY to say such a thing is practicable, and that a person was taken off in broad day light, and in the middle of a large City, though under the protection of an English Major, and seven old French women, and that too, by an individual.* It was

* There are many people now living at Southampton who remember that transaction.

Dr. Grey, long before he died, was perfectly cured of *Jacobitism*, he observed that when the pretender was at Rome, his friends here kept his birth day, and spoke of him with ardour, but when he was in Scotland they seemed to forget him *every day*, now said the doctor, if I had been King, I would have pardoned all those who shewed their mistaken loyalty openly, and hanged all his cowardly adherents who durst not appear to serve him, when their services were wanting; but thank God, that silly business is all at an end, and the Catholicks know, the sweets of living under a PROTESTANT PRINCE, and a free government.

was not a King it's true, who was taken off, nor it was not *a man*, but before the furprife of the Major, and his female party were over, the lady was far out of their reach.

ANECDOTE

ANECDOTE

OF

MRS. GARRICK, WHEN SHE WAS THE ADMIRED MADAME VIOLETTE.

IN the year one thouſand ſeven hundred and forty nine, that lady was at Bath, and though I had not then nor ſince the pleaſure of being perſonally known to her, I never ſaw her but with admiration; her perſonal beauty, and the delicate manner of her dreſs, could not but attract attention, I mean not frippery or finery, but rather the reverſe; mentioning that elegant woman to Lady Vane, who perhaps was the next woman in the Kingdom, to be admired

mired on account of taſte, in dreſs, &c. ſhe agreed with me, and added, her breeding alſo, correſponds with her external appearance. Are you then Madame, ſaid I, acquainted with Madame Violette? no, I am not, but ſhe always paſſes me with good breeding, obſerving that well bred people, betray that, even as they paſs ſtrangers. This juſt obſervation ſtruck me exceedingly, I had often obſerved it in the late Duke of Hamilton, when he paſſed ſtrangers in the public walks; but Lady Vane could not but notice Madame Violette's poliſhed manners, as moſt of the *un-fly-blown* wives and miſſes, uſually paſſed her with a toſs of the head, or a look of contempt, though perhaps at the *bottom of the mixture*, there might have been found a few grains of envy. During Madame Violette's ſtay at Bath, Mr. Naſh was deſired to take her out to dance a minuet, and certainly her dancing there at *that time*, was conſidered by all well bred perſons as a favour. She was accordingly the firſt lady aſked, after thoſe of precedence had danced; and then ſhe danced a minuet, as void of any flouriſhes, as it was full of grace and elegance; but behold! the next lady aſked, refuſed! what! dance *after* Madame Violette? Mr. Naſh took care ſhe

ſhould

ſhould not dance then, nor at any ſubſequent ball, and Miſs returned to her Papa, an Iron-monger at Saliſbury, without ſhewing the beauxs of Bath, what an ear ſhe had for the *muſicks*, for Miſs had learnt to play upon the *ſpinnet*, as well as the ſpinning wheel. Having mentioned the late Duke of Hamilton, I cannot deny myſelf the pleaſure of recording a ſingular inſtance of the quickneſs of his parts, and the readineſs of his addreſs. When he firſt went to Edinburgh with his handſome Ducheſs; his country folks charged them both with ſhewing too much *hauteur*, not only in public, but even at their own table; a charge which *his Grace*, one would think could not merit. However a prodigal Laird, not long deſcended from the mountains, who thought himſelf as *guede a cheeld* as any Duke or Laird on earth, determined to put his Grace to ſhame at a public ball given at Holy Rood Houſe. After the whole *nobleſſe* of Edinburgh were ſeated, and the muſic waiting to ſtrike up, on the *entrè* of *their two Graces*, a rumour was heard at the lower end of the room,—here comes the Ducheſs—here comes the Ducheſs, and accordingly the crowd of gentlemen, moved to the right and left, to give her Grace a paſſage,

paſſage, amidſt their humble and bended bodies, but before her Grace had been ſeated at the upper end five minutes, a ſecond alarm was announced, here comes the Duke—here comes the Duke,—the avenue was again cleared for his Grace's entrance, by all but the *Highland Laddy* mentioned above, but he turning his back to the door, and ſetting his arms *a kimbo*, placed himſelf in the very center of the *Gang way.* The Duke inſtantly perceived who it was; and *why* it *was;* ſo walking ſtedfaſtly up, linked his arm under his champion's, ſaying Mackittrick how do you do? and keeping him in familiar converſation till he had led him to the upper end of the room, and joined his Ducheſs, and there left *Jemmy* to walk back again, an object of as much contempt, when he appeared as the village doctor before Lord Moreton to whom one would think he had been formerly a *Lacque.*†

† During the diſpute between the author of theſe ſheets and the Doctor, the following grub was handed about the City of Bath. How or why a man educated at the *only* univerſity in Britain, capable of *turning out able Phyſicians*, could ſuſpect the grub to allude to him, I cannot ſay, but he certainly offered a reward in the Bath Chronicle of fifty pounds to diſcover the author, he is therefore now informed *gratis*, that Joe Millar was the author, and P. Thickneſſe the editor.

A CAUTION

A CAUTION TO THE CAUTIONED, A true Tale told by Lord M——R——N, Addreſſed to a Medical *Aſſaſſin*, and a *Foolosipher* of Bath.

GOING ſome years ſince into Scotland, ſaid his lordſhip, I ſtopped early at a ſmall town in the north of England, it being winter, and a long evening before me, I conſulted my landlord, what chance I had of finding in that town, a ſociable companion to ſup with me; the parſon, after whom I firſt enquired, was juſt dead; the lawyer was gone to London; and in ſhort, the doctor was the only man my landlord informed me, who was genteel enough to be admitted. I accordingly enquired his name, and ſuſpecting thereby he was a North Briton, I ſent the compliments of a travelling ſtranger to the doctor, and deſired the favor of his company at ſupper with me; the waiter ſoon informed me, that the doctor was in the bar, for having learnt there, that I were a lord, he waited for a ſecond invitation; upon his entering the room, I perceived an uncommon degree of embaraſſment in his countenance, which I endeavored to remove by making an apology for the liberty I had taken, and entreated him to ſit down, and favor me with his company without ceremony; ne,—ne,—replied the doctor, I muſt *declene* that *owner*——no, no, doctor, pray be ſeated; *en troth* my guede lord you muſt excuſe me, for though your lordſhip do *na ken* me, yet I ken your lordſhip *rite weil*; de you not remember your *auld* ſervant *Jemmy Macmurdith?*——what do I ſee Jemmy, in the capacity of a doctor of phyſic!—ſoftly my guede lord, let me *whesler* a word in your lugg, ſpeak low leſt our landlord ſhould hear what paſſes; it is your *auld* ſervant Jemmy who now ſtands before you;—well Dr. Jemmy ſaid my lord, ſit down, however, and let me hear without reſerve, how you became a practitioner in phyſic; Jemmy then acquainted his Lordſhip, that his houſe ſteward having *loſt* a *ſiler* ſpoon the day before he left his lordſhip's ſervice, refuſed to give him a character, and being out of employ, he entered on board a Guinea man, in the ſlave trade, and having, ſays he, a *lettel Laitin* as ye know my lord, we *awe bave* in my guts, I ſoon perſuaded our *South Bretan* ſurgeon, that I knew a little of *phesyeck* alſo, and he gave up the care of *awe* the black devils to me, from *Geuene* to Antigua.——well, and were you ſucceſsful in your firſt outſet? in troth no my lord, I was gelty of *manifold errors*, and we loſt more than a moiety of our *living* cargo; but *fortunatly* for poor Jemmy, the ſurgeon himſelf, (tho' I did the beſt I could for him) died the very day we caſt *ancor* at Antigua,

Antigua, and I returned to Bretan in the *capacety* of ſurgeon's mate, and then got another ſtation to the ſame *clemate*, as full ſurgeon; *thes* my lord, put ſome money in my pocket, and when I returned I purchaſed a deplema, and have practiſed now ſeven years in this town, and the hamlets rouud *about*, as a regular *pheſecian*; well Jemmy and I hope, ſaid my lord, with better ſucceſs than on your ſouthern excurſions? in troth, my lord no, I have nothing to boaſt of in that way neither; but however, let me tell your lordſhip, that I have pretty well revenged the *battle of Flowden Field.*

A ROBBERY

ROBBERY

COMMITTED BY THE LATE ALDERMAN K——N.

MR. K——n, having a pleaſure yatch of his own, often made a trip in her with a few friends to Calais, Boulonge, &c. and happened to arrive at Calais, juſt as I was returned from my Spaniſh Tour to Montſerrat. At this time I had engaged an Artiſt to engrave, from a painting I had got executed at Lyons, a view of that extraordinary mountain, and which I wanted an opportunity of ſending ſafe to England. The late Mr. Redmond Simpſon, of the Queen's band of muſic, being

being in the Alderman's *suite* and a careful honest man, I desired him to take charge of it to London, and to deliver it to my departed and valuable friend Mr. Alexander Whitchurch, who had promised to superintend the execution of the plate; Mr. Simpson, therefore placed the picture with great care, under the green baize, and the uppermost article in his portmanteau. The custom house officers at Dover *knowing their men*, merely for form sake, meant only to lift up the covers of the Alderman and his friend's trunks, but could not even do that without the picture appearing, and then they were, reluctantly enough, obliged to seize it; in vain did poor Simpson plead his readiness to forfeit every thing which was his own, provided the picture, another man's property, and for so particular a purpose, could be delivered up, but all was ineffectual, the picture was seized as contraband, and could not be restored; poor Redmond related his grievances pathetically to the good natured Alderman, but nothing could be done. The next morning, Mr. K——n, visited the custom house, and after talking with the collector and the other officers on different subjects, pray said that gentleman shew me the picture of Montserrat, which you seized yesterday; it was accordingly

cordingly produced, he took a ſlight view of it, and then entered upon ſome other ſubject, till at length, buſineſs called the officers to different part of the office, and then Mr. K——n rolled up the picture, put it under his arm, and walked off with it! a circumſtance which probably was full as agreeable to the officers who had ſeized it, (for it was of no real value) as it was to Mr. Simpſon who had it, and to whom it was reſtored. If this was a crime, it was a crime which muſt be regiſtered among the many generous and benevolent crimes Mr. K——n, was frequently committing, by relieving thoſe who were diſtreſſed in either body, mind, or purſe; he perceived how hurt his friend Simpſon was, and would have given the beſt picture in his houſe to redeem his friend from ſuch anxious concern, ſuch was the diſpoſition of a gentleman, taken off in the prime of life, loved and lamented by all who knew him.

ANECDOTE

OF A

HALF PAY LIEUTENANT OF THE BRITISH NAVY.

WHEN I had the *honour* of ſpending a few months in the King's Bench Priſon, (an honour I am diſpoſed to hope my candid readers may be induced to think I was *led into* from not being properly ſupported for doing my duty with propriety as a ſoldier, and with decency as a ſubject,) * I declined during thoſe three months, any the leaſt acquaintance, with that claſs of people called *the gentlemen of the Bench*, though many of them were in the very laced waiſtcoats

A a which

* Perhaps I might (however wrong it certainly would have been) have confined Captain Lynch before, but that I had reaſon to think Lord Anſon might have landed the Queen at the Fort, certain I am that the Fort could have accommodated her Majeſty better than any houſe in Harwich.

which had procured them their *outward doublets*; *indeed* a *volunteer* female prisoner who accompanied me thither, and a numerous train of visitors would have prevented me, had I been disposed to associate with a worse class of people than even Captain Dunn, or the *scratching family of cock lane*. This rendered me rather obnoxious to the laced coat gentry, to not one of whom I ever spoke. About a fortnight before the day of my enlargement, my female friend left me to prepare a King's Garrison, for the reception of a King's Bench Prisoner! Such are the vicissitudes of human life! During this last fortnight of my durance, I had leisure to look about me, as far as the walls of a prison extended; and though I doubt not there were many wretched beings among my fellow prisoners, one only struck my attention, sufficiently to promote a desire of speaking to him; he always walked alone, smoaked his pipe, and had the appearance of a reduced tradesman. I invited him to drink a glass of wine with me, and found that his mind and his affairs were soon to be made easy, I offered him a little present assistance, which he declined, and desired I would bestow my attention upon a prisoner who was under the same roof with me, a Lieutenant of a man of war who had told him, that

that when my dinner was brought up ſtairs, ſuch was his extreme hunger, that he was often obliged to run down, and walk in the garden, to avoid even the ſmell of it; I deſired him immediately to wait upon that gentleman, and to beg the favor of his company to eat a bit of cake and drink a glaſs of wine with us, which he often did, and the following is the ſtate of his caſe. He was a man of neither family, nor intereſt, but the late gallant Admiral Boſcowen, had taken notice of him as a very active good ſeaman, brought him *aft* upon the quarter deck, and promoted him by degrees to the rank of a Lieutenant. After the peace, being upon half pay, and much better acquainted with NEPTUNE and ÆLOUS, than the artifices of women, as he was ſauntring about the royal exchange he ſaw a *weeded widow* leaning over a hatch, over which was written in LETTERS OF GOLD—— ASSURANCE OFFICE. Pray Madam ſaid *my Lieutenant*, what is it you inſure? Ships, Sir, from the dangers of the ſea, &c. a further converſation enſued, and old *Mrs. Aſſurance* invited the young Lieutenant, in to drink tea with her. The Lieutenant, who was rather *before hand* with his half pay agent, thought he had found a good peace *birth* on ſhore, made proposals to the old lady, married her, and the next week was conducted to an apartment near mine, in the state house of St. George's Fields for her debts. I pitied him, and so I am sure will the reader, and therefore I told the public in a letter printed in the St. James's Chronicle, that being the inhabitant of a goal, and the day of my liberation near at hand, I had deposited a few guineas in Mr. Davis's hands, Bookseller in Sackville Street, to begin a subscription, which I hoped the public would consider due to a young man who had deserved well of his country in war, but now shut up in a prison, and who had lost his only patron and friend the gallant Admiral Boscawen; in short I so stated his case, that Mrs. Boscawen happened to hear of it, and finding it to be truly stated, she nobly supported the collection, and I had not only the pleasure of seeing *my* Lieutenant liberated before I obtained my own, but when I did, I quitted the goal, *on that account*, with the eclat of a general huzza, of my fellow prisoners, at the head of which, was a late Westminster *Justice of peace*, otherwise I make no doubt I should have experienced the very reverse, for I had now and then a letter thrust under my door, to remind me that I was a CRIMINAL PRISONER, and ought

ought to be put on the common ſide, not to mix with the gentlemen of the Bench, who only had been guilty of defrauding every tradeſman who were weak enough to give them credit, for what they knew they were unable to pay.

A

DANGEROUS MOB, OF BATH,

BESET THE AUTHOR's HOUSE AT BATH-HAMPTON.

SOON after I had publiſhed the Proſe Bath Guide, in which I had told ſome *tales out of ſchool*, that proved offenſive to ſome Butchers and diſhoneſt tradeſmen; the mob, like Lord George Gordon's, (who always hold out falſe colours) aſſembled to the amount of ſome hundreds, in order to beſet my houſe, or deſtroy me, under the *pretence*, that I had cauſed my man to be treacherouſly impreſſed at Briſtol.

In order to explain this matter, it may be neceſſary to ſay, that being in want of a man ſervant who could occaſionally work in my garden; an innocent pretty country wench, then in my family, embraced that *favorable opening* to recommend her ſweet heart, the conſequence

consequence of which was what I expected, that Betty would soon become *thin about the nose*, and *thick* about *the waist*, but before poor Betty's *disorder* appeared, John informed me that his father and brothers with-held from him fifty pounds, and would neither pay him principal nor interest, and that he had no other security than a note of hand; but upon the note being produced, I found he had not even that, for it had neither name nor date to it! Such a shameful piece of business, I thought too gross to let pass unnoticed, I therefore employed a reputable attorney, and put John's fifty pounds safe into his pocket. Soon after this transaction, it appeared that John *had given* Betty *a note of word only*, that he would marry her, but having found out *the riddle* without the assistance of the parson of the parish, he would not *sign it*. I took occasion to talk seriously to him upon this subject; offered a two guinea wedding dinner in my orchard, for him and his friends, but all to no purpose; I then observed, that as I had rendered him a piece of justice, I would endeavour also, to render justice to the woman he had so highly injured, and accordingly went to Bristol, and settled my plan of operation with the Lieutenant of a press gang, obtaining at the same time

time his promiſe, that if the man agreed to marry the girl, he ſhould diſmiſs him. The next day I took John to Briſtol with me, and the Lieutenant took him on board a Tender. Soon after my return, being, at Bath, a mile and a half from my houſe at Bath Hampton, I was informed, that a mob, conſiſting of ſome hundreds, were gone to pull my houſe down, I immediately ordered a chaiſe from York Houſe, to fetch my wife and two daughters to town, and followed the empty chaiſe on horſe back, previouſly putting piſtols to my ſaddle, I found men, women and children ſitting upon the road ſide, and aſking them what occaſion brought them thither, they informed me, *I ſhould ſoon know*, and as I paſſed a mow, two men upon the top of it, ſtruck their forks down at me with ſuch force, that had either of them hit me or my horſe, it might have deſtroyed us, when I came within a quarter of a mile of Bath Hampton, I heard the ſhouting of voices, rattling of tins, ſounding of horns, &c. and upon an hundred yards nearer approach, I ſaw a *grimalkin* hanging in a tree, which I ſuppoſed to be a repreſentation of the OFFENDER. Upon entering the town neither I, nor the chaiſe, could hardly approach my houſe, for the numbers which ſurrounded it; I ſaid

I ſaid nothing however, till I had put my family into it, and ſeen them drove off towards Bath. The mob were all infantry, except one horſe mounted by a ſecond repreſentative of the culprit. Upon ſuch occaſions as theſe, in ſpite of whatever apprehenſions may lurk in the boſom, the ſafeſt way is, to pretend at leaſt, not to be apprehenſive of perſonal danger; I therefore ſtood my ground, till all the *mobility* had gathered around me, and then with the appearance of good temper, aſked them the cauſe of their aſſembling, and whether they had any thing to charge me with, from which I could not defend and juſtify myſelf. They ſaid I had, in a moſt treacherous manner, taken my ſervant with me to Briſtol, and ſent him out to buy lemons, in order to throw him into the hands of a preſs gang, who had confined him on board a Tender. As all things under the ſun are governed by women, and as many of my aſſembly were of that ſex, I conſidered it *ſafeſt*, (for I did not think myſelf ſafe) to appeal to them, I obſerved that many of them knew *our Betty*, that ſhe was a handſome, and I will add ſaid I, a virtuous girl, that John had, under the moſt ſolemn promiſes of marriage, ſeduced and ruined her, and now refuſed to fulfil his engagements, that I had rendered

dered him ſervices, and now wiſhed to do ſo by the woman he had ſo highly injured. And as we were in ſight of the tree where my effigies was ſuſpended by a rope, I took occaſion to obſerve, that by the laws of this country, no man ought either to be condemned, or executed without a tryal, and a jury of his countrymen; but as they hanged me *firſt*, I begged they would try me *afterwards*, and inſtantly declared my willingneſs to have a jury of twelve women impannelled upon the ſpot, and that I would ſubmit to a tryal, and to the ſentence of that female jury; for I began to perceive approbation from every female eye; thus encouraged, I further aſſured them, that I was ſo confident of my own innocence, and their impartial juſtice, that I would no longer ſit amidſt ſo many of countrymen armed, as if I were afraid, but truſt my perſon wholly to their diſpoſal, and accordingly threw my piſtols over the hedge. I then re-pleaded the conduct of the baſe deceiver, touched upon the betrayed beauty and innocence of the deluded girl (the caſe probably of *all my jury*, if not of all the females preſent) and in ſhort, I was not only acquitted with honour, but I had the pleaſure of ſeeing *myſelf* cut down from the fatal *tree*, at the root of which the next day I

placed

placed a barrel of ale, and I and my neighbours become better friends than ever. It was the ſenſe however of my jury (may I call them my conſtituents?) that John ſhould be liberated, I therefore wrote to Lord Sandwich (a facetious clever man) ſuch a letter as I thought a proper one upon ſuch an occaſion *to him*, and obſerved therein, that though it might ſeem a matter of no conſequence to his Lordſhip, to whom I was unknown, whether I died in my bed, or was knocked on the head by an enraged mob, yet I begged leave to obſerve, that as it was *mobbing time*; a mob which began with me, might end with his Lordſhip; and I hoped therefore he would order the man to be diſcharged. It is a pleaſant thing to tranſact buſineſs with a man of ſenſe and diſcernment, Lord Sandwich inſtantly ordered the man's diſcharge, *before* he was under the neceſſity of flying from a mob himſelf, of greater magnitude in London; without time, ſcarce to put on his breeches. Such a man ſhould always be FIRST LORD of the ADMIRALTY. The man was accordingly diſcharged, and Lord *George's mob*, ſoon after, convinced his Lordſhip, that my obſervation was not altogether *ill founded*. It is a pleaſant thing I ſay to have dealings with a man of ſenſe. Lord Sandwich felt the truth of my obſervation, he

ſaw

ſaw the reaſonableneſs of my requeſt, and though he did not apprehend any perſonal danger to himſelf, he did as he would be done unto, ſuch men ſhould always be at the head of every department. Men of ſenſe and ſpirit, are infinitely ſuperior to your fine ſmooth flowerly Orators or claſſical ſcholars. Sir John Barnard, without much of either, ſaid more to the purpoſe in plain language, than half the Orators of the preſent Century; we frequently ſee men as great coxcombs in language, as we do others in dreſs.

SINGULAR

SINGULAR

LAW ANECDOTE.

I HAVE ſaid above, that in money matters I have been *always* unfortunate, but I muſt recall that expreſſion; I *once* in my life was fortunate, and that too, under the guidance of a lawyer! but I muſt firſt obſerve, that I had put a chancery ſuit into the hands of an eminent lawyer who treated me with veniſon and turtle, and who kept me at *bay*, till he wanted to make two *peaſants* in *Languedoc*, (if they were to be found) parties to my bill. I knew nothing of law, but I knew that I had no buſineſs with *Meſſrs. Saboe* whatever he had, ſo I called for my bill, paid him fifty three pounds, and found myſelf juſt *where* I was, and *as* I was, except the loſs of my fifty three pounds, and

and the loſs of time alſo. Under this dilemma I happened to ſee an advertiſement in the daily advertiſer, which began thus. "The difficul- "ties, diſtreſſes, embaraſſments of law affairs, "&c. ſpeedily adjuſted by O. Q. who was to "be ſpoke with every day on certain hours at "a coffee houſe upon London Bridge." De- termining that O. Q. ſhould neither toſs me into the Thames, nor jockey me out of another fifty three pounds, I waited upon him, and told him what my *diſtreſſes* and *embaraſſments* were, and deſired he would *ſpeedily adjuſt them.* Mr. O. Q. gave me a very patient hearing, and then with much ſeeming candour and ingenu- ouſneſs informed me, that he thought my cauſe a very good one, but of too great a magnitude for him to undertake, obſerving that *they* only did little matters in the conveyancing way, &c. I was pleaſed with the ſimplicity of his manners, treated him with a diſh of chocolate, and took my leave; but before I had got *terra firma* under my feet, Mr. *O. Q.* purſued, over- took and thus addreſſed me,—" It is plain Sir by your application to me, an utter ſtranger, that you do not know a proper ſolicitor in chancery to undertake your cauſe, and there- fore as I told you before, though it is too much for

for *us* to undertake, yet I can introduce you to a gentleman of reſpectable character, of long and experienced practice in the court of chancery, who will undertake it, and who will carry it to a hearing more expeditiouſly than any man in England; do not ſaid he rely upon my word, but enquire his general character and abilities of his neighbours, I will inſtantly wait upon you to his houſe, and did ſo, and there I found a man of a certain age, with an eye as brilliant as a hawk's, and as deep as a well, with whom my conductor left me, and to whom I communicated my claim, and the manner I had left my *veniſon lawyer*. Have you paid him Sir ſaid he? I have; then Sir your cauſe is a good one, and I am faithfully at your ſervice.

It was now I thought my turn to queſtion him; how came Mr. O. Q. ſaid I, to bring me to you? I do not know, for the man is *almoſt* a ſtranger to me.—Pray Sir what do you think your bill may amount to, in doing this buſineſs? I cannot tell, but at moſt fifty or ſixty pounds, not more, then Sir inſtead of treating me,

* Mr. P—e was well known to a gentleman who now reſides at Bath.

me with turtle and venison, I will treat you with a draft on Mr. Hoare for an hundred guineas to be paid the day after a decree is made, whether I succeed or not.—That replied my *Hawk's eyed* solicitor, is very handsomely said, but it is irregular, and much more than my bill can amount to, but rest assured, I will execute the business with speed and punctuality, and he did so; for by presenting a petition to the master of the Rolls, setting forth that I was an officer going abroad, that it was a matter of great importance to me and my family, to be decided before I went, he got it heard at the master's house (Sir John Strange) previous, I think to seventy causes which stood before it, and in three months time, I had a decree in my favor, and the some thousand pounds in my pocket. Messrs. Wilbarham and Willes were my council, and it had nearly taken an unfavorable turn by the well meant, but ill managed pleading of my old *school fellow*, but as his father was an intimate friend of my fathers, kind to all his children, and had allowed me to send my solicitor from time to time, to consult with him during the proceedings, (beside having given his son the usual fees) as soon as the cause was decided, I put a handsome silver bread basket upon his side board,

board, as a further mark of my regard to his family. A mark however, that gentleman overlooked, when he accepted Lord Orwell's *two guineas*, to become an advocate againſt me, in a cauſe which merited rather the appellation of a *perſecution* than a *proſecution*; indeed it was *after* the death of his venerable father; he would not; he durſt not, have taken it had his father been living. If the reader has not already found out Mr. O. Q.'s riddle, I will give him the ſolution of it; O. Q. was Q. in the corner to my ſolicitor, or what is vulgarly called, *Barker*, to that excellent and adroit lawyer, for during my attendance upon Mr. P——e, I often obſerved Mr. Q. coming or going, with I preſume other Q. in the corner buſineſs; and now as *Mackittrick* has ſaid that Mr. FOOT, of facetious memory, obſerved that I am as ſtupid as an owl, and as ſenſeleſs as a gooſe; I cannot deny myſelf the pleaſure of relating one inſtance of the juſtneſs of his obſervation. *This ſame Mr. Foot*, took it into his head, when he firſt opened his very humourous and entertaining mode of *giving chocolate* to his morning viſitors; of taking off as the *phraſe is* Mr. Counſellor W—s, in the tryal of Betty *Canning* of infamous memory,

 and

and by taking the advantage alſo of his ſqueek-ing voice, and effiminate face, when croſs exa-mining the witneſſes, in what manner their toaſt and butter was ſerved up, or whether buttered on *both ſides*, or only on one, ſet the ſon of my reſpectable friend in a very ridicu-lous light, ſoon after which, Foot, having ob-tained a licence for the little Hay market theatre, I was informed he intended to enter-tain his company there alſo, with a repetition of that *croſs examination* the firſt night of his opening the theatre, I therefore went early to the houſe, got behind the ſcenes and procured an audience with Mr. Foot, I then told him, no man either in the theatre, nor out of it, felt or enjoyed his humourous pleaſantry more than I did, when it was exerciſed to mark, either wicked or infamous characters, but that when he brought before the public, men of reſpectability, remarkable only for the imper-fections of their perſons or intellectual faculties, no man could ſee them with more abhorrence, and as I underſtood he intended that night to exhibit a gentleman who came under one of thoſe denominations, deſired he would *well conſider* what he was about, aſſuring him if he did I would take the ſenſe of the houſe upon

it.

it, and if they would not resent it, I would. I then retired to a place I had secured in a box, near the stage, in which I found Mr. W——s brother, and with whom I had the pleasure of partaking of the evening entertainment, without any thing passing, either painful to him, or to myself; and I am glad of this occasion to record such an instance of Mr. Foot's prudence, good sense, and sound judgment. The night before my tryal came on at St. Edmund's Bury, I wrote a letter to the following purpose to Mr. W——s.

SIR,

"It has been a matter of much surprise and concern, to many of my friends, and to some of yours, that the son of Lord Chief Justice Willes, whose favour, friendship and kindnesses, were always open to me and to all my family, should engage in a paltry and oppressive cause against an old school fellow, and therefore you will excuse me, if I relate a *cause* in which I was engaged in, FOR; not AGAINST YOU." I then related what had passed behind the scenes, between me and Mr. Foot, and suggested, that which it probably prevented passing *before them*. Mr. Willes, who was a good

 tempered

tempered man, felt I believe very awkward upon receiving ſuch an unexpected piece of information, for he inſtantly came to my lodgings, and I believe would have thrown up his brief, had I admitted him, I believe it, becauſe when I appeared to receive the *gentle puniſhments* for my offences, at the bar of the King's Bench, he did refuſe his brief, and thereby offended Lord Orwell, more than, he did even the " *falſe, ſcandalous and infamous* " *libeller*" he had convicted at St. Edmund's Bury. I muſt alſo do Mr. Willes the juſtice to ſay, that I never ſaw him after this tranſaction, either in or off the Bench, that he did not convince me,. that he was either aſhamed or ſorry, for what had paſſed. I will not attribute that colour which fluſhed in his cheeks upon thoſe occaſions, to have aroſe from anger, becauſe when I had the honor of meeting him and his lady at Lord Kilmorrey's table, he was *uncommonly* polite to me, nor was Mrs. Willes leſs ſo to Mrs. Thickneſſe; indeed he was pleaſed to tell me it was right, that he ſhould be counſel *againſt me*, becauſe I might be very ſure, that nothing would be ſaid *ſevere to me* upon the occaſion, and I muſt own, I was *never under any apprehenſions that he would:* but as that tryal

coſt

coſt me a thouſand pounds, I could not help thinking Mr. Willes, ſhould have had ſome little conſideration for *my own bread baſket*, as well as for that which I preſented to him.

A DIGRESSION.

A

DIGRESSION.

THAT Lord Audley might have it in his power to return me the thousand pounds, or insure his life against mine, least I might out-live him, and thereby out-live the real want of the fifty pounds a year, I could not have wanted during my old age, if I had not been too forward in making his youthful days more happy. I sent him that chapter in which he and his brother make no conspicuous a figure; but the only notice taken of it, is contained in the following anonymous letter, I just received from his *baby* brother Philip.

Mr. *Touchet's* compliments to Mr. Thicknesse, Senior, begs leave to recommend to him to erase certain words which he asserts were inserted in an affidavit *written by himself*, though he seems now

now to have totally forgot both the *writer* and the *words* expreſſed therein, namely; "*ſitting him* "*Mr. T. Junior, on a run away horſe;* and like- "wiſe his being of the age *of nineteen or twenty,* "as there is not the moſt diſtant hint of the "former, the latter being totally falſe, as will "appear by comparing the time Mr. T. was "born with the *date* of the affidavit, the firſt "was in 1760 the latter dated 1778, which "makes it clear he was but eighteen years of age "when he was *compell'd* to take it, truth will be "truth, tho' every power may be made uſe of "to oppoſe it. And therefore if Mr. T. Senior, "does not eraſe thoſe words, the *original* affi- "davit ſhall be laid before the public to confute "him. *

"And if he pleaſes *this* alſo may be inſerted, "as he ſeems to be very barren for even "*decent* matter to fill up his *catch penny* publi- "cation.

LONDON, *Nov.* 29, 1788.

"On peruſing this *catch penny* performance "further, Mr. Thickneſſe, Senior, aſſerts *po-*

"*ſitively,*

* Mr. *Touchet* is requeſted to publiſh the affidavit, he was *compelled* to make at *only* the age of eighteen, it was read by Mr. Wright in his preſence, and I believe Mr. Wright knows he made no more objection to ſwear it, than he has now to break it.

"*ſitively*, page two hundred and eighty-five; "that it was not at the age of eighteen, "the oath was taken, which proves he was "aſham'd of it, as well he might, and alſo his "total diſregard to even the ſhadow of "truth!"

To this inſolent letter I ſhall only obſerve, that it is probable the cauſe of his making that affidavit about the *run away horſe*, may not be inſerted in the affidavit, and that the *baby* was only eighteen years of age when I *compelled* him to make it, but he was an independent *baby*, and ſurely would not have made it without ſome real or imaginary cauſe; has he forgot the day on which Lord Audley urged him to go to Sandridge Hill with him, and why I made them both give their word and honour that *he* ſhould return the ſame night to Bath? but finding he did not return, I ſent an expreſs from York Houſe the ſame night, and when *the brothers* came the next day, did he not tell me what an eſcape he *had had*, from a ſtone quarry which had fallen in *upon both*, and nearly deſtroyed him? why was that expreſs ſent? I believe Mr. Lucas of York Houſe knows, I am ſure he knows, that an expreſs *was* ſent, and Mrs. Thickneſſe and I are both ready to ſwear that he charged his brother Lord Audley with thoſe two acts of *fraternal affection.* I hope neither were true, and as he was known throughout BATH, and at Moore's academy, by the name of the *Bruſſell's Gazette,* it is very probable both were falſe, nor will he dare to ſay he did not write to his brother and renounce him, and all correſpondence whatever with him. Why ſhould I have laid the elder brother under ſuch a reſtraint; but that the younger had told me of the *horſe expedition,* and his fears? could a *baby only* eighteen years of age have been prevailed upon, to exhibit ſo d——ble a charge againſt his brother without any foundation? Yes he might, becauſe he has exhibited as vile a one againſt his father, does he even attempt to deny it in his inſolent letter? a ſon who would dare to inſult his father with ſuch letters, and ſuch crimes, as he has done, might eaſily be wicked enough to charge his brother as falſly, and I am now much inclined to believe the ſtory of the run away horſe, is a wicked falſhood. It is a ſad, a melancholy reflection, but what my brother (who has had *hundreds* of children ſays, I fear is too true) Did you ever ſaid he, know *independent* children behave otherwiſe to parents? no, I reply I never did, but I never knew or heard of independent children charging their

parents

parents with committing forgery, taxing them with cruelty, and yet giving them notes of hand, for five hundred guineas, value receiv'd, for an eſtate before it was conveyed, and without mentioning the conditions, there is ſomething novel in ſuch deeds, is there not young Mr. Touchet?

A SINGULAR

☞ The above inſolent letter has determined me to negociate the young gentleman's note of hand, and then if he dares, he may try the validity of it.

A SINGULAR

INSTANCE OF

MINISTERIAL JUSTICE.

PART of a marching regiment being on duty at Land Guard Fort, under my command, an officious and over *pious* Major, commanding the other part of it at Ipſwich, wrote to the Secretary at war, Lord Barrington, complaining that the deputy chaplain to the garriſon, not only omitted his duty there on week days, but frequently on the Sabbath, without even mentioning the matter to the deputy, whom he ſaw every day, and who lived in the ſame city! Lord Barrington did not reply to the pious Major, but wrote to me to know with whom the neglect lay, whether with the proper chaplain, or the deputy? I informed his lordſhip that it was a queſtion difficult to anſwer, but a complaint I apprehend improperly lodged, that

that the neglect, if any, was in the deputy, but submitted it to his lordship's consideration, whether it were not the duty of the regiment chaplain, to attend his own corps, and not expect it to be done by the Fort chaplain, without some recompence; and whether Mr. Lloyd, the proper chaplain, who was Rector of Rotherham in Yorkshire; who had a good paternal fortune—who was chaplain also to a regiment, and who had never even seen Land Guard Fort, ought not to allow his deputy the whole pay, instead of one shilling a day? and lastly whether a gentleman could be expected to ride six and twenty miles, two or three times a week, for so small a pittance? Lord Barrington in reply to this representation, desired I would recommend a proper person, to be appointed chaplain to the garrison, and said he would move the King to supersede Mr. Lloyd, I therefore recommended the deputy, who had been so unhandsomely complained of, as an honest sensible man, with a large family, and much to the honour of Lord Barrington's head and heart he did so; Mr. Layton was appointed chaplain, and was paid a shilling a day also, by the regiment's chaplain for doing his duty. The Major whose duty led him so much astray upon this occasion, was soon after called upon

upon to anſwer at a Court Martial, for a crime of too deep a nature to be mentioned here, and ſuch as led him further *a field*, for rather than appear before the Court Martial, he quitted his country in order to avoid the ſhame and conſequences of ſuch a horrid charge. This ſhews that whenever a man pretends to appear better than his neighbours, there is much reaſon to ſuſpect him ſomewhat worſe, a drunken man is always acting the part of a ſober one; nor was this the only inſtance I could give of Lord Barrington's impartial juſtice, for when a whole corps had ignorantly united to ſend my garriſon orders to Lord Barrington, as being unwarrantable, and exerciſing a power not veſted with me, in order to be laid before the King, which they told me they had done, and lamented the conſequence, becauſe I had in my private capacity ſhewn them many marks of politeneſs, Lord Barrington informed them that there were none of thoſe orders which were not right and proper, and that he was ſorry to ſind that any troops in the Britiſh Army were ſo ignorant of their duty, as not to know, that the governor of a garriſon had the indiſputable command of every officer and ſoldier doing duty therein. Truth however compels me to ſay, that I ſhould at this day have

have been in the ſame command, had not Lord Barrington wrote me ſuch a letter, as I thought incompatible with my honour to ſerve any longer, under ſuch reſtrictions, which he had the candour to inform me, he had recommended to the King to lay me under; and though I do not believe he meant me any injury thereby, yet it was ſuch, that an ignorant attorney of Ipſwich, conſtrued as a diſmiſſion from the ſervice, but the block-head has been often guilty of miſtakes, though not of ſo deep a dye, as the *miſtakes* of his *infamous parſon brother*. I therefore told his lordſhip if I might not be permitted to ſell my commiſſion, I would reſign it. I was told that was impoſſible, but Lord Rockingham (it was in his VIRTUOUS ADMINISTRATION) was kind enough to let me reſign it, with a recompence of two thouſand four hundred pounds from the preſent poſſeſſor, Captain Singleton.

A MADMAN

A MADMAN

CONCEALS HIMSELF BY NIGHT, IN THE AUTHOR'S HOUSE.

ABOUT the year 1747, I rented a houſe of Mr. *Johnny Wadman's*, at Old Sarum, it was a cottage in the form of a roman L, in which my man ſervant's bed-chamber was at the extremity of the upper *limb* of the L, over the brew houſe, and quite detached from the other part of the family, the man going into his bed-chamber without a candle, about ten o'clock, during the longeſt ſummer days, ſaw a human figure ſitting in the chair by his bed-ſide, high over which was the only window in the room; but what added to his fright exceedingly was, that the figure appeared to have two heads! one leap I believe brought him down ſtairs, and he really appeared to me (with his porcupine head of hair) as terrific as the two headed monſter

monſter had appeared to him. As ſoon as he was able to ſpeak, for he could not at firſt, he informed me that a man, or a ghoſt, having *two* heads, was ſitting by his bed-ſide! believing there was only *one head*, and that a bad one, in the buſineſs, I went half way up the ſtairs but whether my heart failed me, or prudence dictated, I cannot ſay (perhaps both had their ſway) I returned and took a highland broad ſword in my hand. On entering the room there was light enough to perceive the double headed monſter, but his hands and arms, being in ſhadow from the ſituation of the chair under the window, it was impoſſible to ſee whether he had any *other arms*. He appeared quite motionleſs as I approached him, with my uplifted ſword, till I took him ſtoutly by the collar, and, then his *upper head* fell to the ground.† He made ſome efforts to recover his bundle, but would not ſpeak a word, not even when threatened and provoked to it, by ſome ſmart blows, with the flat part of the ſword blade. Thus irritated by his obſtinate ſilence, I brought him down into the court yard, where there was light ſufficient to perceive he was a goodly looking man about three ſcore, decently dreſſed in grey cloaths, but ſtill regardleſs of my threats,

† A ſhirt or two, and ſtockings.

threats, he would not ſpeak! at length he pointed to the pump, tc which I led him, and holding him faſt, threw up ſome water to the ſpout, and after he had drank of it, I again aſked him who and what he was, and why he had concealed himſelf in my houſe? he then replied with great moderation; *Sir, I have an impediment in my ſpeech*—but is that a reaſon you ſhould ſecret yourſelf in my ſervant's bed-chamber? why whoſe houſe is this ſaid he, and what is your name? being told; where then ſaid he is my uncle Townſhend? I replied, that a gentleman had lived and died in that houſe of the name of Townſhend, and that I was tenant, and I Sir ſaid he am his heir, and come to take poſſeſſion of my eſtate. It grew late by this time, and not knowing very well what to do with this new heir and viſitor, I took the liberty to lock him into a *little temple hard by*, and told him he muſt give ſome more ſatisfactory account of his embaſſy before we parted the next morning, though I began to ſuſpect his errand, was neither to rob or murther. Soon after I had ſecured my priſoner, a neighbouring farmer who had *prudently* heard the buſtle from a window out of which he would only truſt his head, (upon my telling him what had paſſed *under mine)* ſaid he believed he could in ſome meaſure account for it. He ſaid that the deceaſed Mr. Townſhend had maintained an unfortunate nephew many years in a mad houſe at Box, near Bath, and probably ſaid he this is the man who has broke out, I never ſaw him, but if it be him, he is a clergyman, and his name is *Acourt*. I inſtantly returned to my *priſoner*, and aſking him his name found the farmer's ſuggeſtion ſo far right; I then opened the door, aſked Mr. Acourt's pardon, for the rough manner I had received him, and pointed out the danger both he and I had eſcaped, by his coming to take poſſeſſion of his fortune in ſo private and dangerous a manner, but as he was now in poſſeſſion of it, I begged he would accept of the uſe of that bed which he had choſen for himſelf, I then gave him ſome refreſhment, put him to bed, locked him in, and ſecured the door of the brew houſe beneath. While he was preparing for bed, he told me he always ſlept in the parlour bedchamber in his Uncle's time, lent me his M. S. ſermons which he had wrote at Box, upon condition that I would not take a copy, and *to me* he was very civil and ſenſible too, conſidering his condition, but he had told the ſervants he was not *a ſoldier*, and did not like to be beat. In the morning I found both doors broke open and my prifoner gone; he returned however at night, and lodged with me a confiderable time, always enquiring whether an imaginary wife from Frome had been to enquire for him during the paft day. Pitying more than admiring my new lodger, I applied to the Magiftrates of Salifbury, to confine him, as there was at that time a place for the reception of fuch unfortunate people, but they either would not, or could not perceive, that the poor man was not as *fenfible as they themfelves*, though I fhewed them a hole in his fkull, in which might be feen the working of his brain! he therefore continued my nightly vifitor, (for I never faw him during the day) till I was informed that he had been Rector of Bridge Town in Barbadoes, and that the firft mark of his infanity appeared by his tearing a young child limb from limb. This alarming information to me and my family, fome of whom were young children, determined me to quit the houfe to the ufe of the heir at law. The unfortunate man however did not *break out* of Box mad houfe, he was *turned out*, but *why* he was turned out, Mr. Wadman *the other heir at law*, muft explain, I cannot; for he quitted his abode reluctantly, and the humane keeper of that houfe parted with him reluctantly alfo, and gave him gold

 in

in his pocket when they ſo parted. And now, being upon this, of all others, the moſt melancholy ſubject; I cannot help mentioning a few obſervations I have made on the conduct of mad perſons. No man in his perfect ſenſes contrives to carry his deſigns into execution, with more craft, and ſecreſy than mad men, but however miſchievous or dangerous the acts committed are, they never make any attempts to eſcape or to conceal it. Many of them will converſe for hours together without diſcovering the leaſt ſymptom of a diſordered mind, unleſs that ſubject which moſt affects them is mentioned. Mr. *Guſtaldi*, Miniſter from Genoa to this country, with whom I lived in intimacy in the year 1753, with whom I often ate, and who was a very learned and ingenious man, diſcovered only one ſingle proof of being the leaſt diſordered, and that was lamenting that he was immortal!! I can not die ſaid he, that is my only misfortune. Lord Ferrer's was a mad man, and ſo is Lord George G——n, the former was an object of pity, the latter is ſo, I do not know him, but I lament that his confinement is not more ſuitable to the condition of his mind, and his rank in life. Whom among us can ſay that I ſhall not become a miſchievous mad man? why

then

then ſhould miſchievous mad men ſuffer more than thoſe who are paſſive? The former ſurely are the greateſt objects of pity. It is *actions* more than *words*, by which the ſane, from the inſane are to be known, a dangerous mad man ſhould be confined, but he ſhould not be provoked to a greater degree, by inſulting paragraphs in news papers, or too ſevere confinement, it is enough that he be confined.

ANECDOTE

OF OLD

LORD AND LADY THANET.

THAT Lord and Lady lived upon ſuch bad terms together many years, that at length they could agree in nothing but to part, during the negotiation of that buſineſs, which was tranſacted at NEW BOTTLE in Northamtonſhire, they both frequently viſited my brother and ſiſter Grey at Hinton, to conſult about the meaſures each ſhould take, previous to the ſeparation. My Lady was ſiſter to the late Lady Burlington, and reckoned a great wit, my Lord, much addicted to long ſtory telling, and that garrulity generally attendant upon old age. In one of my lady's conſultations with Doctor Grey, ſhe told him ſome very extraordinary reſolutions ſhe was determined to take, and the Doctor poſitively aſſured her, that if ſhe did,

did, her Lord will do ſo, and ſo, in return; that is impoſſible ſaid my lady he cannot, he durſt not; ſhe accordingly carried her plan into execution and my Lord inſtantly did as Doctor Grey had foretold. My lady highly exaſperated, wrote the Doctor the following letter.

Dear Doctor,

You told me if I did as I told you I would do, my Lord would do *ſo* and *ſo*, and ſo he has, which convinces me, that one tyger always knows what another tyger will do; however we both can agree to ſee you when you have leiſure to viſit *Dull-Bottle.**

I am dear Doctor,

Your Friend, &c.

The Doctor's patron and friend Lord Crew, buried his lady in Steane Chapel, the little rectory mentioned before, and when Lady Crew's monument was erected, he frequently took the key, retired to the chapel, and placed himſelf near her remains, and op-

poſite

* Her ladyſhip always called *New Bottle*, Dull Bottle, where ſhe declared ſhe had heard the ſame dull ſtories told over and over again ſo often, that it was one of her chief reaſons of quitting her Lord and Manſion, pray Mrs. Grey ſaid her ladyſhip, has your huſband any one ſtory that he tells over and over again to every body who approaches him? my ſiſter confeſſed the Doctor had, and as the Doctor himſelf can never relate it again, I will tell it the reader *only once.*

posite the monument, under which he directed his own body to be placed; and there it is presumed, he often contemplated on mortal men, and immortal life, but the sculptor having put a very ghastly grinning alabaster skull at the bottom of the monument, he took an occasion to say to Doctor Grey, I wish Dick that horrid skull had not been placed there? The Doctor, who affectionately loved the bishop, and wished to render his latter days as easy and happy as possible, sent to Banbury for the artist to consult with him whether it were possible to turn the skull into a pleasing, instead of a disagreeable object? after much consideration the sculptor determined that the only thing he could convert the skull into, was a bunch of grapes, and that was accordingly done, and so remains to this day, this was the Doctor's story he so often told.

THE

THE

CONCLUSION.

A PARTICULAR friend of mine, ſays he is often aſked why I have ſo many enemies? he replied you ſhould aſk me why he has ſo few. Some of the preceding anecdotes will account for a numerous liſt of them, but a man ſaid he who lives in abſolute retirement, who never goes into public ſociety, and who never ſpends an evening out of his own houſe, can only look for friendſhip among a few old acquaintance; but I could have furniſhed him with a much ſtronger reaſon, which is that I am known to write occaſionly in a public paper, and conſequently every raſcal, *(and there are a few in the world)* becomes of courſe my enemy. I never made any ſecret that I aſſiſted the St. James's Chronicle, becauſe I have made it an invariable

invariable rule, not to make any perſonal attack upon the character or conduct of any man, without leaving my name with the printer, or being ready to acknowledge myſelf the author if called upon for an explanation, if they were perſons who were eſteemed men of character. One ſingular inſtance of which, I will relate. Ten or a dozen years ſince a gentleman of this city, a man of genius and character, but perhaps like myſelf, rather eccentric, was attacked in the St. James's chronicle, it was a long ſimple letter, and therefore a prating old woman of Bath,* laid it at my door, I was in London when the letter was publiſhed, and there I read it, but ſome parts being local, about tranſactions at Bath Eaſton Villa, I did not even underſtand it, for I poſitively declare I did not then, nor do I now know the author of it. Upon my return to Bath, I was informed the gentleman it alluded to, was much exaſperated, and was preparing a two and ſixpenny poetical reply to it, I was alarmed, I own I dreaded to find my hand ſo near a lyon's mouth, and I deſired a friend therefore, who was intimately known to the offended gentleman, to aſſure him, that I was one of the public, who had been highly entertained by his writings, and

therefore

* Mrs. R——e.

therefore felt myſelf obliged to him ; and that I did in the moſt unequivocal manner, declare myſelf an utter ſtranger to the tranſaction, my friend who delivered this meſſage to the offended party, told me at the ſame time, that my name had been mentioned as the author, and as three months paſſed without any notice being taken of my declaration, I had too much reaſon to fear it had not met with the credit it ought, and I confeſs it was three months painful ſuſpence, for I knew the preſs was *in labour* to chaſtiſe the ſuppoſed author. However when the peeviſh *brat was born*, it was laid at the door of a Rev. Divine, who it ſeems had been all that time under a much more painful ſuſpenſe than I was, not that he was more guilty, for he alſo was perfectly innocent ; but he was in a bad ſtate of health, and ſo oppreſſed with nervous complaints, that his friends thought it would kill him. However he *publickly* declared his innocence, and moſt ſolemnly aſſured the unjuſtly offended poet, that he never wrote a line relative to him, except an elegant poetical compliment which he republiſhed with his defence. The real author of the nonſenſical letter, is to this day unknown. I then became a fellow feeler, as well as a fellow ſufferer with the Divine, and I aſſiſted him

him as well as I could, in every kind of news-paper reprisal which lay in my power, but before I left Bath to make my *wandering* tour into Spain, I wrote the doubly and unjustly offended gentleman a letter, and therein again assured him, I did not write the foolish letter which had given him so much offence, but as he had kept me three months in hot water, at a time he ought to have removed my anxiety, and had wantonly attacked another innocent man, I had made myself a partaker of his injuries, and that I did write my *squibs*, *crackers* and inuendoes afterwards; I must however observe, that the poetical reprisal, was full as contemptible and despicable as the prose accusation. * And now having told my garrulous stories, as well as my age, hurry and *opium* enabled me, I cannot look it over without being reminded by the voice of our town Bell-Man, how much my prose performance resembles his, the Bell man's poetical address to

* If after the unjustly attacked clergyman had in the most solemn manner declared his innocence, nay proved it, by republishing the complimentary verses, the Half-Crown epistle still appeared in the Booksellers windows in London, though it were suppressed at Bath, I shall not dread the bitterest mode of *dissection*, the poet can devise, for having told the tale, I have told it for truth sake, and to deter other wits from leaping before they look, not from personal resentment for I feel none.

to his noble *masters and mistresses.* I therefore like him, beg leave to return my most respectful thanks to the many Noble masters and mistresses, who have so generously contributed to enable me to defend my military character, so falsly attacked by a daring impostor, and to assure them, that I have caused advertisements to be inserted in the Jamaica Gazette, in hopes of finding some gentlemen still living in that Island, who can attest that Mr. Concannen, was the unfortunate gentleman who commanded me, and the soldiers in Spanish River, more than fifty years ago, and that he, not me, had the sole command, and that James Mackittrick is the *sole person*, either there or here, who has dared to assert the contrary; and I hereby pledge myself, if I receive any information from Jamaica on that subject, whatever it be, to lay it before the public in the St. James's Chronicle, the instant I receive it; provided it comes from a gentleman of character with his *real*, not an *assumed name.* If the ingenious Doctor now imagines himself in possession of the field of battle, much good may the laurels he has won do him. I solemnly promise never to engage with such a *valiant champion again*, nor ever to read a line he writes, nor hear a word he puts forth, during the remainder of my days, but as he

has

has ſo falſly ſet forth a *timid tranſaction* of my youth, I will record a bold one of his, in his old age. His own and only brother, who died lately at Wincheſter, ſent for him in his illneſs, and left him and his ſon, at his death, all he had to leave, about a thouſand pounds. Upon Doctor *Adair's* arrival to viſit his brother Dr. *Mackittrick*, the *well Doctor Adair*, perceived that the ſick Doctor Mackittrick, could not *hauld it above a day or two*; Dr. *Adair* therefore with that ſpirit which he has in his *cautions* ſo ſtrongly recommended to his brethren, ſent immediately for the plumber to take meaſure for his brother's *leaden doublet*, but as the poor man was as ſenſible, as he was ſick, his brother would not treat him as a criminal is when he is to be hung in chains, very humanely *laid* before the plumber a ſuit of the Doctor's old cloathes, *for meaſure*, however the *goods* came home too ſhort by *the head*, and the poor doctor, thought not hung in chains, was buried with a *wry neck* as if he had been a malefactor? This is not a wild *Negroe ſtory*, nor one without head or tale, I pledge myſelf to produce a Lady of faſhion and character, an inhabitant of Wincheſter, and one who had much regard for the *wry necked Doctor*, who was ſo ſhocked at this

this inſtance of *fraternal affection*, that ſhe left the town the day of the funeral, to avoid ſeeing ſo painful a proceſſion.

But I have been ſince told the ſurviving Doctor *Adair*, ſays that the dying Doctor *Mackittrick*, deſired he might be "*coffined as ſoon as he was dead, and buried as ſoon as he was cold.*" The ſpot where the departed brother's cold remains lie in St. Michael's Church Yard, is marked from the pen of the living brother thus, "*Jn° Mackittrick, M. D.* 1784." And as I dare ſay the living Doctor will cauſe his remains to be laid by the ſide of his dear departed brother, I think the following epitaph written by our Bell man would not be amiſs.

Here lie the bodies, bleſs their Skill,
Of two Scots Brethren, of the Pill,
Pray Mr. Devil, have an eye to James,
Don't let him Nick you by changing names.

And now, that the turbulent ſcene of life, nay of life itſelf, is nearly over, I would not have it thought that I conſider myſelf ſo much an unfortunate, as an unlucky man; I ſet out in life, without any patrimony, and in ſtruggling through it, I have obtained that

that which every man aims at, but few acquire; SOLITUDE and RETIREMENT, and have not only been in poſſeſſion of for ſome years, but have been ſenſible that it is the only line in the laſt ſtage of life, where with a few friends a man can find peace. The duplicity of mankind; and the ſatiety of enjoyments, all tend to ſhew, that even the ſplendid ſcenes which ſurround the palaces of wealth and greatneſs, are never thought compleat, unleſs marked by ſome ſhady Cave and the abode of an imaginary Anchorite, nor is all the magnificence of Architecture diſplayed in Temples, Columns, and Porticoes, ſufficient to adorn our modern Edens, without the contraſted form of ſome humble Cot, where ſolitary ſanctity might be ſuppoſed to retire, for where is the man whoſe lot has been caſt in the active ſcenes of the world, who has not often in the midſt of them, exclaimed with the prophet Jeremiah; *O that I had a place in the Wilderneſs?* though there are but few who have the reſolution to obey the impulſe which would guide them thither; ſome lurking paſſion yet unſatiated; ſome idle hope yet unextinguiſhed, ſome natural weakneſs yet unremoved, keeps moſt men halting between the engagements or pleaſures of life, and the leiſure of retirement, till it is too late.

Whether

Whether I have found ſuch a retreat, the reader will be able to judge when he has read the following feeble attempt I have made, to deſcribe my humble *Cabane*, in the following letter to a friend at Bruſſells. I flatter myſelf he will think I have, becauſe I can aſſure him, it is ſome years that the ſun has not ſet upon it, without my being preſent, and a ſpectator of the nobleſt ſight of GOD's wonderful WORKS.

YOU aſk me, dear Sir, * to ſend you a *deſcription of my delightful Hermitage;* and though your reſidence in another kingdom, and my deſire to oblige you, urge me to attempt it, yet I muſt apprize you, that it is impoſſible to comply with your requeſt.

Deſcriptive writing is, of all others, even with an able pen, the moſt difficult, and though I might ſucceed a little in the deſcription of *Montſerrat*, (an object ſo ſingularly novel,) yet I feel myſelf utterly incapable to deſcribe ſuch a ſpot as this—a ſpot ſo fortunately placed, ſo irregularly marked, and a little improved by my own hands. For when all is ſaid that can be

* Sir John O'Carroll, Bart.

be ſaid, the beſt deſcription would convey but a very imperfect idea of the place.

Suppoſe, for inſtance, I had never ſeen your beautiful daughter, and you were to write me a particular deſcription of her perſon, features, &c. I could only conclude, that ſhe is a very charming and beautiful woman; but yet I could not know her when we met by that deſcription. If then, the feature of a human face or perſon cannot be deſcribed, how can the aſpect of hills, dales, wood-lands, incloſures, rivers, buildings, &c. be otherwiſe delineated, than with an able pencil, inſtead of a pen? and therefore I can only ſay, that the ſituation is inferior to few ſpots any where, that the *tout enſemble* renders it in my eyes a little *bijou*, and obſerve that moſt ſtrangers are pleaſed with it.

It commands a ſouth-weſt proſpect, and hangs on the ſide of Lanſdown hills, and ſo cloſe under a high tump to the north, that we are perfectly ſheltered from the ſevere winds of that quarter, and in a great meaſure from the eaſt winds alſo; for though it is a quarter of an hour's ſteep walk from the weſt end of the Royal Creſcent in Bath, and commands juſt ſo much proſpect that the eye can take in the verdure,

verdure, and no more, yet Lord THURLOW was pleased, in *pleasantry*, to name it *Gully-Hall*.

From my little study window, however, I look down upon BATH with that indifference, which age, and a long knowledge of its contents, or rather discontents, have furnished me, and with infinite pleasure on a mile and a half of the gentle AVON gliding down the vale, and now and then, seeing the swelling bosoms of deep-laden barks freighted with merchandize; which I consider as returning messengers, whom I have sent forth to fetch me Tea from Asia, Sugar from America, Wine from France, and Fruit from Portugal.

But to return to *Gully-Hall;* for when great rains fall on the mountains which so shelter us from the northern winds, yet they do not hinder a very rapid stream which sometimes tumbles down with mighty force indeed; but by being kindly attended to, and invited to take a few turns between a variety of little *breast-works*, with which the buxom valley is adorned, I rather consider it an ornament than a defect; though none of the *bosoms* on the banks are barren, and some yield a constant stream of the purest water, in or near Bath.

No little ſpot of ground can be more beautifully irregular, broken, and divided, than this dingle; and no wonder; for it is as GOD formed it, and as He willed the ſtately trees to grow, which ſhade it, and who cauſes the whole ſurface annually to be covered with the primroſe, violet, and all the elder ſiſters of the ſpring. I have therefore taken a few ſteps about it, but with caution, to avoid diſturbing ſuch adorable marks of the founder of all things viſible and inviſible; and my eyes are as often turned upwards as downwards, with delight and gratitude, that ſuch a walk, narrow and humble as it is, and limited as I am, is to be my laſt ſcene on this ſide the grave.

The inſolence of a fellow who poſſeſſes more land than manners or honeſty, once drove me out of this ſequeſtered ſhade, and I ſold it to my youngeſt ſon; the houſe I then left upon it (if a houſe it could be called) he was pleaſed to *improve*, and now its front reſembles Alderman Pudding's houſe, over againſt the Pack-Horſe on Turnham-Green, and therefore the incloſed drawing is ſketched from a point, in which only a bit of the houſe is ſeen, peeping through the trees. You will ſee however, the hermit's hut, built on the ſide of the dingle, at which we chiefly reſide in the ſummer.

So

So much for a little art and nature:—but I muſt inform you, that from the great quantity of broken urns which were turned up, whereever we opened the ground, on a little lawn which overhangs the dingle, I was led to ſuſpect this to be the ſpot where the ROMANS buried their dead, when they inhabited BATH; and upon *deeper* enquiries, I found my conjecture eſtabliſhed beyond a doubt. But unfortunately the SAXONS, or ſome ſucceeding race, made the ſame uſe of it, ſo that I have never met with a perfect urn, but thouſands of their fragments, and many of the convex ſtones which covered the tops of the urns to prevent the incumbent mould from mixing with the aſhes of the dead.

Three ſtone coffins have been dug up, two Saxon, and one Roman; the latter had the body in it, quite perfect, and ſome of the fleſh on the ſkull. It had been covered with a pickle, which preſerved it.

Faſt fixed (and never more to *move*) on the ſide of my hermit's hut, is ſecured the body of my old *Wandering Shaiſe;* and on an old decayed oak, which grows through the roof of the

the kitchen, the following lines are engraven on the rind, as a *memento* to Man :—

" Stranger, kneel here, to age due homage pay!
When first Eliza held Britannia's ſway
My growth began :—the ſame illuſtrious morn,
Joy to the hour, was gallant Sydney born.
Sydney, the darling of Arcadia's ſwains,
Sydney, the terror of the martial plains,
He periſh'd early; I juſt ſtaid behind
An hundred years, and lo! my clefted rind,
My wither'd boughs, foretell deſtruction nigh,
We all are mortal;—Oaks and Heroes die.

Near a rude arch, on all ſides embraced with the twiſted eglantine, is a perforated rock-ſtone, from which conſtantly runs a ſmall ſtream of the pureſt water imaginable, that falls into a Saxon coffin dug up hard by; from the length and narrowneſs of which I have diſpoſed myſelf to believe the body which I found in it to be that of a beautiful Saxon virgin; ſo that inſtead of being hurt with the idea of its original uſe, it is become only a memento of what we muſt all come to. And who knows but " ſome kindred ſpirit" may, a thouſand years hence, make the ſame uſe of my departed daughter's coffin; which alas! lies hard by, and in cloſe contact with the old Roman knight's mentioned above, which is to receive what remains of myſelf.

Now

Now do not wonder! for I muſt inform you, that ſome years ſince I had ſcooped out a cave on the ſide of the dingle, under the ſpreading roots of an aſh tree, and turned a rude arch in front of it; and there placed, cut in relief, the head of that wonderful genius THOMAS CHATTERTON, with the following lines beneath it.

"Sacred to the Memory of
T H O M A S C H A T T E R T O N.
Unfortunate Boy!
Short and Evil were thy Days,
But the Vigour of thy Genius ſhall immortalize Thee.
Unfortunate Boy!
Poorly waſt Thou accommodated,
During thy Short Sojourning among us.
Thou lived'ſt unnoticed,
But thy Fame ſhall never die."

Since which, the long, painful, and hopeleſs illneſs of my daughter, which had worn her down to death, and her parents to ſuch a deep ſorrow, that the idea of the proceſſion of removing her remains down the hill ſeemed to us but one remove leſs painful than that fatal remove between LIFE and DEATH; and therefore, as ſhe was virtuous, dutiful, and not void of ſome genius, we have depoſited her body beneath the only monumental ſtone raiſed in *Britain* to the greateſt Genius *Britain*, or or perhaps any other nation under the ſun, has produced: apologizing, however, for ſo bold a ſtep, by the following beautiful lines from Pope, and fulfilling, in ſome meaſure, the offerings propoſed:

" What tho' no ſacred earth afford thee room,
" Nor hallow'd dirge be mutter'd o'er thy tomb;
" Yet ſhall thy grave with riſing flow'rs be dreſt,
" And the green turf lie lightly on thy breaſt.
" Here ſhall the morn her earlieſt tears beſtow,
" Here the firſt roſes of the year ſhall blow;
" While angels with their ſilver wings o'erſhade
" The ground now ſacred by thy reliques made."

Since which, ſome (unknown) admirer of my daughter publiſhed in one of the Morning Papers, the following lines, which he modeſtly terms 'Elegiac Lines' offered to her memory. They were too flattering to be neglected, and therefore on the model of the Lyons *Taurobolium*, which guards the unhallowed ſpot, they likewiſe are impreſſed, and are as follows:

" Reader, if Youth ſhould ſparkle in thine eye,
" If on thy cheek the flow'r of Beauty blows,
" Here ſhed a tear, and heave the penſive ſigh,
" Where Beauty, Youth, and Innocence, repoſe.
" Doth Wit adorn thy mind, doth Science pour
" It's ripen'd bounties on thy vernal year?
" Behold, where death has cropt the plenteous ſtore!
" And heave the ſigh, and ſhed the penſive tear.
" Does Muſick's dulcet notes dwell on thy tongue,
" And do thy fingers ſweep the ſounding lyre?

" Behold

" Behold, where low she lies! who sweetly sung
" The melting strains a Cherub might inspire.
" Of Youth, of Beauty, then, be vain no more,
" Of Musick's power, of Wit, and Learning's prize,
" For while you read, these charms may all be o'er,
" And ask to share the grave where Anna lies."

I cannot, however, quit this melancholy subject, without mentioning an accidental object, which, on a superstitious mind, might operate very forcibly. The workmen, in turning this rude arch, put by the stones unhewn, in the most irregular manner; yet it so happened, that two whitish stones, something of a bastard alabaster kind, were so laid, that *since* my daughter's death, and the place becoming more an object of serious attention, I perceived that those stones, at a certain oblique point of view, offer a very striking figure of a winged angel, and consequently are now emblematical of the lines, which almost touch the " silver " wings" of this natural piece of sculpture.

It is a pleasing idea and no unnatural one, I hope, (however it may savour of Popery) to suppose that there are an host of saints and angels offering up their prayers to GOD in behalf of departed spirits. Surely then the inhabitants of an hermitage may so far join in the prayers or faith of the Catholic Church,

that

that however divided we are *here*, as to particular points of faith, that by their interceſſion we may all meet hereafter: for alas! I fear there is little probability of you and I meeting here.

I am, dear Sir,

&c. &c.

P. S. Dr. Young, author of the *Night Thoughts*, being introduced where I was on a viſit in London, he attracted the attention of all the company, but in a particular manner that of an elderly lady, who was ſo aſtoniſhed to find him a cheerful lively old man, inſtead of the gloomy being ſhe had conceived him to be, that ſhe could not help expreſſing to him her agreeable ſurpriſe. "O Madam," replied the Doctor) "there is much difference between *writing* and *talking*:"——

So, that you may not conclude me altogether loſt in ſorrow and ſadneſs, I muſt give you the epitaph on one of my fellow travellers. He was a very honeſt fellow, as the following lines will teſtify:——

True to his maſter, gen'rous, brave,
His friend, companion, not his ſlave;
Fond without fawning, ſtill the ſame,
When fortune ſmil'd, or when the dame,
Led the poor Wanderer ſuch a dance,
An exile ſad, thro' Spain and France.
Bluſh then, ye human ſons of b——s,
Who fawn on raſcals for their riches,
Yet grudge the tribute of a tear,
To the poor dog which ſlumbers here.

Mrs. THICKNESSE, who preſents her compliments to you and your's, calls out " *Pray put me in*, for I am afraid I ſhall die ſoon." So I repeated to her the following Epigram:

My ſickly ſpouſe, with many a ſigh,
Oft tells me " PHILLY, I ſhall die."
I giev'd; but recollecting ſtrait,
'Twere bootleſs to contend with fate;—
So reſignation to Heaven's will,
Prepar'd me for ſucceeding ill.
'Twas well it did;—for on my life,
'Twas Heaven's will to *ſpare my wife.*

You will conclude, my dear ſir, that a ſpot which is ſo reſpectable for *modern* as well as *ancient endowments*, and which is to be farther enriched with *kindred aſhes*, will not be left liable to the precarious diſpoſal of an auctioneer's wooden hammer:—No, ſir; if no child of

our's

of *our's* ſurvive us to enjoy it, it ſhall devolve to a moſt reſpectable Gentlemen of Bath, or to his heirs; a Gentleman, with whom I never ate or drank, and for reaſons he, or they, will *then* know; but which I will carry to the grave with me.

The following lines, which are in a little receſs at the foot-path gate, are too applicable to be omitted, though they may be rather out of place:——

Here let Time's creeping winter ſhed
His hoary ſnow around my head;
And while I feel, by ſlow degrees,
My ſluggard blood wax chill and freeze,
Let thought unveil to my fix'd eye
The ſcenes of deep Eternity;
Till life diſſolving at the view,
I wake! and find thoſe viſions true.

St. Catherine's Hermitage,
Feb. 1ſt. 1786.

Since

*** Since the preceding Sketch has been printed off, the following IMPROMPTU, written by the ingenious Mr. TASKER has appeared in the *European Magazine*; and I own I am too much pleaſed with the compliment paid to the Quick and the Dead, to omit it on that account. So, by way of *Codicil* to my Letter, I add that, and the Hermit's Prayer.

IF breath of mortal fame can pleaſure yield
To ſhades of Genius in Elyſian field;
—Spirit of injur'd CHATTERTON! rejoice,
And hear of fame the late applauding voice!
Chill penury depreſs'd thy Muſe of fire,
And SUICIDE's rude hand unſtrung thy lyre.——
Tho' all the Muſes ſmil'd upon thy birth,
And ſhew'd thee as a prodigy on earth;
Lo! ſuch the hard conditions of thy fate!
Living deſpis'd, lamented when too late:
Thy thread of life (by too ſevere a doom)
Was early cut, e'en in thy youthful bloom,
Nor was thy name yet honour'd with a tomb.
O CHATTERTON! if thou mayh'ſt deign to ſmile
On one receſs of thine ungrateful iſle;
Suppreſs a-while thy juſt indignant rage,
And view well pleas'd the WANDERER's Hermitage;
There thy delighted eye at laſt may ſee
The grateful monument ariſe to thee:
One worthy individual thus ſupply'd
What all thy boaſted patrons have deny'd.

THE

THE

HERMIT's PRAYER.

GOD of my Life, who numbereſt my days, teach me to meet, with gratitude or patience, the good or ill which the tide of time ſhall float down upon me; but never, O God, I humbly beſeech Thee, withdraw from me thoſe native ſpirits which have been the cheering companions of my exiſtence, and have ſpread a gliding even upon my misfortunes.

Continue to me, O GOD of Life, thoſe powers, that I may view with rapture the inexhauſtible VOLUME of NATURE, which Thou haſt ſpread before mine eyes; in every page of which, I read the impreſſion of thy omnipotent hand.

It is with inexpressible concern that I now find myself under the Necessity of adding to the above Description, to my *paradisiacal* Abode; the following Advertisement, but I have lived to perceive, that two Events are not very remote, and if either of them happen in my Life, it will render my Residence here, incompatible with my scanty Income.

ADVERTISEMENT.

On the 15th of JUNE, 1789, will be Sold by Auction, ST. CATHERINE's HERMITAGE, near Bath.——For further Particulars, enquire of Mr. FORES, Bookseller, in Piccadilly; or of Mr. PLURA, Auctioneer, at Bath.

THAT I may finish this motley performance with a tail piece, to tally with the *occasional introduction;* I will do it by congratulating my country men under the present melancholy condition of the Sovereign, that the Prince his son is vested, though imperfectly, with that regal power which is not only due to his ROYAL HIGHNESS's birth, but consistent also to his PRINCELY ENDOWMENTS.

It seldom falls to the lot of any Kingdom, to see a Prince at the head of it, who has mixed with mankind, and thereby gathered that worldly knowledge which cannot be taught in private, as it is to be observed, when that has happened, it has proved fortunate to the people so governed. The education of Princes in general, is so different from that of private gentlemen, that when they possess power it is often without sufficient knoweldge to exercise it it with judgment; and then, ſome bold daring miniſter wreſts the Sceptor in a manner from his hands. Did THE PEOPLE imagine from the late violence, the two parties conducted themſelves before the Regency was ſettled, aroſe purely from a deſire to promote the welfare of the ſtate? if they did, they were egregiouſly miſtaken, I doubt not by a few good men on both ſides, were ſo actuated, but at ſuch times, it is particularly neceſſary to keep a watchful eye upon the moſt clamourous, and more particularly on ſuch men who endeavour to be thought *better than their neighbours*, as they are in general ſomewhat worſe.

A drunken man is always acting the part of a ſober one, and a man may be as much intoxicated with power, as with wine, and not only think himſelf upon an *equality with his Prince*, but unguarded enough to avow it publickly. A Nation governed as this HAS, IS, I hope always will be governed, ſince the GLORIOUS REVOLUTION, ſhould never veſt too much power in the hands of ſuch arrogant men; it is a fooliſh wiſdom ſays Mr. HUME "which is ſo "carefully diſplayed, in unvaluing Princes, "and puting them upon a level with the meaneſt of mankind; though it be true, that an

"Anatomiſt

" Anatomist finds no difference in the greatest " Monarch, than in the lowest day labourer or " peasant, for what do all these reflections tend " to? we all of us still retain these prejudices in " favor of high birth, and family, and in our seri- " ous occupations, and most careless amuse- " ments, can never get rid of them." It is for the welfare of society it should be so, and we may justly pronounce such men who deliver sentiments contrary to it unworthy of power, nay dangerous to be trusted with it. The subject who declares himself equal to his Prince, would become his superior if he could. It is a matter of very little consequence who is prime minister in such a Kingdom as this, if the sovereign be a man of sense, and though I have long since ceased to entertain any very high opinion of Mr. Fox further than of his parliamentary Knowledge, yet were that to happen here, which did happen two thousand years ago, at *Athens*, between ESCHINES and DEMOSTHENES, I should not wonder if he were to do, as the victorious statesman did there, who having by his superior eloquence caused his competitor to be exiled, followed him privately, soothed him with topicks of consolation, and offered him money to console him under his misfortunes, whereupon the banished statesman exclaimed,

exclaimed, alas! with what regret do I leave a country, and my fellow citizens; where my very enemies are ſo generous.

If what Mr. Sheridan declared in the houſe, and which ſtands uncontradicted be true, may we not ſay with Sir John Harrington.

Ferro, non auro, vitam cernamus utrique,
Vos ne velit, tel me regnare hera quidve ferat ſors.
Try me with glittering WORDS, not glittering Gold,
Which of *us two*, the HIGHEST SEAT SHALL HOLD.

THE Author, unable to bear the imputation of having ſhamefully fled from his colours, as fully charged by the daring impoſtor, put forth the dedication prefixed to this book, as ſoon as it was printed; and the following paper was laid at the bookſellers by its ſide, a paper which needs no comments, for HE IS THE MAN, who thus has replied to a charge brought againſt him, for writing, printing, and ſecretly publiſhing, a falſe, ſcurrilous and wicked untruth. I know not which of the two to deſpiſe moſt, whether the worthleſs author, or the ungrateful printer.

"Doctor Adair has been lately informed that Mr. Meyler has exhibited for the amuſement of his cuſtomers a *dedication* worthy of the illiterate and malignant driveller who publiſhed it. A— has not read it, nor will he, until it is prefixed to that precious morſel of biography, the ſpeedy publication of which Thickneſſe, has announced

announced in his mumping ſubſcription advertiſement, though the dunce has been a hackney ſcribler *for* half a century, yet his letter to A— exhibits in every page ſuch groſs ignorance of grammar and even of orthography as would diſgrace a footman or a cook-maid, A— therefore advise *(fas eſt ab horte doceri)* that as he has quarrelled with his old friend C—s, whom he formerly employed to correct his blunders, he would put his M. S. into the hands of ſome perſon who is qualified to tranſlate his jargon into tolerable Engliſh, and that in his narrative he will tell the whole truth, and nothing but the truth, otherwiſe one of his grub ſtreet brethren will certainly be employed to publiſh a cheap edition of his life embelliſhed with genuine anecdotes, and explanatory annotations. It is expected that Mr. M. will evince his impartiality by allowing this paper a place on his ſhop table."

March 14th.

ERRATA.

The Author is in his Seventieth Year and never pretended to be an accurate Writer.

THE END.

www.ingramcontent.com/pod-product-compliance
Lightning Source LLC
Chambersburg PA
CBHW030947110726
47900CB00004B/1164

* 9 7 8 3 3 3 7 2 6 7 0 0 1 *